Cathryn Grant

THE DEMISE

OF THE

SOCCER MOMS

A Novel

Published by D2C Perspectives

This book is a work of fiction. Any resemblance to actual events or persons, living or dead, is entirely coincidental. Artistic liberty has been taken with the city of Sunnyvale, but I got the restaurants right, and that's the most important part.

ISBN: 978-0-9831868-1-6
ISBN: 978-0-9831868-0-9 (ebook)

Dedication

C 2 D

Prologue

THE DOORBELL WOKE Amy from a feverish sleep. The sun was well above the horizon, causing her bedroom curtains to glow like a paper lantern. She heard the front door open and her mother's voice, calm and friendly. A man spoke, but Amy couldn't decipher his words. The front door closed. After a moment of silence, a thud shook the walls of the living room and the hallway outside Amy's bedroom. Her mother yelped. Amy rolled onto her back. The walls shivered again. There was a thick, damp sound like the pounding of her mother's meat tenderizer on a piece of beef. The man growled, "Shut up."

Amy sat up and clutched the comforter around her shoulders. "Mommy? Mom?"

Her mother whimpered.

Amy pushed the blankets to the foot of the bed and swung her legs over the edge. Her flannel nightgown was damp with sweat. She tiptoed across the room and opened the bedroom door. The air in the hallway was icy on her neck and face. She crept toward the living room. She dragged her fingertips along the wall, even though she and her sisters were told to keep their hands off the walls.

The man grunted. It was the same sound she heard coming from her parents' bedroom every Friday night. According to her oldest sister, it was the sound of their parents having sex. She wished her sister would shut up about that. They shouldn't be listening to their parents when the bedroom door was closed. Her sister said, How can we not?

A man wearing a white, long-sleeved shirt blocked Amy's view of her mother's face and most of her body. His black hair was shaved close to his head so his scalp was visible, like her father's Navy buddies that came over to drink beer and watch football games. His gray slacks were loose around his knees. Below the edge of the shirt was his bare butt, almost as white as the fabric. He drove his hips against her mother's body as if he wanted to hammer her into the floor. Amy shoved her fingers into her ears, but she could still hear her mother's mewling, and the animal noises that burst out of the man's open mouth.

Her mother's blonde-streaked hair was spread across the carpet, silky as the fur of the neighbor's cat. The man had her mother's arms pinched against the floor so they bent at an awkward angle. One arm looked like the broken wing of a seagull Amy had seen on the school playground.

Amy backed away from the doorway. What if he saw her? What if he pushed her to the ground and pounded his hips against her? Sweat spread between her shoulder blades and her nightgown felt as heavy as a winter coat. All the air had gone out of her lungs. She should help her mother, push the man off, punch him, bite him. She had to stop those sounds; he was trying to kill her mother. But he was huge, taller than her father, with shoulder muscles that showed through his shirt. She was so thin. *Spindly as a sparrow*, her father always said, telling her mother, *you need to make that girl eat more.*

Amy wanted to scratch the man's face, make him bleed, but she couldn't move. Why did her feet feel as if they weren't attached to her legs? They wouldn't even slide along the carpet. Her bones felt hollow, as if her body lacked substance. The pounding and grunting drilled into her head. Should she sneak up from behind, or rush at him screaming? Then what? A sob heaved up from her ribs, but she plastered her hands over her mouth so no sound could escape.

With her shoulders pressed against the wall, she could still see a sliver of the living room. The man rolled off her mother's body and yanked her hair, snapping her head sideways. He whispered in her ear. Then he smacked her face with the back of his hand. He stood and tugged up his pants, buckled his belt, and walked across the room. He picked up a briefcase that leaned against the wall and went out the front door. The screen slammed closed behind him.

Tears drained down the sides of her mother's cheeks and into her ears, but she didn't lift her hand to wipe them away. There was a smear of blood near her bottom lip, and her right eye looked as if the socket couldn't hold it in place. Her sundress was bunched around her waist and her underpants were a tiny streak of white across her right ankle.

Amy still couldn't manage to move her feet. Maybe her mother didn't want to know she was there. The only sound was a bee outside the screen door, circling the Fuchsia that hung in a pot from the porch roof. The front door was open and her mother wasn't doing anything about it. Anyone could walk past and look inside. Her mother's chest moved as she gasped for air like she'd been under water. Tears spread around her neck, making her skin glisten.

After a few minutes, Amy tiptoed back to her bedroom. She opened the closet door and pushed the clothes to one side. She scooped up her shoes and put them on top of a box. There was barely room for her to squeeze herself into the open space and settle on the floor with her legs crossed. She grabbed the bottom edge of the closet door and pulled it closed. The air was stuffy, but the warmth felt good. Her feet weren't quite as numb and she could wiggle her toes now.

When the cough from her bronchitis started up again, Amy came out of the closet and climbed into bed. Soon her mother would bring the cough syrup and a glass of apple juice.

HOW STUPID TO invite a stranger inside the house. That's what everyone said. He didn't threaten to kill her. She could have fought harder, couldn't she? Was it really rape if she didn't fight back? Had Amy seen the man's hands around her mother's neck? She wasn't sure, but she wasn't sure of anything, only what appeared in her dreams, and those were fluid. One night the sensation of her feet gripped in a tub of cement, the next night nothing but the animal-like cries of pain.

You dress like a slut. Her father spoke so casually, stating an indisputable fact, like he did with all his edicts. *No wonder the scumbag thought he could do what he wanted. You were asking for it.* In the months after she was raped, Amy's mother shuffled through the house, trailing her fingers along the back of the sofa, across the kitchen table. When she spoke, her voice was a whisper, as if she'd been strangled and could no longer generate sound from her vocal cords. She ate nothing but raw vegetables and apples. Most of the flesh melted off her formerly curvy body. She wore thick sweaters and slacks that looked like men's pants, cinched at the waist by a woven belt. There were no more shopping trips, no more mother-daughter chats. She no longer polished her nails, treating Amy to a dab of clear polish on her pinkie. Instead, Amy's mother cut her nails to the quick and they never seemed to grow.

The neighbors stared when Amy's mother left the house. Conversations stopped when she walked down the front path, but she didn't seem to know they were gossiping about her. After a while, she didn't hear what her husband said and she didn't hear Amy, or her sisters, chattering about their days.

AMY KNEW THAT life would be different for her girls. They wouldn't watch their childhood evaporate in front of their eyes. Their mother would not turn into a ghost. They wouldn't experience divorce and the rotting away of their security. Already, their scrapbooks proved their lives were different – a record of happy memories, photographs taken at the edge of Lake Tahoe, smiling in front of the Christmas tree, posing with one foot on a soccer ball, confident grins stretched across their cheeks in every image.

Chapter One

AMY SET HER HAND across the top of her sunglasses to reduce the glare. Her diamond ring slid to the side, resting on her pinky finger and she flicked it back into place. A woman she'd never seen before was sauntering across the school playground. The woman's short, light brown hair was gelled so that it stood out from her head, the tips dyed black. She wore a gauze skirt paired with *Doc Marten* boots that made her look like a hybrid of Tinker Bell and a thug. As she walked, her breasts bounced and swayed, barely contained by the fabric of her spandex shirt.

"That woman's not wearing a bra." For a moment, Amy didn't realize she'd spoken out loud.

Rachel turned to look.

"Don't stare at her," said Amy. The woman couldn't possibly be a mother, dressed like that. Yet she looked as if she was rushing toward the fifth grade classrooms, anxious to arrive before the dismissal bell rang. Maybe she was a nanny. The hair and boots were bad enough, but advertising the fact that she wasn't wearing a bra was too much. Did she want men to stare at her?

Amy hadn't been married to Justin for nearly sixteen years without noticing the male obsession with breasts. The first time she'd met Justin, she caught him looking at the opening on her shirt as if he were willing her to unbutton it. Although she prided herself on her slender shape, there was a prick of fear when she noticed him sneaking a glance at a woman with larger breasts. His eyes would fall out of his head if he saw this woman dancing across the blacktop.

"*You're* staring," said Kit.

"Why would anyone dress like that?" said Amy.

"Maybe she doesn't know how it looks," said Rachel.

"I think she knows," said Amy. The woman couldn't be oblivious to the impression she was making. All the mothers, scattered around the picnic tables, were trying hard not to stare. The few fathers waiting for their children weren't trying as hard. The casual movement of the woman's arms and her loping stride didn't fool Amy. Most women were more calculating, more self-conscious than they let on. There wouldn't be thousands of clothing stores and endless aisles of cosmetics, magazines devoted to fashion, and nail salons on every block, if women weren't packaging themselves to project a desired image.

As the woman drew closer, she slowed her pace. This made her breasts move more seductively. When she reached the area where Amy and her friends were seated, she paused and turned to an empty picnic table. Instead of sitting with her back to the table as the other women did, she climbed onto the bench. Her boots clanged on the metal as she turned and sat on the table, using the bench as a footrest.

Amy lowered her voice, "She has a diamond stuck in her nose." From the corner of her eye, she saw Kit's face stiffen. "There's nothing wrong with that. I just think it's unusual." She hadn't intended to sound judgmental and she wasn't even sure why she felt so hostile. Mostly, it was the missing bra. The woman's appearance screamed that she was trying to look different, as if she didn't care whether she fit in. It was rude to whisper, but she couldn't help it. Seeing a pierced nose on a mother was worth noting, even if Kit didn't think so.

Kit leaned back and turned to face the athletic field that stretched out from the edge of the playground, merging into the park adjacent to the school. She ran her fingers through her dark hair. A strand caught in the hinge of her sunglasses. She turned back toward Amy and Rachel. "Did you read about that rape and murder on Benton Court?"

Amy nodded. Her reflection wavered on the surface of Kit's sunglasses. She touched her collarbone. Moisture spread across her scalp, as if the image was melting into her brain – a woman limp on the floor, her blood covering the tiles, staining the grout. Amy pinched her thighs together until they ached. It was impossible not to feel the violation in her own body. It had always been that way. When she watched movies, the violent sequences rippled through her flesh until her stomach felt like a pocket turned inside out. She closed her eyes and tried to blot out the imagined scene. That morning, she'd read the newspaper coverage. The attack had taken place only six blocks from her house. The article quoted the victim's husband and his stunned attention to unimportant details as he explained that the smell of burned carrots told him something was wrong the moment he entered the house. His wife had been assaulted on her kitchen floor, three feet from the stove. The rapist had stabbed her twenty-three times.

Amy knew Rachel and Kit would discuss the rape and murder as if it was a curiosity – nothing more than a news item. They'd want to talk about the reported details – the woman's torn shirt, her missing shoe, and the placement of the knife wounds. They would avoid the soul-shattering horror of a man forcibly stabbing himself into a woman's body. They'd try to categorize it as an isolated event, far removed from their lives, something they didn't have to worry about. They wouldn't feel it in their bones. Why would they?

"You don't think of someone being murdered in the middle of the day," said Kit.

"There's nothing sacred about daylight," said Amy.

"But you tend to think of crime happening in the dark." Rachel stretched her legs out and pointed her toes as far as her leather sandals would allow.

Amy folded her hands on her lap. She unfolded them and ran her palms down her thighs, hoping the moisture didn't leave marks on her Capri pants. She crossed her legs. Her sandal dangled off her foot.

"I don't see why he had to kill her," said Kit.

"So if all he did was rape her, it would be ok?" Amy knew her voice sounded too sharp, but there was something inside her that wanted to provoke her friends to feel more frightened.

Their voices sounded detached, as if the violence had nothing to do with them, could never happen to them.

"That's not what I meant," said Kit.

"Sometimes death might be better. If it's too painful to go on," said Amy.

"How can you say that?" said Rachel.

"They say stabbing is a crime of passion," said Kit.

"Then she must have known him," said Rachel.

Amy closed her eyes. Her friends didn't know what they were talking about, tossing out opinions as if they were discussing the next soccer game or planning the fall carnival. Did they think they could sit around the picnic tables and determine the motive? They didn't understand that you couldn't possibly know why, even if it happened in your own house. You could spend your whole life trying to find a reason, and never discover the answer.

"Do you think they'll catch him? If she knew him?" said Rachel.

"I can't imagine knowing someone with that potential for violence," said Kit.

Rachel and Kit went on talking. The words swarmed around Amy's head like gnats. She wanted to smack them between her hands. The whole thing made her feel light-headed. It might be a good idea to talk to Justin about getting her gun out of the safe deposit box. Now that the girls were older, there was no need to keep it locked away.

Rachel pushed her sunglasses into her hair, using them to keep the spiraling curls off her face. She leaned toward Amy. "Are you okay? You look like you're going to be sick."

The dismissal bell rang and the doors of the classrooms swung open. Children poured out onto the playground. Amy and her friends all stood at the same time. The stranger remained perched on the edge of the table like one of the crows that clung to the branches of redwood trees throughout Sunnyvale.

Amy watched as Amanda, the eldest of her twins, emerged from the classroom clutching two paperback books in her hand. A smaller girl walked beside her. She was thin with reddish hair that reached past her waist in a snarl of untrimmed fluff. The girl's hair hung oddly on the left side because it was combed over a small bald spot. She wore a pink jumper with a turquoise tank top, and clutched a purple backpack like she was carrying a puppy. Tucked between the backpack and her chest was a stack of books. The girl stroked Amanda's arm. "See you tomorrow." She smiled with a giddiness that seemed to hint at hyperactivity. Amy knew her imagination was out of control again. Somehow, she also knew the girl belonged to the bra-less woman, even before the stranger stood and climbed down from the picnic table.

"How was school?" Amy put her arm across Amanda's shoulders and squeezed gently. Amanda tugged away. "I made a new friend."

Amy smiled, but her lips felt stiff, like they might split open if she didn't apply a coat of gloss. She wanted to be kind, so it was best to say nothing. She was used to swallowing her fears, determined to make sure she was an easy-going mom, supportive of her daughters, but still guiding them in the right direction. There was nothing to be concerned about. The new girl would find other friends. Soon, the soccer season would begin. Amanda and Alice would spend their time with the girls on the team, the girls they'd known all their lives, the daughters of Amy's closest friends.

Chapter Two

CHARLOTTE'S FEET WERE SWOLLEN inside her *Doc Martens*. She'd forgotten how the temperature settled into the eighties and low nineties in the south bay during August and September. Puddles of sweat formed between her breasts and inside her armpits. After twelve years in the fog of San Francisco, she'd forgotten a lot of things about suburbia, not just the weather. Watching those women sit on the picnic table benches, as if they had paid for them like box seats at a baseball game, yanked her thoughts back to high school – the geeks at this table, the artists on the front lawn, the popular kids setting up camp at the center of the quad.

The three women who had watched her walk toward Meadow's classroom kept their expressions hidden behind sunglasses, but their lowered voices indicated Charlotte was the topic of conversation. There was no doubt her unconventional hair and clothes prompted the whispering. So what? She was an artist, and even though she was forced to live for a while in a community that personified conformity, she refused to change her style. In the area around their Haight-Ashbury apartment, *Doc Marten* boots and spiked hair had been conservative fashion choices.

Charlotte carried Meadow's backpack and Meadow skipped ahead as they turned onto a curved half-mile stretch of Palmdale Avenue. The houses were serene behind mature trees. The streets were wide, nearly empty of traffic at three-thirty in the afternoon. Parked cars were hidden inside garages. Even the dirt in the gardens looked clean, the soil damp from automatic drip watering systems.

"I like all the trees and grass," said Meadow. "When I woke up this morning I heard about fifty birds outside my window."

Charlotte placed her hand on Meadow's head, feeling the warmth of her scalp. It was easy to imagine her hand tingling with the thoughts racing along the nerves of her daughter's brain, like electricity pulsing through the power lines buried beneath the streets. In four months Meadow would turn eleven. For how much longer would she allow her mother to put her hand on top of her head? Charlotte wove her fingers into the tangle of hair at the base of Meadow's skull. Meadow's entire being felt so vulnerable to damage. For a moment, she longed to tighten her grip and pull her daughter's body back inside her own. "There are a lot more songbirds here," she said. "Or maybe we notice them more because it's so quiet."

Meadow shook her head, dislodging Charlotte's hand.

"How was your first day?" said Charlotte.

"A boy got suspended because he brought his pocketknife to school."

"Suspended?"

"Zero Tolerance. Remember that paper we had to sign?"

Charlotte remembered the policy; it was just hard to believe it had been enforced for a boy with a pocketknife. Did parents and school officials really think they could control everything? The school policies emphasized that if a child brought an aspirin to school it would be confiscated to ensure a drug-free campus. Perhaps the drive to create a perfect world for one's children was simply part of human nature. Wasn't that exactly what she was trying to do for Meadow, moving back to the suburban neighborhood she'd been so anxious to escape when she was eighteen?

At Redwood Avenue they paused to wait for the traffic light that separated their new neighborhood from the houses surrounding the elementary school. The area around Charlotte's rented house was an eclectic collection of 1950s cottages, duplexes, and small apartment buildings. If there were railroad tracks through this section of Sunnyvale, their home would definitely be on the wrong side. Still, it was a neighborhood free of crime except for the occasional theft of a bicycle or a laptop computer. On some level, she believed the wide streets and manicured yards guaranteed that Meadow would forget the violence she'd witnessed last spring. She'd grow up safe, whatever safe meant. When the light turned green, they started walking across.

"I made a friend."

"The girl who came out of the classroom with you?"

"Her name's Amanda. She's a twin."

They passed under an oak tree growing near the entrance to a group of townhouses. Acorns were scattered across the sidewalk. Meadow squatted and scooped up a handful of satiny nuts. She crept along the concrete, stuffing acorns into her pocket. "Amanda said I should join the soccer team."

A breeze wound through the oak tree. The branches swayed above them. Hot air blew against Charlotte's skin, but goose bumps ran down her arms. "You've never mentioned wanting to play soccer."

"Almost everyone at this school plays soccer. All of Amanda's friends. Their team is called the Emerald Tigers. Sign ups are on Saturday."

"I didn't know you were interested in soccer."

"How do I know if I'm interested? I never tried it."

"I thought you wanted to take dance lessons."

"Can't I do both?"

Of course she could do both, but Charlotte didn't want Meadow turning into one of those kids with a schedule as tight as a corporate attorney's. Children should have lots of free time to read, or simply fiddle around. She was a firm believer in daydreaming. "Let's start with one thing and see how it goes."

"Then I want the one thing to be soccer."

If Meadow learned to dance, she would acquire a skill that would give her pleasure throughout her life. She had a narrow body that seemed designed for dance, with supple limbs and an ethereal quality that made her appear to float when she walked. Kicking a soccer ball was such an aggressive act. "Those girls have probably played soccer for years. You might not be able to join the same team as Amanda."

"The teams are by age. Everyone gets to play – it's a rule," said Meadow.

"Let's wait and think about it." She wanted Meadow to make friends, but not like this, not by blindly participating in the same activity as everyone else.

"Why do we have to think about it?"

"Because this is the first time you've ever mentioned it."

"I thought I got to pick what I'm interested in."

"You do."

"I want to play soccer with my new friend."

Charlotte was determined to let Meadow make as many decisions as possible. A few nights a week Meadow planned the dinner menu, even when it meant unusual combinations, like flour tortillas stuffed with fruit. Meadow had been selecting her own clothes since she was eight. But Charlotte had assumed her daughter would choose only among the offerings she was exposed to by her mother, at least for a few more years.

They turned the corner onto Crestview Way. The two-bedroom cottage where they'd lived for less than a week had a small front yard of pale grass that struggled for life because the sun was blocked by a large magnolia tree. The white paint on the trim was flaking in some spots and there were no drapes for the living room window. She couldn't afford to replace them. More truthfully, she didn't want to spend her limited cash on a problem that could be taken care of by tacking an enormous woven blanket inside the window frame.

She unlocked the front door. The thud of her boots sounded solid on the living room's hardwood floor. The wood was scuffed, but so much more pleasing than a carpet that hid the dead skin and sweat of previous tenants. The house, more of a cottage, actually, was eleven hundred square feet and exuded a slight odor of mildew. She kept the windows open night and day.

Meadow dropped her backpack and paperback books on the floor. She inched toward the kitchen and disappeared around the corner. Charlotte sat on the couch and unlaced her boots. Meadow returned clutching a spoon and a plastic container of raspberry yogurt. Meadow's eyelids trembled with the desire for her mother to reflect a sudden enthusiasm for soccer. Was Charlotte making a mistake, allowing her daughter to grow up in a world she had found constricting? She had even played soccer for a few months. Should she tell Meadow about her experience? It hadn't gone well.

When she was ten years old, everyone said she ran like a leopard. Her long legs carried her around the track with a fluid motion. She loved stretching her muscles and tendons with graceful strides, but on the soccer field it wasn't about beautiful running. Hidden lumps under the grass waited to twist her ankle. The chalked lines made her feel confined. The other girls pressed so close, pushing in front of her to get at the ball. All the while, the coach shouted at them, *play your positions, girls!* They weren't individuals to her, just chess pieces. Charlotte was a fullback, rarely allowed to even attempt a score.

Then there was that perfect day – Charlotte had gotten control of the ball. For once, it stayed where it belonged, bobbing back and forth between her feet as she trotted down the field. She felt good, she knew what she was doing, putting distance between herself and the others so that she didn't feel the heat of their skin, the puffing of their breath on her neck. She ran, increasing her speed with each step. The ball rolled and bounced in front of her. That scratching voice faded behind her. *Play your position. Pass the ball. Pass!*

She didn't want to pass the ball. For once, she was having fun; she might even have a chance to score. She ran all the way to the end of the field and gave the ball a solid whack. The ball flew into the net. She turned, grinning.

"God, Charlotte. Are you stupid?"

The grin slid off her face.

"You were supposed to pass."

"But I scored."

"It's not your job to score."

The girls turned and walked back to their starting positions. Not once, for the remainder of the game, did the ball come within five feet of Charlotte. Instead, she danced back and forth, running slightly with nowhere to go. Did they have any fun at all, or did they just echo the voices of their parents about how important it was to do it right? Follow the rules, play your position. Why? So they could win a trophy of a fake-gold-plated girl kicking a ball? So they could shout, we won! After she quit soccer and decided sports weren't for her, the soccer players no longer seemed interested in being friends with a girl like Charlotte. She wasn't on their team. They were athletes, competitors, they had an identity – *we're soccer players*. It still hurt more than she wanted to admit.

She smiled, hoping her face hid the memories racing inside her head. Maybe it would be different for Meadow. Maybe not. She'd moved to suburbia to give Meadow a safer world, but had managed to forget about the pain that could be inflicted on Meadow's psyche if she didn't conform. "You're right, you won't know if you like soccer unless you try." Her words sounded hollow, echoing against the walls of the half empty room.

Meadow grinned, unaware that a droplet of pink yogurt clung to her lower lip.

Chapter Three

THE SOCCER FIELD WAS a wash of colors. Rachel's eyes ached from the crowd of parents and children, dressed in shirts and baseball caps speckled with the logos of colleges and professional sports teams. It was late Saturday morning and already the scent of broiled hamburgers filled the air. She and Greg had agreed on a plan to divide and conquer – Greg would take Sara to register for fall soccer with the fifth grade girls while Rachel stayed with Trent. As they walked, Trent tugged at her hand, restraining her forward movement. She slowed her pace, hoping to instill confidence so he didn't feel he was being dragged like an unwilling dog to the vet. They stopped at the end of a short line. Trent pressed his toes on the outer edge of her foot. Rachel jiggled to the side. He stepped closer, placing his toes back where they'd been. She wasn't sure what she'd expected, that he would show sudden enthusiasm for the game? Last year, as she'd watched him scuttle down the edge of the field, a kindergartener nervous about the flying ball, she'd worried that his sole desire was to blend into the chalked sideline. She'd been certain he'd have more confidence this year.

"There's Brian, at the front of the line," she said.

Trent pressed his feet harder on the side of her foot. She lost her balance and stumbled sideways.

"Careful." She smiled and put her hand on his shoulder. For two weeks now, Trent had whimpered that he didn't want to play soccer. Yet every evening when he and Greg went out to the back yard to practice, Trent kicked the ball hard, laughing as it slammed into shrubs and the posts supporting the patio roof. Rachel was convinced he was enjoying himself. This morning during breakfast, Trent hadn't mentioned soccer. As they backed out of the driveway and Sara chattered about her plans for improving her skills, Trent had been silent.

Greg insisted there was nothing to worry about. *He's sensitive, more creative.* She couldn't argue with that. Trent spent hours drawing with fine-tipped felt pens. The drawings he produced were intricate, down to accurately rendered shadows cast by figures and buildings. *Let him find his own way,* Greg said.

Because he was a software developer, immersed every day in writing the codes that made computers work, Greg saw everything from a logical point of view. He seemed to think numbers could account for every part of life, explaining behavior and dictating that each human being followed a code like a computer followed a series of numerical instructions. In his view, a child who didn't want to play soccer was programmed differently and should discover his own interests. He stared blankly at Rachel when she explained that soccer was important for a lot of reasons. By participating in a fun activity, children improved their coordination and learned to compete and accept loss. Most important of all, they made friends with their teammates.

When Rachel started dating Greg during their first year in college, she felt she'd finally discovered a best friend. All the loneliness of her childhood dissolved. Perhaps spending every afternoon with her three brothers had destined her to identify more closely with boys. Maybe friendships with females had proven too treacherous. Through college and their early marriage Greg was her closest friend. They talked for hours while they ate dinner and sipped beer on the back porch of their condo on hot summer evenings. Greg made her feel as if she didn't need anyone else. They shared the newspaper over their morning coffee and bowls of Cream of Wheat. He made her laugh until she choked on her cereal as he read news reports in a high-pitched voice threaded with alarm, telling of newly released studies stating the obvious – *study finds more coffee is consumed by people addicted to caffeine.*

Pregnancy had changed everything. Suddenly, Rachel craved the similar experiences of other women. After Sara was born, she realized Greg couldn't possibly know how she felt when the baby fussed for two hours before succumbing to a nap. He couldn't coach her on how to relax so her breast milk would flow. He couldn't laugh until tears gushed out over the discovery that an imported beer smelled like a wet diaper. The women she'd met at Lamaze class could do all those things.

It wasn't that their marriage was strained; they just drifted around each other as if they were floating on a vast lake. Sometimes the sides of their rafts bumped together, other times he was barely visible on the horizon. Right now was one of those times. How could she let Trent find his own way when he seemed content to isolate himself? Her heart ached when she saw him walking alone, studying the toes of his shoes. He didn't seem to care whether he had any friends.

Today's sign-ups for soccer were a formality. It could be done on-line. This was a chance to get re-acquainted, and an excuse for a barbeque. She hoped seeing the other kids would spark Trent's desire to play. She picked up the pencil tied to the metal tab of the clipboard.

"What are you writing?" said Trent.

"We're signing up for soccer."

"I don't want to play soccer any more. It's boring."

"It's not boring." He was too young to be bored, wasn't he?

"I don't want to."

"Everyone loves soccer." She knew this was a lie.

"I hate it."

"Remember when you kicked the ball to Brian last year and he scored? You helped win the game."

"It hurt my foot."

She wrote his name on the line. Trent grabbed her wrist. "No. I hate soccer."

"You've had fun kicking the ball with Dad. It's important to keep trying."

His hand was so tight she thought her bones might break. She pried at his fingers, but as she peeled one away from her wrist, he curled the others back around.

The woman behind her spoke in a loud voice, "I don't think he wants to play."

Rachel kept her eyes focused on the clipboard. "Let's give it one more try."

Trent grabbed the pencil out of her hand. He stabbed it on the table. The lead snapped with a crunching sound.

The teenage boy seated at the table handed her another pencil.

Trent kicked her ankle. Tears rushed into her eyes, but she blinked them away.

"Can you hurry up," said the woman behind them. "My son wants a burger."

Rachel took a deep breath. "Trent, you're not being polite. Let's sign the paper. You can always change your mind later."

"I hate soccer. It's stupid."

Rachel placed the pencil on the clipboard. "We'll sign up on-line." She stepped away from the table. They crossed the field and she collapsed on a bench to wait for Greg and Sara. "Most of the boys your age play soccer. That's where you'll make friends."

Trent stared at her as if he didn't understand the meaning of the word. His eyes were wide and clear, dark chocolate centers surrounded by white as pure as whipping cream. She loved looking into his eyes. Sometimes, she wondered who was looking back at her. Who resided inside that small, quiet body? He wasn't the kind of child that mindlessly followed the other kids. She should be glad, but instead, it scared her. What would happen to him if he grew up friendless, unable to compete or interact with his peers? Soccer was supposed to be fun. All that was involved at his age was running up and down the field, practicing dribbling, and kicking the ball. Quitting wasn't the behavior they should be encouraging, but once Greg heard about the incident with the pencil, he'd say that was enough. Soccer was over for Trent. She was suddenly hungry. She scanned the field, looking for Greg and Sara.

Trent squatted on the grass in front of her. He stroked the shell of a snail with his index finger. He rubbed his finger across the tip of the antennae. The snail didn't seem to be bothered by Trent's finger on its flesh, but Rachel shuddered. She was impatient to get her mind off that woman's tone, judging her, as if Rachel didn't love her son more than her own life. "Come stand on the bench, Trent. I need help looking for your Dad and Sara."

He placed the snail on the palm of his hand and scrambled onto the bench.

"Put the snail back on the grass."

"No. He's my friend."

She closed her eyes. "Do you see them?"

"Yup. They're at the food hut." He climbed down and put the snail into a tuft of grass under the bench.

A few minutes later Greg and Sara arrived with two flimsy cartons of food. The four of them settled on the grass to eat. "All signed up for soccer?" Greg handed Trent a hotdog. Trent plucked the meat out of the bun and dropped the ketchup-coated bread onto the grass. Greg swooped it up and tossed it into a nearby trashcan.

"I'm not playing soccer," said Trent.

Rachel looked at Greg and sipped her coke.

Greg nodded. "Changed your mind?"

"No. I never wanted to play."

Greg took a large bite out of his burger. He chewed slowly while they all held their breath, waiting to see which way this would go.

"I love soccer," said Sara. "You didn't try hard enough to learn the game."

Talking around the burger in his mouth, Greg said, "It's not for everyone."

Rachel ripped open her bag of chips and ate one. She took another sip of coke. The cold made her teeth ache. So, that was how it would be. Greg wasn't going to charm Trent into a playful mood, even though she knew he could – she'd seen him do it a hundred times.

"You could play baseball," said Sara.

"I don't like games with balls." Trent reached over and picked up the snail that he'd left under the bench. He put it on the inner side of his thigh.

"Ew. That's disgusting," said Sara.

Rachel set her burger on the cardboard box. She drank her soda and tried not to look at the other families. There was a sharp pain, as if one of the chips was stuck inside her lung. If Amy were here, she would understand. Rachel wouldn't have to explain that it wasn't just about soccer. It wasn't only about being a team player and exercise and competition. Soccer was the glue that held kids together. Without a group where they felt connected, children drifted alone. Anything could happen. Being part of a soccer team formed a safety net, protecting children from the threats that lurked in the darker corners of a mother's imagination.

Greg pointed at her burger. "Are you going to eat that?"

"You can have it," she said.

He put his hand on her ankle. With the other hand, he picked up the burger and devoured it in five bites. He squeezed her ankle. Rachel closed her eyes and tried not to think about the snail crawling toward the hem of Trent's shorts.

Chapter Four

AMY'S FINGERTIPS WERE TINGED gray from newsprint, the layer of grime slick and powdery, like charcoal. She concentrated on the scissors. Sliding steel against paper was comforting. It put space between the horror of the printed words and the fluttery rhythm of her heart. There was a thrill in using a potentially deadly tool for the simple act of cutting paper. She knew that gluing crime stories into scrapbooks was strange, possibly even demented, but Justin didn't complain about her compulsion. *Everyone has their quirks*, he said. That made it okay, didn't it? She didn't like to think of herself as quirky, but he meant it as reassurance. It wasn't as if he laughed at her, or suggested she get rid of the scrapbooks. For the most part, he forgot about them. He never went into the spare room where she stored them.

Her friends didn't know about the scrapbooks. They would not view her habit as an endearing flaw. She pictured Kit smirking and lifting her left eyebrow, Rachel biting her lip, asking if it was really necessary to glue the stories into a scrapbook, couldn't she collect them in a large envelope? Jane would laugh with that barking sound she made. She'd point out that if Amy had enough free time to catalog her fears in a scrapbook, maybe she should find something productive to do during the day. If Amy knew this about her friends, did that mean that deep inside she knew there was something unbalanced about her need to clip the report of every violent crime and secure it on the pages of a scrapbook? She clung to Justin's word – *quirky*. Everyone had secrets, parts of their lives kept hidden.

She placed the cutout story to her left. The article concluded on page four. It was admirable that the newspaper published stories so they were easy to clip and save. Rarely were they printed back to back. She was grateful for that. She slid the shears up the center of the paper to remove the section she wanted, and then trimmed it into a rectangle.

Along with the initial crime reports, she saved each article that provided a revelation of new information. Once the entire story unfolded, crimes didn't seem as messy. The follow-up articles often hinted at mistakes on the part of the victims – unlocked doors, visits to rough neighborhoods, and unsavory acquaintances. It made her feel better when she realized most crimes weren't random at all. It was comforting to read about the victims' carelessness, their involvement in situations where exposure to violence was more likely. There was nothing to fear, she reminded herself, if you lived your life with caution.

She was reassured once she learned a perpetrator had been caught. Many of the murder stories she'd collected ended happily, but too many of the rape stories glued in her scrapbooks had nothing more than an artist's sketch. Those stories often failed to point out errors on the part of the victim. Sure, there were some women who were in bad neighborhoods or out at strange hours of the night, but she also read about women attacked in supermarket parking lots and women overpowered by men who came to the front door, sweet-talking their way inside, pretending to want something reasonable. Sometimes the women knew their attackers. Although she felt compelled to save each and every report of violent crime, she didn't like how it reminded her of the attack on her mother.

She went to the sink and turned on the faucet. While she waited for the water to get warm, she depressed the plunger on the almond-scented soap, squirting an ivory puddle onto her palm. She moistened her right hand under the running water and rubbed her hands together, turning the foam to a gray-tinged color that looked like sludge from a corroded pipe. She rinsed her hands and wiped them on a linen towel. She grabbed a glass and filled it with water, drinking quickly. It was better not to think about her mother. It had been over ten years since her mother's suicide. Something else it was best not to think about.

She returned to the table, pulled the cap off the glue stick and turned the dial at the bottom. A smooth wedge of glue rose above the edge of the container.

The doorbell rang. She set the glue stick on the table. She only had to hold her breath and wait. A stranger would ring once and leave, but if it were one of her friends, they wouldn't give up as easily. Rachel would push the bell five or six times before she'd accept that Amy might not be home. Kit wouldn't ring quite as many times, but she would query Amy later, demanding to know, *where were you?* Amy didn't like to lie, even if it was a lie where she wouldn't be caught.

The bell rang again. She laid the pieces of the article inside the scrapbook, twisted the glue back into the tube and replaced the cap. She opened the cabinet door, shoved the scrapbook, scissors, and glue on top of her baking dishes and then stuffed the excess newspaper into the trash. The bell rang a third time. She rinsed her hands.

In the living room, she stuck her finger into the opening between the drapes and created a slit wide enough to see the front porch. It was Kit. Sometimes she wondered why Kit Shepherd even paid attention to her. Kit wasn't like Amy's other friends. For one thing, her husband was now a vice president of engineering. All the men in their group earned lucrative salaries working in the high tech industry, but Aaron Shepherd was in a class by himself. Kit drove a *Mercedes* and they owned a second home in the Sierras. They belonged to a club where Kit played tennis and Aaron golfed. It wasn't just the money, it was Kit's entire life that made her different. Kit had graduated from Stanford University. Amy hadn't gone to college at all, and sometimes she felt as if she didn't understand what Kit was talking about. It was difficult to tell whether Kit was deliberately obscure, or if she really read all those novels Amy had never heard of, books that Kit learned about on *National Public Radio*. Still, she liked Kit. She admired her clothes and her braininess. Despite Kit's aloofness, the almost imperceptible distance she kept between herself and the other moms at Spruce Elementary School, they'd been friends for what seemed like forever.

Amy stepped into the foyer, turned the deadbolt, and opened the door.

"What took so long?" said Kit.

"My hands were wet."

Kit looked past Amy's shoulder as if she expected to see an explanation more believable than wet hands. "I brought your dish back." She handed Amy a glass pan.

As Amy took the pan, it started to slide out of her grip. Kit grabbed it. "I guess your hands are still wet."

Amy ran her palms down her thighs.

"Thanks for the casserole," said Kit. "All the meals everyone brought over made me feel like I had a mini vacation instead of a back spasm."

Amy took the pan, "You're welcome."

"Can I come in? I have something to tell you."

Amy hesitated, unable to put the scrapbook out of her mind. It was important to get the story glued in place and the scrapbook shelved in the closet of the spare room. It was the only way to settle her thoughts. "I need to get some things finished," she said.

"Aaron finally agreed to put our house on the market," said Kit.

"Now? This is a terrible time to sell your house."

"We've been there almost twelve years, so it's still worth a lot more than we paid for it. And it's a perfect time to find something in Palo Alto for a more reasonable price."

"I suppose."

"He suddenly realized that if we're ever going to move, now is the time," said Kit. "Before Carter starts junior high."

"Is it because of the rape? And the stabbing?"

"No, we've talked about it for quite awhile. It's because of Carter's age."

"Well his age isn't any different than it was two weeks ago. Something must have made Aaron change his mind."

Kit shrugged.

"If something that horrible can happen here, it could happen in Palo Alto too." Amy looked out across her front yard. If Kit was afraid, but didn't want to admit it, what did that mean? Amy hugged the casserole pan to her chest. She wasn't sure if she wanted Kit to feel the same fear or reassure her. Announcing plans to move away was not reassuring.

"It's not because of the murder. We've been talking about this forever."

"I know you have, but it seems sudden."

"It's not," said Kit.

She didn't think Kit was telling the truth. It made no sense to decide during the first week of the new school year that now was the time to uproot your children. Kit was more afraid than she wanted to admit. She sounded keyed up, as if she couldn't wait to escape. "I suppose Renee would be on a different soccer team," said Amy.

"I'm thinking of starting them in tennis. Soccer is kind of a kid thing. Tennis is a sport they can still play when they're adults."

"Moving. Quitting soccer. That's a lot of disruption."

Kit backed to the edge of the porch. "Since you don't have time for me to come in, I should go. I can still run a few errands before school's out."

Amy wanted to hear more. She wanted to find out whether Kit could be persuaded to re-think her plans. She was sure that somewhere under this sudden decision, after talking about it and doing nothing for years, was the urge to find a safer community. It was upsetting, knowing that Kit was afraid. Amy wanted to find out what Aaron had said about the attack, but she had to finish the scrapbook before the twins were out of school.

Kit waved. "See you."

It only took twenty minutes to carefully glue the article onto two fresh pages. She read the story again. There had been no sign of forced entry – the police speculated that the woman had invited her attacker into the house, or left a door unlocked. Amy turned the album page to read the rest. As she lifted the page, her hand shook so badly that she had to grab her wrist with her left hand. The bones felt thin under her fingers, as if they were filled with air. The woman had been attacked with her own carving knife, which indicated the stabbing was unplanned. The police officer quoted in the article didn't come right out and say this, but there was another expert interviewed who said that since the man didn't carry a weapon, he hadn't intended to kill her. Something happened that wasn't in his plan. Perhaps the woman resisted more than he'd expected, or she'd torn a mask he might have been wearing. It was all speculation. They didn't really know anything.

Amy closed the scrapbook and put her supplies in the kitchen drawer. She paused in front of the open window above the sink. She smelled the dry odor of late summer after months without rain. The air burned in her nostrils and she had a sudden longing for crisp autumn weather. Instead, they were stuck with this constant, oppressive heat. She closed the window. How could a woman be raped in her own house? Uninvited thoughts slid through her mind. *How stupid to invite a stranger inside. Why didn't she fight harder?*

She carried the scrapbook upstairs. Sunnyvale was supposed to be one of the safest cities in the country. She didn't have a single friend or neighbor who had been the victim of even a petty crime. She was confident the articles over the next few days would explain that the woman had done something foolish, had involved herself with some kind of shady character. Once the story was complete, the ending pasted in her scrapbook, she would feel calm again.

Chapter Five

CHARLOTTE REMOVED THE LENS cap from her camera and peered through the viewfinder. At four on a weekday afternoon, Crestview Avenue was devoid of human life. This was the first chance she'd had to take photographs since she and Meadow moved into their new home. Even if she couldn't work on her photo essay right now, at least she might be able to find some images to submit to the stock photography company that purchased her freelance work from time to time. She scanned the street, looking through the tiny rectangle for an interesting angle. All she saw were bland apartment buildings and condos. As she continued scanning the opposite side of the street, a woman came into view. She was pushing a shopping cart loaded with her possessions.

To ease the sting of hot concrete on her bare feet, Charlotte stepped off the sidewalk onto a flat, spreading weed growing through a crack in the gutter. Even from across the street, she saw that the woman's skin bore the grayish color of old leather. A homeless woman seemed so out of place here. In

San Francisco, the homeless had been everywhere. When she'd walked Meadow to and from school and when they strolled through the park, they passed people living on the street. She'd been sickened on a regular basis, forced to step over sleeping bodies as she went into the local market.

This woman's legs were puffy beneath the hem of a brown plaid coat. Her ankles were reddened from rubbing on the top edges of athletic shoes that were too large. Charlotte aimed her Nikon at the woman's feet and pressed the shutter release. The woman whipped her cart to the side, shoved it over the curb and rushed across the street. She slammed the cart into Charlotte's legs. "Don't be taking my picture."

Charlotte jumped back and lowered the camera to her hip. She bent over and rubbed the broken skin on her leg. "I was just trying to…" What was the right thing to say? That she wanted to build a photography career on the image of a woman who was barely surviving? She looked into the woman's eyes. They were bright blue, without the milky cloud of alcohol or madness that Charlotte was used to seeing in the eyes of a homeless person. "I didn't think you'd mind."

"You have no right to take my picture."

"I'm sorry."

The cart was filled with plastic bags stuffed so they looked like shiny black pillows. Wedged between the garbage bags were smashed aluminum cans and several books, including *Harry Potter and the Half-Blood Prince*. Meadow wanted to read that book; she'd finished book five in the series a few weeks ago.

"I just wanted a few photographs of your feet. I'm working on a photo essay. It includes people who … live outdoors."

"I don't live outdoors."

"Oh, right. I mean people who ..."

After years of seeing so many homeless as part of the daily scenery, she'd had the idea to build a photo essay that would portray their humanity. She wanted people to see the homeless as human beings, not as a frightening or annoying intrusion. She wanted to make people look beyond the thickened skin and carts piled with rags and cans. In Charlotte's mind, their feet illustrated the decay of their bodies, of their entire lives. She hoped contrasting those images with photographs showing the smooth feet of babies and children would illustrate how every person started out fresh. The photographs would evoke memories of the sweet scent of a baby's feet. Difficulties arose in every life, but life hit some people harder and with more frequency. A relentless stream of setbacks left some with no other choice than living on the street. By including photographs of children's feet, her collection would show that some of those children could fall off the desired path of a stable life. Some children would grow up to become homeless, battered, living on the fringe of society. How did she explain all of that without making this woman feel like an object?

"I didn't mean to offend you," said Charlotte.

The woman started back across the street, the wheels of the cart clacked and rattled on the blacktop. "Go take your pictures somewhere else, girly."

"Wait. I'd like to buy your copy of Harry Potter. Would that be a fair exchange for taking a few pictures?"

The woman turned back. "Harry-who?"

Charlotte walked closer. The pavement burned her feet. She curled her toes to minimize contact. She poked her finger through the side of the cart and tapped the book. "The book about Harry Potter. My daughter wants to read it."

"It's not for sale."

"But don't … couldn't you use some cash?"

"Not for sale." The woman shoved the cart, straining under its weight as it went up the slight incline at the center of the street.

Charlotte lifted the camera and framed the woman's heels. She moved the camera to follow her progress. The woman stopped at the curb, tilted the cart back and lifted the front wheels onto the sidewalk. Charlotte snapped three pictures. The woman whirled around. She opened her mouth wide and raised her face toward the sky. "Stop taking my picture or I'm calling the cops!" She lifted one hand off the handle and the cart tipped sideways. One of the garbage bags and her books spilled onto the ground.

Charlotte ran across the street. "I'm sorry. I'm really sorry. Let me help."

"No. Get away from me. Don't touch my stuff." The woman straightened the cart and picked up the bag. She stuffed it into the cart, making sure all the corners were tucked in. She nestled the books into the spaces between the bags.

"I want to show how hard your life is. It will help people understand."

Once again the woman lifted the front wheels of the cart onto the sidewalk. She hoisted the back end up and proceeded down the street. Charlotte darted back across the pavement and leaped onto her front lawn.

A man in the yard next door held the nozzle of a hose near a slightly faded rosebush. His skin was almost as leathery as the homeless woman's. "Hot day to be barefoot," he said.

Charlotte smiled. "I know."

"You're new here."

She nodded.

"That's Linda. She likes to be left alone."

"I didn't mean to upset her. I'm working on a photo essay."

"So I heard."

Charlotte snapped the lens cap back in place. "How long have you lived here?"

"Since 1978. You shouldn't take pictures of people without asking."

"I said I was sorry. Usually people like to be photographed."

"You're exploiting her."

"I'm not. Really. I care about showing the human side of the homeless."

"See, listen to the way you say that – the homeless – as if it's a disease."

The grass was like crumpled paper under her bare feet. They still burned from the blacktop. She wanted to ask her new neighbor to point the hose in her direction. Maybe she'd take a few shots of her own feet to show a gradual progression from childhood. "I won't be exploiting her."

He moved the hose to the next rosebush. It was filled with pale pink buds, a few blooms going to seed, and one perfect blossom. "You can't take pictures of anyone you choose."

He sounded cold, as if he had no interest in starting a neighborly relationship. Maybe she was imagining it, still shaken from the woman's anger. "Thanks for the advice," she said.

"Good luck on your essay." He lifted his hand in a wave, but kept his head down, staring at the water seeping across the bowl of dirt he'd dug around the base of the roses.

She climbed the porch steps, fit the camera inside her bag and zipped it closed. It wasn't fair to accuse her of tainted motives. All she wanted were a few anonymous photographs. It wasn't as if she was trying to put Linda in a bad light, just the opposite. None of the homeless people in San Francisco objected when she photographed them. Either they hardly noticed or they welcomed the attention. Were the homeless in suburbia different? More private?

She went inside and locked the screen door behind her. She felt as if her photography career was stalled yet again. The small income from her stock photo submissions would only cover a few extras. Sure, she had help. After Mark's sentencing, when she knew she couldn't afford their apartment on her own, his brother had offered free rent on this cottage. But if she was going to launch a career as a photographer, it was now or never. She had a clear vision for the facets of life she wanted to capture. Was it so wrong to show human beings struggling to survive? She didn't think that was a bad thing. Until today, she'd thought it was a noble desire.

Chapter Six

CHARLOTTE PUSHED OPEN the door of *Valley Camera*. A set of Tibetan bells tied to the handle clanged against the glass. A man with thick, wavy gray hair and heavy black-rimmed glasses was on the opposite side of a large opening in the wall, the front end of a framing studio. A red-haired woman stood with her narrow hips pressed against the counter. She held samples of blue mat board spread between her fingers like a fan.

Meadow leaned close to Charlotte and whispered, "That's Amanda's mom."

The counter was covered with mat board in varying shades of blue and green. Lying at the center was a twenty-by-twenty-four inch photograph of Amanda and her twin sister. "I'm just not sure," the woman said.

Meadow walked down the steps that led to the section of the shop displaying other merchandise – photo albums, frames, books, and photography equipment. Charlotte studied the woman's back. She wore white jeans, a dark green top and matching sandals with three-inch heels. Her hair was expertly cut and straightened so that it brushed the tops of her shoulders. A single section that had not taken well to the precision cut stuck out at an awkward angle. The woman picked up another piece of mat board. "I don't know. I'm just not sure."

Charlotte saw how this indecision could go on for quite some time. "Excuse me, I just have a quick question."

"I don't know if I want to bring out the color of their eyes or have more contrast," said the woman.

Charlotte moved closer so she was touching the counter. She held up the memory stick. "I need to get some black and white prints."

Amanda's mother placed the samples on the counter and turned.

"Our daughters know each other," said Charlotte. "Spruce Elementary? Your daughter invited mine to join the soccer team." From the corner of her eye she saw Meadow had stopped wandering around the aisles and was facing them, listening.

The woman smiled. "Your daughter's a soccer player?"

"No, but ..." She glanced at Meadow. A grin spread across Meadow's face and she made eye contact, waiting to hear what her mother would say about her soccer aspirations.

"I thought she looked a bit delicate for soccer. Amanda told me she's very smart. Did she skip a grade?" The woman tilted her head to the side and smiled. Her lips glistened with burgundy-tinted gloss.

A bit delicate? What was that supposed to mean? Especially coming from someone equally thin. The woman's wrists were like twigs and her pelvic bones were visible through the fabric of her pants. "Meadow will be eleven in a few months. She may be small, but she's strong." Charlotte immediately regretted the words. She wasn't required to prove Meadow was capable of playing soccer.

The woman extended her hand. "Amy Lewis. I didn't mean to upset you."

Charlotte shook Amy's hand and introduced herself. "I'm not upset," she said.

"You look very upset." Amy's voice was soft and her smile seemed genuine.

"I'm not," said Charlotte.

"I assumed your daughter was a dancer, or something."

"She's interested in a lot of things."

Amy stared at her, still smiling. Her eyes were ringed in light brown liner, making her look frightened, or dismissive, Charlotte wasn't sure which.

"The girls on our team have been playing soccer together since kindergarten."

"Well, she's already signed up," said Charlotte. It looked as if Meadow had grown bored with the conversation because she'd moved to the end of the row and picked up a metal tree that had tiny picture frames stuck to the ends of the branches.

"Good for her." Amy's voice was loud. She lowered it to a whisper. "You know, I couldn't help noticing. What happened to her hair? That little bald spot. Is she ok?"

"It's nothing." Charlotte glanced across the store again. Meadow was combing her fingers through her hair, moving it around so the exposed skin was covered. Charlotte wasn't sure whether it was an unconscious movement. She'd seen her do it before.

"I just wondered. If you don't want to say, that's ok. I didn't mean to pry." Amy looked at Charlotte's left hand, still clutching the memory stick.

"Are you a single mom?"

"I ... what? Not really. My ..." She never knew what to call Mark. Boyfriend? That sounded like they were in high school. They'd never thought getting married was that important. They knew they loved each other and that was enough. It wasn't as if marriage guaranteed a satisfying relationship. "Not single, but Meadow and I are here alone, for now."

"Is your husband in the military?"

"No, he's not..."

"You don't have to explain it. That's ok. I'm sure it's painful. I can't imagine trying to raise a child by myself. And now with the rape and everything. You must be scared to death. Two females alone."

"We're fine. We can take care of ourselves." Charlotte straightened her shoulders and smiled. She should have prepared herself for questions like these. She'd forgotten that everyone here was clearly labeled: Married. Divorced. Soccer player.

Amy turned to the clerk. "I'll go with the sapphire."

The clerk looked at Charlotte. She placed the memory stick on the counter. "I'd like the images on this printed as eight by tens." The clerk handed her an envelope to fill out her contact details and said she could pick up her prints after seven that evening. She filled out the form and stepped away from the counter. "I guess we'll see you at soccer practice."

Without turning, Amy lifted her arm and flicked her fingers. "Bye-bye."

Charlotte walked down the steps to the other half of the shop.

"Can I get this?" Meadow held up the pewter tree.

"Not today."

Meadow put the tree on the shelf.

Outside in the parking lot, Charlotte plucked at her T-shirt, stuck to a damp spot on her lower back. She put her hand in her pocket and gripped her keys, squeezing hard until the teeth dug into her palm. After she opened the *Jetta's* passenger door for Meadow, she settled into the driver's seat and jammed the key into the ignition. She should have defended Meadow, but against what? All Amy said was that she looked too delicate to be a soccer player. Well she wasn't a soccer player, so what was wrong with that?

It was the comment about Meadow's torn hair. The look on Amy's face implied Meadow had some kind of disease. The whispering to emphasize there was something to be ashamed of – *If you don't want to say, it's ok.* Amy's words hinted that Charlotte was hiding the truth, that there was something wrong with Meadow that couldn't be discussed. Her insistence that Meadow was too delicate seemed calculated to press Charlotte into admitting Meadow couldn't keep up with the other girls. It was almost as if Amy didn't want Meadow to play soccer. The words lodged in her mind, *too delicate.* Wasn't that what that cop had said? No, she'd said fragile. She'd said Meadow looked fragile but kicked like she was in the NFL.

Last spring, when the cops had come to arrest Mark, Charlotte hadn't been focused on Meadow. All she could think about were the three police officers moving around her living room as if they had every right to do as they pleased. Another officer dug through cabinets, searching for the packages of pot Mark had prepared for his customers. They'd ordered Mark to lie down, his face pressed to the floor.

He doesn't have a gun. Why are you making him do that? She asked that question several times, but they ignored her.

As one cop snapped handcuffs around Mark's wrists, Meadow had come flying out of the bedroom. Her hair was tangled and her San Francisco Giants shirt clung to her legs. She leaped onto the officer's back, and shrieked, "Let go of my Daddy!"

The officer jerked his head toward the female cop. "Get her off me."

The female officer tried to pry Meadow's arms from around the other cop's shoulders. Meadow screamed and grabbed at his ears. He bellowed and swung his body hard, letting her fall to the floor with a thud. Charlotte screamed. Mark pleaded with them to leave Meadow out of it. The pain in his voice, the hint of tears froze Charlotte's thoughts. In all their years together, she'd never seen him cry.

The female cop told Mark to stay quiet. Meadow was still lying on her side where she'd fallen, but that didn't slow her down. She kicked at the cop's shins, his knee, thrashing her legs with the same intensity she used when she swam in water over her head. She wrapped her body around the cop's leg. Then the other male cop stepped in. He grabbed her hair and pulled. There was a sickening tearing sound. Meadow screamed. A chunk of hair came out of the side of her head. Blood bubbled up in tiny dots on the bare skin. The officer dropped the clump of hair on the floor. Charlotte heard a whimper from her own lips. "Don't hurt her."

"Then get control of her."

Charlotte dropped to her knees and stroked Meadow's head. She laid her fingers on the exposed piece of scalp.

"What a little hellion," said the female cop. "She looks as fragile as a freakin' bird but kicks like she's in the NFL."

Charlotte looked at Mark. Tears ran down his face.

Before Mark's arrest, Charlotte had thought of herself as a peaceful person. She believed in kindness, in looking for the good in people. The only violence she'd ever witnessed was a fight in the girls' bathroom when she was in high school. Now, a violent world had spilled into her own living room. She shouldn't have been surprised, given Mark's method of earning a living, but she was. Whether she was deluding herself or not, she thought of pot as a harmless drug, a high favored by hippie types, a tool for the pursuit of a mellow frame of mind. She associated violence with alcohol.

Meadow had been trusting and open with everyone she met, but trying to defend her daddy, not understanding what was happening, she'd been repaid with brutality. Maybe it was good that she wanted to play soccer. It would make her feel strong, in control.

Meadow waved her hand in front of Charlotte's face. "Are we going?"

Charlotte turned the key, released the brake, and wrenched the gearshift into reverse. Amy's steady flow of words had made her feel she might be missing something important. There was a glitter in Amy's eyes that hinted at the kind of violence that didn't leave physical wounds.

Chapter Seven

RACHEL BACKED HER *RAV4* out of the garage and gunned it down the street. She'd barely managed to escape the house without grabbing two of the oatmeal cookies she'd baked before dinner. It felt like she was running for her life, escaping the lure of chewy flour and sugar that offered to sooth her ricocheting nerves. She'd left Sara and Trent with the dishes, Greg with homework supervision.

She looked forward to her evening walks with Amy – two nights a week, when they could manage it – a chance to unload all the feelings she didn't want to talk about when Kit or Jane were around. Although since Jane had started working full time, she missed half their conversations. During their walks, she could tell Amy the kind of thoughts that were reserved for a best friend. Amy was on her side, and Amy would confirm that for once, Greg was wrong. Why couldn't he see that playing team sports was critical for Trent? She wanted both her children to have all the things she'd missed when she was a kid.

Straight A's had been important to her parents, not delivering a trophy or a ribbon. From sixth grade on, she spent her after-school hours studying and watching out for her younger brothers. Instead of spending time with friends, she was responsible for making sure her brothers finished their homework before their parents arrived home from work. She never had a chance to feel the closeness of a team that won and lost together. She never learned to take control of a ball. Even now, she ducked when a ball raced through the air in her direction. Worse, she was stuck with a body that carried fifteen pounds of extra weight, a sense of clumsiness, and the nagging feeling that she never quite belonged to any group.

She pulled up to the curb in front of Amy's house. A few months ago it had occurred to her that the house looked a bit like a castle. It was built on a slight rise so it dominated the cul-de-sac. It featured a stone façade and the slate roof was sharply peaked. The wrought iron fence surrounding the front yard had posts shaped like spear tips that reached past Rachel's shoulders. White roses stood out sharply against the black painted iron.

She unlatched the gate and walked up two steps to a stone path that wound its way to the porch. The doorbell resonated like chimes in a church tower. After a few seconds, she pressed the button again.

Amy opened the door and stepped onto the porch. She slipped off her nylon jacket. "I guess I don't need this. Why is it still so hot?"

They walked down the path to the edge of the yard. Rachel opened the gate and held it for Amy. They turned left, as always, walking a half block to Birch Avenue, then right onto Dennison. They followed a route that made a swath around the elementary school and the adjacent park, as if they were marking out the territory at the center of their lives.

"Trent refused to sign up for soccer." The words burst out of Rachel's throat like a ragged cough.

"He'll change his mind once he gets out on the field with the other kids."

"I don't think so. He says he hates soccer. How can he hate it?" said Rachel.

"Take him to the first practice. Once he sees the other kids, he'll be fine."

"He had a melt-down at the sign-ups. He kicked me."

"Then ask Greg to take him. I think boys need their fathers more."

"Kit's always taken Carter to practice. He doesn't seem to need his father there."

"Maybe Trent is more bonded with his Daddy," said Amy.

If only that were true. Rachel's throat tightened. Afraid that her voice would tremble, she spoke softly. "Greg thinks we shouldn't force him."

Amy stopped at the corner of a yard edged with river rock. She pushed her toe against a rock that had separated from the others to move it back into place. "I suppose some kids don't like soccer."

Amy sounded as unconcerned as Greg. Why couldn't anyone feel the pinch of fear that appeared in her chest the minute she woke in the morning and stayed with her all day? "If he doesn't play soccer, how will he make friends?"

Amy slowed and moved toward the edge of the sidewalk, close to slipping off the curb into the gutter. "He's just different. A loner."

"But I'm scared for him."

"I can see why you'd be worried," said Amy.

Suddenly Rachel didn't want to walk any further. Amy was trying to be sympathetic, but everything she said made it worse. She might as well say there was no hope for him. He was just a little boy, how could he be heading down such a lonely path already? Rachel wanted to yank him back, but her grasp was slippery.

"Guess who I saw today at *Valley Camera*," said Amy.

"I told him he should give it one more try," said Rachel.

"Greg should do drills with him."

"He has. Greg thinks it's no big deal if he doesn't play on a team."

"Then it probably isn't a big deal. You haven't guessed who I saw."

Rachel folded her arms and gripped her elbows, pressing them close to her ribs. She didn't know how to describe her fears for Trent without exposing raw feelings of her own – the occasional awareness that there might be some unidentified, yet vital ingredient missing in her personality, making her feel she existed on the periphery of her group of friends. Was there an invisible flaw that she'd passed on to her son? Why were friendships so difficult? It wasn't that way for all women. Kit, for example. Some people were just more comfortable in their own skin, breezing through life without analyzing their relationships. "I'm trying to talk to you about Trent," she whispered. "He acts like he's terrified of the game. Of the other kids."

"Maybe you should take him to therapy."

"No."

"I'm trying to help," said Amy.

Rachel thought about the oatmeal cookies. They were still warm when she left the house. Chewing on one right now would keep tears from spilling out of her eyes. "The only thing he's interested in is drawing. And snails."

"Snails?"

"It's a new thing."

Amy stopped and turned to face her. "Then you need snail bait."

Rachel decided not to tell her that he let the snails creep along his bare skin, leaving a trail of slime like soap scum.

"That's disgusting," said Amy. "Snails. You really should think about therapy, just to make sure there's not something seriously wrong."

She shouldn't have told Amy about the snails. She didn't want a stranger poking around in Trent's head. How would that make him feel? He would know she was worried about him. That couldn't be good for a child's self-esteem, knowing your mother thought you were in need of professional help. Besides, Greg would never agree.

"Since you won't guess who I saw, I'll tell you. That woman who doesn't wear a bra. Her name is Charlotte Whittington. Apparently Amanda invited her daughter to play soccer and she's all signed up."

"So?"

"Did you notice the bald spot on that girl's head?"

"No."

"I wonder what it's from," said Amy.

"I don't know. It's not really any of our business."

"I don't think it's a good idea for her to play soccer on our team," said Amy.

"Why not?"

"For one thing, she's never played before."

"That doesn't matter," said Rachel.

"The more new players there are, the harder it is for the girls to win."

"Well there's nothing you can do about it."

"I also think Charlotte is a bad influence."

"On who?"

"She dresses like a ... like she wants men to stare at her."

Rachel walked faster. The sky was turning to a deep navy blue as the light drained out. The trees shifted like spilled ink into silhouettes. All she wanted was to get home and eat one or two of those cookies, too bad if it set back her effort to streamline her thighs.

"Don't walk so fast," said Amy.

"I want to get home."

"We can cut through the school. That'll save time. Just slow down."

Rachel kept up her pace. Her stomach twisted into a hard pasty ball like a tissue left in the pocket of Greg's jeans when they came out of the dryer.

"Her daughter wants to be friends with our girls," said Amy. "If Charlotte starts hanging around, we'll have to watch the guys drool all over her."

"I don't think that will happen."

"My father said women who dress like that are asking to get raped."

"That's a horrible thing to say. And it's absolutely not true."

"Well that's what he told me and my sisters."

"It's not true. Rape is about violence. It has nothing to do with how you're dressed, nothing to do with sex."

They turned at the parking strip in front of the school and cut through the courtyard. "I forgot how scary it is here at night," said Amy. Her voice echoed between the buildings.

"It's not that bad," said Rachel.

"Cutting through was a mistake. Someone could be hiding behind any one of these buildings. It's not as well-lit as I remembered."

"We'll be fine."

"So what do you think we should do?" said Amy.

"Walk faster."

"I meant what should we do to keep that girl off the team?"

"That's cruel." Rachel knew she should say more, but it required too much effort. All she could think about were Trent's arms, gripping her knees, making her body heavy, pulling at her so she couldn't move. They emerged from the cluster of buildings and started across the blacktop toward the park. The metal picnic tables glistened under the nearly full moon.

"Just wait until the first time Greg sees her walking across the soccer field with her boobs bouncing all over," said Amy.

Rachel closed her eyes. She stumbled on a rough spot in the grass. Greg was oblivious. He probably wouldn't even notice Charlotte.

Chapter Eight

CHARLOTTE STOPPED AT THE EDGE of Rennert Park. She watched Meadow walk toward the designated area for soccer practice. Every few steps, her soccer shorts slid down her hips and she paused to tug them back into place. As she approached the group of girls at the center of the field, her steps slowed. Finally, she moved deliberately into their circle until she was indistinguishable in the cluster of white and green uniforms flickering in the afternoon light like leaves dancing in the breeze.

Since the day Meadow had first mentioned she wanted to play soccer, she'd talked about it constantly. At dinner, she spoke while she licked salad dressing from her lips. *I won't be the only new girl, so I might not be the worst player on the team. Don't you think, Mom?* Charlotte nodded. She tried to suppress images of Meadow – unable to keep up with the others, or getting smacked in the back of the head by a ball. The other girls on the team had been dribbling balls and learning the rules for years. It had been painful watching Meadow stumble around the clumps of dried grass in their backyard. When she kicked, her foot sometimes missed contact with the ball. Other times, the soccer ball bounced off her toe and crashed into shrubs or the lower branches of the pear tree. When she picked up the ball to experiment with drop kicks, her hands looked like baby mice crawling across the black and white panels.

Charlotte shifted her backpack so the weight of the camera was centered on her spine. Near the side of the field, a group of women sat on low-slung lawn chairs, their legs stretched out in front of them. Most wore sandals, boasting professionally painted toenails that shimmered like gems against the grass. They leaned toward each other, talking, turning to watch the girls scatter out on the field for warm-up drills. Amy and another woman stood near a picnic table that held a large blue and white ice chest. Amy glanced at Charlotte and gave her a half-smile. Was it the sunglasses, hiding much of her face, or something else that made the smile look blank? Charlotte paused. Seeing that rusty colored hair, sun glinting off the highlights, brought Amy's words to a simmer in her mind. *She looks a bit too delicate for soccer.*

She wasn't up to fielding any more of Amy's questions and didn't have a lawn chair that would allow her to join the other women. She could sit on the grass, but that was a huge commitment, planting herself with them for the entire practice. She lifted the straps of the backpack off her shoulders and held the bag in one arm while she unzipped the main compartment and pulled out the camera and looped the strap around her neck. She removed the telephoto lens and zipped the bag closed.

The woman standing next to Amy was dressed in a pale green jacket over a white silk blouse. She wore pumps and jeans. A corporate badge dangled from one of her belt loops. Blonde hair cascaded away from her face when she tipped her head back to take a long swallow from her can of soda. She walked toward Charlotte. "Hi, I'm Jane."

Charlotte shook Jane's extended hand.

"That's a huge lens," said Jane.

"I'm a photographer."

"Are you here to shoot team photos?"

"No. I'm working on a photo essay."

"About soccer?"

Charlotte hesitated. "It's kind of hard to explain."

Jane smiled but looked confused. She tucked her hair behind her ear. "You're new at Spruce?" She nodded toward the field. "That's my daughter, Dana, with the blonde braids."

"I grew up here," said Charlotte. "My daughter and I just moved back last week."

"Did you play soccer when you were a kid?"

"I wasn't really into sports."

"It's a great outlet for the girls, don't you think?" said Jane.

It was difficult to imagine, thinking there was nothing better than watching your daughter fight for a chance to kick a ball, hoping she'd be able to contribute something to the team. Charlotte smiled. "Meadow can't talk about anything else."

"Has she played before?"

"This is her first time," said Charlotte. She glanced at Amy who was inching closer while fiddling with the cap of her water bottle.

"It's an *everyone plays* philosophy," said Jane. "So you don't need to worry about her not getting a chance just because she's new."

Amy removed the cap from her water bottle and took a sip. "Although it is more fun for the girls when they win." She smiled. Her lips were slick with gloss the color of dark red wine, as if she'd just applied a fresh coat.

The shouts of the girls drifted into the endless blue sky behind Charlotte. For a minute, no one spoke. Finally, Jane murmured, "It's not about winning. It's about building team skills. There's plenty of time for more competition in a few years."

"Only if they do well at this age," said Amy.

Charlotte's heart pounded so hard she was sure Jane and Amy could hear the sound thumping out of her ears. She smiled. "Nice meeting you. I'm going to take some photographs."

"Sure, talk to you later," said Jane.

Charlotte walked to a wooden bench behind the goal line. While she fitted the camera with the 70-200mm lens, she took slow breaths to steady her hands. She popped the lens cap off and put it in the pocket of her skirt. She walked along the end of the field and stopped fifteen feet from where the goalie crouched. The movement of the goalie's head tracked the ball as it raced from one girl to another, rebounding off toes and ankles.

The coach called out, "Don't clump around the ball! Play your positions." Charlotte pointed the camera and snapped multiple shots, aimed at capturing the girls' feet and the tangle of legs.

As she concentrated on varying the composition of each photograph, time dissolved. The world was condensed to the tiny rectangle in front of her eye. She liked the feeling of distance, observing from outside the action. She focused on details – a sock with a hole in the side and an untied shoelace. While she watched through the viewfinder, Amanda slid her foot across the grass into the path of her twin sister, who skidded and sat down hard. She got up, but it was too late. Another girl moved in and took control of the ball.

Charlotte made her way around the field, keeping a wide distance between herself and the chalked sidelines. When she reached the centerline and lifted the camera, Jane appeared in the viewfinder. Charlotte adjusted the distance for a tighter shot around Jane's ankles and the heels of her pumps. Photographs of the mothers' feet would make an excellent juxtaposition for her other images – women insulated from sweat and grime, the rough spots pumiced off their feet so they could display them in sandals with polished toenails. The puffy skin of the homeless, the plump skin of babies' feet, the ankles of the girls, thick with shin-guards, and the well-groomed feet of their mothers would tell a more complete story. She crept closer. She stayed far enough back to utilize the magnification of her lens and avoid being obvious that she was photographing them.

Squatting on her heels, she focused on the women's smooth leather sandals. Of course the colored nail polish wouldn't show up in black and white, but the gloss and the perfectly shaped nails would be evident. Some of the women were standing now, so she moved the lens up their legs, trying to duplicate the angles she'd used for the girls. With a slight shift of position she was able to snap pictures framed to show their hips – all different, some of them swollen by the effects of carrying and delivering children. Others were so slim they hinted at frantic exercise and a strict diet.

Amy's voice rose above the background sounds of the practice game. "What are you taking pictures of?"

"She's getting photos of her budding soccer star." Kit's voice floated across the distance between them, clear as a wind chime tapped by the breeze.

Amy marched across the thick grass. Her feet wobbled on open-backed sandals. The narrow high heels sank into the turf, slowing her progress. "My friends might think you're photographing your daughter, but I saw that camera pointed at us."

Charlotte pulled the camera close to her stomach.

"I don't want my picture taken," said Amy.

"Why not?" said Charlotte.

"You can't take pictures without asking us first."

Amy was dangerously close to her camera lens. Charlotte took a step back. "Why do you assume I was photographing you? I hardly know you."

"Exactly. So either take pictures of your daughter or put the camera away."

"I don't need your permission."

"You do if you're taking pictures of me and my friends."

No faces appeared in the shots she'd taken, no one was identifiable, but Amy probably wouldn't care. Charlotte slipped the backpack off her shoulders and unzipped it. It was a shame to give the impression of yielding to Amy's demand, but she'd lost her focus. There was no point in continuing out of spite. There would be plenty of other soccer practices.

"Thank you," said Amy.

The other women had their heads turned toward the action on the field. Charlotte wondered if they'd heard the exchange. She watched Amy step back across the grass to where the others were seated. Charlotte lifted the camera and snapped three pictures of Amy's narrow feet, her toes clenched to keep the sandals in place. She zoomed slightly for a closer shot of Amy's taut Achilles tendons and her squashed heels spilling over the edges of the sandals.

Chapter Nine

AFTER SOCCER PRACTICE, Amy had a few minutes before it was time to start dinner. Once Alice and Amanda were settled down with their homework, she walked along the upstairs hall to the spare bedroom. She clutched the key, warmed by the perspiration on her palms, then unlocked the door and went inside. The blinds were closed, the room cold and filled with gray light. The simple act of closing the door behind her calmed her thoughts for a moment.

No one else ever entered this room. The twins were not allowed inside and Justin ignored its existence. Occasionally he mentioned that her need for the room, and its contents, caused him to worry about her. But when she explained how important it was to be prepared for emergencies, he reassured her that if she felt she had to have all that stuff, he would leave it alone. The room contained all the things necessary to keep daily life running smoothly, as well as the supplies she kept on hand for a potential disaster. Her scrapbooks and the twins' photo albums were stored in the closet. The wall immediately to her right was lined with metal shelves, stacked with blankets, batteries, canned food, and cases of bottled water. She also had pellets to purify water once the bottled supply ran out. The food and water were kept nearest the door for convenient rotation through her kitchen cupboards. There was a tightly packed tent large enough to sleep six, and extra boxes of sanitary pads and painkillers. Her family was prepared to remain holed up almost indefinitely in case of an earthquake or a national disaster.

The entire floor space contained rows of plastic storage bins, stacked in towers. They were filled with new towels and sponges, socks for the girls and Justin, and sheets and mattress pads so that she could quickly dispose of anything that became stained or worn. Seeing all these things eased her ragged breathing. Her father had always insisted that emergency supplies were critical to a family's security. *You can't rely on the government to take care of you if something bad happens.* He never spelled out what something bad might be, but Amy had developed a pretty good idea of it from listening to her father – a major earthquake that was *overdue*, a widespread power failure that would *cripple the city*, the *under-funded* national defense. It was important to be prepared.

About two years after her mother had been attacked, eight months after her father moved out to his own apartment, Amy had gone to the kitchen one afternoon, thirsty for a glass of orange juice. A search of the refrigerator turned up nothing but a pitcher of water. Usually her mother brought in a fresh gallon of juice from the supply in the garage as soon as the jug in the fridge was down to a few cups.

Amy opened the door from the kitchen to the garage. She wriggled past the bicycles and walked along the back to the room her father had built inside the garage to house their emergency supplies. She pulled on the knob of the flimsy door. It popped open more easily than she'd expected and she stumbled back. A few blankets and boxes of batteries were stacked neatly on one of the bottom shelves, but there wasn't a single jug of juice or a can of soup. The bags of rice, the canned fruit, and the toilet paper were all gone. She ran back into the house without closing either door.

Her mother was asleep on the living room sofa. Amy shook her mother's arm, "Mom!"

Her mother opened her eyes and smiled. She propped herself up on her elbow and wiped at her eyes. "Hi honey, what's wrong?"

"All the earthquake food is gone."

"I know."

"We're supposed to buy more when we use it," said Amy.

"What do you need? I'll run to the store."

"Dad said you have to stay on top of it."

"Well Dad's not here, is he."

"What if something happens?"

Her mother put her arm around Amy's hips and pulled her closer to the sofa. "When was the last time we had an earthquake?"

"You never know when there's going to be an emergency," said Amy.

"It would be nice to be over-prepared, but we can't afford it right now," said her mother. She stroked Amy's arm and then took her hand. "We'll be okay."

"No we won't! There could be a huge power failure or we could be attacked."

"Don't shout, please. Not everyone is as nervous about disasters as your father is. But he never thought someone would assault me right in our own living room, did he?"

Amy didn't like her mother mentioning that. She backed away from the sofa and waited. After a few minutes, her mother shifted her position and closed her eyes.

Amy went into her bedroom and took her flashlight off the nightstand. She opened the closet door and wedged herself into the narrow space between boxes of her sisters' outgrown clothes and the wall. She sat with her knees pulled up close. She turned on the flashlight, pulled the door closed and tugged a copy of *Seventeen* magazine from behind the boxes. She turned the pages slowly, imagining herself smiling, with the wind blowing through her hair like the girls in the pictures.

It wasn't until dinnertime that she'd remembered she was thirsty.

Amy surveyed the contents of her spare room. Running out of emergency supplies would never happen in her home. She was doing a good job taking care of her family. In the opposite corner from where she stood was a wingchair. There was a table with two drawers on one side of the chair and a small refrigerator on the other side. She used to keep a few cheese sticks and a bottle of wine in the refrigerator, but recently she'd removed all the food. Now she carried the bottle upstairs when she wanted to relax in her room.

She wound her way through the stacks of boxes and collapsed in the confines of the chair. Thoughts pressed on her head like needles pricking at her brain. The image of the woman on Benton Court, raped and stabbed, flashed across her mind. The rapist was out there. He was watching, considering his next victim. She'd tried to bring up the subject at soccer practice, but no one wanted to talk about it. She was pretty sure Kit was lying about her sudden decision to move, that she was nervous. But Jane was so nonchalant, acting as if they were immune. Jane didn't seem to understand how easily it could happen. Any one of them could be next. It wasn't as if any of her friends kept a handgun in the kitchen drawer with the scissors and pushpins. Was it her imagination that both horrifying events – the murder and Charlotte's arrival – had happened on the same day?

Charlotte and her camera had spoiled soccer practice. It was creepy the way she snuck up on them, pretending it was only the girls she was photographing. Amy had felt that tingling sensation wind its way across her shoulders and down her spine, the sure knowledge that she was being scrutinized. Turning around to see that enormous lens, like the protruding eye of an alien, had been terrifying. Her friends smirked at her reaction to the staring lens. They didn't know what it was like to have people watching you, studying your clothes and the expression on your face, judging you. Having all that recorded by a camera was so much worse.

It had been different when Justin used to take photographs of her. He waited while she styled her hair and put on fresh makeup. He made sure to adjust the lighting and gave her plenty of time to arrange herself in a flattering position with good posture and a pleasant smile. He allowed her to look through the images first and delete the ones she didn't like. His soothing voice made her feel loved and his photographs made her look more beautiful than she was in real life. Of course, that was before the twins were born, before her fears emerged out of nowhere, battling for control every day. Where had she put those photo albums filled with revealing pictures of her? They weren't stored in the spare room. She'd have to look for them when she had more time. They weren't appropriate for the girls' curious eyes.

Obviously Charlotte was here to stay. From now on, she'd be showing up at games and school events. Justin and the other men would pretend they were paying attention to their wives, while their eyes slid casually in the direction of a woman dressed like she was waiting to hop into a bed where she didn't belong. Apparently Charlotte never bothered to wear a bra. Did the others think they were so spectacular-looking that their husbands wouldn't cast a second glance?

She felt like the world was decaying around her. Television shows served up a steady flow of crude jokes, violence, and inappropriate sex. People allowed weeds to infest their yards and left their garbage containers sitting at the curb for hours after they were emptied. Parents allowed their children to dress in sloppy clothes and use disgusting language. If you let children do as they pleased, they grew up thinking it was acceptable to expose their breasts with skin-hugging tops and pierce their bodies in odd places, like Charlotte did. Amy imagined a fat needle sliding through her nostril and shuddered. She would not allow the innocence of childhood to be stolen from her daughters. It was her job to protect them from the threats breathing down, pressing closer every day.

She stood and turned the wand to angle the mini blinds for more light. She leaned over the small refrigerator and peeked out through the slats. A woman was pushing a stroller around the curve of the cul-de-sac. A small boy walked beside her. They stopped at the edge of the yard next door. The woman bent down and plucked a dandelion that had gone to seed. She blew at the fluffy white weed and then held it for the boy to do the same. Seeds scattered across the ground under Amy's rosebushes. Amy knocked on the window, rattling the blinds. Neither one looked up. She pounded her fist on the glass. They continued to the corner of the cul-de-sac and down the street. Amy backed away from the window breathing hard as if she'd raced up the stairs. Why was her life suddenly over-run with undesirable people?

Chapter Ten

CHARLOTTE PLACED THE LAST framed photograph into the box on the kitchen table. The collection contained fifteen eight by tens. All she needed now was a place to display them. She tried not to think about how difficult that might be.

The images from soccer practice had turned out just as she'd envisioned – a perfect completion to her photo essay. The girls' clean, well-fitted cleats contrasted with the cast-off sneakers worn by the homeless women she'd photographed. The shot of Amanda sticking her foot in front of her sister's was a well-balanced tangle of feet and lower legs. In the next shot Alice was on the ground, her legs splayed, the nubs of the cleats prominent, like large blisters.

The pictures of the girls' mothers focused on ankles that were smooth, with a slight gloss from moisturizing lotion, a beautiful comparison to their daughters' legs that all bore a delicate growth of hair. The women's feet were also a jarring contrast to the homeless women's splotched and swollen skin. There was a seductive quality in their pedicured toes. Rachel's nails were unpainted, making her feet look naked and vulnerable next to the others. Some of the shots were low angles of the women's hips. They provided variety from the photographs of feet, and added a new dimension to the story. The point might be too subtle for the casual viewer, but in her mind, it illustrated the cycle of life. She would put them first in the sequence, showing the bodies that had given birth, and their vigilance, hovering at soccer practice as if their presence ensured successful futures for their daughters. No mother expected her child to grow up and disappear into the ranks of the homeless.

There was a purity and sense of mystery in black and white photographs. Black and white had a way of stripping off the distractions that prevented a clear view of reality. It had an intrinsic quality that forced people to slow down, to look at an image with a meditative spirit. It created a sense of time standing still. Maybe the eye had to work harder to process a black and white image. She really didn't know. All she knew was that it was the way she liked to capture the world.

She pressed her hands on the edge of the table and leaned over. Tucked inside the two boxes was some of the best work she'd done. Yet now she was cut off from her old life where she'd had relationships with the managers at a neighborhood coffee shop and a deli that displayed and sold her photography. She couldn't go back to San Francisco. It was too far to drive, leaving Meadow home alone for several hours. If she took Meadow with her, she might come across as a hobbyist. A professional photographer wouldn't bring a child along on what amounted to a sales call. Besides, she didn't want to run into any of Mark's old associates. This was a new life. She had to find a local place that was interested in her work. Her first step would be to survey the restaurants and bars in downtown Sunnyvale.

She pulled out two framed photographs to take with her, one of the homeless woman, Linda, and the other a shot of Jane's feet in her black leather pumps. She left Meadow with a bowl of almonds and raisins to snack on, reminding her for the hundredth time not to answer the door. She drove to the downtown area, a single street lined with restaurants and small shops. She parked in a lot behind a Mexican restaurant. She walked down the alley that ran from the parking lot to Murphy Street, and turned onto the main street, walking slowly. There was a Thai restaurant and an Irish-themed pub. The pub was an unlikely candidate; it was too dark.

"Hi Charlotte."

She turned and saw Jane Goodman walking behind her, a few yards back.

"Are you here for a late lunch? Or an early dinner?" said Jane.

Charlotte shoved her hands in her pockets. "I'm looking for a place that might be interested in displaying my photography."

Jane pushed her sunglasses to the top of her head, scooping waves of blonde hair off her face. "Your photo essay from soccer practice?"

"It's more than that – I've been working on it for awhile." She didn't want to try to describe the idea. The point of a photo essay was to communicate without words. Explaining it would destroy the impact. "I use different images of feet to show how life progresses, how circumstances can change."

"Feet?"

"Baby's feet, small children. The girls' feet while they were playing soccer." No matter how much Jane squinted and twisted her lips into an expression of curiosity, Charlotte wasn't going to mention the homeless people.

"So what kind of place are you looking for? A gallery?"

"Not exactly. When I lived in San Francisco I displayed my work in coffee shops. I was hoping to find a place here that might be interested in a similar arrangement. They get free artwork and the photographs are marked for sale. If something sells, I replace it. Of course, I hope there would be a buyer for the whole collection this time."

"Have you sold a lot of your work?"

"Some."

"So you're pretty good?"

Charlotte wasn't sure how to respond. Agreeing would sound arrogant, while disagreeing would sound as if she was begging for praise.

"Don't answer," said Jane. "You must be good or people wouldn't buy your work." She pulled her phone out of her purse and tapped the screen. "I don't know of any place around here that does that kind of thing. I've heard of some office buildings up the Peninsula that feature local artists in their lobbies. There are a few small art galleries in the area."

Charlotte looked down the street – a Chinese restaurant, a Sushi bar, and another Mexican restaurant. Probably all of them offered décor that was in keeping with the cuisine.

"Don't look so discouraged."

"I'm not. It's just hard … starting over."

"How about asking to display them at the school? Since they're about soccer."

Jane looked pleased with her helpful suggestion. Charlotte felt like crying. She wasn't sure how she'd left the impression the pictures were about soccer, but she wasn't going to try to correct Jane's description. "That seems a little needy," she said. "Showing them at the school."

"I know it's not what you were hoping for. You couldn't price them for sale, but it's a way to get them out there."

She patted Charlotte's arm. Jane's fingers were warm and dry. For the first time since Charlotte had arrived in Sunnyvale, someone was actually interested in her, possibly even wanted to be a friend. Still the idea was almost humiliating.

"I can talk to the principal for you," said Jane. "And you could sign up to be in the silent auction at the fall carnival. Offer a photo session. The proceeds go to the school, but it's another way to get your name known."

"I don't really do portraits." Charlotte knew her voice sounded cold. Jane was trying to be friendly and she was responding as if she wanted to argue, as if Jane was deliberately dismissive of her work, when it was just the opposite. It seemed she'd forgotten how to make friends, she was so used to socializing with Mark's buddies.

Jane pulled her sunglasses down to the bridge of her nose. "You have to start somewhere."

"That's true." Charlotte smiled. "Maybe I'll try the school, for now."

"I need to get back to the office. See you at Saturday's game. Call me if you want me to suggest the idea to the principal." Jane darted across the street, turning to wave before cutting into an alley.

Charlotte continued walking. There was a single coffee shop, but it had a corporate feel. She looked inside. The walls were crowded with historical photographs of Sunnyvale. In suburbia, perhaps the elementary school was the center of the social and artistic world.

Chapter Eleven

WHEN AMY ARRIVED AT THE school playground on Tuesday afternoon, Kit and Rachel were standing near the picnic tables rather than sitting in their usual spots. They looked as if they were waiting for an appointment and Amy was late. She didn't like them studying every step as she walked toward them. It made her suddenly aware of how her legs moved. The angle of her back felt skewed. She straightened her shoulders and slowed her pace. She paused a few feet away. "What are you waiting for?"

"I have something to show you," said Kit. She turned and walked toward the multi-purpose room at the center of the school complex.

Amy and Rachel followed, taking rapid steps in order to keep up with Kit's long, liquid strides. Kit stopped in front of two display cases mounted on the half wall outside the multi-purpose room. "You were right, Amy. Charlotte wasn't taking pictures of her daughter at soccer practice, she was photographing us."

A breeze rushed through the covered corridor. Amy shivered. She stepped closer to the display case at her left. Behind the glass were six black and white photographs with narrow black frames. The first picture showed three women, shot from a low angle, the camera aimed upward at their thighs and hips. There were two pictures of a baby's bare feet and then a shot that captured a tangle of girls' feet and lower legs, nearly identical in thick white socks and shin guards. In the next picture, one girl was kicking her foot at the ankle of another player. In the last image, a girl was shown from the waist down, sitting on the grass with her legs spread out. Amy recognized a scab at the top of the girl's shin – Alice. The girl kicking her ankle in the previous picture was Amanda.

She moved sideways to look at the photographs in the second display case. There was a shot of a child's feet, half covered with sand. Another picture was a close-up of Trent's fingers fumbling with his untied shoelace. A photo of a woman in high-heeled pumps followed this.

"Look at these. Pictures of homeless people." Kit's voice was rushed, describing the subject as if they couldn't see for themselves.

The breeze died down. In the garden area just past the display cases, a bee circled the agapanthus. Its buzzing drilled into Amy's skull. She tried to focus on what she was seeing, but the black bee circled in her peripheral vision so that she felt there was something lodged behind her contact lens, even though she knew that wasn't possible. She moved back to the first display case. The picture in front of her showed a cluster of women's feet and calves – each woman was easily identifiable by her shoes. Compared to the images of her friends, Amy's feet and ankles looked scrawny and silly.

"Do I look fat?" Rachel's breath was dry on Amy's arm. Strands of Rachel's hair tickled Amy's bare skin. She swatted her hand and Rachel stepped back.

"That picture makes Jane's feet look huge," said Rachel.

Amy folded her arms, curling her fingers around her elbows. Jane's feet always looked enormous. Did that mean the pictures were telling the truth? The camera doesn't lie. She wished that it did, that it blurred the edges or automatically filtered the light. Instead, everyone who glanced at these photographs would see that she had the feet of an old woman. But that couldn't be right. Her feet didn't look old. Every two weeks she received a pedicure. Twice a day she rubbed lotion along the sides of her feet where the skin tended to get dry and flakey. Once a week she used a pumice stone to slough off the dead stuff. Shot from the back, her heels looked like slabs of raw chicken breast spilling over the edges of her sandals. What if Justin saw these? He'd be disgusted that she was no longer the woman he used to photograph with such loving attention.

Blood rushed to her neck. She could feel the puffiness around her eyes that probably meant her face was erupting in red splotches. She put her hand to her throat, hoping to cool her skin, but the burning was below the surface. She didn't know which was worse, the shots that made her look anything but exotically thin, or the picture that betrayed Amanda's aggression toward her sister. What would the other parents say when they saw the images of her twins? The words hummed in her mind — *bully. Not a team player.* Charlotte had no right to sneak up on them and take these pictures.

In too many ways, the photographs reminded her of the last time her life had been torn open for public inspection. It was three days after her mother's rape. Amy's father pulled the *Pontiac* into the driveway and entered the house through the side door. It was only 4:30 in the afternoon and Amy was seated at the kitchen table, drawing tiny eyeballs along the lines of her ruled paper. She made the oval formed by the lids and the whispery strokes of the lashes first, then shaded the iris and filled the pupil with solid black. The eyes filled three lines of paper, but there wasn't a single word of the book report she was supposed to be writing. Her mother was resting in the darkened living room.

Her father strode through the kitchen. The walls shuddered as he stomped down the hall to the master bedroom. A few minutes later he passed through the kitchen again with yellow fabric wadded up in his hands. The dress her mother had been wearing on that day.

Amy slid off her chair and went to the window. Her father appeared at the side of the garage. He dragged the black plastic trashcan down the driveway. The dress was tucked in his armpit. Theirs was the only trashcan on the street. Its companions wouldn't appear until after dark. No one liked the garbage cans sitting out during dinner. He lifted the lid and stuffed the dress inside. The can was full so the lid barely fit in place. He walked back to the side of the house and disappeared behind the garage. How had he not noticed that the skirt hung out one side, garish against the black plastic? She should go out there and push the dress into the can. Or take it and bury it in the back yard. The sun had moved slightly and shone directly into the kitchen, revealing the rain spots and dust on the surface of the glass, spreading across the table like a cloth. Amy shifted to the side so the sun wasn't in her eyes.

A girl came into view – Heather Morton – who lived two houses down. Next to her was a boy from the junior high school. An expensive-looking camera hung from a strap around his neck. Amy didn't know his name but she'd seen him walk down her street before. He was cute, hot, according to Heather. Amy saw Heather lean into the boy, bumping against his side. When they reached Amy's house, Heather stopped. She glanced at the living room window. She said something to the boy, and then she took the lid off the trashcan and pulled out the dress. The boy twisted his mouth in disgust.

Amy gripped the sill. Her nails scratched against the metal frame of the window. If she went outside and tried to grab the dress, Heather might say something about the attack. Lots of people seemed to know about it. Amy didn't know how they'd found out. She and her sisters certainly hadn't told anyone. How did they know?

Heather held the dress up to her collarbone. One of the straps was broken and it dangled in a thin line down Heather's arm, bright against tanned skin. Heather's short black hair looked like a spray of ink as she danced around. She flung herself on the scrubby grass of the parking strip and writhed like a snake. The boy lifted the camera and snapped a picture. Then he pointed the camera at the house. Amy closed her eyes and tried to make her tears drain back into her sinuses. She pressed her forehead against the corner of the wall until she felt a crevice was opening in her skull. When she looked again, Heather and the boy were gone. The dress lay on the apron of the driveway. She went outside and grabbed it. She shoved her arm into the trash up to her shoulder, until the dress was buried in the center of the mass of garbage.

Outside the multi-purpose room, the bee in the agapanthus sawed at Amy's thoughts. The droning grew fiercer as it probed at the small purple blooms shaped like fluted champagne glasses, determined to get what it desired. The hum echoed through the corridor, carrying the volume of ten bees in one fat, shiny body. Why would someone take such intrusive pictures? Spats between sisters should be worked out inside the walls of their home, not photographed and hung in public. Pictures were meant to be posed. People should be given fair warning. The images in the display case were designed to show the most unflattering angles and awkward positions, preserved forever.

Rachel cleared her throat. "I look fat."

Kit moved closer and laid her hand on Rachel's shoulder. "The angle is distorted. No one would look good with the camera pointing up like that."

Amy turned to face them. Easy for Kit to say, there was only one picture of her narrow feet in flat sandals, a chain slack below her anklebone. Amy hoped the dark stain of blood had drained from her face. "What should we do?" She knew what she wanted to do – break the glass and throw the pictures in the dumpster. That's what she would do if her friends weren't watching.

"I need to get going," said Kit. "Carter has an orthodontist appointment. I'll see you later." She turned and walked toward the sixth grade classrooms.

Rachel continued staring at the photographs. She licked her lips. They were bright red, raw as a scraped kneecap.

"We should do something," said Amy.

"What can we do?" said Rachel.

"We should complain to Ms. Shafton. Tell her we want them taken down."

"What if she says no?" said Rachel.

"She won't."

TWENTY MINUTES LATER they sat in chairs facing the principal's desk. Amy felt like a child called in for punishment. The blinds were closed and the primary source of light was Ms. Shafton's computer screen. Surrounding the computer were handmade gifts that children had given to her over the years – clay animals painted orange, blue, and pink. The principal pushed her chair back and smiled. "What can I do for you?"

Amy folded her hands on her knees. She sat at the edge of her chair with her spine straight and her shoulders back. "There are some photographs hanging in the display cases that were taken without our permission. We'd like them removed."

"Pictures of us and our children," said Rachel.

"You're talking about Charlotte Whittington's artwork?" said Ms. Shafton.

Amy stared at a pink triceratops at the edge of the desk. Art? Art should be beautiful – colors, scenes of mountains or water. Pictures of soccer practice weren't art, even if the girls' faces were visible, which they weren't. "I wouldn't call it art," she said.

"I suppose the definition of art is subjective," said Ms. Shafton.

"She didn't ask our permission to take the pictures," said Rachel.

"Since no faces were visible, I don't think it matters," said Ms. Shafton.

"It matters to me. To us," said Amy. She could sweep her arm across the cluttered desk, sending the clay figurines crashing onto the floor. That might remove the condescending smile from the principal's face. Ms. Shafton could be so obstinate. When the twins were in the third grade, Amy had asked to have them placed in the same class, but Ms. Shafton had refused. *It's better to have them individuate at this age.* They were twins; they should be together. There was plenty of time for *individuating* when they were older. Ms. Shafton seemed to think all educational decisions belonged to her.

"Charlotte wanted a place to display her art," said Ms. Shafton. "Since it focused on soccer, I thought it was a fantastic community-building idea."

Amy leaned forward. She didn't know why she was bothering. Ms. Shafton's mind was made up. "We've been involved with this school since our children were in kindergarten. Don't you think our feelings are more important than her photographs?"

"The pictures are embarrassing," said Rachel. "No one looks good."

Ms. Shafton rolled her chair closer to the desk. She rested her hand on the computer mouse and glanced at the screen. She let go of the mouse and looked at Rachel. "I'm sorry you don't like the photographs, but there are no faces, so I don't think they're invasive. They'll only be on display for two weeks."

Amy's throat felt like it was clogged with one of the clay snakes. There were tears collecting in the corners of her eyes, but she refused to cry in front of this woman. It wasn't fair that Charlotte could walk in and hang up anything she wanted without thinking of how other people might feel. For the next two weeks, children and parents would stop in front of the display cases and stare at Amy and her daughters. She might as well leave her drapes open all night. This couldn't be legal, could it? There had to be some law about privacy. She unfolded her hands. Her fingers trembled, so she laced them back together. Didn't she have a right to decide whether someone was allowed to take her picture? Surely she had a right, a duty, to protect her children from that nosy camera lens.

After a few minutes, Rachel stood and edged out of the small space between her chair and the desk. She leaned against the wall. "There's a picture of my son, a close-up that shows his cuticles all bitten up."

"Lots of children bite their nails. No one will even recognize him." Ms. Shafton smiled, but her attention had wandered back to the computer screen.

Amy stood and picked up her purse. Her throat was tight. She wouldn't be able to speak without crying.

"Charlotte's a single mother; we should be supportive," said Ms. Shafton.

Amy and Rachel walked out of the office without saying anything else.

The corridor outside the main office was empty. The air was cooler, as if the sun had raced toward the horizon while they'd been inside. Amy shivered. Her skin felt dry and her rings were too loose. She flipped the diamond around and held it in place with her right hand. At least her fingers had stopped trembling.

"It looks like we'll have everyone staring at us for two weeks," said Rachel.

"I can't ..." Amy's throat tightened again.

"She isn't going to get rid of the pictures."

"I'll see what Justin says. It has to be illegal to hang up pictures when you don't have permission to take them." If it wasn't illegal, it should be.

"Won't more people see them if we make a big deal about it ... if we try to force her to take them down?"

Amy looked across the courtyard at the empty playground. A plastic bag danced across the blacktop. She turned and walked toward the display cases. Rachel followed, dragging her heels on the concrete. Amy wiggled the lock at the center of the doors. She tugged harder and rattled the glass. It was secure, as if they expected thieves to be interested in the notices that were usually posted there. She couldn't live for two weeks with those pictures hanging where every single parent and all the teachers would see them. There had to be a way to get them removed.

Chapter Twelve

THAT EVENING RACHEL STOOD in front of Amy's open front door while Amy tied her shoelaces. The sky was bluish-black, but the streetlights hadn't come on yet. Amy stepped out and closed the door. She held an eighteen-inch long flashlight. "Let's walk to the school."

Rachel stepped off the porch. Her nylon jogging pants made a sound like tissue paper being crumpled. "I don't want to see the pictures. I'll just get upset again."

"I don't have to see them to get upset," said Amy.

"Did you talk to Justin about it?"

"No. He just got home."

The darkening sky made the neighboring houses look clean, as if they'd been freshly painted. They walked quickly. Rachel could hear Amy's breath, short and rhythmic as their footsteps. By the time they reached the front drive of the elementary school, most of the light had drained out of the sky. Rachel's legs were hot against the thin flannel lining of her pants. Her blood pumped close to the surface of her thighs, making her skin itch. They walked around the circular driveway, past the concrete planter filled with shrubs and clusters of cyclamen, the petals nearly colorless under the fluorescent lights. Rachel followed Amy as she cut across the plot of grass behind the planter. The features of the school that stayed in the background during daylight appeared more prominent – the brushed silver knobs and the white numbers glistening on each door. They walked past the office.

"The more I think about those pictures, the angrier I get," said Amy. "I feel like she's watching us, poking into our lives with that oversized camera."

"Let's cut across the playground. I don't want to look at them again," said Rachel.

"We can't put our heads in the sand and pretend they aren't there."

Rachel licked her lips, already chapped and sore. The images in the photographs were burned into the backs of her eyes. Until now, she'd believed her skirts and longish tops shaped her body into a smooth line. How wrong she'd been. Next to Amy and Kit, she looked like she was hiding water balloons under her skirt. Why did she always have to feel awkward and uncertain? When the other girls at school hung from the climbing bar by one knee and swung around in frantic circles, she sat and watched. No matter how hard she tried, she couldn't hurl her body down and under the bar, gaining momentum for the swing upward. She wasn't sure if it was fear of hurting her self, or a lack of ease with her body.

The soles of Amy's athletic shoes squeaked on the concrete as she stopped abruptly in front of the display cases. She held the flashlight at an angle to illuminate one of the photographs of the twins. "This makes it look like Amanda is trying to hurt her sister."

Rachel peered at the photograph of Trent. He sat alone on a bench. It was shot from the end, so the bench looked desolate, and his body small, only the toes of his shoes touching the ground. The torn skin of his cuticles looked painful. She rubbed her arms. "I don't think you need the flashlight."

"Yes I do." Amy pressed the switch and the light went out. She raised her arm and smashed the flashlight against the front of the case. The glass cracked.

Rachel shrieked. "What are you doing?"

"I don't want these pictures here." Amy swung her arm over her head and struck the crack she'd created with the first impact.

Rachel backed up. Her heels tipped over the concrete into the grass area on the opposite side of the corridor. "Stop. Someone will hear. Isn't there a security guard?"

"Not this early."

Amy swung the flashlight and ducked. The glass crumbled into small beads, skittering across the concrete like hailstones. She beat faster as if the tinkling glass energized the movement of her arm. She danced sideways to the second case and slammed the flashlight against the doors. Glass sprinkled on the tops of her shoes and clung to the laces.

"Amy, stop. Please don't."

"It's not right that she can take pictures of me, of my children, showing our worst sides, and put them up so the entire school can ridicule us."

"I don't think the entire school will ridicule us." Rachel wished she believed that.

"You don't know how it is." Amy was sobbing.

Rachel stepped away. Amy's shoulders trembled as if she was standing in an icy wind.

"After my mother was raped, people whispered about us. Right in front of us."

"Your mother was raped?" Rachel felt a sudden, piercing ache at the base of her skull. "When? How? You never said."

"*How?*"

She heard the sneering tone in Amy's voice and felt foolish. "What happened?"

"I don't want to talk about it. She was stupid to let that man in the house."

"It's not like it was her fault."

"That's not what my father said."

"Then he's ignorant."

"People stared at us. They pitied us. Private things should be private. They shouldn't be broadcast to the whole world."

"I'm so sorry. Why didn't you ever tell me?"

Amy whipped the flashlight at the last panel like she was swinging a baseball bat. The glass shattered and a shard pierced her hair. It shimmered like a barrette.

"Please stop. Someone will hear you. This won't accomplish anything, unless you're planning to carry all these photographs back home."

"That's where you come in." Amy pounded the flashlight on one of the photographs. The glass and the thin wood frame cracked.

It was the image of Trent, his fingers bloody, his shoelaces in a large tangle as if he didn't quite understand the concept of securing his shoes to his feet. "I don't want anything to do with this," said Rachel.

"It's too late. Try it. Take your keys and rip this picture until it's unrecognizable."

"I can't."

"Yes you can. We can't allow her to get away with this. It's like she stole part of us and used it for her art career."

"We'll get caught. We could get arrested."

"She should have been arrested for taking these pictures."

"It's not the same thing."

"That's your son up there, pinned on the wall for the whole school to pity."

Rachel felt queasy. Inside her pocket, her keys were warm with sweat. She closed her fingers around them, letting one key protrude between her index and middle fingers. Amy was right about that. She had to protect Trent from the criticism of other parents. They were so unforgiving, so ready to shun a child who wasn't meeting all the standards in the classroom or on the sports field. And blame the mother. It was the mother's fault if a child wasn't the star of the team, if the child was slow learning to read, or in the average math group. Average wasn't good enough around here. In the picture hanging in front of her, Trent didn't even appear to measure up to average.

She walked back across the corridor. She ran the key across the surface of the photograph. It scraped easily, pulling up ink that curled like iron shavings, leaving a long scar. She had the chance to wipe away what the camera had seen, to punish

Charlotte for exposing her fears. With a few more keystrokes, the moment would be erased as if it had never happened. She raked the key across the photograph, tearing away the image of Trent's gnawed fingers, scratching out his feet. No one would look at her son and judge him.

Amy smashed the flashlight against the glass covering the other photographs. Rachel followed, thirsty for more destruction. The key obliterated the pain of seeing her body frozen in time. She scratched across the pictures of Amy's feet and ankles and destroyed the picture of Amanda tripping her sister.

Rachel felt she and Amy were linked in a new way – by a shared secret. She never let herself go wild. Was there any part of her life that wasn't filled with constant planning? Nothing she did happened on the spur of the moment, where her body took over, following unspoken desires. This was how millions of other people lived. They didn't spend their days going to the grocery store and shuttling children to their games and appointments, making dinner and folding laundry. Instead, they went out at night, cut loose, followed whatever instinct arose.

Amy's eyes glittered in the thickening darkness, making her look like a mountain lion that had emerged from the surrounding foothills, hungry for prey. Her hair was damp at the roots and her shoulders heaved as she gulped in air. They stepped away from the display cases. Glass crunched beneath their feet. Rachel looked around, trying to peer through the shadows. Any minute a security guard might walk past. Or maybe it wasn't patrolled after all.

The first person to see this mess would call the police. The date and address would appear in the police report of the weekly paper: *property destruction*, or maybe, *vandalism*. What kind of person was she? In a few minutes' time she'd destroyed public property – at her children's school. But it was so satisfying, dragging her key across those hateful pictures. For those few minutes she'd felt like a teenager, impulsive and unthinking. She'd never done anything crazy when she was young. Her life was filled with studying and following the rules and taking care of her brothers. She overheard kids in the hallway, talking about parties she hadn't known about, late night trips to the beach with illegal bonfires. She was nothing more than an observer of her own high school years. They'd passed by without her really being there.

Her keys slipped out of her hands and clattered on the concrete. "We should leave. What if someone comes by?"

"What a relief," said Amy.

The air rushed out of Rachel's lungs as if they were collapsing. Suddenly she felt tired. She bent to pick up her keys. Even if they weren't caught this minute by a neighbor out for a walk, they would be found out. Hadn't they practically announced their plans by complaining to Ms. Shafton? Spruce Elementary had never been the target of vandalism. What had they been thinking? "It's not a relief. It will be obvious we did this."

"They can't prove anything."

"Even if they can't prove it, they'll know."

"Know what?"

"That it was us."

"But they can't prove it."

They walked across the littered pavement. The glass snapped beneath their feet. Their steps made scraping sounds from the fragments stuck in the grooves on the bottoms of their athletic shoes. Amy turned on the flashlight. She stopped and shone it on the bottom of one foot. "Let's sit down and pick out this glass."

"No. We should do it at home. If we touch it, we might leave fingerprints."

"They're tiny slivers. There aren't any fingerprints."

"How do you know? We need to get out of here," said Rachel. All she cared about was crawling into her bed and pretending the past half hour was an inexplicable dream. No matter if there was proof or not, Ms. Shafton and all their friends, Greg and Justin, their children, would know who destroyed the photographs. "We'll be caught," she gasped as she jogged along Dennison, following the route back to Amy's.

"You worry about the wrong things," said Amy.

Rachel stopped at the corner. She gripped the pole that held the street signs. "I feel stupid. Everyone will know it was us."

"So what? Our friends will think we're awesome because we stood up for what's right."

"But Kit didn't care. Jane doesn't even know about it. We're the only ones who were bothered by it."

Amy stepped off the curb and started across the street.

"We'll keep it a secret though," said Rachel.

"If that's what you want." It seemed as if Amy wasn't concerned whether everyone knew. She almost seemed proud of what they'd done.

Chapter Thirteen

RACHEL SHOVED THE TOOTHBRUSH into the corner behind the toilet and scrubbed at the grout. Her fingers and the back of her hand ached and her knees were sore from the pressure of the tile floor. The bathroom had needed a good scrubbing for two weeks now and she'd hoped the vigorous work would take her mind off the previous evening. She'd thought working her shoulders and arms might ease her mind into a drifting state. Instead, it spun viciously around thoughts of the photographs she'd scraped out of existence. All the things that hadn't bothered her while she scratched her keys across the images had consumed her thoughts since the moment she stopped tearing at the pictures – the questions her children would ask once the news burned its way through the school. The janitor was usually on the school grounds by seven. She wondered whether he had swept up the mess or called the police to let them see it as it had been left – the crime scene. Would Ms. Shafton summon them to the office, immediately suspicious? By 8:45 all the children had probably known about the vandalism, the parents on volunteer duty at the school today would have heard within minutes after that, followed by the teachers. What if Greg found out she'd participated? She could see the horrified expression on his face.

She sat back on her heels. The bristles of the toothbrush were flattened. It was time to toss it in the trash and start with a new one. She dreaded going to the school that afternoon. She didn't want to see the other mothers and listen to their speculation. She didn't think she could act surprised or shocked without the skin of her face twitching, without suddenly shouting – *It was me! I did it! I'm sorry.*

When she arrived at the school, the picnic table where she usually sat with Amy and Kit was empty. The air felt dirty from the layer of fog that had lingered most of the day. It added to the grit on her hands left from cleaning the floor. A soiled dampness had soaked beneath her skin and no matter how many times she soaped and rinsed them, no matter how many layers of hand cream she applied, her fingers still looked water-logged and slightly unclean. She sat down to wait.

After a few minutes she saw Kit walking across the playground. She wore a tennis skirt that highlighted the length of her tanned legs. Once a week Kit played tennis with another group of friends – women Rachel had never met. Rachel suspected they had parties that didn't include Kit's friends from Spruce. Kit's tennis friends were probably all tall and slim. No one had flabby thighs or kinky hair that couldn't be controlled. She supposed all their children were super-achievers in sports and school. Those women didn't come unglued over a few unattractive photographs. Of course, they most likely had never seen themselves in an unattractive photograph. There wasn't a vandal among them.

"Cold day," said Kit. "But perfect for tennis. I didn't get all hot and sweaty."

"Did you win?"

"We did. My partner and I."

Rachel couldn't think of anything else to say. Her mind was crowded with the sound of shattering glass. She pictured Kit's pale pink lips curving into a sneer.

"What's new with you?" said Kit.

Rachel lifted her heels so the balls of her feet pressed hard against the ground. This had the effect of lifting her thighs off the bench so they appeared slimmer. "Not too much. I hate it when the fog hangs around all day. It's depressing to have this blank sky that makes you feel like you're closed in a box." She looked up and saw Amy approaching.

When Amy reached the picnic table she sat on the edge of the bench as if she was eager to start talking. "Tennis day, I see."

No one said anything. Rachel stared at Amy. All these years she'd considered Amy her best friend. Hearing that Amy's mother had been raped was more than disturbing. Why hadn't Amy ever mentioned it? Maybe that wasn't something you told your friends. Still, Amy had blurted it out last night like it was at the forefront of her mind. Rachel couldn't help looking at her with new eyes, wondering what else Amy hadn't told her. It kind of explained why she was so afraid of so many things.

"I hate this weather," said Amy.

"What's with the weather complaints from you two? It's just fog," said Kit.

"Did Rachel tell you what happened?"

"Amy! Don't." Rachel's heart pounded erratically. Others might guess, but no one should know for certain who had destroyed the photographs. It was their secret. Kit would never understand.

"I solved the problem," said Amy. "No more ugly pictures. Rachel helped, of course."

"What are you talking about?" said Kit.

"You promised," said Rachel. Her breath caught in her throat and her voice sounded too high-pitched.

"We didn't promise anything. And Kit needs to know."

"I need to know what?"

"Ms. Shafton refused to take down the pictures. So we took care of it ourselves."

"She gave you the key?"

"Of course we didn't have the key. I told you, Ms. Shafton refused. We smashed the glass and tore up the pictures."

Kit collapsed back against the table. She opened her mouth but said nothing.

"Can you believe it?" Amy laughed. "It felt amazing. I'm sure the mess is cleaned up by now. There was glass all over the ground."

"Tell me this is a joke."

"It's not a joke. I smashed the glass with my flashlight. Rachel used a key to rip up the photographs so you couldn't recognize anything. You saw what terrible angles she used. She didn't even let us pose."

Kit stared. Her mouth was still partially open. Her lips formed a narrow slit that showed the edges of her teeth in a thin line. "Are you crazy?"

"She had no right to take those pictures and hang them in public."

Rachel scooted down the bench. Amy's voice was shrill in her ear, like the whining of a drill boring into the soft tissue of her brain. If Kit were shocked, what would the others think? What would Greg say about their violent behavior? Kit clearly thought they were idiots. Disgust was plastered across her face. It was childish, the thrill of doing something wrong and enjoying it. Now, as she stared across the school grounds at the blue roofs of the buildings, stark against the white sky, there wasn't a particle of enjoyment.

Kit stood and folded her arms. She glared at Amy. "I showed you the pictures so you wouldn't be blind-sided. I didn't think you'd destroy someone's property."

"We told you we were going to get them removed."

"And did you?"

"Yes. Ms. Shafton laughed at us."

"No she didn't," said Rachel.

"She treated us like we were anti-art."

"That's not exactly how it was," said Rachel.

Amy jerked around to face Rachel. "That's exactly how it was. She put that woman's pathetic attempt to be some kind of artist ahead of our feelings. We've supported this school for years. Suddenly Charlotte bounces into town with her army boots and tight shirts and acts like she owns the place. If you aren't outraged, there's something wrong with you."

"There's nothing wrong with me," said Kit. "If you'd been patient and worked with Ms. Shafton, you might have achieved what you wanted. Now you'll be lucky if you don't get charged with a misdemeanor."

"That's ridiculous. How would they find out?"

"It's completely obvious. Photographs of the four of us are hung in the display cases and overnight they get smashed to pieces? Who else would do it?"

"There were pictures of the whole team," said Amy. "At least pictures of their feet." She laughed.

"Do you think they'll arrest us? I guess…" Rachel coughed. She swallowed the hard chunk of phlegm in her throat. "I didn't think of that."

"You didn't think at all."

Amy stabbed her index finger at Kit's arm. "Don't tell anyone."

Kit lifted her arm out of Amy's reach. "You've crossed a line."

"I saved us from being humiliated."

"You're not going to tell, are you?" said Rachel.

"No. But I feel like I don't know you," said Kit.

Rachel looked at her friend – classy, elegant Kit. One rash act had snapped the fragile ties between them. She could feel their friendship sliding between her fingers, as slippery as uncooked rice.

"I won't be staying at soccer practice today. I'm dropping off Renee and then I have to take Carter back to the orthodontist," said Kit.

"I can drive Renee to practice to save you a trip," said Rachel.

"No, that's fine. But thanks for the offer." The words sounded hollow, tacked on, like Kit had remembered her manners and would never allow her disgust to prevent her from being polite.

Rachel lifted her hair off her shoulders. Her neck was perspiring despite the fog. Why was she only now realizing that polite behavior and following the rules, controlling yourself, was the glue that made friendships work? In a single breath it was gone.

Chapter Fourteen

CHARLOTTE WALKED TOWARD the courtyard at the center of the school. The breeze drifting through the covered corridors was cool on her arms. Her heart thumped faster as she approached the display cases. She wanted to take a quick look at them to reassure herself the photograph collection looked as sophisticated as she remembered. As she drew closer to the wall where they hung, something didn't seem right. The reflection she expected to see from the panels of glass wasn't there. She stopped about six feet away. There was no reflection because the glass was missing. It was like staring through the eye sockets of a skull. Her photographs were gone. A few tacks remained and a thin shard of glass protruded from the side of one of the corkboard panels. Had the principal changed her mind and removed them? But that made no sense. Maybe her mind was playing tricks on her. The school must have two sets of cases and this set didn't have the glass doors. She glanced across at the multi-purpose room. No, this was the right place. Why would someone remove her photographs? She turned and jogged back to the school office. Inside, she wove through the cluster of children. She expected the secretary to call her back, asking about an appointment, but there was too much activity. Charlotte slipped around the corner unnoticed.

Ms. Shafton was on the phone. Charlotte paused in the doorway. The principal looked up and waved her into the office. Charlotte walked around one of the chairs facing the desk and sat down.

Ms. Shafton put the receiver into the cradle. "I meant to call you, but it's been so hectic. By now you've heard we had some property damage."

"Property damage?" said Charlotte.

"The display cases were vandalized."

"My photographs were stolen?"

"No. The glass on the cases was smashed," said Ms. Shafton. "I'm afraid your photographs were destroyed."

Charlotte leaned forward. She pressed her hands on her knees. Her palms were damp and her hands slipped to the side. "Where are they?"

"They were unsalvageable. The frames were splintered and the photographs were … torn."

Charlotte stood. An ache formed in her chest. The pressure was so tight she could only take shallow breaths. She tried to steady her thoughts, hoping the principal was exaggerating, hoping this wasn't really happening. "So where are they?" she whispered.

"They were disposed of. There was really nothing left. The photographs were mutilated. I'm so sorry. The police are investigating."

Charlotte swallowed. Tears burned behind her eyes.

The principal spoke faster. "Hopefully they'll be able to identify a local gang. But it might have been younger kids. Random destruction. I'm very sorry. I truly meant to call."

"It doesn't sound random at all. As far as I can see, the only thing destroyed was my photo essay."

"And the display cases," said Ms. Shafton.

"Well yes, but to get at my photographs."

"We've never had anything like this happen before. The police are ..."

"There's nothing to investigate. I think I can guess who did it."

Ms. Shafton leaned back in her chair. "There aren't any suspects right now."

"It wasn't a gang. That makes no sense."

"It's the most likely explanation."

"No it's not. I bet Amy Lewis knows something about it," said Charlotte.

"Why would you think that?"

"She didn't want me to take her picture. She was very insistent."

"Ms. Whittington, you can't stand here and accuse one of our parents of a crime without any facts."

Charlotte clenched her hands and pressed her knuckles on the edge of the desk. "Why would a gang walk through an elementary school, stop and tear up a bunch of photographs they couldn't even see in the dark? Either they would break into classrooms looking for computers, or they would do more damage. My photography was the target. How can you not see that?"

"You're understandably distraught, but that doesn't mean you can leap to the conclusion that a mother vandalized school property. She's a *very nice, community-minded* woman. Calm down and listen to yourself."

The office was too warm. Charlotte felt the fabric of her shirt growing damp under her arms. She thought she could smell her own sweat and she imagined Ms. Shafton sniffing at her grief. What chance did Charlotte have against a very nice, community-minded woman? Apparently Ms. Shafton would rather fool herself into thinking that a roving group of vandals wandered onto the school grounds and paused in the dark to tear up a collection of black and white photographs.

"Perhaps a witness will come forward."

A witness? From that group of women that moved and spoke like a single organism? She turned sideways to wriggle between the other chair and the desk. What if someone hurt a child under the school's care? Would Ms. Shafton exhibit the same nonchalant attitude? Her attitude was so casual she might have been talking about a misplaced library book.

Ms. Shafton stood and extended her hand across the desk.

Charlotte ignored the gesture. Ms. Shafton was acting as if they were concluding a parent-teacher conference instead of discussing a crime.

"I'm sure the police will let us know what evidence they find," said Ms. Shafton.

Had she emphasized the word *evidence*? Charlotte didn't believe there was any evidence. There was nothing to disprove the easy answer. There was no need to stir up gossip by suggesting something ugly might have happened at such an upscale elementary school. This was a place that had never witnessed violence, didn't really know what to think about vandalism, and the principal reflected that. She would smile, pretend it was an unfortunate aberration and hope everyone forgot about it.

Charlotte turned and walked out of the office and down the short hallway. She pushed open the door to the courtyard and let it fall shut behind her. Ms. Shafton was too weak to do anything, but Charlotte was not going to simply put it behind her and accept it as an unfortunate incident that could only be resolved by the police. She would force Amy to confess. As she crossed the playground, headed to where Amy and the others were seated, her heartbeat accelerated to a rapid flutter. The moment she saw them, huddled together across from the fifth grade classrooms, she knew it wouldn't be so easy. Amy would never admit what she'd done.

She stopped beside the bench where Amy was seated. Her skirt brushed against Amy's kneecap. Amy shifted her legs to the side and flicked her fingers at Charlotte's skirt.

"Do you know what happened to my photographs?"

"What do you mean?" said Amy.

"My photographs were destroyed."

"What photographs are those?"

"I had a photo essay hanging in the display cases. Someone smashed the glass and destroyed my work. I think you might know something about it."

"Why would you think that?" said Amy.

"Because you didn't want me to photograph you." Charlotte knew she was being rash, but her gut insisted it was Amy. There was something chilling and frantic about this fragile, over-dressed woman that wasn't quite right.

"You can't accuse someone of vandalism without any proof."

Charlotte shoved her hands in the pockets of her skirt. Her fists bulged like growths on the sides of her thighs. "Wouldn't the right answer be; *I didn't do it?*"

Rachel and Kit were silent. This nice suburban woman had taken some kind of weapon to school property and destroyed a beautiful series of photographs, and no one was going to do anything about it. Charlotte could feel them closing together, mortar hardening in the crevices between them. Rachel stared at her toes. Kit leaned back and shook her hair off her face. Why were they protecting Amy? Had they been involved? She was convinced Amy had ruined her work, but she wasn't sure about the others. It was too fantastic to believe a group of suburban women would set out to vandalize their children's school, yet she knew she was right. She would stand here until one of them said something. They couldn't all be as cold as Amy.

"I'm sorry about your pictures," whispered Rachel. "Maybe you could ..."

"Maybe I could ... what?"

"I don't know. You said you have a photo essay," said Rachel. "You could show that somewhere, if it's of something nice, something uplifting, not people's feet. That's not very interesting."

"I think it's interesting," said Charlotte. Amy's evasive words had made it clear she knew something about the vandalism. If Rachel or Kit had been there with her, if they had any regrets, there might be a crack in their united front. She planted her hands on her hips and glared at Rachel. "Do you know what happened to my photographs?"

Rachel lifted her heels off the ground, arching her feet. She shook her head with a slight movement that looked like a tic.

Charlotte looked at Kit but couldn't read her expression. She hadn't realized how much of her soul lived in the design of each shot, the cropping, the framing, and the planning of what she wanted to communicate. And that didn't count the money she'd spent. Seeing those hollow cases felt like a hole had been carved in her chest. "I think you know."

Amy stood slowly. The top of her head came up to Charlotte's nose. "You have no right to accuse us of some kind of crime. We don't know anything about your pictures."

"You destroyed something that belonged to me."

"Those were tabloid photos," said Amy. "And if someone destroyed them, you should be talking to the police."

"I know you did it." Charlotte hated the slightly hysterical vibration of her voice. She swallowed and lifted her chin to keep tears from pooling in her eyes and spilling down her face. She would not cry in front of them. She put out her hand to keep Amy from creeping closer. Her fingers brushed against Amy's wrist.

"Don't hit me."

"I didn't hit you."

"Amy, don't," said Rachel. "Please. Maybe we should …"

"Maybe you should pay what you owe for destroying my work. Is that what you were going to say?" said Charlotte.

"I already told you we don't know anything about it," said Amy." Now leave us alone."

Charlotte wanted to hammer her fists against that defiant mouth, the only part of Amy's face not covered by her large sunglasses. The desire for violence pumped through her blood vessels as if she'd been injected with a drug. Would she feel better if she kicked Amy's skinny ankles and tore at her hair? She longed to rake her nails across that smug face. It was the only thing that would satisfy her.

Amy grabbed her pink straw purse off the bench. As she walked away the heels of her backless sandals hit the blacktop like pellets from a bee-bee gun.

Charlotte called after her, "I'm not giving up on this."

Amy turned. "Is that a threat?"

Charlotte lifted her shoulders and relaxed them in an exaggerated shrug. "If it feels like a threat, it's because you know you're lying."

Amy continued walking. Rachel stood and hurried after her. Kit leaned back against the edge of the table. She folded her hands on her right leg as if she was posing for a picture.

"Amy did it, didn't she?" said Charlotte.

Kit uncrossed her legs and stood. "Let it go." She walked toward the building. Her hair swung across her shoulders like a curtain of dark water.

Chapter Fifteen

RACHEL PULLED A FISTFUL of spaghetti out of the package. She snapped it in half and dropped the pasta into the boiling water. She broke two more handfuls into the pot, stirred it, and turned to scoop up the felt pens spread across the kitchen table. Trent's sketchpad lay open at one end of the table. A drawing of a snail consumed the entire nine by twelve-inch page. The shadows drawn in light strokes of moss green and several shades of brown to define the curves of the shell gave the creature an unbelievably life-like presence. She heard Greg's key in the front door and closed the cover. She put the pens and pad on the window seat behind the table.

Greg walked into the kitchen. "Smells good."

Lately, when he spoke those words, all she could think of was the murdered woman, her stew hardening into a thick glob while she was assaulted and stabbed on the kitchen floor. Rachel turned down the gas under the sauce and meatballs until there was only a thin line of flame visible. Greg walked up behind her and slid his arms around her waist. His lips on her neck were smooth and dry.

"Mmm, spaghetti. I'll slice the bread." As he picked up the serrated knife, a chill slithered through her spine.

"We had vandalism at school," said Trent.

She hadn't even noticed Trent had entered the room. He sat at the table, waiting.

Greg sawed the knife through the bread crust. "What happened?"

"Someone smashed up a bunch of glass. I got to see it," said Trent.

"That's not good." Greg glanced at her and hacked off another slice of bread. "How many windows?"

"It wasn't windows. It was the display cases."

Greg continued to saw at the bread, pressing too hard so the loaf was squashed. She wanted to take the knife away from him, but all she could do was stare at the white foam on the simmering water and try to keep her gaze steady. Of course Trent would want to talk about the vandalism. It was probably the biggest news of the day and much more interesting to first graders than anything happening inside the classroom.

"Someone smashed up all the display cases and ripped up some pictures."

"Really? Do you know anything about it, Rachel?"

She put her face close to the steam hovering over the spaghetti pot. "The glass was broken in the display cases near the multi-purpose room."

"I heard that part. I wonder if it was kids from our school," said Greg.

"I'm sure not," said Rachel.

"What else was damaged?"

"Nothing," said Rachel.

"Just the pictures," said Trent. "Pictures of soccer."

She turned away from the pot. Trent's eyes sparkled as if he expected a wrapped gift to appear on his placemat any minute. "Will you set the table, Trent."

Trent slid off the chair and went to the drawer and yanked it open. The utensils rattled in the tray. "No one ever did something that bad at our school before."

"What soccer pictures?" said Greg.

"Some lady took them," said Trent.

Rachel dumped the pasta into the colander and ducked her head to avoid the blast of steam. "Dinner's ready. Please go tell Sara."

"You told me to set the table," said Trent.

"Finish it up and call Sara." She ran cold water over the pasta.

She had hoped the activity of putting a bowl of salad and the bread on the table, scooping spaghetti onto their plates, and Sara's arrival would divert the conversation, but before she could lift a forkful of pasta and half a meatball to her mouth, Trent was back on the topic of vandalism. "There was lots of glass. It looked like ice."

"Did they send a notice home to let us know what's being done?" said Greg.

"The janitor cleaned it up and the police came," said Trent.

Greg stared at Rachel, waiting for an answer to his question.

"What can be done? They filed a police report," said Rachel.

"It doesn't exactly inspire feelings of safety for our kids. Especially after the other thing," said Greg.

She tried to catch his eye, but he was looking down at his plate. Why was he bringing that up? Talking about it would prompt questions from Trent and she didn't want to explain rape and murder to a six-year-old. The room was too hot, her skin damp from the steam that still lingered from the boiling pasta. Her son, disinterested in everything little boys should care about, was now enthused over the destruction of school property. She set her fork on the plate. How would Trent react if he knew his mother was one of the vandals? She closed her eyes and saw herself again. Had that really been her own hand scraping her keys across beautifully composed black and white photographs, carving ugly scratches, watching as the ink curled into metallic-like shavings that fell to the ground? Listening to her family talk, she had no idea how she'd gotten caught up in such a frenzy of anger and destruction. She felt her life was suddenly unrecognizable.

"Do you?" said Greg.

She looked at him.

"I said, do you think the school will do anything?"

"What can they do? If there are any clues the police will track them down. I'm sure it was an isolated event."

"It's still disturbing. I'm surprised you're not more concerned."

She put a piece of butter lettuce in her mouth. It was thin, soaked with too much oil and vinegar, clinging to her tongue.

She stabbed her fork into the spaghetti, twirled thick strands of pasta around the tines and stuffed them in her mouth before she'd swallowed the lettuce. She chewed for several seconds. The taste was soothing, soaking up the vinegar. "I don't know what we can do about it."

"Do you think the kids are safe?"

Why was he was asking these questions right in front of Sara and Trent?

"It's no big deal, Dad." Sara slunk down in her chair and rested her elbows on the edge of the table. Her pale brown hair fell forward, covering her jaw. The light of the sun, moving toward the horizon, came through the window and played across her hair so the blonde streaks glowed. She lowered her eyelids, gazing at her parents with a bored expression.

Although it was nice to have Sara on her side, downplaying the event, the deliberate change in her posture terrified Rachel. Sara looked like a teenager, overly aware of the power of her body. She looked smug with her ability to show nonchalance by a simple shift in position.

"Finally something interesting instead of boring old soccer all the time," said Trent. He reached across the table for a piece of bread. His elbow tapped the side of his glass and it tipped over. Milk ran across the wood, pooling in the split at the center where the table pulled apart for expansion leaves and pouring over the edge like a waterfall.

Rachel jumped up. Sara shoved her chair back and grabbed her plate.

While Rachel yanked paper towels off the roll, Sara strolled over to the counter. "Nice work, Trent. Now we'll have a sour milk stink for the next two days."

As she wiped up the milk, Rachel's mind crawled with imagined looks of shock if anyone found out what she and Amy had done. It wasn't even a secret any more, with Kit knowing. How long would it be until Amy felt compelled to share her victory with someone else? Rachel's hands smelled like milk and her pasta looked gaudy on the plate. She was no longer hungry. At some point, she was going to have to tell Greg what they'd done.

UPSTAIRS IN THEIR bedroom, after Trent was tucked in and Sara was settled in bed reading, Rachel took off her shirt and jeans and left them on the bathroom floor. She turned her back to the mirror. She unclasped her bra and let it fall on the pile of clothes. She pulled her nightshirt off the hook on the back of the bathroom door and tugged it over her head without turning to face the mirror. Seeing the extra flesh around her ribs and the roundness of her hips would remind her of how justified she'd felt destroying the pictures. What had made Charlotte think a photograph of the lower halves of women's bodies was interesting? A better question was, what made Ms. Shafton think those pictures were worth displaying on the walls of their elementary school? One minute Rachel felt her actions were justified, and the next, she was terrified Greg would find out, that everyone would know she was so uncomfortable with her body, so insecure about her son, that she lost control and damaged public property. Not to mention how she'd hurt Charlotte.

After she brushed her teeth and hair and washed her face, she turned off the light and crawled into bed.

By the time Greg came into the bedroom, her cheeks were stiff with tears. She turned so that her back faced his side of the bed. She pulled her legs up at a right angle. It felt safe, her breasts and belly protected inside the circle of her arms and legs. She'd been drifting to sleep, but now she was wide awake as Greg knocked around the bathroom like an animal in a cage. He banged the shower door, rattling the glass in its frame. He bumped the towel rack. At six feet, four inches tall, everything was a bit too close to his elbows. Nothing fit. She didn't fit either. He should have a longer, leaner wife. A wife that was easy-going, like him. Not a wife who was so obsessed with her son's hatred of soccer, so afraid her hips were too round, that she was driven to destroy a few harmless photographs. She squeezed her arms more tightly around the pillow and tried to slow down her breathing, as if that would make sleep come.

Greg came into the room and climbed into bed, rolled on his side and slid his arm under hers. He inched closer so his chest was pressed against her back.

"You know I love you, don't you?" He folded his hand around her breast, stroking it, then slid his palm down her ribs and up under her nightshirt. He tugged the fabric away from her body so he could make contact with her skin. She pulled her arms more tightly around her curled up legs, but that didn't stop him. He pushed and wriggled his hand until he found her breast under the nightshirt. "You feel nice. Do you love me?"

She sighed. He wouldn't stop until he received an answer, almost as if he needed reassurance. Or did he simply want acknowledgement she was in the mood to make love? It was the last thing on earth she wanted right now. All she could picture behind her closed eyes was that photograph, her enormous ass at the center. His wrist bumped against the folds of skin on her belly. She straightened her back and uncurled her knees, stretching out so he didn't feel he was poking his hand into a bucket of rolled up flesh.

"You feel so good. Tell me you love me."

She moved away and rolled halfway onto her back. "I love you," she said.

"Take off your shirt. I want to see your scrumptious body."

"You mean my fat body." Without warning, a gulping sob burst out of her throat.

He tightened his arm around her. "Hey. Why are you crying? You're not fat. I've told you a thousand times, you look spectacular."

"Don't lie to me. My thighs are too thick, my butt is too..."

"Stop." He squeezed her so hard she couldn't take a full breath. "You hang around with a bunch of sticks." He stroked her nipple and she felt it harden in spite of everything pushing to the forefront of her mind, thoughts demanding attention like a crowd of children waiting for snacks.

"My friends look nice. Their clothes fit perfectly."

He pulled her toward him again, tugging so hard she was forced to move. He kissed her wet cheeks and slid her nightshirt up to her waist, pulling until she yielded and he could lift it over her head. "I know what I like, and it's not some anorexic girl from the cover of a magazine, all skin and bones. I want you."

There was no point in saying anything more. They'd had this conversation hundreds of times. He refused to relent in telling her how much he loved her body, as if the extra flesh on her thighs didn't exist, as if the curve of her belly was sexy. According to him, it was. She should be glad. At least his blind admiration made Amy's words ring hollow, her insistence that the men would all be panting after Charlotte. Not Greg. For some reason she could never fully grasp, he thought she was the most attractive woman on earth. She relaxed her shoulders and let him stroke his fingers around her breasts, but as they made love, a small corner of her mind spun nervously. She worried Kit would stop speaking to her, that Greg wouldn't find her quite so sexy if he knew what she'd done. She tried to block out the picture of Trent that had become a permanent shadow in the back of her mind. The image flickered behind her eyelids – a child destined to sit on the sidelines, biting his fingers and looking scared. Just like his mother.

Chapter Sixteen

CHARLOTTE HELD HER CAMERA near her stomach, the strap loose around her neck. The school day wouldn't be over for another half hour. She'd come early to be sure she arrived before the other mothers. She walked across the playground to the climbing equipment. A white sweatshirt was draped over the edge of the grayed wood border that surrounded the equipment area. There was something about the sweatshirt and the empty playground that emphasized her sense of desolation. She lifted the camera, framing the sweatshirt so the darkest part of the wood was visible. She took a few shots and lowered the camera. She'd come early with a vague idea that she would intimidate Amy by getting in her face with the camera. It wasn't a very good plan. Amy wasn't easily intimidated. In fact, Charlotte might end up looking ridiculous, but she couldn't pretend nothing had happened.

The temperature was in the mid-eighties. A strong breeze, like hot breath, whipped across the athletic field. Just as quickly, the breeze died back. She closed her eyes and let the sun stroke her bare arms. She still wasn't used to the warm south bay weather, and when she felt this kind of heat on her skin, it had a way of stirring up her longing for Mark. She could almost feel his hands on her. Her muscles melted, as if they were preparing her body to wrap itself around him. Her knees were soft, unable to support her. She sat on the wood frame next to the sweatshirt. Three years was such a long time to be separated, close to a third of Meadow's life so far. She didn't know how she was going to survive.

When Mark first started selling pot, it seemed harmless, a little extra cash on the side. She wasn't even sure when he'd gotten in so far over his head. They were both nineteen when they moved to San Francisco, in love with each other and with their artistic desires. It was easy to share a sleeping bag on the floor of a friend's loft. Mark played his sax on street corners, and occasionally as a fill-in for bands in small clubs. Charlotte brought in a little money working for a graphic designer editing photographs. They got by, but then she found out she was pregnant. Somehow, when she wasn't quite paying attention, Mark developed a full time business selling pot. He was never involved with dangerous substances, and really, how bad was pot compared with alcohol? There was no difference in its use – a desire to relax, unwind, and let the mind drift aimlessly on a weekend evening. The rationalizations were easy, and with half her mind, she still believed them. Mark's partners were all nice guys, they didn't seem like drug dealers, criminals. They read stories to Meadow, admired her drawings, and one guy built her a rocking horse. They were friends.

All that time, she never stopped taking photographs. Once Meadow started kindergarten, Charlotte threw herself back into her work, determined to succeed as an artist. She was excited about her success with the stock photography companies and finally she landed the consignment arrangements with the coffee shop and an Italian bistro. She should have paid more attention to the income that was paying their rent and buying their food, but she didn't. How could a confident, independent woman have been so blasé, ignorant really, about the risks her partner was taking to earn a living? But she was. Blame it on the total absorption that was motherhood, blame it on her blind passion to look at the world through a camera lens. For whatever reason, she was completely unprepared for the police officers swarming into their apartment.

Right now, she needed to focus on the future. She couldn't allow her thoughts to keep wandering back over the ways their lives had gotten off track.

The playground was no longer empty; a few other mothers were seated at the picnic tables. One woman was reading a book and another stood under a tiny tree, trying to get a scrap of shade, holding a one-year-old that was wrestling to be let out of her arms.

Rachel emerged from between the buildings near the school office. As she walked, her hair blew across her face. She batted it back. Charlotte raised the camera and snapped a picture, focusing tightly on Rachel's hands. She aimed lower, catching Rachel's skirt plastered against her thighs.

Rachel stopped a few feet away. "What are you taking pictures of?"

"Whatever interests me."

"Why do you show the worst side of people?"

"I don't try to do that, but I like details."

"Please stop pointing the camera at me."

Charlotte lowered the camera. "Most people like to be photographed."

"Your pictures are cruel," said Rachel.

"You hated them so much you destroyed my work?"

Rachel settled herself on the bench, grabbed her hair and pulled it back from her shoulders. She twisted it into a knot, but the moment she let go, it tumbled forward. Loose strands danced in the breeze.

Charlotte backed away, aimed her camera and snapped three shots.

"Please stop," said Rachel.

Charlotte looked up and saw Amy scurrying across the blacktop. A part of her wanted to slip away into a safe corner of the schoolyard, while another side of her longed to punch Amy's face. All her life she'd considered herself a tranquil person, but since Mark's arrest, these unfamiliar urges for violence churned inside her on a regular basis. The sensations frightened her and she wanted them to go away. There was an animalistic instinct to protect her daughter, her art, from Amy. Was there some deeper knowledge, below conscious thought, warning her of something sinister? Or was she feeling fragile and slightly paranoid with Mark ripped out of her life?

"What are you doing?" said Amy. "We already discussed this. You can't take our pictures. You're not making yourself very welcome around here."

"I grew up here." She had no idea why she'd said that. The words sounded absurd. It was the tone of Amy's voice, the territorial attitude and the barely veiled assertion that Charlotte and Meadow didn't belong. She implied that Charlotte lacked whatever quality was required to be a member of their club. Perhaps an extreme sense of entitlement was the ticket in. Whatever it was, she didn't want it. She wanted an apology, and payment, or something. She wanted them to admit they'd hurt her. They could afford to pay for her prints and frames ten times over. They didn't have budgets so tight they could hardly breathe. Her savings, the free rent, and a little extra cash from Mark's brother was all she had. They acted as if her loss was nothing, pretending they didn't know what she was talking about. She lifted the camera to her face and pointed it at Amy's knees where there was a tiny smudge of grease on her white jeans.

"Stop." Amy lunged at her.

Charlotte snapped the picture at the same instant Amy's shoulder crashed into her. The sharp heel of Amy's shoe scraped the surface of Charlotte's boot.

"Watch what you're doing."

"I lost my balance," said Amy.

"You tore my boot."

"Prove it."

"What does that mean? Look at it," said Charlotte.

"You seem to like making accusations without any proof," said Amy.

Charlotte took a few steps back. She pointed the camera directly at Amy's face. Her wine-colored lips were pressed into a frown; her jaw so tight there was a small lump in front of her ear.

Amy lunged again. She stumbled and hit the camera, causing it to dig into the bridge of Charlotte's nose. Tears rushed to Charlotte's eyes.

"Amy. Please, don't," said Rachel.

Rachel sounded as if she was reciting lines from a script, knowing she was obligated to intervene, but not overly concerned.

Charlotte's forehead ached where the camera had slammed against her face. It had been a lame idea to think she could force Amy into an admission of guilt by pushing her to lose control. She pulled the camera close to her belly again, turned, and walked away.

Behind her she heard Amy's sharp tone, "You have no right."

As Charlotte walked, she pulled the backpack off her shoulders, unzipped the top and shoved the camera inside without replacing the lens cap. She wanted to be back in San Francisco, with Mark and his friends and their girlfriends – mostly with Mark. More than that, she wanted a world where a woman like Amy Lewis didn't exist. The dismissal bell rang. Doors slammed open and children swarmed out. With her eyes still watering, she couldn't focus or even remember which door belonged to Meadow's classroom. She looked across the waves of children.

Finally she saw Meadow walking toward her; recognizable by the pink baseball cap she'd worn that morning. Charlotte swallowed the moisture that had collected at the back of her throat. "How was your day?"

"We have to plan a science project and I was thinking I could put out food for the birds in our back yard. I could find out what kind of birds like which kinds of food."

Charlotte nodded.

"What do you think, Mom? Is that a good idea?"

"Yes. That's a good idea." Her mind circled around her desire to build a career as a photographer. The warmth of her longing spread through her with the same intensity as her ache for Mark's body. She smiled at the comparison, but it was true. There was nothing else she wanted to do and nothing was going to stop her. The only things Amy had destroyed were paper and glass and wood. It was expensive, but she'd simply start over, this time with a proper venue. She wasn't backing down, no matter what Amy did.

Chapter Seventeen

IT WAS CLOSE TO eleven o'clock when Amy arrived at the soccer field on Saturday morning. The twins' game was already in the second half. She regretted sleeping so late, but lying on her back staring into the darkness from two-thirty until the alarm buzzed at six-thirty that morning had left her exhausted. Most nights she was awake when she would have preferred to be sleeping. Instead, her mind raced – was that a footstep on the first floor? Had the wall shuddered in the hallway? Was Justin dreaming about women more alluring than her? While the rest of the neighborhood slept, she worried about the possibility of a major earthquake, her daughters' grades, their teen years, and the fragile economy. She drifted off like an infant when she first went to bed, but sometime around one or two in the morning her brain sprang into active duty and she couldn't seem to find the off switch. Justin was unsympathetic to her inability to sleep through the night. In his view, it was a simple matter of refusing to worry about things she couldn't control.

But that was the whole point – if she could do something about all those potential problems, she wouldn't be awake.

Justin wasn't likely to forgive her for missing the first game of the season. He wouldn't say anything to criticize her, but his averted eyes and his eager description of the twins' successes would tell her she'd let them down. Alice and Amanda wanted both their parents cheering every move.

He was at the far end of the field, standing next to Greg Matthews under a fruitless mulberry tree behind the goal line, clutching a *Venti Starbucks* cup. From a distance she could see his lips and jaw working furiously. His eyes were fixed on the girls, running with their ponytails flying behind them. She knew he and Greg were analyzing the game, talking about offensive strategy as if the two men were planning a military maneuver. She walked along the edge of the field. When she reached his side, she stood on her toes and kissed his earlobe.

"All rested?" Justin kept his eyes focused on the field.

"Yes." She glanced at Greg and laughed.

Greg smiled but didn't look at her.

Her friends were seated in their lawn chairs near the sideline. While she watched, Jane jumped up to shout her approval of a well-executed pass. "Bye. I'm off to sit with the girls," said Amy.

Justin didn't respond. Why did he ignore her like this? Didn't he understand how his silence stabbed at her chest, causing a sharp pain that lingered? It gave the impression she was a burden, that she was the least important part of his life. She took his hand and lifted it to her face. She brushed her lips across his knuckles. "I'll miss you."

"OK. I'll fill you in on the game later," he said. "We're ahead by two."

She lowered his hand. Her chest tightened as he let his arm fall like dead weight. Sometimes she felt like she was a fixture in his life, that she'd lost her ability to capture his undivided attention. It wasn't her fault she couldn't sleep. She had to make up for it during the day or she'd be useless taking care of Alice and Amanda. She smiled to show she wasn't upset and walked toward her friends.

As she made her way across the grass, she glanced around the field. Charlotte must be at the game, but she wasn't seated with the mothers of the Emerald Tigers. A cluster of parents from the other team stood close to their goal line, many of them sipping coffee drinks from green and white *Starbucks* cups. She shaded her eyes to see if Charlotte was seated with the parents from the opposing team, but she didn't see the spiky, black-tipped hair. She took quick steps, trying to avoid muddy spots. It was getting hot and the damp ground gave off a farm-like smell. She breathed through her mouth, afraid the odor steaming out of the soil would make her nauseous.

Then she saw Charlotte, far from the sidelines. She wore faded low-cut jeans and a short top that left a strip of skin exposed. She moved methodically down the field, snapping pictures of the players as if she hadn't heard a word Amy had said, as if the damage to her work hadn't ruffled a single spike of hair. Amy had to hand it to her, Charlotte wasn't going to give up her picture-taking project. Amy slowed her pace. Was she planning to take pictures of the men today? It was hard to believe she would be brazen enough to photograph their butts like she had done to the women. The camera appeared to be aimed at the girls, but Amy couldn't be sure. Charlotte's breasts wobbled with every step. Amy looked at the men. Every single guy had turned his head slightly, watching Charlotte's progress along the sideline. Their mouths were carefully closed, but she was sure their pupils were dilated as they hungered to touch, all their thoughts of soccer erased by those seductively dancing breasts.

Amy hurried to her friends and settled into an empty chair. "Look at that."

"What?" said Jane.

"All the guys are staring at Charlotte."

Her friends glanced at the group of men.

Jane leaned back in her chair. "They're watching the game."

"If you think that, you don't know much about men," said Amy.

"I don't know about Justin, but my husband is watching our daughter," said Jane.

Amy closed her eyes. Her head ached from the heat and she longed for the darkness of her bedroom. The way Jane's husband was ogling Charlotte should make Jane shiver with fear, but she was too obstinate, deluding herself into thinking he didn't notice that goddess striding down the length of the soccer field. Charlotte had a confident, gliding walk because she didn't need heels on her shoes. She was almost as tall as Jane's husband, who was just under six feet. Her shoulders were muscled without being bulky and her breasts were round and perfectly symmetrical, no need to be re-shaped with snug fitting wire and lace and satin. She had a small, straight nose and high cheekbones, a face that could carry off the look of short, spiky hair. She was beautiful. "Are you blind?" said Amy.

Jane ran her fingers through her hair. Blonde waves slid across the backs of her hands. "Even if they're staring at her, it doesn't mean anything. That's how men are. You know that."

"You notice your husband staring at another woman and you sit back and say, that's the way it is? How can you do nothing?"

Jane laughed and nodded toward the group of men. "Look who's staring the hardest. What are you going to do about it? Are you going to rush over there and pull down Justin's baseball cap so he can't see? Pluck his eyes out of his head?"

Amy refused to look. She wouldn't give Jane the satisfaction. The others stared at her, their faces illuminated with the worst possible expression – pity. Why was Jane trying to hurt her? They used to be close, but since Jane started her job writing press releases, traveling for her employer, she'd changed. She'd never been a person who worried much, but now she acted as if she was fearless. "Never mind," said Amy. "You can't really see his face; it's so dark in the shade. But if I caught him leering at her, I wouldn't chirp about boys being boys."

"Let's talk about something else," said Rachel.

"Yes, let's," said Kit.

The conversation turned to game schedules. Amy said nothing. A woman was nearly dancing in front of their husbands and all they wanted to talk about was soccer? She watched Charlotte's progress around the perimeter of the field. She could only hope Charlotte was aiming at the girls instead of at Amy's feet, or up the insides of her legs, for that matter. She stretched out her legs and pressed her knees together. There was no good way to sit or stand with that camera tracking every move.

The coach for the other team had his mouth open, watching Charlotte squat and stand, her breasts bouncing like tennis balls. It was so easy for men to stop thinking, to behave like animals, and Charlotte knew how to take advantage of that. Amy pressed her fingers to her forehead and wiped at the moisture collecting along her hairline, hoping her movements were discreet. She wanted the game to be over. She wanted to be home, not out here, exposed, with Justin drifting beyond her reach where she was unable to probe his thoughts.

Chapter Eighteen

THAT EVENING AMY SURVEYED the remains of the meal on the kitchen table, the pan that contained only a third of the lasagna she'd made, the empty salad bowl with a white puddle of dressing, and crumbs from the baguette scattered on the plates. She felt satisfied. For once, she'd been hungry. She'd finished a heaping plate of lettuce with chopped vegetables and two slices of bread. She didn't care for the bloody-looking lasagna, but Justin and the girls loved it. She picked up her glass of Chardonnay. "Alice and Amanda, it's time to do the dishes."

The girls pushed back their chairs. The sound of wood scraping on tile gave Amy chills, but she smiled and said nothing. Amanda stacked her plate on top of her mother's and carried them to the counter. It was so nice to see them do their chores without whining. She knew it wasn't that way with many children. She was fortunate her daughters were so cooperative, although she liked to take a little credit for teaching them good manners.

"Let's finish our wine out back." She opened the French doors and went out onto the patio. It was still hot even though the sun was below the horizon. She sat on the edge of one of the wrought iron chairs surrounding the table.

Justin stepped outside.

She lifted her wine glass. "I'm almost empty, will you get the bottle."

"Do you need another glass?"

"I want to unwind and talk."

"You need another glass of wine in order to talk to me?" said Justin.

"It's a glass of wine. Why are you being so difficult?"

He trudged back into the kitchen and returned with the bottle. He looked like a little boy with his dark blonde hair falling over one brow. His *San Francisco Giants* T-shirt that was so old it sagged down over one hip, making him look thinner than he was. "There's not much left anyway." He splashed the rest of the wine into her glass.

"Aren't you going to sit down?" she said.

"I thought we'd let the girls watch a movie and go to bed early." He winked.

Why did he have to do that? It made her feel like a woman he'd picked up in a bar. Why couldn't he be a little romantic, sip some wine and talk until she felt more relaxed? He should seduce her instead of flashing that cheesy wink, the only effort he seemed to think was required to let her know it was time to hurry upstairs and take off her clothes.

He dragged a chair out from its place at the table.

The iron feet scraped on the stone and her arms erupted in goose bumps in spite of the warm air. "You weren't very nice to me at the game today," she said.

"What do you mean?"

"I was trying to be affectionate and you pushed me away."

He laughed. "Your timing is off. You want to be affectionate in the middle of a soccer game in front of the other guys? But when I want to make love, you want to drink wine and chit chat."

"It's not like that."

He sipped his wine. His glass was almost full, which meant she'd consumed most of the bottle herself. Was he trying to make it look like she drank too much? "It's humiliating when I touch you and you shake me off like I'm a fly crawling up your arm," she said.

He reached across the table and laid his hand on hers.

"I didn't shake you off. Pawing each other at a soccer game is creepy."

"Touching your wife isn't creepy. Running around without a bra is."

"What?"

"Never mind," said Amy.

"Why do you have to climb all over me when there are fifty people standing around watching?" he said.

"I want them to know we have a happy marriage."

Justin laced his fingers behind his head and leaned back. "What gives you the idea they're thinking about your marriage?"

"*Our* marriage. It gives a bad impression when you act like I don't matter."

"Why don't we go upstairs? I won't push you away now."
He winked again.

She raised her glass to her lips and closed her eyes. It was
impossible to get through to him. She wasn't sure if he was
being deliberately obtuse, if he was teasing her, or if he truly
didn't grasp what she was saying. Jane had implied that Amy
was the only one worried about her husband staring at
Charlotte, wanting to touch those perfect breasts, imagining
what she looked like without her tee shirt. "Will you promise
not to do that any more?"

"I'd really prefer if you wouldn't hang on me in front of
other people," he said.

"I want our friends to know how much you love me. That
you would never be interested in another woman." She was
treading on dangerous ground; she didn't want to bring up his
lapse. It had been nothing, really, only that one time. He hadn't
actually cheated on her, he said. It wasn't cheating because there
was no sex, he said. But he'd kissed that woman, and that was
the first step. In Amy's mind, it was still cheating. He wanted
someone else, even if he stopped himself in time. It meant Amy
wasn't enough. He insisted that kissing a woman he met at a
tradeshow didn't mean anything because she was a stranger.
Besides, he'd confessed. That meant he wasn't going behind her
back, which meant he wasn't cheating.

Amy had no idea what the woman had looked like. She
tried to draw a composite in her mind based on the body types
of the women she caught him glancing at when they were out
together. She had a pretty good idea the woman wasn't thin and
delicate, that she probably had much larger breasts. Amy didn't

know the woman's name. She'd never asked. If she asked, he would know how badly he'd hurt her, and she would never allow him to see that pain, still there, glowing inside like a candle that sometimes flickered but never went out. He'd been drunk; it was just a few pecks with a sales manager from a partner company. It didn't mean anything. The woman lived in Chicago and he never saw her again.

For months after he'd told her, she was tormented with the image. She even imagined the physical sensation of his lips pressing hard, sucking a stranger's tongue. In her mind, she saw him kissing a woman who didn't have to work so hard to enjoy his touch, to drink three glasses of wine before she could even think about letting someone invade her body. She thought of how aroused Justin got when they used to kiss for hours. Kissing made people limp with desire, turned their legs to pudding if they did it long enough. Especially when it was fresh and there was a new body to explore. The kiss settled itself in her brain and wouldn't let go. It presented itself in her dreams and woke her up in the pre-dawn hours, when the only light was the tiny flicker from a few stars peeking in the narrow window just below the rafters.

Justin stared at her. She could tell by the tremor in his upper lip that he was straining to avoid an argument, considering how quickly he could guide her up the stairs and into bed.

She stood, picked up her glass and gulped the rest of the wine. It bit at the tender flesh at the back of her throat. She coughed. "If you want to make love at the blink of an eye, you should be more affectionate. Women can't instantly turn it on and off like that."

"Some women can," he said.

"I'm the only woman that matters."

He rose from his chair and walked around to stand behind her. He took her glass out of her hand and set it on the table. He wrapped his arms around her waist. "I can feel your ribs. You should have eaten some lasagna."

"It's fattening. Four hundred and fifty calories in one piece."

"Some meat on your bones would be nice." He curved his hands around her breasts.

She wrenched away from him and tripped backwards over the leg of her chair. "Why don't you love me the way I am? I keep myself thin for you. Were you looking at that woman? Is that why you suddenly don't like my body?" She coughed again.

He pulled her back. "I love your body, I just want you to get enough food. Sometimes you hardly eat."

"You were looking at her."

"Looking at who?"

"The woman who doesn't wear a bra. You were staring. Everyone noticed."

He nuzzled his face into the curve of her neck. "I don't know what you're talking about. Let's not fight. I'll try to be more affectionate. Now let's settle the girls in front of their movie and go upstairs."

"Can't we sit out here awhile longer? We could open another bottle of wine."

"I thought you wanted affection?"

She couldn't answer. There was affection, talking and cuddling, but he didn't want any of that. He said *affection* but he meant *sex*. He wanted the sweating, the thrashing around, and all the mess. It wasn't that she didn't enjoy touching him or having him hold her close, it was just that it never seemed to go the way she'd hoped. She wanted to enjoy making love. If he wouldn't rush her, maybe it would be better. Or maybe not.

One more glass of wine would dull the helplessness of being at the mercy of a man who seemed to forget, at some point in the process, exactly who she was. She wrapped her hands around her arms, hugging herself. Her body felt raw. She let him nudge her toward the back door.

They left the glasses and the empty wine bottle on the kitchen table and settled the twins in front of *The Parent Trap*. She loved introducing the girls to old movies. Normally they weren't that excited to see a movie from another era like this 1961 classic, but they loved the twins in *The Parent Trap*, they liked the idea of trading places with an identical sister. They'd seen the movie four or five times and still hadn't grown tired of it. Amy regretted she wouldn't be watching it with them. It felt cold, leaving them alone with the screen and a bowl of pretzels and fish crackers. Justin said it was good for them – it made them feel independent. At ten years old? She wasn't sure about that.

In their bedroom, Justin flung the mauve satiny bed cover away from the pillows. It slid off the foot of the bed. She grabbed the slippery stuff and folded it into a rectangle across the bottom third of their king-sized bed. He stripped off his shirt, jeans, and boxers and dropped them near his dresser. He climbed into bed.

He was such a gentleman when he dressed in a suit and headed to the office. Why did he have to be transformed into a beast when he was alone with her? She wanted him to stay clean and well behaved, not this gamy, aggressive person emerging from his clothes.

She went into the bathroom. After she undressed and hung her clothes on the hangers dangling from the hook on the back of the bathroom door, she removed her contact lenses, placing them into the container that kept them rinsed. She removed her eye makeup and washed her face with cleanser. She brushed her hair, letting the bristles scrape along her scalp to dig out the dead skin. She scrubbed and flossed her teeth. Next, she spread lotion down her arms, around the knobs of her elbows and wrists. She went to work on her feet and legs, rubbing it up over her hips and around the surface of her butt. She covered her belly and breasts. There was one spot in the center of her back that she couldn't reach, but she tried not to worry about it. She slipped her nightgown over her head. It was the color of coffee, with a creamy lace bodice, but Justin wouldn't appreciate it at all. He'd pull it off, not taking care with the delicate fabric. She looked down at her breasts, flattened by the lace, tiny mounds like apricots. Would he be thinking of Charlotte while they were in bed? He claimed he didn't know who she was, but something prompted him to talk about having more meat on her bones. Such a disgusting word – *meat*. She turned off the light.

While she was in the bathroom, he'd thrown the blanket over the carefully folded comforter. She slid under the sheet and closed her eyes. Justin turned on his side and laid his leg across her hips. Her breath shortened under his weight. Muscle pinned her to the mattress, hands slid over her nightgown, pulled at the fragile straps.

"Be careful, you'll tear it."

"Take it off."

Her throat tightened as she slithered out of her nightgown. Her head felt heavy on the pillow. Her neck and shoulders were stiff. All she wanted was sleep, the few hours she was allotted each night to escape her thoughts. By the time he was finished playing around, the whispering presence of sleep would have evaporated and she'd twist from side to side for the rest of the night while her mind swam in ever narrowing circles.

"Relax, your shoulders feel like a two-by-four," he said.

"That's flattering."

He rubbed the muscle along the top of her spine then ran his hand over the length of her body. His touch was demanding, stroking her skin with too much pressure, then too lightly, like a thread of ants creeping up her ribs. She scratched at her waist and pushed him away.

"What's wrong?" said Justin.

"Your hands make me itchy."

"You had two or three glasses of wine, I though you'd be loose."

"You want a loose wife?"

"Why do you deliberately misinterpret what I say? Do you want a backrub?"

"No thanks." She looped her arms around his neck and willed herself to forget about the sensations on her skin. She loved him, she really did. She wanted to please him, to feel safe in his arms. His desire wasn't anything like that thing with her mother. Not even close. She didn't understand why those thoughts had to squirm around in her mind when Justin wanted to make love. The sound of that man grunting, pounding himself into her mother as if he wanted to split her in two. She heard her father mumbling, *you asked for it*, her mother crying, *I didn't*. It was so confusing. She squeezed her eyes tighter, pushing the words out of her skull, tightening her brain into a knot so nothing could penetrate.

Justin's breath was steamy on her face. The force of his need consumed her. She wanted him to be finished, to be happy with her because she made him feel good. No matter what she did, he seemed content, so loving and affectionate after. If she could get through this part, get to where she could climb out of bed and hurry to the bathroom to wash herself. Then she could return to bed and curl up next to him.

She slid her arms down to his waist. She sighed. He liked that. All she had to do was keep her mind empty, no complaining that he was crushing her or hurting the tendons along the inner sides of her legs. She held him gently. Only a few more minutes.

Chapter Nineteen

CHARLOTTE LAY ON HER yoga mat in the corpse pose. The intent of the pose was to observe her breath moving in and out of her lungs, feel the tension unwind from her limbs. Instead, she was consumed with the memory of Mark lying on top of her, how content she felt as his weight pressed her spine to the floor and his hips grew hot against hers. Tears ran down her cheekbones and trickled into her ears. She didn't wipe them away, wanting to feel the discomfort of her loss, liking the tangible evidence of grief.

The house seemed to echo with the sound of her breath. Meadow was sleeping late, tired after her soccer game followed by a two-hour hike in the foothills the day before.

Finally her tears stopped. For a few more minutes she remained on her back, her arms partially off the mat so her wrist bones touched the hardwood floor. She pictured Mark lying on a cot in a tiny cell. She imagined him feeling the same ghost-like sensation of her body pressing against his. It comforted her to know their minds were connected, both feeling the same aching emptiness. The loss of her photographs made her feel even more alone. It wasn't simply the physical destruction of her work that hurt – it was an assault on her vision, on something so personal she felt ripped open. She could print the images again, purchase new frames, but she couldn't erase the hostility toward something she cared about, the desire of others to obliterate her work, hoping to ensure that no one saw those photographs, as if the images had existed only in her own mind.

She turned on her side, sat up, then knelt on the floor and rolled her mat into a tube. She secured it with a ribbon and stood it in the corner behind the portable CD player. She went into the kitchen and filled the teakettle. While the water hissed and sighed like a living creature, she sat at the round oak table and stared out the window. The magnolia tree was heavy with thick leaves that blocked the sun from reaching the window. The street was empty of traffic and pedestrians. The absence of harsh sounds was pleasant, but isolating.

The kettle whistled. She got up and poured the water into a cup, hanging onto the string of the tea bag so it wasn't sucked beneath the steaming surface.

"Can I have cocoa?"

Charlotte jerked her hand back at the unexpected sound of Meadow's voice. Hot waster splashed onto the counter.

"Sorry I scared you," said Meadow.

"You didn't."

"You jumped like someone kicked down our door and barged in with an Uzi."

"How in the world do you know what an Uzi is?"

"I read a lot." Meadow laughed. "So can I have some cocoa?"

"Sure." Charlotte restarted the gas and put the kettle on the burner for a moment to bring it back to boiling.

"How come you jumped?"

"I was thinking about my photographs getting destroyed."

"Can't you print more and hang them up again?"

"I can, but that's not really the point. My work was destroyed and it feels like I was attacked."

"You always say not to exaggerate."

Charlotte pulled another mug out of the cabinet, emptied powdered cocoa into it and filled it with boiling water. She rattled the spoon hard against the sides of the mug so the powder would fully dissolve. "I'm not exaggerating. When someone ruins something you care about, it feels like you've been attacked. It hurts inside your stomach. And knowing a mother of your classmates did this is kind of scary."

"But it could have been anyone," said Meadow.

"It could have. But it wasn't."

"Then why aren't the police arresting her?" said Meadow.

Her shoulders sagged, pulling at the muscles of her neck so it ached. She couldn't even answer the question herself. The unanswerable questions were the most difficult part of raising a child. It was one thing to provide a steady stream of answers to questions that were clear and simple – *Why do we have to wash fruit before we eat it?* But when it came to matters such as injustice or other shadowy areas of life, Charlotte was at a loss for words. She didn't want to brush off Meadow's questions, but it was hard to explain why some things happened – why baby birds fell out of nests and why some children were cruel and why some people didn't have homes and had to sleep on the sidewalk.

Mark was good at explanations and answers. He seemed to have an endless supply of information on how the world worked. He was so patient; he would answer Meadow's questions repeatedly. It was probably because he didn't try so hard to offer precise responses. Charlotte couldn't bear the confused look in Meadow's eyes, and often talked too much, hoping she could make that vulnerable look go away. She couldn't explain why it was legal to stock an entire supermarket aisle with wine and liquor so anyone could consume as much as she pleased. People could make themselves sick and crash cars and kill others, but Meadow's daddy was arrested for selling pot. Meadow's teachers told her alcohol was a drug. Why didn't they arrest people for selling it? She asked over and over, and Charlotte's weak explanations, words she didn't believe herself, never provided satisfaction. So Meadow asked again. And again.

"Why, Mom? If you know it was her, why wasn't she arrested?"

"It seems that what's obvious isn't good enough. They want proof. Fingerprints, or a witness."

"Oh. That makes sense."

"Not really. If it involved broken windows or graffiti, then it would make sense. But Amanda's mother freaked out about having her picture taken. One of the other moms told me Amy tried to make the principal take them down. It's obvious she decided to get rid of them herself."

"But there's a chance it could be someone else. So they want fingerprints," said Meadow.

"There's no chance it could be someone else."

"But without the fingerprints, there's no proof. Right?"

"Never mind. I don't want to talk about it any more." Charlotte refused to believe she was the one who was blind. It was impossible to accept that the vandalism was a random act. Amy might as well have signed her name in spray paint.

Showing the pictures at the school had been a bad idea. She'd had doubts about it but rushed into it anyway, and look where it had gotten her – nearly three hundred dollars, gone. If the principal would at least offer to reimburse her, she might feel slightly better.

"Do you want anything to eat?" said Charlotte.

"I'm not hungry. Can we sit on the couch with our drinks?"

"Sure." The tea would calm her. She needed to shift her attention to Meadow, let herself heal for a few days. Then, she'd have to swallow the loss of money and start again. This time she would listen to her instinct and find a legitimate place to show her work, not some silly display case in the hallway of an elementary school. Maybe Mark's brother would have some suggestions. He owned this house; he must know people in Silicon Valley. Since he'd been so eager to offer the cottage, giving them a safe place to live while they waited for Mark, surely he'd be willing to introduce her to people. There must be some place that would be interested in her work. Amy could rip apart the photographs, but she couldn't take away her talent or destroy her ideas.

Chapter Twenty

GREG PULLED INTO the parking lot adjacent to the Rennert Park soccer field and turned off the ignition. Before Rachel could unlatch her seatbelt, Sara flung open the back door and jumped out of the SUV. She ran to join her teammates in pre-game drills. Her pale brown and blonde streaked ponytail swung across her shoulders and her movements were so graceful it appeared that she might lift off in flight. It was such a relief not to worry about Sara, to know she'd enjoy the game. Even when her team lost, when she didn't score for an entire game, she bounced off the field smiling. The pure act of running, kicking the ball, breathing the same air as her friends, was enough for Sara.

Rachel and Greg opened their doors at the same time.

"I know a secret," said Trent.

"What's that?" said Greg. He swung one leg out and turned to face Trent.

"The kids said someone from our school smashed up the display cases."

"What kids said that?" said Rachel. "One of your friends?"

"I heard them talking."

"Were you playing with Brian and the other boys?" She tried to steady her breathing. She turned and smiled at Trent. She knew she sounded too eager to find out whether he was interacting with other children.

"Since there wasn't any tagging on the walls, the police don't think it was a gang. And it was targeted."

"Really?" said Rachel.

"What's targeted?" said Trent.

"When you choose something specific to focus your attention on," said Greg.

"The police came and talked to the principal," said Trent.

"I thought that was all done with," said Rachel.

Trent grinned. "Someone in our school might be a criminal."

Rachel slid out of the SUV. She ducked her head back inside, "Let's go." She stood and closed the passenger door.

Greg climbed out. "Don't brush him off," he said.

"He should be interested in something besides vandalism. And snails," she said. "The damage was minor. It will cost less than a few hundred dollars to repair the glass and reimburse the photographer."

Greg looked at her. He didn't move to close the door. "Why are you acting like you don't want to talk about this?"

"I don't," she said.

"Usually you're all over every detail of what happens at the school."

"They won't be able to figure out who did it."

"How do you know?"

"The glass was crumbled. How are they going to get fingerprints?" said Rachel.

"There are other ways to solve crimes than with fingerprints."

"Such as?"

"If they keep asking, a witness might come forward."

"I doubt it," she said.

"You seem awfully sure."

She opened the back door. "Come on Trent, the game's starting."

Trent unbuckled his seat belt, wriggled to the edge of the seat, and hopped to the ground. "Do you think they'll catch him?"

She sighed, relieved to hear him refer to the male gender. "Probably not."

"Or her. It could have been a girl," he said.

Greg walked around the car. "It's scary to think kids that young might be involved."

"Maybe it wasn't a kid," said Rachel.

He pressed the button to set the alarm. "So you do talk about it. What do the other moms think?" He put his arm around her shoulder and buried his face in her hair.

She grabbed her hair and coiled it over her opposite shoulder.

They walked to the picnic table at the edge of the field. Trent darted to the end of the table and squatted. He plucked a snail out of a tuft of grass and set it on the bench. Rachel turned away. She supposed it would be more comforting if she thought of him having a future as a biologist. But when she saw his fingers drifting down the slimy neck that stretched out as the creature tried to find its way back to the moist ground, all she felt was horror. "Put the snail back in the grass. He needs to be near something he can eat."

"How do you know it's a boy?"

"Ok, put it back on the ground."

"I like to watch them climb down the bench and find their own way back." He plucked up another snail from under the table.

How did he find them? They seemed to come out of the earth when he was around. She never noticed that many snails when she was working in the yard, or sitting on the sidelines during practice.

Amy turned and waved. She pointed to an empty chair next to her. Despite the cloudy sky, she wore sunglasses and her red hair was combed into a ponytail that clung to the nape of her neck. She stood and started to walk toward them.

Rachel didn't want Amy anywhere near Greg. Not right now when the vandalism was fresh in his thoughts. If he brought it up, she didn't trust Amy to keep her comments noncommittal. Amy would be too eager to spew out opinions about Charlotte's invasion of their lives. Greg would figure it out in an instant. Already she felt he was probing at it, seeming to sense that she knew more than she was saying. It was difficult, sometimes, to keep secrets in a fourteen-year marriage, although it didn't seem to be difficult in a long-lived friendship. She nodded at the men standing behind the Emerald Tigers' goal line. "There are the guys, I'll see you later."

Greg squeezed her neck. "Are you trying to get rid of me?"

She ducked out from under his arm. He trailed his fingers down the side of her neck. "Go hang out with the guys," she said.

From the corner of her eye she saw Amy weaving around the scattered chairs, walking on her toes to keep the heels of her sandals from sinking into the ground.

"If you won't tell me the gossip, I'll ask Amy. She always has something to say."

Rachel's heart pounded. Why was he acting so flirty? Usually they arrived at the game and he plodded off across the field after a quick peck on the cheek and a pat on her butt. In some way she couldn't figure out, the vandalism was piquing his interest.

She glanced at Trent. There were now five snails creeping along the length of the bench. Great. She could guess what Amy would have to say about that. She'd declare the benches unfit for sitting and hint that Trent was disturbed. Rachel walked over to the picnic table. "That's quite a collection, but I really think they would be happier on the ground."

Amy was now a few feet from Greg. "Ew. Get them off the bench," she said.

Greg stepped closer to the table. He squatted next to Trent and peered at the snails. "Too bad you don't have your sketch book, buddy."

Rachel sat at the end of the table, well away from the snail parade. She swallowed hard. Aversion to the snails' gooey bodies was probably learned behavior, but she hated sitting on the bench with them. She wasn't sure how fast they could move.

Amy rubbed her arms and shivered with an exaggerated twitching of her shoulders. "Come sit by me, it's more comfortable." She turned away and tiptoed back to her chair.

Rachel smiled, but her throat still felt tight. Greg's interest in the vandalism would re-emerge sooner or later and she wouldn't be any more prepared to deflect his curiosity.

Chapter Twenty-one

CHARLOTTE HADN'T WANTED to go to the fall carnival, but she wasn't about to send Meadow into that crowd all by herself. As they entered the multi-purpose room, the sound of hundreds of children talking and shouting assaulted her ears. The walls were covered with painted pictures of clowns, stars, and confetti. Streamers dangled from the ceiling and balloons had been taped to string that stretched diagonally across the room. Meadow pointed out the clown she and Amanda had painted. With a rainbow of polka dots on its clothing and blue spiked hair, it was a mix of classic clown and punk. Tables lined the perimeter of the room. Each table hosted a game – darts for popping balloons, a lollipop pull, a ring toss, and a cakewalk. One table was filled with tiny bowls, each containing a single goldfish that shimmered under the fluorescent lights. Children tossed ping-pong balls, trying to hit the open mouth of a bowl to win a fish.

Charlotte purchased a string of tickets and handed them to Meadow. "What should we do first?"

"I'm going to look for Amanda. I thought you were helping with the games."

She was pleased with Meadow's show of independence. She'd worried that Mark's arrest, his incarceration, and the move to a new town would leave Meadow feeling insecure. Apparently not. After only a few weeks, Meadow acted as if the school belonged to her. Was it possible soccer had boosted her daughter's self-confidence? "I'm supposed to help, but Jane wasn't sure where they'd need me."

A shadow flickered across Meadow's eyes.

"Don't worry, I'll figure it out. Go win a fish."

Meadow scurried across the room to the goldfish table.

Jane and three other women were at the dart game, pinning up small balloons. "We don't need any extra hands after all," said Jane. "Why don't you take some photographs? We could use some new ones on the Spruce website." Jane lowered her voice, "I'm so sorry about what happened to your photo essay. Hopefully the school reimbursed you."

Charlotte smiled. "Thanks." If the principal planned to pay for the cost of frames and printing, that was news to her. She turned and looked across the crowd. At the front of the room, Amy stood behind a table serving punch. Charlotte was thirsty but both the server and the pink stuff in the bowl looked unappealing. She slipped off the straps of her backpack and pulled a mini bottle of water from the side pocket. A long swallow soothed her throat, even though the water was room temperature. She moved toward the back corner, unzipped the bag and lifted out her camera. Balancing the bag on her knee, she attached the wide-angle lens. She squeezed herself further into the corner between two tables that hosted gift baskets and spa certificates for the silent auction. She held the bottle in her left hand, sipping more water, and lifted the camera with her right hand. She kept it unfocused so she could capture the crowd as a chaotic blur. A man jostled her elbow and she snapped too soon. The image would turn out crooked, but that might not be so bad.

The tall, blonde man who had bumped her arm grinned at her. "Sorry about that."

"No problem," she said.

"Really? I thought for sure you'd bite my head off for messing up your shot. Forever missing that Kodak moment."

"Far from it. There's always another one waiting." She didn't really want to talk to this guy. She wanted to take photographs. She slipped out the lens cap and snapped it in place.

"That's a serious camera for a kids' carnival."

"I'm a professional photographer," she said.

"So can I bid on a studio sitting?" He nodded his head at the silent auction.

"My photographs are considered slightly off-beat by most people."

"No smudged blue background and side lighting?"

"I don't think so. My style is more blurred crowd shots."

He laughed. "So I'm helping your career."

"It looks that way." Was he actually taking her seriously, or teasing? His tone sounded almost flirty, but he wore a wedding band, so maybe just friendly.

"What subjects are you interested in, besides crooked crowd shots?"

"I want to capture scenes no one else wants to look at or every day things – like trash collecting in the gutter. Images that make you stop and think about life. They're basically photo essays, in black and white."

She felt him staring at her. He lowered his voice, as if he was talking to himself. "You aren't the one who took the black and whites that caused the big brouhaha, are you?"

"Yes. Although not the reaction I'd hoped for."

"My wife sure was pissed. You managed to get the worst pictures possible. At least to hear her tell it."

A chill rippled across Charlotte's scalp and down her neck. The hair on her arms stood up. Of all the parents in the room, this was the man who bumped into her? She could hope he was Rachel's husband, but somehow, she knew he belonged to Amy. She looked at the toes of her boots. The roar of voices, adults talking, and children shouting across the room, swelled as if there had been a sudden influx of a hundred people. It sounded as if he didn't know anything about the vandalism.

"I guess you're angry about the complaints? One of those *two sides to every story* situations?"

"My photographs were ripped to shreds."

"What?"

"Someone destroyed the cases where they were displayed. They smashed the frames and glass and scraped a knife or something across the photographs."

"Shit."

He looked across the room, staring at a spot she couldn't identify. "It's such a quiet neighborhood. Nothing like that has ever happened here," he said.

She closed her eyes. Now he'd blame it on a gang.

"We're so far from the major arteries. You don't even know the school is here unless you're looking for it." He shoved his hands in the pockets of his jeans and continued to stare blankly at the crowd.

She allowed herself a thread of hope that he would wonder what part his wife had played. "It makes me so angry," she said. "I can't stop wondering who would do something like that."

"Are the police looking into it?"

"Yes. But without some kind of evidence, they won't do anything. I suppose they're looking for a witness." She wanted to come right out and ask him what he thought, but it would be more satisfying if he came to the right conclusion on his own.

"I guess there's not a lot you can do then," he said.

"I'm going to make new prints."

"That's good."

"I need to find a place to show them. Obviously the school was a bad choice." She laughed, but it sounded harsh.

"A friend of mine is in commercial real estate. He might be able to get you some contacts that would consider displaying your work in corporate lobbies."

"Really?" Her throat seemed to swell with pride or desire, or some other feeling she couldn't define. The room suddenly looked different, softer, and the noise wasn't as grating. Even the punch looked slightly more refreshing. She lifted the water bottle to her lips and took a long swallow.

He held out a business card. "Let's get together so you can show me your work."

She slid the card into her pocket. "Thanks. You don't even know me."

He extended his hand, "Justin Lewis."

She took his hand, "Charlotte Whittington." She smiled.

"I used to be a photographer," he said. "Not a professional or anything, but I liked experimenting, trying to create art with a camera. Portraits, mostly. Now I pretty much stick to documenting family history. Although I guess those are still portraits, there's just not much time to think about lighting and composition and things like that."

***

AMY AND RACHEL stood in the school kitchen, pouring grapefruit juice into punch bowls. Rachel released a tray of ice cubes into the first bowl and Amy added a bottle of clear soda. Even though it was pink, the punch reminded Amy of juice that had oozed from a rotten peach. Her arm ached from holding the ladle at the awkward angle required to spoon the liquid into small cups. How had she gotten sucked into this? There was sticky residue all over her hands. "Do I get a break?"

"No, we don't get a break," said Rachel.

"I don't know why we didn't just serve root beer and coke," said Amy.

"This costs less, so we can raise more money."

It was so much unnecessary energy. If they all wrote checks to the school library, they could forget the carnival. What was accomplished by all this extra work? A few dollars made selling tickets? Most of the profit came from the silent auction.

"This is full." Amy lifted the bowl. "Can you open the door for me?"

She took small steps. The punch lunged close to the edge of the bowl. She paused to let it settle. The last thing she needed was gunk slopped down the front of her new tan slacks and sleeveless top. Until she'd started mixing punch, she'd felt elegant and clean. She set the bowl on the table with a thud, but nothing sloshed out. Her fingers were stiff from clutching the edges of the bowl and her arms were shaky. Rachel moved to the table next to her where a line of children waited to hand over tickets in exchange for a brownie or an oatmeal cookie.

Amy squinted at the mass of people. Where was Justin? It was difficult to see any individual person as children darted from one side of the room to the other and adults huddled around the booths, some working and some chatting. She walked along the length of the serving table, trying to see past the shifting crowd. Finally, she saw him – at the opposite end of the room. Standing next to him, much closer than necessary, was Charlotte Whittington. Amy bit her lip and tried to think what to do. Charlotte stared into Justin's eyes like she wanted to slide into a pool of warm water. She was talking, fiddling with her camera. What could she possibly have to say to him? They'd never met before. Or had they? Charlotte leaned closer. Her shoulder bumped against Justin's. She shifted the camera to her left side and cocked her hip to support it. The thin fabric of her shirt did nothing to control her breasts. Justin looked down, gazing with adoration at the gentle movement of her flesh.

Amy stepped out from behind the table.

"Where are you going?" said Rachel.

"I have to take care of something."

"But there's no one to serve."

"You can do it," said Amy.

"I can't. I have to manage the cookies and brownies."

"If anyone wants punch, they can serve themselves." Amy pushed through the crowd. She couldn't believe Charlotte was flirting with him, right in front of hundreds of people, all of them watching him stare at her breasts with raw desire. Each time Charlotte took a breath, her breasts came close enough to brush against his arm.

Amy knew she'd let him down the other night, like she did nearly every time they made love. She wanted to please him. She tried so hard, if he would just be more patient. She loved him so much it made her chest ache. She wouldn't allow Charlotte to take him right out from under her nose. That terrifyingly beautiful face, with no need for makeup to make her skin smooth. Her legs, carved like those of a Grecian statue, and her loose breasts inviting every man in sight to reach out and stroke them, the irresistible male urge to touch round pieces of women's flesh.

She reached his side. "Justin!" She clutched his bicep as if he'd stepped too close to the edge of a cliff.

"What's wrong?" said Justin.

"I need your help."

"With what?"

She didn't know. She couldn't say. Not with Charlotte standing there, her hip jutting out, a smirk on her face as if she'd won some kind of game.

"I need your help with the punch. The bowl is too heavy for me."

"I'm in the middle of a conversation."

"What are you talking about?"

Charlotte smiled. "Photography."

Amy gripped Justin's arm more tightly and pulled him closer. "You probably don't have much in common. Justin isn't a professional. Like you are."

Charlotte was silent for several seconds. Her gaze was so steady, Amy had to look away.

"He was giving me ideas for where I might display my photographs. Since it didn't work out at the school."

Amy tried to decipher Charlotte's tone. Had she complained to Justin about the vandalism? Was this a trap? Her entire body felt like it was covered with melted sugar, as if it had seeped into her pores and was coming back to the surface in sheets of perspiration. She let go of Justin's arm and scrubbed her hands on her slacks, leaving damp smears on the silky fabric. Even her beautiful diamond appeared to have a film of punch residue. She rubbed the stone with her thumb.

Charlotte dug around in the bag and pulled out an index card. She extended her hand and found Justin's as if he'd been waiting all evening to touch her slim fingers. She handed the card to him. "Here's my cell number."

Justin stuffed the index card in his pocket.

"Just because your husband or whatever isn't around, doesn't mean you can start sniffing around my husband."

"Amy!" Justin pried her fingers off his arm. "What's wrong with you?"

Charlotte zipped her backpack with a ripping sound like gnashing teeth. "Nice talking to you." She turned away.

"Not so fast," said Amy. "I have something to say to you." She grabbed Charlotte's skirt. There was a tearing sound, but nothing came loose.

"You ripped my skirt."

"Find some other guy to discuss photography with," said Amy.

"He's the one who started the conversation, I think you're angry at the wrong person." Charlotte walked away.

Amy turned back to Justin. He put his arm around her shoulders, squashing her body close to his. "You're hurting me," she said. She tried to wriggle away, but he squeezed harder. He pulled her, stumbling after him, to the doors at the back of the room. The children waiting for the cakewalk to start stared eagerly. They looked more entertained by the tussle than the chance to win a cake. They'd frozen in their spots, watching the two mothers fight. Drama like this never happened at school events. The best they could hope for was a child eating too many sweets and throwing up on the floor. Justin tugged her into the corridor that ran along the back of the building and pressed her against the wall. He put his hands on her shoulders. "What's your problem? That was the most humiliating thing I've ever experienced."

"Then you're lucky." He knew nothing about humiliation. Words hissed through her head, scratched at the edges of her mind. *She asked for it. She should have fought harder.* She couldn't think, couldn't understand why her father's words were echoing their way through her memory right now. Why did they rush to the surface when she least expected?

"Why did you talk to her like that?" said Justin.

"She was falling all over you."

"We were talking about her photography. Which I understand was destroyed."

She couldn't let him start asking about the pictures. She coughed, gagging slightly. "Don't tell me she doesn't know what she's doing. She realizes you're staring at her breasts the whole time, wondering what they feel like, comparing them to mine." She whimpered softly, turning her head to the side and pressing her cheek against the wall.

"You're imagining things," he said.

"And you can't see what's right in front of your face."

He folded his arms.

She held her breath. In a moment, he would say how he loved her, that he adored her, that he only wanted her. That's what he used to say. For several minutes he said nothing. His eyes were dull and his skin tinged with gray around his jaw.

"You need to apologize to her," he said.

"What are you, my father?"

"Maybe that's the problem. You didn't have a father around to teach you how to look at the world rationally."

She gasped. Tears pooled in her eyes until his features appeared to dissolve.

"Stop feeling sorry for yourself," he said. "Stop letting your imagination run out of control." He turned and walked down the hall and disappeared through the double doors. The sound of children shrieking drifted into the hallway, piercing her eardrums like knives. He acted as if there was something wrong with her. She ran her pinky fingers gently along the skin under her eyes to wipe off the tears without smearing her mascara. He wasn't going to make her feel like she was the one behaving badly when Charlotte was the one dressed like a slut.

***

RACHEL STOOD BEHIND the table, watching over the trays of brownies. Was Amy ever coming back to help serve? Luckily, the demand for punch was minimal.

Kit stood near the end of the table. She picked up a brownie, broke it in two and put half back on the tray. She nibbled at the piece in her hand.

"I hope you're planning to pay for the whole thing," said Rachel.

Kit reached into her tiny leather purse. She pulled out a ten and dropped it on the table. "There. Does that cover it?"

"It's only a dollar. But this is a fundraiser, we need to make as much as we can," said Rachel.

"I don't even know why I'm here. I should be contributing to Renee and Carter's new school."

"Why are you so anxious to get away from us?" said Rachel.

Kit bit off a speck of brownie. "We're not moving to get away from anyone. We want to give Carter and Renee more opportunities."

"It doesn't feel like that. Since the ... since Amy mentioned that we ..."

"Turned into vandals?" said Kit.

"It feels like you're judging us. And that you can't wait to leave."

"We made the decision to move before your ethical lapse."

"Is that what you think it was?"

Kit took another tiny bite of the brownie. "I don't know what it was."

"I wish I could go back and un-do it," said Rachel.

"You can't.

"I know that. I'm saying it was a mistake. I don't know what came over me."

"Amy came over you. She's obsessive," said Kit.

"She felt invaded. We both did."

"It's nice of you to defend her, but I know how wound up she gets and I know how you'll go along with almost anything."

Rachel stepped over to the food service window that opened into the kitchen and picked up another tray of brownies. She lifted off the foil as if she was unwrapping a blanket from a baby's body. She put the tray on the table and let the aroma fill her nostrils. The urge to eat one was overwhelming, but once she took a bite she wouldn't be able to stop. Saliva formed on her tongue as she thought of the soft chewy stuff filling her mouth. "I don't go along with everything," she said.

"It's not necessarily a bad a thing, you're a very agreeable person," said Kit.

"I really feel badly about it."

"You should apologize to Charlotte, not to me. At least offer to reimburse her."

"No one knows I did it."

Kit laughed. "They will soon enough."

"Are you going to tell?"

"No, but it's not hard to figure out. Charlotte knows you did it. I bet Ms. Shafton does too." Kit patted Rachel's wrist. "Don't worry. Everyone knows Amy is the crazy one."

"She's not crazy," said Rachel. Would Kit be more compassionate if she knew what had happened to Amy's mother? How did a person survive something like that? And how had she managed to hold it inside all these years? Didn't it help explain her behavior? Rachel could see how living with that memory, hearing people whisper about your family, hearing your father speak such vicious lies, blaming your mother, would make you anxious, self-conscious. Even obsessive.

"Something's not right about her," said Kit. "She's fixated on Charlotte, and she's more upset that the woman on Benton was raped than that she was murdered."

Rachel put her hands in her pockets. She should defend Amy, but she couldn't. If it had taken Amy all these years to speak about her mother's rape to her best friend, she obviously didn't want anyone to know. It didn't matter anyway because Kit would be gone soon. "I just can't believe you're moving. I always thought we'd watch our children grow up together," she said.

"Nothing's forever."

"Aren't you worried that Renee will miss her friends?"

"She'll make new friends."

Kit made it sound so easy. As if making friends was as simple as pinching your fingers around the edges of the one you wanted and lifting her off a tray. She watched Kit nibble at her brownie. Her tiny bites of chocolate went nowhere. Her hips were a smooth curve of bone and muscle. Her jeans hugged her flat belly without a hint of loose skin to indicate she'd given birth – twice. Why did some women pop out babies without any impact to their hips or thighs? But who was she kidding? Her body was too round before she'd ever thought of having children. From the moment she'd hit puberty, everything had gone haywire and she'd never gotten it back under control. Too much flesh everywhere, pressing against the seams of her jeans, poking over the waistbands of her skirts, and nearly spilling out of her bra. She could avoid brownies the rest of her life and never look like Kit. She picked up a brownie, bit off half and closed her eyes as the chocolate melted into her.

"I thought we weren't supposed to eat the profits," said Kit.

Rachel ate the other half of the brownie. She glanced around the room. Children crowded every game booth. That was a good sign. Trent was second in line at the ping pong toss. Next to him was a boy she'd never seen before. The boy pointed at one of the goldfish bowls. Trent nodded and said something. Perhaps he was capable of making friends after all. As Greg said, he needed to find his own way. Suddenly, the sting of Kit's eagerness to move away dissolved. For the first time in weeks Rachel felt content.

"What do you think Amy was all fired up about a few minutes ago?" said Kit. "She looked like a vulture, diving into the crowd."

"I don't know," said Rachel.

"Probably something to do with her obsession over Charlotte," said Kit.

"She's not obsessed."

"What would you call it? I've never seen a woman so overly concerned with another woman's body."

It only took three bites for Rachel to chew and swallow another brownie. If she wasn't careful, she'd wind up eating everything on the tray. She should have asked to be assigned to a non-food booth. Her mind hovered over the brownies, trying not to think about what Kit was saying. There was a small dot of shame humming in the center of her chest, shouting that there was also something wrong with her, constantly evaluating the bodies of other women. Even though she was only about fifteen pounds over what was considered her ideal weight, she felt enormous next to her friends. But that wasn't the same as Amy's fixation. It could be that Justin gave Amy good cause to worry, to obsess. Who knew what went on in another woman's marriage, behind the bedroom door? "Someone with breasts that large should wear a bra," she said.

"Why? And what business is it of Amy's. Or yours?"

"It seems inappropriate. For a mother," said Rachel.

"So once you're a mother, you don't get to have a sexual side any more?"

"It shouldn't be so public. And she's single."

"This is the twenty-first century," said Kit. "Women aren't required to wrap their bodies in boning and layers of petticoats, even if they're single moms."

"I'm not saying a mother can't be sexy. But there are rules," said Rachel.

"It's not like there's a dress code," said Kit.

"You don't think there are any unspoken standards?"

"Like what?" said Kit.

"You don't think it looks kind of like she wants to attract attention?"

"It's not any different than Amy in her stilettos."

"That's so unfair," said Rachel.

"Isn't it just as unfair to ostracize a woman because she doesn't wear a bra?"

"It's not just the bra," said Rachel.

"That's what started it."

Rachel ate another brownie. She had to stop, but part of her didn't even want to. She couldn't see the point. Kit was moving on, and now she was suddenly critical of her old friends. She acted as if her own opinions were more enlightened. She was turning into a snob. Or maybe she had always been a snob and Rachel was just noticing for the first time. She popped another smallish brownie from the corner of the pan into her mouth.

"Are you going to eat the whole tray?"

Rachel made a face, but she couldn't speak with her mouth full. Let Kit move away. Part of having friends was accepting them with their flaws, and if Kit couldn't do that, good riddance. Let her find perfect people in her new community.

Rachel swallowed the brownie, tasting the salt of tears mixed with chocolate.

Chapter Twenty-two

AMY PUT TUNA SANDWICHES on two small plates and carried them into the dining room. She set them on the placemats in front of Alice and Amanda and seated herself in Justin's chair at the head of the table.

"Aren't you eating dinner, Mom?" said Amanda.

The fishy odor and the oily sheen of the mayonnaise made Amy's stomach shudder until she thought she might heave up the apple and yogurt she'd eaten for lunch. "I'm not hungry right now."

The temperature had hit over ninety degrees this afternoon. Relief wasn't expected until Wednesday. She took a sip from her glass of Chardonnay. The crisp taste cooled her lips and eased the bloated feeling in her tongue. Even though it was dusk, she'd kept the light off, hoping the room would stay cooler. It seemed as if the air seeped relentlessly through invisible crevices in the walls of the house. If she turned on the ceiling fan, it would simply push hot air down into their faces. She already felt as if she was suffocating. Her skin and hair, bones and muscles, all felt as soft as hot wax. She looked at her girls – two nearly identical blonde heads on opposite sides of the long table. The darker streaks in their hair were more visible in the shadowed room. Her daughters were the reason for her existence. Her breath caught in her throat when she thought of anything happening to them. She couldn't bear it when they cried, when they were frightened. They looked so fragile – their unblemished skin, the soft downy hair near their ears, their smooth lips. The older they got, the more frightening the world became. There were so many things that could go wrong, so many hurtful and violent acts that could enter their lives and she was helpless to stop it. She took another sip of wine and listened to their voices, chattering with each other as if their thoughts came from a single mind.

By the time the girls had finished their sandwiches, Amy was thinking about uncorking a second bottle of wine. She scooped the remaining tuna fish from the mixing bowl into the trash, tied the red straps of the plastic sack into a bow and hurried out to the garbage can. She didn't need rotting tuna stinking up the house. She rinsed the dishes and put them in the dishwasher.

When she heard Justin's *BMW* rumble into the garage, she went into the living room and sat near the middle of the long sofa. She placed her glass on the stone coaster. She recoiled from touching it. The perspiration on her hands mingled with the sweat on the outside of the glass, creating a slimy texture that made her think of a salamander's body. Justin's key scraped at the inside of the lock and the door from the garage to the pantry opened. She heard him walk into the dining room, set his briefcase on the table and step back into the kitchen. The refrigerator door opened. Several seconds passed before she heard it close.

"Amy?"

"I'm in the living room."

"Is there anything to eat? The fridge looks barren." He walked into the room and stood behind the sofa. "Did you eat with the girls?"

She shook her head.

"What did they have for dinner?"

"Tuna sandwiches."

"Where are the leftovers?" he said.

"I threw them out so the house wouldn't smell fishy."

She heard the scrape of fabric as he slid his tie out from under his shirt collar. He tossed it on the leather wing chair. It slid to the floor but he didn't pick it up. He perched on the arm of the chair. "I'm hungry."

She sipped her wine and set the glass back on the coaster. "Charlotte was falling all over you at the carnival the other night."

"I thought we finished that fight."

"We're not fighting." She took another sip of wine.

"It's not a good idea to drink too much when it's this hot," said Justin.

"Do you know how it makes me feel to see you flirting with her?"

"I wasn't flirting."

"She was."

"No she wasn't."

"She's not married, did you know that?"

He stood and walked into the dining room.

"Where are you going?"

"I'm getting some water. I guess there's no dinner for me, unless I want a fermented banana."

"There's an apple and some string cheese."

When he returned he was holding a handful of fish crackers and a bottle of water.

"Those are for the girls' snacks."

He sat on the edge of the chair and gulped down half the bottle of water. He popped the crackers into his mouth. "They get to eat but I don't? Am I being punished?"

Her glass clinked on the coaster as she set it down with too much force. Wine splashed onto the coffee table. "Charlotte's boyfriend is in prison. Amanda told me. Who knows what other dangerous people she hangs out with."

"You're over-reacting."

"Alice and Amanda are being exposed to a girl whose father is a criminal. Doesn't that scare you?"

"You can't keep them away from every kid who doesn't have a background you've personally checked and approved. Are you planning to inspect all their friends for the next eight or nine years?"

"They're only ten. I think we should still influence their choice of friends. That's the point of soccer."

"I thought the point of soccer was to play soccer." He stood and inched toward the dining room.

Why did he have to argue with everything? It was perfectly clear that Charlotte was a bad influence. And she was obviously flirting with him. If he would only recognize the problem, she could relax. "Can't you sit down so we can finish talking?" she said.

"You're conjuring up things to worry about."

"I'll try to explain it better if you'll sit down."

He walked back and settled on the arm of the chair, with one leg stretched out to the side to steady himself.

"Can't you sit like you're planning to stay?"

"It's hot in here."

She sipped her wine then held up her glass. "Will you give me a re-fill?"

"Do you …"

"Don't lecture me," she said. "I'm tense and I need to unwind a little."

He took her glass and left the room. When he returned, he was carrying two half-filled glasses of wine. He sat next to her. He put his arm around her shoulders and pulled her toward him. "I'm sorry. I didn't mean to give the impression I was flirting. Can we forget it now?"

"Why am I the only one who sees that she has her eye on you?"

He put his wine glass on the table. She picked it up and set it on a coaster.

"You're always worrying. Crime, earthquakes, terrorist attacks. And now Charlotte. It's exhausting," said Justin.

She pushed away from him and scooted to the end of the sofa. How could he not see what Charlotte was up to?

He stood and walked to the picture window. He yanked the cord to open the drapes. He pressed the release for the lock and slid open the window.

"What are you doing?"

"Getting some air in here. I can hardly breathe."

"I don't like having the drapes open. Anyone walking by can look inside."

"We're sitting right here, it's fine."

Amy picked up her wine glass.

Justin turned to face her. "Do you know anything about Charlotte's photographs getting trashed?"

She took a long swallow of wine. She wiped her finger down the side of the glass to remove the excess water. "Not really."

"It's strange, don't you think? We've never had vandalism at Spruce."

She took another small sip of wine. "We never had a rape either. Or a murder."

"Do you know what happened to her pictures?"

"I said, no."

"You said, *not really.*"

She swallowed the last of her wine.

"It doesn't sound like simple property damage," he said. "Since the photographs were shredded."

She wished he would stop going on about it. He wouldn't see it her way; he wouldn't understand why they had to be gotten rid of. "It's a horrible world," she said. "Rape. Murder. Gangs. People freaked out on drugs. Dangerous men let out of prison every day."

"None of that has anything to do with Charlotte."

"It has to do with why I don't want our living room window hanging open."

"It's too damn hot. I'm not closing the window."

"Will you stay away from her? For me?" said Amy.

"We should help her find a place to display her work."

Amy stood. She spun her rings around her finger. She stared at him. His eyes were red around the lower lids. "Why would you do that to me?" she said.

"I'm not doing anything to you. Her work was destroyed. It would be nice to help her get back on her feet." He picked up both glasses and walked out of the room.

She wanted to grab her glass out of his hand. One more glass of wine would steady her pulse so she could breathe, but if she asked, he would tell her she'd had enough. She flopped back onto the sofa and twisted her hands together. Her diamond dug into the palm of her right hand. At least he'd stopped asking what happened to the pictures. If he wasn't going to stay away from Charlotte, she was going to have to find a way to keep Charlotte away from him. An idea would come to mind soon. If not now, then in the quiet hours of the night, when the air cooled down and no one was around to tell her she was imagining things.

Chapter Twenty-three

RACHEL SAT OUTSIDE THE fifth grade classrooms trying not to worry. There'd been another rape. A single attack could be written off as an anomaly, but this second assault changed everything. This meant the theory that the woman knew her attacker was wishful thinking. It was a theory that had made Rachel feel safer. The second woman had been attacked in the early afternoon. The streets were quiet at that time of day, most people were at work and the stay-at-home moms were gardening or cleaning or gluing remnants of their children's lives into scrapbooks. Who thought a chime of the doorbell meant someone was moments away from slamming you onto the floor?

At least this woman hadn't been stabbed. That's what you got for fighting back, twenty-three stab wounds. According to the news, the stabbing in the first rape baffled the police. They expected crimes to remain static or become more brutal with repetition. There was now a partial description of a suspect – a white man, five feet ten inches tall wearing a tan uniform. The uniform was what enticed the latest victim to open her door – the khaki shirt and slacks, the cap with a logo that looked like the electric company or the cable company or the phone company. Maybe a delivery service. Did anyone really know what those various uniforms were supposed to look like? The bill of his cap was pulled low so that no description of his eyes, his brow, or even his nose was possible. All that the woman remembered was his thick lips. Thick, bright red lips. He carried a clipboard and wore a communication device on his hip. There was so much detail and so little information.

IT WAS SO HOT. She wiped her hand across the back of her neck. The afternoon temperature was still in the high eighties. When was the fall weather going to make an appearance? It was almost October. Would the rapist break in through an open window if he knew a woman was home and she didn't answer the door?

She looked up and saw Amy. She wore low-heeled black patent sandals that slapped at her heels as she walked. Her pale yellow slacks and black and yellow striped top, fitted at the waist, proved there wasn't an ounce of fat anywhere on her body. Her small black purse was shaped like an envelope.

Amy dropped her purse on the table and sat down. "Jane's here today. She's on her way over as soon as she finishes her phone call."

"Why?" said Rachel.

"Maybe this attack finally freaked her out. I think she took the afternoon off so she could pick up the kids herself."

"Kit's probably too busy house-hunting to help carpool," said Rachel.

Jane strolled across the playground. She wore a sundress and flip-flops in place of her usual jacket and heels. She settled herself on the opposite bench.

"Isn't it horrible about the latest attack?" said Amy. "I'm not answering the door any more. If someone needs to look at the cable line, they can find it without my help."

"So much drama," said Jane.

"I don't want to feel like a prisoner in my own house," said Rachel.

"They'll catch him," said Jane. "If he does it again, they'll get a better description. His odds of getting caught increase each time."

"Each time? What if he rings *your* doorbell the next time?" said Amy.

Jane set her cell phone on the bench and crossed her legs. "I'm not usually home during the day."

"So you don't care if someone else, one of us, gets raped?" said Amy.

"That's not what I said. It's unnerving, but I know they'll catch him."

"How can you be so sure?" said Amy.

"Guys in tan uniforms are on every woman's radar now. He'll feel the pressure and move on to another area."

"I'm so tired. I'm not getting any sleep," said Amy. "A rapist stalking us, a woman trying to seduce my husband..."

Jane laughed, then grimaced. "From rape to seduction. That's quite a leap."

Rachel's stomach tightened. Any minute Jane would start poking at Amy's fears as if she enjoyed watching Amy come unglued. It didn't used to be like this, but lately, Jane seemed to enjoy making Amy look silly and hysterical. Some of Amy's concerns were legitimate. There was nothing wrong with being scared.

Jane uncrossed her legs. "It's so hot out here." She lifted the hem of her dress and flapped the fabric across her legs. "You are so funny, Amy. Don't you ever relax and enjoy life? You're freaked out about getting raped by someone at your front door, even though you don't answer it any more. You think because a woman doesn't wear a bra, she's after your husband. Why don't you focus all that energy on something useful? Your kids are getting older, you should get a part time job."

"My job is raising my daughters," said Amy. "I want to do one thing really well instead of trying to do everything. And right now, I want to protect my girls from a bad influence. I wish I had some support from my friends."

"You sound like a vigilante. Let's all go after a woman who … what? Exactly what is her crime? Not wearing lingerie?"

"You know the girl's father is in jail, don't you?" said Amy.

"So? How does that affect you?" said Jane.

"I don't like the families of criminals having children in our school. That girl thinks it's okay to have a father who broke the law. And we don't even know what he did. Who knows who his friends are? What will happen when he gets out of prison? This is supposed to be a safe town, and suddenly we have all this crime."

"Her boyfriend has nothing to do with the stabbing or the rapes. And there were only two. It's not a crime wave," said Jane.

"Only two? Is that how you'd feel if it was you?" said Amy.

"No. But you can't invent a phony connection to Charlotte's boyfriend. And her daughter is completely innocent, so leave them alone."

Rachel closed her eyes. Why couldn't they stop arguing? They both had a point, but why did they have to fight about it? They acted as if they didn't even like each other. "How do you know her boyfriend is in prison?" said Rachel.

"Amanda told me. She's very friendly with that girl – Meadow." Amy stood and backed away from the table. She wiggled her feet to adjust her sandals and put her hands on her hips. Her diamond ring slipped to the side, glittering in the sun. "Charlotte was falling all over Justin at the carnival. Are you going to help me figure out how to keep her away from him, or is Rachel the only friend I can count on?"

The metal bench, exposed all afternoon to the sun, continued to absorb heat. It was too hot to be sitting out here. The temperature and the arguing made Rachel irritable. Her group of friends was unraveling every day, one thread at a time. "Please don't fight," she said. "You're both right, but Amy has a point. It seems like maybe Charlotte was flirting with Justin. She just has a different view of the world than we do."

"Don't make excuses for her," said Amy.

"I'm not," said Rachel.

"I can't stick my head in the sand and pretend she's not trying to seduce him. Are you going to help me figure out how to get her to move away, or are you too P-C to speak out and say it's not right for criminals to send their kids to our school?"

Jane laughed. "It's a public school, Amy."

"I know what can happen when someone with a criminal background is allowed to mingle with normal families," said Amy.

Rachel leaned forward. Her back was slick with sweat. She wanted to get up and walk over to the buildings where there was a thin strip of shade. "What do you mean?"

"Why can't you leave her alone?" said Jane. "Stay away from her if you think she's such a bad influence."

"Because that's not enough. Her daughter is on our soccer team." Amy grabbed her purse strap. The purse bounced down and hit the bench before she swung it over her shoulder. "We chose to live here because it's safe, because it was a nice city. And it's not nice anymore."

Chapter Twenty-four

CHARLOTTE FOUND A CURBSIDE table in front of *Dish Dash*, a Mediterranean restaurant on Murphy Street in downtown Sunnyvale. She settled in one of the chairs, her back to the curb, facing the open doors of the restaurant across the sidewalk. Her reprinted photographs, still unframed, were tucked inside her portfolio. She leaned the black case against the legs of the chair.

A moment later she heard Justin's voice behind her as he stepped onto the sidewalk. "Hi there." He pulled out the opposite chair and sat down. "I have terrific news. I talked to my friend. Bruce. He's definitely open to showing your work in one of his office buildings."

Charlotte laced her fingers together and straightened her arms, feeling the need to stretch her muscles to contain the thrill that rushed through her. She suppressed a grin. "That's great." As she absorbed his words, she wondered whether the destruction of her work had almost been worth it. If she hadn't told Justin what had happened, would he have thought to help her find an even better opportunity?

The waiter appeared with a plate of *Naan* and a bowl of olive oil mixed with herbs. Justin ordered two glasses of Cabernet. He picked up a piece of the flatbread, tore off a corner and scooped up a bit of oil and herbs. "I don't think you mentioned, where did you show your work in San Francisco?"

"A few coffee shops and this deli slash bistro-type place."

He nodded. "Did you sell much?"

"Three single photographs. I also sold a photo essay."

"What was that one about?"

"It was a series of empty liquor bottles around the city – on window ledges and in gutters. It also included photographs inside upscale bars. I was trying to show how a lot of the energy of the city revolves around alcohol."

"You definitely go for unusual subjects," said Justin.

The wine arrived. Justin lifted his glass. "To the next step in your career." They both drank then set their glasses down at the same time.

"You know, you're making me think about my own photography. I'm wishing I'd done something with it," said Justin.

"You still can," said Charlotte.

"I'm not as inspired as I used to be."

"If you start thinking about the things that haunt you, you might be surprised."

He looked directly into her eyes. She met his gaze for a moment, and then looked away. She stroked the tines of the fork lying on the white linen napkin. She felt him staring at the

side of her face. It seemed there was something else he wanted
to say. The silence was thick and heavy as the noontime air. Was
he considering the elusive nature of artistic inspiration or
something else? Maybe he knew for certain that his wife had
damaged someone's property, ruined something beautiful. Was
he planning to confess on Amy's behalf? Maybe he would
apologize or offer to reimburse her.

He tore another piece of flatbread, popped it into his
mouth and spoke while he chewed, "Aren't you going to eat
anything?"

"I'm too excited." She sipped her wine. "I know I
shouldn't say that. I should be more detached and professional,
but it's hard starting over. This is the first good thing that's
happened to me."

"When did you move here?"

"Three days before school started."

She picked up a piece of *Naan* but didn't dip it in the herbs;
she didn't want oily fingers when she showed him her
photographs.

"What made you decide to move? It sounds like you were
off to a good start in San Francisco."

She placed the bread on her plate without eating it and
took a sip of wine. "I wanted a safer environment for Meadow."

"It must be unnerving with the murder and everything.
That, and having your work destroyed. Really, this is a nice
place." He grinned, looking apologetic, as if he wanted to sell
her on the idea of living in Sunnyvale.

His smile was so charming. It transformed his expression
from the intensity she'd seen stretched across the faces of most

people working long hours in high tech. He could be a kid standing on the beach with a surfboard, despite his white shirt and slightly loosened gray tie. He must be in sales – most of the engineering types stuck to jeans and, from what she'd seen, didn't appear to own a single tie. Confidence hovered around him like an aura. He was friendly, easy-going, and most likely, very smart. How on earth had this guy ended up with Amy? She picked up her portfolio and unzipped the case. "Do you want to see these?"

Justin pushed the plates to the side and picked up his wine glass to make more room on the small table. He moved his chair so it was touching hers, his back to the street.

She pulled out the stack of prints and placed them in front of him. Their knees bumped and she turned her legs to the side.

He studied the first picture – the women's feet. He set it aside and picked up the shot of the little girl's feet. Sand lay across her toes and the edges of her sandals were half-buried.

She had hoped he would comment on each one, but then decided she was impressed that he looked without talking, taking in the whole series before he spoke. The entire collection consisted of thirty-two photographs. She'd hung only a small selection at the school. She sipped her wine slowly, letting it fold around her tongue. She tried not to study his expression, looking for a signal of what he was thinking. He paused for several minutes over the picture of one of his daughters tripping her sister. Slowly he flipped through the stack to the shots of the homeless people she'd taken in San Francisco, then to the woman she'd met in front of her house. Looking at the photographs of Linda was a reminder of yet another unpleasant experience since she'd moved in to her new home. But maybe all that was about to change.

"These are fantastic," he said. "You have an amazing eye."

"Thank you."

He handed the photographs to her and she slid them back between the sides of the portfolio, zipped it closed and set it near her feet.

"It makes you think," he said. "Life can change so fast from upward momentum into something else entirely."

"That's exactly what I'm trying to show." This all seemed too good to be true. If it worked out, the display in an office complex was so much better than the coffee shops. She shoved aside the thought of the expense of producing larger prints and framing them. She imagined them hanging in a building lobby spacious enough to hold the complete series. They would look magnificent. Each one would stand out, not crammed into a few display cases or shoved up close to the patrons' faces in a coffee shop. This would be a place where people could walk around slowly, quietly studying each photograph, spending time absorbing the details. Viewers would take time to contemplate the images, almost like they would in a gallery.

"The whole concept is fascinating," he said. "It knocks you back to see the feet of an infant right next to a homeless person's toes, all grungy. It's so easy to forget they were children once." He leaned his elbows on the table.

He was so close his breath brushed across her cheek. She picked up her glass again and sipped the wine. It was rich and smooth, warming her throat. The muscles in her shoulders were softening. Tension drained out as she thought of the possibilities, felt the warmth of his flattering comments. The sun had inched across the sky and their table was no longer in the shade. Her skin was growing hot. She fiddled with the stem of her wine glass, and then let go when she saw their fingers were only a few inches apart. She leaned her elbows on the table and was suddenly aware of her breasts touching the sides of her arms. She sat up straight again. She picked up her glass and licked a droplet of wine off the lip. "It's nice hearing positive comments about my work. Thanks."

"You're an excellent photographer. I'm not doing this just because I feel bad about what happened."

She wasn't sure she believed that. Somewhere beneath his initial interest, before he'd seen the photographs, there had to be a certain amount of guilt. He'd said Amy had freaked out about the display. He must suspect she could have destroyed them. Would he do anything about it? Not that it mattered any more. This chance to expand her audience was more than enough. She no longer cared about Amy and her irrational fear of the camera.

"I suppose the reason I don't feel inspired any more is because the only time I have my camera out is at soccer practice or when we're on vacation." He swallowed more wine. The waiter appeared and asked whether they were ordering lunch. Justin shook his head. "I have to get back to the office."

The waiter turned to the next table.

"That's why I take my camera everywhere," said Charlotte. "It gets cumbersome sometimes, but I'm always ready."

Justin picked up another piece of *Naan*. "I used to take portraits of Amy. I thought I might enjoy doing more of that, capturing a woman's essence or something like that. But once we had kids ..." He picked up his glass but didn't drink.

Charlotte slid her bracelets up her arm and lined them in even circles, pressing against the bone on the underside of her forearm. Was he suggesting he wanted to do boudoir portraits or something similar? She had to suppress a laugh, imagining how Amy would respond to that idea.

"Anyway, that's in the past. But maybe I should think about picking it up again, at least beyond all the soccer shots that are filling my back-up drive now." He smiled, but his eyes were unfocused. After a minute, he shifted his gaze and stared at the last bit of wine in his glass. "I should get going. I have a customer meeting. Better get some gum or breathmints." He grinned.

She reached into her pocket and pulled out a memory stick. "Here are some pictures to show Bruce."

"It might be about two weeks before you hear from him. He's traveling in Asia. But he'll absolutely call you once I let him know how good these are." He stood and dropped a few bills on the table. "See you later." He walked quickly to his car, parked at the curb behind her.

Charlotte looked down at her portfolio. How would she control her anticipation for two weeks? The best thing to do was to get busy thinking about another project. She sipped the Cabernet. The texture had changed as the air had grown warmer and it felt sharp on her tongue. She picked up a piece of Nann and took a bite. Hopefully she would be able to make a trip up to visit Mark soon.

Finally she had something exciting to tell him, something that would make them both feel as if their lives might be turning around.

Chapter Twenty-five

THE CHIMES OF AMY'S doorbell echoed behind the front door. Rachel shifted her weight to the opposite foot, feeling like a supplicant. After a few minutes she pressed the button again. A series of tones cascaded up and down the scale. Why was Amy taking so long? Rachel had called that morning to tell her she was coming by this afternoon. Finally, the deadbolt turned, grinding out of its casing as if it resisted letting loose its grip on the frame of the house. The door opened. Amy's left eye was red and swollen so that her eyeball seemed to swim in the socket. Her nose was bright red. She held a dishtowel, lumpy with ice cubes, against the left side of her head.

"You look awful," said Rachel. "Are you sick?"

"I have a migraine." Amy edged the wadded up towel closer to her temple. Water dripped down her forearm. "My ice is melting." She opened the door wider.

Rachel stepped inside. "I thought you had medication for your migraines."

"I didn't get my prescription filled in time and the pharmacy didn't have any on hand. I have to wait until four o'clock."

"Can I do anything? Rub your neck or something?"

Amy blinked. "That's a little weird." Her voice was a hoarse whisper, lacking the authority that usually drove her words home like knives. "You could get me more ice." She handed the sopping towel to Rachel and sidled over to the couch. She stretched out on her back, wiggling around to settle a tube-shaped pillow under her neck. Her head lolled back, making her neck look longer and whiter than usual.

Rachel went in to the kitchen and dropped the towel and melted ice into the sink. She pulled a fresh towel out of the drawer and filled a bowl with ice. She dumped the ice into a plastic bag, wrapped it in the towel and carried it to the living room. She watched Amy's pulse throb in her neck. "Do you want me to pick up the girls after school so you can rest?" said Rachel.

"Could you? That would really help." She closed her eyes.

"I should leave if you don't feel good," said Rachel.

Amy didn't answer.

Rachel moved to the wing chair and settled on the edge. She didn't want to leave yet. She had to find out what Amy had been talking about the other day. Her words had sounded so ominous – *I know what can happen when the relatives of criminals live nearby.* Did Amy know more about Charlotte than she was saying? If she had a reason to believe for certain that Charlotte was capable of hurting them, she owed it to her friends to tell them what she knew. "I just wanted to ask what you meant when you said we can't ignore Charlotte."

"She's dangerous."

"Why?"

"Her boyfriend is in prison."

"So. Has *she* done anything wrong?"

"Well she puts up with it.

"How do you know that?"

"She thinks it's ok." Amy's voice filled the room, no longer a whisper, no longer sounding as if she could hardly speak. "You can't have a criminal sending her kid to our school. You can't let people like that live around your family."

"People like what? What do you think is going to happen?"

"I don't know. Anything could happen."

"You made it sound like you know something else."

"I know what happens when everyone pretends criminals are rehabilitated, or whatever." Amy turned onto her side to face Rachel. She stared out of her good eye. The swollen eye was nearly closed. "You look blurry," said Amy. "Can you scoot the chair closer?"

Rachel leaned forward. "What do you mean about not getting rehabilitated?"

"The guy who raped my mother had been in prison."

Amy spoke the words in a firm voice. When she'd first blurted it out a few weeks ago, she'd sounded as if she could hardly speak; now she said it casually, as if she was talking about a trip to the mall. "It's so terrible. I can't even imagine," said Rachel.

"I knew him."

"What?"

"The guy who raped my mother. I knew who he was."

Rachel swallowed. She'd hardly digested the idea of a child witnessing her mother's rape. Amy knew him? It was beyond horrifying. "What did they do when you told them?"

"I never told. I never even told anyone I saw it."

Rachel leaned back in the chair. The leather was hard against her shoulder blades. "Why not?" she said.

"I don't know. I was scared. My father wouldn't have believed me."

"His wife was *raped*. You were a child."

"The guy was his friend."

"Then why didn't you tell?"

"My father was so angry. Because she didn't fight hard enough."

"That's disgusting. What kind of person thinks like that?"

"You don't know how he was."

"I guess not." Rachel stared at the coffee table. In the center was a large glass vase filled with sunflowers. Silk, but so well made they looked real. Every time she sat in Amy's living room, she was overcome with a desire to touch one of the petals, as if she had to reassure herself it wasn't real.

"The guy who attacked her … he had already been in prison for beating up another woman. I found that out when I was older."

Rachel licked her lips. She had a hard time getting her head around the idea that someone would blame a woman for her own rape. It was so sick, such a distorted view. How could Amy accept all that as if it made any sense? It sounded as if her father had almost brainwashed her.

"So I know you can't take any chances," said Amy.

"Take chances on what?"

"Are you listening?" Amy sat up suddenly. She looked child-like on the enormous blue sofa. "You can't think criminals are going to change."

"Charlotte isn't a criminal."

"But we don't know what her boyfriend did. You don't know what kind of people they associate with. Isn't it strange that we never had any violent crimes around here. Then, she moves in and all of a sudden there's a guy raping women? Someone is murdered?"

"It's not connected. They think he's a delivery guy."

"Someone *dressed up* as a delivery guy. It's too much of a coincidence."

She couldn't follow Amy's logic. Perhaps the migraine had twisted the capillaries of her brain and her mind was creating erratic patterns out of nothing.

Amy held the ice pack on her lap. Her eye was still so swollen that only a thin slit of her iris was visible.

"Shouldn't you be lying down?" said Rachel.

"This is too important. I want you to realize that we have to do something."

Rachel couldn't even think about Charlotte, all she could do was wonder why Amy had never told anyone what she'd seen. How could she let her mother suffer while she hid the identity of a rapist? "I don't understand why you never said anything."

"What good would it have done?"

"They would have punished him. It might have helped your mother find some peace of mind."

"My dad said it was her fault. She wore clothes that made men look at her in that way."

"What you wear has nothing to do with it." Rachel stood up. She crossed her arms. She ached for Amy's mother, and for Amy, growing up with a man who had such perverted ideas.

"My dad said she dressed like a slut."

"It's not like that. He's wrong. More than wrong. His views are sick."

"It doesn't matter anymore. All that matters is figuring out how to get rid of Charlotte."

Rachel put her hand on the back of the chair, hoping to steady herself. "She hasn't done anything."

"Do you want to wait until one of her boyfriend's gang buddies moves in? How do we know the rapist isn't a friend of hers? You don't even know who else lives in that dump."

"How do you know where she lives?"

"I looked it up on the soccer sheet. I drove by." Amy closed her eyes but didn't pick up the ice pack.

"That's going to make a wet spot," said Rachel. "Do you want me to put it in the kitchen?"

Amy nodded.

Rachel carried the towel into the kitchen and set it in the sink. She looked out the window. The branches of an apricot tree brushed against the glass. A small birdhouse with a tray of seed hung in the tree. She didn't recall noticing it before. A

Finch, its breast bright orange against the grayed wood of the birdhouse, perched on the edge of the trough, pecking madly.

She went back into the living room. "I'm really sorry about your mother."

"It's ok."

It wasn't okay. Rachel wondered what Amy's sisters thought, if they viewed it the same way. Of course, they didn't know what Amy knew, but still, they'd grown up listening to the same garbage. They'd heard their father turn rape into something sexual, blaming their mother for a brutal attack. She wondered if Justin knew about any of this. Now she understood at least part of why Amy's mother had killed herself. She walked to the end of the living room and up the step to the foyer. "I'll bring the twins home."

"What are we going to do?" said Amy.

"Nothing. Leave her alone."

"I can't. You need to help me. Like you helped with the pictures."

Rachel put her hand on the door handle. There was a hardness in Amy's voice that made her words sound intimidating. What did Amy think they would do? Charlotte wasn't a person who backed down easily. She wouldn't suddenly move because they made her life uncomfortable. "Let's forget about the pictures. It was a terrible mistake."

"No it wasn't. You have to help me. If you're my friend."

"You're not feeling well. Let's talk some other time."

"Tomorrow." Amy rose slowly to her feet. She shuffled across the carpet to the foyer. She stopped and leaned against the wall.

"You shouldn't be up," said Rachel.

"I have to lock the door after you leave."

Outside, the air smelled smoggy from too many days of unrelieved heat. Rachel longed for the ocean fog to move back inland. Should she tell Greg what she'd done? She couldn't risk Amy telling him, spreading the news to everyone she knew, proud of the damage they'd caused. It almost sounded like Amy was threatening her. How could she have been so stupid, getting so caught up in her insecurities over Trent? She leaned against the iron gate. There was no one she could talk to, no one who would understand and help her figure out what to do.

Chapter Twenty-six

AFTER RACHEL LEFT, Amy settled back down on the sofa. She turned from one side to the other; worried she was staining the dark blue fabric with even darker spots of sweat. She was tired of resting and it hadn't made her feel any better. The pain still stabbed at the back of her eye and ran down her neck. She slid her legs over the edge of the sofa and sat up slowly. The simple change in position intensified the throbbing in her skull. She stood and trudged across the room. She started up the stairs. At each step, she stopped for a moment before moving to the next.

In the master bathroom she splashed cold water on her face and patted it dry. She stripped off her wrinkled blouse and replaced it with a white T-shirt. The soft cotton made her feel cleaner, somehow victorious over the knifing pain. She went back into the bathroom and applied moisturizer, a light covering of foundation, and lip gloss. Her left eye continued to weep, preventing her from using mascara or liner. She put the contact lens in her right eye. That would have to do. She swallowed three ibuprofen capsules and then remembered the acetaminophen with codeine that Justin hadn't used up after his root canal. She swallowed one tablet, picked up her purse, and went back downstairs, taking firmer steps this time.

Out in the garage, she climbed into the *Expedition* and pressed the button to open the door. She backed out and hit the remote again to close the door. She wasn't really sure where she was going, but now that Rachel was looking after the twins, she had a few hours to focus on the Charlotte problem.

She drove out of the cul-de-sac, down Birch, past the school and across Redwood to Crestview Way. Cars lined the curbs in front of the apartment complex across from Charlotte's tiny house, a shack, really. The front yard was nothing but dried grass. Instead of drapes, a red, green, and orange woven blanket was tacked inside the window frame. If she walked on to the front porch, she would probably be able to see right into the living room because there were gaps on either side where the blanket sagged.

Curious as she was to learn the details of Charlotte's living room and discover who else might be staying in the house, it wasn't worth getting caught. Besides, she didn't want to get out of the *Expedition* even though the migraine had started to subside. The codeine was helping. The tears had stopped flooding her vision and all that remained was a dull knot behind her eye. She continued to the end of the street and turned toward downtown. She wasn't really sure where she was headed. An idea was slowly forming in her mind. If she sent a package to Charlotte, to be delivered by a uniformed carrier, it might make Charlotte wake up and see what an easy target she was.

Was it possible to frighten her into realizing it was risky for a single woman to be living in such a flimsy house? It was a perfect idea. She would buy something small and ship it from the office supply store. But first, she'd stop and have a quick lunch of chicken salad at *Tao Taos*. Migraines made her ravenous, and her cravings usually leaned toward a blend of sweet and salty. She turned onto Murphy Street. It was eleven-thirty, early enough to hope for a curbside spot.

She stopped while the car ahead of her maneuvered into a parking space. A small Mediterranean restaurant was on the right. She had wanted Justin to take her and the girls there. She'd have to remind him again. She glanced at the tables arranged on the sidewalk. Only three were occupied this early. Charlotte Whittington was seated at the last table. Next to her was a man who looked eerily like Justin. It must be the ache behind her eye, still disturbing her vision, or maybe her missing contact lens. That couldn't be Justin's blonde hair. He had that same way of propping his hand on his hip when he was seated at the table waiting for dinner.

The traffic started moving again. When she reached the end of the short street, she tapped the brake then veered around the corner and up the half block to make another right. She sped into the parking lot behind the row of restaurants and shops and lurched into an empty spot. Chicken salad no longer sounded appealing. She might think about eating after she'd double-checked what she thought she'd seen; to reassure herself it couldn't possibly be Justin. His office was a thirty-minute drive from here. Her friends were right. She spent too much time thinking about Charlotte and her mind had conjured up something that wasn't there. Still, she had to check.

She crossed the parking lot and entered the alley that led back to Murphy Street. In the spot where the alley opened up onto the sidewalk, she had a clear view of the Mediterranean place. She stayed in the shaded area near the building and looked down the street. Charlotte's black-tipped hair was prominent, but now a waiter blocked the man from Amy's view. Then she realized it wasn't necessary to see the man. Parked at the curb, right behind him, was Justin's silver *BMW*. Even if she forgot the numbers of the license plate, the XXV on a silver *BMW 7-series* was enough. She swallowed. The yogurt and granola from breakfast burned in her throat. She tried to breathe. She folded her arms around her waist and felt the sharp points of her elbows in her palms. She'd been right after all. She never should have listened to Justin's words of denial when she'd first asked him if he'd noticed Charlotte and he'd acted as if he didn't know who she was talking about.

Charlotte's chair was scooted around the table, close to Justin's. She held a stack of photographs in one hand and a wine glass in the other. She handed the photographs to Justin. She leaned toward him and her breast moved gently, brushing against his arm.

Amy jerked around to face the building behind her. She didn't need to see any more. She had been stupid to listen to his protests of innocence. Stupid to listen to her friends who implied she was too judgmental, that she was wrong to assume Charlotte's choice of clothes advertised that she was looking for sex. Amy stepped further into the alley. She leaned over a trashcan and let the liquid from her stomach pour out into the plastic-lined container. She pulled a tissue from her purse and wiped her lips.

The clacking of her heels echoed between the walls of the buildings as she hurried down the alley. By the time she reached the *Expedition* she was running, stumbling on the slender heels of her sandals. The alarm beeped and she yanked open the door. The powerful engine felt safe as she gunned the SUV out of the parking lot. She sped toward El Camino Real. The tears from her migraine had dried up, and her stomach was settled. Sending an anonymous package was the perfect idea. Why hadn't she thought of it sooner? She would pay cash, set it up so the package had to be signed for. That way, it wouldn't be left on the porch while Charlotte was running around taking pictures, or seducing other women's husbands. She drove slowly into the parking lot of the office supply store. Her headache had disappeared. It seemed like a miracle.

It took less than half an hour to have a small box wrapped and labeled for overnight shipping. When she left the store, her feet felt like they were gliding above the rough surface of the parking lot. Her body was relaxed and light. Now she was so hungry that she needed more than chicken salad. Besides, she certainly wasn't going back downtown. Her hunger was a massive emptiness that would only be satisfied by a juicy hamburger and a bag of soft, salty fries.

Chapter Twenty-seven

CHARLOTTE UNLOCKED THE DOOR and stepped into the living room. She set two bags of groceries on the floor then closed and locked the screen door behind her. Meadow sat on the edge of the couch holding a copy of Dracula. Her eyes darted across the pages as if she couldn't read the words fast enough. Next to her was a small box wrapped in brown paper. Nearly the entire surface of the package was shiny from multiple layers of clear packing tape. Charlotte went into the kitchen and set the grocery bags on the counter. She returned to the living room and sat on the floor to unlace her boots, eager to feel the cool hardwood on the soles of her feet.

"We got a present." Meadow put her book face down on the couch.

"I see that. Where did it come from?"

"It was delivered."

"You're not supposed to answer the door, Meadow. You know the rules."

"It was a delivery guy, so I thought it was okay."

Charlotte swallowed. A delivery person? She hadn't said anything to Meadow about the murder or the second rape. Would Meadow have heard about it at school? Did she know what rape was? She certainly knew about murder, about stabbings, they had happened from time to time in their old neighborhood. She had thought Meadow would follow the standard rule to not answer the door when she was home alone. Now she realized it was a mistake to assume a ten-year-old would follow instructions to the letter. Obviously it was no longer safe to let her revel in her growing push for independence, at least not until someone was apprehended. "The rule doesn't change depending on who's at the door," she said.

For the thousandth time, she ached for Mark's presence, exhausted by the fine distinctions in the delicate balancing act of parenthood. Should she tell Meadow about the rapist dressed in a non-descript uniform, deliberately scaring her, because a little bit of fear was crucial to survival? Or should she keep her mouth shut and treat Meadow like she was five years old, never leaving her home alone, even for twenty or thirty minutes? One part of her felt she shouldn't terrify Meadow without reason. She didn't want a child who was afraid to open the door, scared of every man in a uniform. Did she need to explain rape? Usually she relied on Meadow's questions to introduce new ideas, to talk about sex or other complex adult experiences. But should she expect a child to ask about rape, or was it her job to provide that information before the question came up? "I make the rules to protect you until you're old enough to decide for yourself when something is dangerous."

"Sorry."

"It's easy to be lulled into thinking this town is safer than the city. In some ways it is. But in some ways, it's not."

"What does *lulled* mean?"

"To make someone feel safe when they aren't."

"Who's lulling me?"

"It's not a person, it's the atmosphere – because all the beautiful yards and parks make it look so peaceful and quiet. That can make you feel safe and it's not always safe."

Meadow nodded, but her eyes were focused on the box. "Can I open it?"

"Sure."

"But it's for you."

"Go ahead and open it. You'll do better with all that tape."

Meadow picked at the tape with her fingernails. She put the box close to her mouth and tried to gnaw at a small peeled-up section.

"Don't use your teeth."

"It's too tight."

Charlotte went into the kitchen. She pulled a paring knife out of the drawer and brought it to Meadow. "Be careful it doesn't slip."

"I know that, Mom." Meadow slid the blade under the tape and sliced along the seam.

Charlotte's heart fluttered. "Give that to me for a minute."

"It's almost open."

"I want to feel how heavy it is."

"It's not heavy," said Meadow.

"Light enough that you think it's a piece of paper, or not heavy because you're able to hold it in one hand?" Her heart beat faster. She reached over and grabbed the box, frightened of the possibilities for what it could contain.

"Why did you do that?"

"I just want to feel it." What was wrong with her? The box was light, but she was still anxious. She handed it back to Meadow. If Mark, or even his brother, sent her something, they would put a return address. And it wasn't her birthday. She hadn't ordered anything. She couldn't think of a single reason she would be receiving a package. The idea of something dangerous, something explosive inside this tiny box was absurd, and yet her hands continued to tremble as Meadow worked at the tape.

Finally, Meadow was able to remove the shell formed by the layers of tape. She lifted off the top and pulled out a plastic bag. It contained an apple core that was soft with age and several candy wrappers smeared with chocolate.

"Why would someone send us garbage?" said Meadow.

"I don't know." But she did know. A single name fluttered across her mind like a scrap of paper. Meadow blinked several times, as if she was trying to wipe away the confusion while she waited for an explanation. Charlotte's heart folded in on itself. She wanted to take away the hurt that caused her daughter's eyelids to quiver. She should have followed her instinct and not allowed Meadow to open the package. She moved onto the couch next to Meadow and stroked her hair. "It was sent to me, not you. So try to put it out of your mind. Can you do that?"

Meadow's lower lip trembled. She nodded.

Charlotte picked up the mess of tape and grabbed the plastic bag. She walked slowly down the hall and out the back door. She opened the lid of the trashcan and dropped the packing materials and the garbage inside. It landed in the empty plastic bin with a thud. When the lid fell closed, she turned quickly. She could call the delivery company and try to find out who the sender was. But would they tell her? Were there rules or laws about sending anonymous packages? She didn't know. It didn't make any difference. Only one person could be responsible for such a cruel gift. Amy knew that a uniformed delivery person would make any woman afraid, even if only for a few seconds.

Chapter Twenty-eight

THE LOCAL PAPER REPORTED that a third woman had been assaulted. The news left Amy shaking, terrified to leave her house. All she had to do was walk out through the pantry and get into the *Expedition*. She whimpered as she flung open the pantry door. She kept her eyes focused on the shadowy corners of the garage while she locked the deadbolt and darted to the SUV. She scrambled inside, slammed the door closed and locked it. She gripped her right wrist with her left hand to prevent it from shaking as she inserted the key into the ignition. She pressed the door opener, half expecting to see a man waiting to overpower the SUV. He would smash the windows with a crowbar, and drag her out onto the pavement, tearing her white silk blouse. The jagged glass of the broken window would rip her skin as viciously as it shredded the silk. She gasped for air, jammed the gearshift into reverse, and gunned the engine so the *Expedition* shot out of the garage. It wobbled from the sudden burst of speed. She managed to back slowly out of the driveway, but her hands slid around the steering wheel as if it was greased. She punched the button to close the garage door.

At the school playground, she dropped her purse on the table and sat down next to Rachel, across from Kit. Charlotte was seated on a nearby table, using the bench as a footrest, fiddling with her camera. She wore a shrunken pale green tee shirt and long shorts with her usual boots.

Amy closed her eyes. "I guess you heard about the latest rape?"

"You'd think women wouldn't open the door to a guy in a tan uniform," said Kit.

"They might not know," said Rachel. "Not everyone gets the newspaper."

"It's their responsibility to stay informed," said Kit. "Don't you think?"

"You sound like Jane," said Amy. "You don't care if he keeps attacking, as long as it's not you?"

"That's not what I meant," said Kit.

Already Amy wondered why she'd even mentioned the attack. Kit and Jane both seemed to think they lived inside some kind of a protective bubble. They thought there was no need to worry because they were more intelligent than other people. Maybe it was because they'd never actually experienced violence. For a fleeting moment, Amy considered telling Kit what had happened to her mother, if only to see the look on Kit's face. She wanted to watch Kit struggle to find a viewpoint that would allow her to continue feeling immune. But she already regretted telling Rachel. The rounded, bulging look of pity in Rachel's eyes had made her feel vulnerable. Keeping it secret made her feel stronger. Still, she knew she was utterly helpless. It didn't matter if the man had been seen in a tan uniform, he could change his method on a whim. She was definitely going to get the gun and put it back in the spare room. She didn't need Justin's permission. It was a matter of protecting herself and her daughters.

Her father had given her the gun when she was twenty years old. She'd just moved into an apartment with two girlfriends. He insisted that she had to watch out for herself. Unwrapping the package that contained the gun, learning to shoot, was one of only a few pleasant memories of her father. Twice a week she'd met him at the shooting range. She fired round after round until she learned to keep her arm steady, learned how to aim correctly. The gun had remained under her bed until she got married. When she and Justin bought their home, she'd stored it in the spare room. After the twins were born, Justin suddenly remembered it was there and insisted she get it out of the house.

"He'll be caught soon," said Kit.

"How are they going to catch him?" said Amy. "Arrest every service guy?" She glanced at Charlotte. Had Charlotte been frightened when the delivery guy showed up with that package? If she wasn't scared, she should be now. Still, Amy had the feeling the package hadn't accomplished much. It was a huge disappointment. If Charlotte had felt even a tremor of fear, she certainly hadn't changed her behavior. Her face looked calm, her shoulders relaxed.

"They probably have clues that aren't published in the paper," said Kit.

"Every time I see a truck, every time the doorbell rings, my heart starts racing," said Amy. "I've had to tell the twins over and over not to answer the door. Ever."

"You don't ever let them answer the door?" said Rachel. "Even when Justin's home?"

"How can I?" said Amy. "If I'm not constantly in the living room, looking out the window, how would I know? It's easier to tell them never."

"I can't live like that," said Kit. "But as soon as the house sells, I guess I won't have to think about it."

"I thought the rapes had nothing to do with your moving plans," said Amy. Did Kit remember what she said from one time to the next, or did she just like to sound confident so everyone else felt worse?

"There's no crime in your new neighborhood?" said Rachel.

"Let's stop talking about this," said Kit. "It's a gorgeous afternoon."

"The whole thing makes me feel sick," said Rachel.

"It should," said Amy.

Kit stood up. She took off her sunglasses, ran her fingers through her hair and put her sunglasses back on. "Why don't we have a hot tub party at my house Saturday? We haven't had a moms' night out in ages. It would be great to get together before the nice weather disappears. Before I start packing."

"How can you think about sitting in a hot tub when that guy is out there?" said Amy.

"Because I refuse to live my life in fear, constantly reminding myself of every single thing that can go wrong. If you thought about it, you'd never set foot outside your house. You'd never get married. Never have children."

Rachel nodded.

Amy wanted to hit both of them. Why weren't they scared? "You're ignoring what's happening right in front of our eyes. If you'd ever known someone who was raped, you wouldn't be so casual."

"I'm not going to let it consume me. So, how about it? I'll call Jane and let her know," said Kit.

Rachel nodded again.

She looked like one of those bobble-headed dolls, wiggling her head in affirmation each time her chin was poked.

Kit walked toward the classrooms. She called back over her shoulder, "Seven on Saturday. I'll provide the wine and you can all bring snacks. Ok?"

Amy pinched the inside of Rachel's forearm.

"Ouch."

"How can you not be scared?" said Amy.

"I check who's there before I answer the door."

"What if he waits outside until you go to pick up the mail?"

"I don't know. That's not how it usually happens," said Rachel.

"Planning for the worst never hurts." Amy lowered her voice. "Like I'm planning to make sure Charlotte stays away from Justin."

"Please don't start that again," said Rachel.

"I saw her drinking wine with him. She was rubbing herself all over him."

"You saw him with her? When?" Rachel shifted sideways and turned to stare at her.

"Don't you believe me?" said Amy.

"Of course I believe you. If you saw them. But I'm sure it didn't mean anything," said Rachel.

"How do you know that?" Amy was constantly amazed at how clueless her friends were. Didn't they ever wonder what their husbands were thinking? Didn't they worry about their husbands' female co-workers?

"Because … I."

"You don't know. And I don't know what's been going on behind my back."

The dismissal bell rang.

"I want you to promise to help me," said Amy.

Rachel stood and edged toward the first grade classroom. "I have to get Trent. He gets worried if he can't see me when he comes out."

"I need you more than Trent does right now. I can't fight her by myself. She's too strong. It's almost like she's a supernatural force."

Rachel scowled, then turned to look across the waves of children.

Amy tried to grab the edge of Rachel's skirt, but missed. "Do you promise?"

"You need to stop thinking about her so much. You're taking minor incidents and inflating them out of proportion."

"No I'm not."

Rachel waved at Trent then turned back. Her body cast a shadow across Amy's face. "Can't you talk to Justin?"

"I tried. You have to help me. You're already in on this, with getting rid of the pictures, and everything."

"Why do you keep bringing that up? I want to forget it." Rachel's voice sounded breathless, nervous.

"Because you helped before. You can't let me down now." Amy smiled. Mentioning the destruction of the pictures again was a smart move. She had to keep reminding Rachel that she was committed. Like Kit said, they had already stepped over a line. Both of them. Doing more to intimidate Charlotte wasn't so bad. Not that it had to be criminal, but still, you never knew.

"Okay. We'll talk about it next week, after Kit's party."

"You said that before," said Amy. "You have to promise."

"Ok," said Rachel.

"Say it."

"I promise," said Rachel.

Chapter Twenty-nine

RACHEL WATCHED THE GOLDFISH swim in circles inside its five-inch bowl. It really needed a larger container. Trent never seemed to tire of watching his pet circle its glass cage, opening and closing its mouth, but its movements made Rachel think it was making a popping sound, audible only beneath the water. The poor thing didn't have many choices in life, and yet, it didn't seem frantic or disturbed. There might be some comfort in a brain that didn't know how close it was to danger, how easily its life could slip away with a sudden gesture from the human world.

She ripped the last of the lettuce and dropped it into the salad bowl while Greg hovered behind her. "Should I be scared?" she said. "Three rapes? A woman murdered?"

Greg plucked a slice of cucumber off the cutting board.

"Please don't eat the salad before it's made," said Rachel.

"I thought they decided the first woman knew the guy who stabbed her. Do they know for sure it's the same guy?"

"If it's not, it would be a weird and horrifying coincidence. There's hardly ever any violent crime around here, and now two different rapists?"

He popped a cherry tomato into his mouth and bit down. Pulp and seeds squirted across his chin.

"Stop eating and tell me what you think."

"About what?" said Greg.

"Amy is terrified. But Kit thinks it's no big deal. I don't even know how I feel. Should I be more afraid?"

"If you have to ask, you already know the answer."

"Amy's really freaked out."

"Amy's always freaked out. She reacts the same whether someone gets stabbed or she chips her nail polish."

"No she doesn't."

"Yes, she does. There's something not right about her."

"How can you say that? She's my best friend."

"You asked what I thought. I think your reaction is reasonable and I think Amy likes to create drama."

"Maybe they won't be able to catch him."

"He's so predictable now, if you're careful, there's nothing to worry about. Creeps like him aren't very bright. He'll give himself away at some point."

She held the bowl up to the cutting board and scooped cucumber, cherry tomatoes, and chopped red onion on top of the lettuce. She opened the refrigerator and pulled out a plate of sliced chicken breast. "You don't understand. It eats away at you."

"It's eating at Amy. You sound fine – completely rational."

She shoved the salad tongs into the bowl and set it on the table.

"Should I call the kids?" said Greg.

"You're acting like it's no big deal that three women have been raped."

He moved behind her and wrapped his arms around her shoulders, folding his body around hers. "I know it's scary."

Greg didn't get it. On one level, Rachel recognized that Amy was overwrought, thinking too much about her mother, and making unreasonable connections with Charlotte's boyfriend. Rachel had a strange sense that she was standing outside her life, watching herself react but feeling numb.

"Just keep your eyes open, but don't let it traumatize you."

"I hate it that someone can go around destroying women's lives like this. Amy's afraid to leave the house. Or answer the door."

"Amy's more frightening than a rapist."

Rachel shoved her elbow into his stomach and pushed out of his arms.

He grabbed at her, but she scuttled next to the counter and pressed her hips against the edge.

"I'm sorry. I shouldn't have said that. But, come on. She's afraid to answer the door?" said Greg.

"That's easy for you to say. You're a man."

"You noticed." He moved up behind her again and curved his hands around her breasts.

She slapped his wrist. "Don't. It's not funny."

"Don't get caught up in her hysteria," said Greg. "Can we eat now?"

She put the basket of rolls in the center of the table and pulled out her chair. It sickened her that Greg could joke around while she was talking about something as serious as rape. There was good cause to be afraid. Maybe Amy was the only rational one. But if that was true, why was Amy making veiled threats? Twice she'd reminded Rachel about their lapse of judgment, as if she expected something in return for keeping quiet about it. Every time Rachel recalled that night, smashing Charlotte's photographs, her legs went damp and gummy and her heart raced. During those few minutes it had taken to scrape the ink into dark clumps, she'd completely lost her sanity. What had made her think, even for a moment, that destroying the pictures could ensure no one would view her son in a negative light?

Was Amy threatening her? Would she tell Greg what they'd done? Rachel couldn't even guess what he'd say. After being married to the man all these years, she was no longer sure she could predict his reaction to anything. All summer she'd thought he was on her side, determined to help Trent succeed at soccer, then suddenly he'd shrugged his shoulders and said it wasn't important. She had to find a way to tell him what she'd done, before Amy did.

Chapter Thirty

RACHEL HANDED KIT THE bowl of guacamole and two bags of tortilla chips. She stepped through the open door into Kit's atrium and took a deep breath. The air smelled of jasmine and damp earth. The pebbled concrete floor of the atrium flowed seamlessly into the foyer so that when the sliding glass door was open, the foyer and the atrium appeared to be a single room. The entire back wall of the *Eichler*-designed home was constructed of floor-to-ceiling glass so the house felt as if the gardens surrounding it were part of the interior as well. She followed Kit into the kitchen. "What can I do to help?"

"Nothing. It's all under control. Why don't you go outside and enjoy the water. Jane got here early." Kit lowered her voice and smiled. "She's already starting her third glass of wine, so you need to catch up." She placed a glass with a long thin stem and a larger than average bowl at the edge of the counter. She poured it half full of Chardonnay and handed it to Rachel.

The glass was so thin, Rachel was afraid it would snap if she gripped it too hard. She took a small sip. No wonder Jane was on her third glass – the wine was soft and buttery. A single bottle probably cost more than Rachel and Greg spent on wine over the course of a month. She lifted her glass. "To friends."

Kit picked up her glass and raised it. "To friends." She set it back on the counter without drinking.

The backyard was crowded with tropical plants that grew up past the top of the fence, hiding the surrounding single-story homes, and giving the yard the feel of a secluded resort. Rachel dropped her purse on a chair near the back door. She walked around the pool to the hot tub nestled in the far corner of the yard near three palm trees and a few plants with enormous leaves that drooped over the chairs. A low table and several wrought iron patio chairs were arranged near the edge of the hot tub. She greeted Jane and settled herself into one of the chairs. She kicked off her flip-flops. She sipped her wine and leaned back to look at the sky, darkening to a deep blue.

"Come on in. The water feels divine," said Jane. "It takes all the kinks out of your back in about three minutes."

Rachel took another sip of wine. "Let me relax with my wine first." The last thing she needed was Jane staring straight up at her thighs, watching her struggle to pull the denim shorts down her legs, exposing hips that weren't completely restrained by her navy blue swimsuit.

"Bring the wine in. It's great. It gives you a very nice buzz." Jane laughed and took a long swallow from her glass. She held it up high so the rumbling water wouldn't splash it.

"I don't think you're supposed to drink too much alcohol in a hot tub," said Rachel.

"That's right," said Amy. She had slipped out the back door. Kit followed, carrying a bottle of wine and a chiller. Amy teetered around the edge of the pool in sandals with three and a half inch cork wedge heels. She wobbled across the uneven flagstone, collapsed in the chair next to Rachel, and let her shoes fall off her feet. She stood up again, lifted her turquoise mini-dress over her head in a quick sweep and dropped it on the back of the chair. "I'm going in before I drink any wine," she said. She lowered herself into the tub. The water swallowed her pale skin. Only the turquoise of her swimsuit was visible, making it look slightly disembodied.

"A few glasses won't hurt you," said Jane. "I drink wine in my hot tub all the time. It's fine, as long as the temperature's not set too high, which this isn't."

Rachel scooted her chair closer to one of the palms to make room for Kit to walk past. She took another small sip from her glass. Jane drank wine like it was water. She never complained of a hangover, and she never seemed unsteady on her feet or troubled by slurred speech. But three glasses in less than an hour was a lot of alcohol, and she showed no sign of slowing down. Why did her friends suddenly seem so messed up? Angry, snobbish, and argumentative. Self-absorbed, drunk, and downright mean. They used to have so much fun together. Didn't they? Rachel longed for their former selves, more focused on their children, less fierce. She took another sip of wine.

Kit stepped out of her skirt, uncovering the rest of her black bikini. She sat on the edge of the tub and slid into the water.

Jane shrieked. "Your feet are like ice. Get them away from my leg." They laughed and some of the tightness in Rachel's stomach unwound itself.

"Come on, Rachel. Hop in," said Jane. "Or we'll pull you in."

"Just a few more sips," said Rachel.

Kit started talking about her new house in Palo Alto. Their offer had been accepted and, despite the sluggish economy, they had received two offers on this house.

Rachel stood and yanked off her shorts. She sipped more wine, hoping to erase the certainty that they were all watching, judging the shape of her body. She pulled off her shirt and eased herself into the tub between Jane and Amy. She hoped the conversation would change, that it would soften around the edges now that all four of them were drifting in the churning water, free of children, and for Rachel, free of concern over how her body looked, now that it was hidden below the surface, blurred by frothing water. For a brief moment she felt they were equal, all essentially the same.

"I wish we could move somewhere safer," said Amy. "We can afford it, but I don't want to disrupt the girls' stability. It would be nice to go somewhere with less crime."

"We have one of the lowest crime rates in the country," said Jane.

"She's not talking about the crime rate in general, she's talking about the rapes," said Kit. "She's obsessed with them."

"I'm not obsessed."

"Then stop talking about it," said Kit.

"Have some wine," said Jane. "Don't think about it. They'll catch him."

"I'm scared. And you should be too, instead of pretending nothing bad can happen to you." She climbed out of the tub. Water streamed down her thin body, dripping off her kneecaps.

"You're not leaving already, are you?" said Rachel. So much for the hope they could still enjoy each other's company. Even if they managed to avoid an argument, this might be their last night together.

***

THE BREEZE AGAINST Amy's wet skin was chilly. She shivered. She picked up her towel and draped it over her shoulders. Maybe she should leave. She was tired of them. She tugged her towel around her shoulders. Explaining the truth was exhausting. If they were really her friends, they wouldn't be constantly criticizing her. "I'm not leaving," she said. "Although I guess I'm the only one who thinks three rapes is something to be concerned about."

"Oh Amy, don't get so pissy," said Kit. "We're just a little tired of hearing you talk about rape; and go on and on about Charlotte. You seem obsessed, that's all."

"While you're up, fill my glass." Jane lifted her wine glass and tapped it against Amy's kneecap.

Amy dribbled wine into the glass.

"Don't be stingy."

"It's a big glass," said Amy. She splashed in enough to fill it two thirds full and poured half a glass for herself. She put the bottle back in the chiller.

Jane took a sip of wine. She stroked the stem of the glass with her index finger. Her short nails looked unnaturally pale from soaking in the water. "I think you have a rape fantasy."

The words sliced through Amy's head, strangely echoing her father's voice – *You were asking for it*. That ugly word haunted her life. She would never escape. As if an eleven-year-old wasn't supposed to know what that word meant. How could she not know, when she'd seen it with her own eyes? The gossiping neighbors, the looks her friends gave her when they thought she wasn't paying attention. They didn't know how her thoughts, her legs, her arms, her entire body froze at the sound of that word. They didn't know she'd seen that man's white, glaring flesh, the thick, black hair on his thighs. She understood exactly what that word meant. No one fantasized about rape and Jane was evil for even thinking such a thing. Her legs shook so hard that her knees tapped against each other. Her stomach rolled, sloshing the salad and vinaigrette she'd had for dinner. She touched her collarbone with one hand, willing the food to stay in her stomach. The wine glass slid out of her other hand and shattered around her feet.

"It's okay," said Kit. "I'll get you a new glass. Don't move." She climbed out of the tub and wrapped a towel around her hips.

"That's a horrible thing to say." Amy's voice was hoarse, her throat inflamed as if she'd already spewed out the bile that simmered in her belly.

Jane sipped her wine. "What else are we supposed to think? You can't stop talking about it. No one else thinks about it as much as you do."

"No one fantasizes about rape," murmured Rachel.

"Oh yes they do," said Jane.

"How do you know?" said Rachel.

"People have all kinds of bizarre fantasies. Rape happens to be Amy's. She secretly wonders what it would be like. It gets her adrenaline flowing, thinking about the loss of control. It makes perfect sense for someone as repressed as Amy. I'm guessing she thinks it's not ok to get excited about sex. Conjuring up rape scenes means she'd be overpowered, that she isn't a bad girl for wanting it, loving it."

The towel came loose and slipped off Amy's shoulders, down her back and onto the chair behind her. "Don't say that!" she cried.

Kit returned wearing sandals, carrying a wine glass and a hand-held vacuum cleaner. "Don't move." She went to work sucking up slivers of glass.

Amy stayed rooted to the spot in front of the chair.

"Sit down." Kit poured wine into the glass and handed it to Amy. "Have some wine, and take a deep breath."

Kit bent to pick up the vacuum cleaner. "Ow!" she cried. "Damn. I tweaked my back again." She straightened slowly.

"Come back in the water," said Jane. "It'll relax the muscles."

Kit nodded. "Maybe." Her voice was strained. "Let me put this away." She pressed her hand against her lower back and limped back around the edge of the pool. As she reached the sliding glass door, the phone rang. It echoed across the dark yard, bouncing off the water so the sound was deeper and louder than normal.

Amy took several large swallows of wine. She felt like smashing the glass against Jane's lips, slicing through that smirk. She lived an admirable life. She was a good mother; she dressed and acted like a classy woman, not someone asking to be raped. She had a lovely home and the best looking husband around, a man who respected her and valued her for things besides sex. Although right this minute, she couldn't think what those things might be.

Kit called out from the kitchen, "Rachel, Greg's on the phone. He tried your cell, but you didn't answer."

Rachel climbed out of the hot tub. Her breasts bulged out of her wet swimsuit. Amy looked away. Why didn't Rachel buy a larger size so she wasn't falling out of her suit into everyone's face? Amy picked up the bottle of Chardonnay and filled her glass. She leaned over the hot tub and poured more into Jane's glass. Maybe Jane would pass out and Kit would drag her out of the tub, call Peter to come get her. As she set the half empty bottle down, her hand shook so that the bottle rattled against the glass-topped table. Right next to it was a freshly uncorked bottle. She was drinking too much; they were all drinking too much.

Rachel pulled on her T-shirt. Her flip-flops slapped on the flagstone as she walked around the edge of the pool.

Now Amy was stuck out here alone with that bitch. She should get up and go home right now, but she didn't feel like leaving right when she was starting to enjoy the effects of Kit's delicious wine. The alcohol had deadened her limbs. And why should she leave anyway? Jane should leave. Kit should tell her those vicious comments were out of line. Besides, she wasn't in the mood to face Justin again. She still hadn't told him she'd seen him with Charlotte, and wasn't sure when, or how, to best bring up the subject. Clearly he was planning to keep it a secret.

Rachel reappeared near the palm trees. "I have to go home. I'm sorry."

"Don't say you're sorry," said Jane. The bubbling water muffled her voice. "Women say they're sorry too much. For nothing."

"Trent fell off his bike and he won't stop screaming. He wants me."

"You baby that boy," said Jane.

Amy wondered whether Jane was ever going to stop talking. She was always full of opinions, but tonight was worse than usual. Why couldn't she shut up? She must be drunk. The sky was darker now and Amy couldn't see Rachel's face. She wanted everyone to stop talking so she could sip her wine and relax. It relieved the shakiness in her hands. The alcohol threaded its way through her brain, numbing her until she was drifting, not thinking, trying to quiet all the words hammering inside her skull.

"He's only six," said Rachel. Her wet swimsuit had soaked through the front of her tee shirt. She struggled into her shorts and picked up her towel.

"I should go too," said Amy. She lifted her glass. Was it already empty?

"No. Don't leave," said Rachel. "I'll be back in less than twenty minutes. There's all that food. We haven't even touched it."

Trust Rachel to worry about the food instead of how Amy might be feeling. Instead of defending her, staying to be supportive, Rachel thought it was more important to run off to her needy son. Amy put her glass on the table and emptied the bottle into it.

Jane's eyes were closed as she sipped from her nearly empty glass.

Amy picked up the fresh bottle and filled Jane's glass. Without opening her eyes, Jane smiled. Her fingers squeaked on the damp glass.

"I'll be back. I promise." Rachel walked around the pool and went inside.

Amy pulled her towel over her legs. Her limbs were spaghetti-like. It was the same sensation she had all those years ago, standing outside the living room, hearing her mother whimper like that dog the neighbors tied on a leash that was only three feet long. She'd been too scared, too ashamed to move a muscle to help. Not that she could have helped. What would she have done? All the same, she should have done something. She never even did the one thing that might have helped afterwards – reveal his identity. Instead, over the weeks that followed, alongside the nightmares, understanding leaked into her conscious thoughts. It was a confused understanding, darkened by her father's insistence that her mother had brought it on herself. *There's no point in seeing a doctor. What's done is done*, he said. *Maybe now you'll stop dressing like a slut.* Her mother cried – all the time. *You used to like the way I dress.* He turned his back to her. *You weren't a mother then.* When she thought no one was listening, her mother began talking to herself. *It wasn't my fault,* she whispered. *What could I have done? If only I hadn't been home. If only Amy wasn't sick. If only I'd been a moment faster, told him to go away. It wasn't my fault.*

No decent woman fantasized about rape. Again, Amy felt the urge to smash the wine glass against Jane's face. No, the entire bottle. The glass would shatter, ripping at her sneering lips. Blood would flow into the water, making her shut up permanently. Amy never thought about sex. *Fantasized.* That wasn't something nice women did. Mothers filled their thoughts with plans for their children and caring for their homes.

All she could see when she forced open her eyes was the backlit blue of the swimming pool to her right. She closed her eyes again. The yard was silent except for the rumbling of the water in the hot tub. The world felt so quiet, a dream where voices were difficult to hear, buried under thick quilts, the voices of her father, her mother, the stabbing of Jane's accusation. She felt as if wet clay was plastered across her eyelids.

AMY TRIED TO open her eyes, tried to focus, but all she could see was that blue water and the light from the house. The giant, clammy leaf of the plant behind her brushed against her shoulder. She felt for the table and set her glass down. It was so light; it must be empty. She couldn't remember when she'd taken the last sip. Her hand was cramped, and letting go of the stem was a relief. She'd been pinching it too tightly. She tried to focus her eyes. Apparently Rachel wasn't coming back after all. And where was Kit? She pushed herself forward. Slowly she rose to her feet, keeping her fingers wrapped around the arms of the chair. The circulation had slowed in her lower legs. Her feet were cold and stiff. A wave of blackness passed behind her eyes and she sat back down for a moment. It finally dissipated and she stood, grabbed her dress off the back of the chair and pulled it over her head. As she slipped her feet into her sandals, she squinted at the hot tub.

Jane looked funny. Amy blinked, trying to clear her vision. Jane's arms were no longer draped along the edge of the tub. Instead, they rested gracefully just below the surface of the water. Her face was hidden. Her hair floated around her head, drifting across the milky white of her arms like seaweed. Amy gasped. She glanced at the back of the house. Where had Kit gone? She was supposed to be watching over her guests. What a rude hostess, abandoning them like this. Leave all the wine and a few plates of snacks and disappear? What was she doing? Was she even inside the house? Jane might need help and Kit was nowhere around. She was fairly certain Jane was unconscious, perhaps even something worse. Her heart raced, skipping beats, shuddering inside her chest as she sucked in air like her throat was a narrow straw. She leaned over the tub and poked her finger at Jane's shoulder. The flesh was warm, normal, whatever that meant, not squishy like a dead octopus as she'd imagined.

What was she supposed to do? Jane wasn't her responsibility. She'd told them not to drink wine in the hot tub. It wasn't safe. Something about hot water all over the body? The lack of oxygen in the blood? It really didn't matter, the problem was that Jane drank too much. She always had, and she seemed to have fallen under the water. It had nothing to do with Amy. She had enough problems with Justin and Charlotte. All her useless friends had drifted away. Some party. She grabbed her towel and walked past the vast, staring eye of the swimming pool. She picked up her purse and went around the side of the house to let herself out through the gate.

Chapter Thirty-one

RACHEL POURED A SECOND cup of coffee. She went into the family room and sat on the couch. Light poured in through the sliding glass doors. She unlocked the door and slid it open a few inches to let fresh air into the room. It was only eight in the morning and so far she hadn't heard the click of bedroom doors opening upstairs. She put her feet on the coffee table and picked up the Style section of the Sunday paper. Not returning to the hot tub party last night had been flakey, but by the time Trent settled down, she'd lost her desire to spend an evening with her friends. The conversation was already deteriorating when she'd left, and joining back in hadn't seemed worth the effort. She'd tried to call all of them – Amy's cell, Jane's cell, Kit's cell, and Kit's house phone. No one had answered. Maybe they were annoyed with her, disgusted that she'd caved to Trent's uncontrollable tears. Maybe they thought she'd spoiled the evening. Although, she was pretty sure Jane had managed to spoil the mood without any help from Rachel or Trent.

The doorbell rang. She heard Greg answer the door and then she heard a woman's voice. She carried her coffee into the foyer. The tile was cool on her bare feet. Greg turned. "Rachel. This is Officer Roberts – from the Sunnyvale police."

The coffee shivered in Rachel's cup. Even though the fear of being connected to the vandalism hovered at the base of her skull every day, she suddenly wondered how they knew. Or did they?

The officer held a leather case that contained a heavy-looking badge. "*Detective* Roberts." She had brown hair cut to her chin and dark brown eyes. "May I come in?"

"Of course." Greg stood back and held the door for her.

"Can we sit down? This should only take a few minutes."

"Sure." Greg gestured toward the living room.

Rachel took a deep breath. There was no need to panic. She would simply answer one question at a time. She followed Greg and the officer into the living room, pulled a coaster toward the edge of the coffee table and set her cup down. Had they found fingerprints after all? Someone must have seen them. She'd known it was a huge risk – people from surrounding homes cut through the school grounds all the time, walking their dogs, kids skateboarding, shooting baskets. She wanted a sip of coffee but was afraid her hand would shake if she picked up the mug. She sat on the love seat, facing the officer settled at the end of the couch.

"I have a few questions about the party you attended last night."

This wasn't about the vandalism? Rachel picked up her mug and cradled it between her hands. Why would they care about a moms' night out?

"You attended the party at Kit Shepherd's home last night?"

"Yes."

"What time did you arrive?"

"What's this about?" said Rachel.

"We'll get to that in a minute. What time did you arrive?"

"About seven."

"And who else was there?"

"Kit, of course. Amy Lewis. Jane Goodman."

"What time did you leave?"

"Why does it matter?"

"There's been a drowning."

"Drowning?" Rachel's stomach contracted. She put her mug on the coaster. It made a scraping sound and sat off-center, in danger of tipping over.

Greg leaned forward and centered the cup on the coaster. Rachel heard his breath, smooth and deep.

"Who? When?" she said.

Greg reached across the space between the sofa and the love seat. He patted her leg. "Calm down."

She stared at him. Why was he acting like it was normal to be sitting in the living room on a Sunday morning answering a police officer's questions?

"Ms. Goodman drowned last night. We think it was sometime between 8:30 and ten."

"How can that be? I don't understand. We were all there. She … I …"

Tears filled her eyes. Dead? Did the officer say dead? This couldn't be happening. Words spun through her mind but wouldn't form into sentences. Her tongue felt thick. Drowned?

"What time did you leave?"

"I don't know."

"What time did you arrive home?"

"I didn't notice. Greg called to tell me our son fell off his bike and he was …" She didn't want to tell this detective that their son was squalling like a two-year-old. "I planned to go back, but it took … I was tired. I tried to call Amy to tell her I wasn't coming back, but her cell was off. Or she didn't answer. That happens a lot, she puts it on vibrate and doesn't notice it. I called Kit, and Jane. No one answered." She should stop, she was babbling, she didn't even know what she was saying.

"Can you estimate what time you left? Nine? Ten?"

"Not ten. Maybe eight?" said Rachel. Greg offered no help at all. The officer stared at her. Suddenly, she was angry. Angry with Jane, for drowning, angry at Greg for being absolutely useless while this detective implied Rachel was guilty of something. Why did it matter what time she'd left? "Why are you asking me these questions?"

"It's routine. So you weren't at the party very long?" said the detective.

"No. I told you, my son needed me to come home."

The officer wrote on her notepad. Rachel couldn't help feeling as if the notes were comments on her life.

"When you left, were Ms. Lewis and Ms. Goodman alone in the backyard?"

The officer's questions sounded as if there was a specific goal. It seemed that she already had an opinion about what had happened, as if she was accusing Rachel, or her friends, of doing something wrong. It was a terrible accident. Did that mean the police were allowed to trample all over her thoughts, peek into her life, and write down what she said?

"Amy wasn't in the hot tub."

"But the two women were alone in the backyard, correct?"

"I suppose. When I left, Kit went back outside."

"How do you know Ms. Shepherd went back out to the hot tub?"

"Why wouldn't she? It was her party."

"Ms. Shepherd experienced a severe back spasm after cleaning up some broken glass," said Detective Roberts. "She took a muscle relaxant and went into her bedroom to lie down. She fell asleep."

The room was quiet. Greg's breathing roared against her eardrums. Was the detective suggesting that Amy had something to do with Jane's drowning? Frail Amy? And Jane so muscular, an athlete? She gasped. A thought whispered at the edge of her mind. Had she actually considered the possibility of Amy holding Jane under the water? It was the detective's tone of voice. Her unemotional expression, the dull quality of her questions managed to eliminate any room to explain normal behavior.

"Why did you gasp?" said Detective Roberts.

"I didn't," said Rachel.

"Yes you did," said Greg.

She looked at him. He raised his left eyebrow, waiting for her answer. Both of them stared at her as if they were trying to peer through her forehead, wanting to pluck out her thoughts against her will. How could she think about anything except the fact that her friend was dead, lying on a cold table somewhere? This couldn't be happening.

"How many drinks did you have?" said the detective.

"A glass of wine. I don't think I finished it."

"And what about Ms. Lewis?"

"A glass or two."

"Can you be more specific?"

"I didn't notice," said Rachel.

"But it was more than one glass? While you were there?"

"I'm not sure."

"And Ms. Goodman?"

"I don't know."

"More than one?"

"Yes."

"Two? Three?"

"I don't count how many glasses of wine my friends drink," said Rachel.

"Did the two women argue?"

"What two women?"

"Come on, Rachel," said Greg. "You know what she means. Amy and Jane."

The detective was trying to make her friends look like bad people, trying to blame someone, anyone, for a terrible accident. She couldn't believe Jane was really gone. Her poor children.

Tears blurred the detective's face. It couldn't be true. Jane was a good swimmer. How could she drown? The water wasn't even over her shoulders, unless she passed out."Did Ms. Lewis and Ms. Goodman have an argument?"

"I don't understand why it matters what we talked about," said Rachel.

"Please answer the question," said the detective.

"They're always arguing. It wasn't anything different than usual."

The detective let out her breath as if she was getting impatient. "So they argued. What was it about?"

"We were talking about the rapes."

"What did they actually argue about?"

"They were saying Amy is obsessed with it. With the rapes."

"Is that all?"

The detective acted as if she knew more. Surely Kit hadn't told her the awful thing Jane said, claiming Amy fantasized about rape. Rachel wasn't going to betray her best friend by repeating those malicious words, even if Kit already had. Even if that made it seem like she was lying. The detective could stare down her nose and scribble in her book all she wanted. Rachel wasn't saying another word. It was a horrible, tragic accident. Asking all these questions wouldn't bring Jane back to life. Tears dribbled across her cheeks. She was too young to have a friend die. "Yes. That's all," she said.

The detective stood. She closed her notebook and shoved it into the pocket of her slacks. She pulled a business card out of her shirt pocket and handed it to Rachel. "I'm sure you're in shock right now. If you think of anything, or remember more details about the argument, please call me. Thank you for your time." She left without waiting for Greg to show her to the door.

Rachel slumped in the love seat. Tears washed down her cheeks.

"You weren't very cooperative," said Greg.

"I don't want to talk to you. My friend is dead. And you joined right in, acting as if one of us must have done something wrong."

"You can't avoid her questions."

She glared at him.

"Why were you so evasive?" said Greg.

"It's none of her business."

"If someone is dead, it is her business."

"Someone?" She sat up straight. "That someone is Jane. And it's a terrible accident. That detective is acting as if it was our fault."

"She's just doing her job."

Rachel's lips quivered. She pressed her fist against her mouth to hide her contorted features. He wasn't even trying to understand. From the cop's point of view, women didn't accidentally drown in hot tubs. Either they drank too much, didn't pay attention, or worse. The questions about an argument meant the police hoped to blame someone for losing control. "Jane is dead, and all she cared about is how much wine we drank."

"Do you know something you're not saying?" said Greg.

"No." She stood. "How can you even think that, much less ask?"

"If Amy did anything out of line, I hope you're not protecting her."

She grabbed the coffee cup off the table. Coffee splashed at her face, down her arm and onto the carpet. She hurled the mug into the front hallway. It shattered on the tile.

"What's wrong with you?" He grabbed her wrist.

Rachel yanked her arm out of his grasp. "I don't know what you're trying to say about Amy, but I don't like it."

"Calm down. You refused to give straight answers to simple questions. It sounded like you're hiding something. For all you know, this could be a murder investigation."

"Murder? That's ridiculous."

"I want you to be careful. If she had something to do with Jane's death, it's not just about you and Amy. It affects our whole family."

Chapter Thirty-two

THE DOORBELL CHIMED. Amy stood in the living room, unsure what she should do, trying to suppress the rush of fear. Who would be at the front door at quarter to nine on a Sunday morning? At least she had the gun tucked away now in her spare room. But would it keep her safe? The only sure way to protect her family was to move away, like Kit. That would solve two problems, leaving the rapist behind and being rid of Charlotte. But it wasn't fair that she should be forced to move, uprooting Alice and Amanda, tearing them away from their friends, their soccer team. And she adored this house. She and Justin had shopped for ages for a house in which they could raise their children. Amy had been pregnant, trying not to worry about the enormity of giving birth to twins. The minute she had stepped into the cream tiled foyer and looked up to the second floor, she had known this was her home.

The bell chimed again. Justin was home. Nothing could happen to her.

It had been a strange morning so far. She felt somewhat foggy about last night. She wasn't really sure what had happened with Jane. Eventually Kit must have gone out to check on her guests, if only to pour more wine. It was so irresponsible, supplying all that wine without any concern for their safety. If something had happened to Jane, wouldn't Kit have called? Amy had practiced in the bathroom last night, whispering shocked-sounding phrases to the mirror. The less said the better – that had been her conclusion. Why hadn't Kit called?

She poked her finger into the opening between the drapes. A woman stood at the edge of the porch. She wore a light blue shirt and gray slacks. She pulled back the cuff of her sleeve and looked at her wristwatch. Amy walked through the dining room to the kitchen and sat at the table.

"Amy?" Justin's voice was faint from the upstairs hall.

If she remained seated, he would come hopping down the stairs to answer the door. Sure enough, the bell chimed a third time and his feet thumped on each step. The front door opened. She heard his voice but couldn't make out the words. Then he thudded through the dining room and in to the kitchen.

"There's a police detective here. She wants to ask you some questions about Kit's party."

"Can't you make her go away?" Amy folded her hands and stared at her nails, the red stark against her pale skin.

"Aren't you curious?" he said.

Amy was not curious. She had a pretty good idea that a police officer at the door meant that Jane was dead. She pushed out her chair. There must be a way to get rid of her, but Justin wasn't going to help. Amy's mind was empty and quiet, as if it was filled with icy water. She followed him through the dining room. The detective was seated on the sofa. Amy stopped at the edge of the living room. Justin walked into the room and sat in the wingback chair.

The detective turned. "Please have a seat Ms. Lewis. I'm Detective Roberts."

This woman was telling her to have a seat in her own living room? Amy straightened her shoulders and took a small step through the archway into the living room. "I can answer the questions from here."

The detective looked at Justin.

"Just sit down. Let's get this over with," he said.

Amy trudged into the living room. She squeezed herself onto Justin's chair so that one hip rested on his lap.

The detective frowned. "I have a few questions about the party you attended last night at the Shepherd residence."

"What's wrong?" said Justin.

"Jane Goodman drowned in the Shepherds' hot tub. We're asking a few routine questions."

Amy widened her eyes and parted her lips. She leaned back against Justin. "How awful to have someone drown in your pool. Poor Kit."

The detective stared at her.

"That's so terrible," said Amy. "I wonder why Kit didn't call me."

"We asked her not to."

That couldn't be good. What had Kit said? It wasn't as if Amy was to blame. Jane was the one at fault – she drank too much. She was irresponsible. So was Kit, for that matter, abandoning her guests when the party was just getting started. What could Amy have done? Tried to drag a sopping wet woman out of the water? Jane outweighed her by at least forty pounds. And what would that have accomplished? She didn't know anything about CPR.

"What time did you arrive at the party?"

"I don't remember."

"An estimate is fine, for now," said Detective Roberts.

"I really don't remember."

"I understand the party was scheduled for seven. Did you arrive before that?"

"I don't remember."

"Ms. Shepherd said you arrived around seven-fifteen."

"Then why are you asking? If Kit told you seven-fifteen, that must be right."

"And what time did you leave? Approximately?"

"I don't know. I didn't wear my watch."

"Did you go directly home?"

"Yes."

"Then what time did you arrive home?"

"I didn't look at the clock."

The detective pursed her lips. "Approximately."

"If she didn't notice, she didn't notice," said Justin.

Amy leaned harder into his shoulder.

The detective looked at Justin. "Do you recall what time she arrived back home?"

"I was asleep. I fell asleep reading about eight-thirty, I think."

"So you didn't arrive home until after eight-thirty." The detective scribbled on her pad. "Who else was at the party when you left?"

"I'm not sure."

Detective Roberts tapped the pen against her thigh.

"My wife didn't even know anything was wrong, why does she need to answer all these questions?"

"We're talking to everyone who was at the Shepherd home. Who else was there when you left, Ms. Lewis?"

"I'm sorry I can't remember every detail. I didn't pay that much attention." Amy's hips ached from being pressed between the arm of the chair and Justin's legs. Her answers sounded weak, as if she wasn't very bright. On the other hand, they also sounded logical – she never went to the party thinking she would have to account for every minute, talk to the police about what she'd done all evening. Never in her life would she have dreamt a police detective would be seated on her royal blue sofa, practically accusing her of murder.

"Knowing who was at the house when you left is not a lot of detail. Let's make it easier – was Kit Shepherd there?"

"She must have been."

"Did you see Ms. Shepherd when you left?"

Amy closed her eyes. The evening was a complete blur. She wasn't even sure she'd actually seen Jane floating in the hot tub. It was almost unbelievable to think that Jane might have died right in front of her. The wine and the broken glass all blurred together into a hazy dream. Unclear images flickered through her head, the backlit pool, bright blue in the darkness like a giant staring eye, the rumbling of the hot tub, the huge tropical plants. Rachel's bathing suit that didn't adequately cover her body, Jane's mocking laugh and her outright glee once she hit on the disgusting lie that Amy fantasized about being raped. To think that she, that anyone, would voluntarily conjure up the imagined experience of the ultimate violation was beyond comprehension. All she could remember was that the evening ended badly. Jane might have been dead, she didn't know that for sure, and even if she did, it had nothing to do with her. It didn't seem fair that she should have to remember all the details. She opened her eyes. "Did you talk to Rachel already?"

"We're questioning everyone who was there."

"Was Ms. Shepherd in the hot tub when you left her home?"

"I don't understand why you're asking me if you already *questioned* Kit."

Justin moved out from beneath Amy's hip. His *Blackberry*, attached to his belt, scraped against her thigh. He stood. "What are you trying to get at here?"

"When there's a suspicious death, we question everyone who was there. Was Ms. Shepherd outside in the pool area?"

"I don't remember."

"Ms. Lewis, try to think. Was Ms. Matthews still at the party when you left?"

"I don't know. They might have gone in the house for awhile."

"Who went into the house?" said the detective.

Amy flapped her hand near her ear. "I don't understand why any of this matters."

"It matters because a young woman died. We need to establish a timeline."

"Why?" said Amy.

Justin shoved his hands in his pockets. "That's a fair question."

His hair flopped over his brow as he turned his head. Amy had the sudden urge to slide her fingers through it, pushing it out of his eyes. He was so protective of her, she wanted to be equally caring toward him, to stop taking him for granted. "It sounds to me like everyone left the party and Jane passed out in the hot tub," she said.

"How much did Ms. Goodman have to drink?" said Detective Roberts.

Amy settled back into the chair and curled her feet up under her. "I can't remember all these details."

"Were you drinking?"

"I had some wine."

"How many glasses?"

"I'm not supposed to drink much with my medication." The minute she said it, she knew it was a mistake. She nibbled at her lip, scraping the lipstick with her teeth.

"What are you taking?"

"I don't think that's important," said Justin.

The detective stood and placed a business card on the coffee table. "I'll be contacting you again. Perhaps your memory will refresh itself."

"I didn't think I would have the police asking me questions. I didn't pay attention to every minute-to-minute thing that happened. You can't expect me to remember."

"Thank you for your time," said Detective Roberts. She went in to the foyer, opened the front door and walked out, pulling it shut behind her.

"Well that was rude," said Amy.

Justin flopped on the sofa. He put his bare feet on the edge of the table. "Why can't you remember anything?"

"Are you going to question me now?" She stared at his feet. His bare skin would leave smudges on the table.

"It sounds like you can't remember anything," said Justin.

"I didn't know I'd have to. Do you remember every detail of every single day?"

"I remember what time I leave places and who else was there."

"I don't see why it's any of her business. This is a nice neighborhood. It's yucky having the police asking questions. Do they think one of us killed her or something?"

"I'm sure they don't think anyone killed her, but you should try harder to remember what happened. She's not going to stop asking questions until she's satisfied."

It made no sense, a man was out there raping women but the police were wasting energy trying to find out who was at a hot tub party? Just because Jane got drunk and passed out? They should be talking to Peter, trying to find out how much she drank on a regular basis. "It's dangerous to drink alcohol in a hot tub," said Amy. "I told her that, but Jane was too stubborn to listen. She thought she was smarter than me. Well maybe she wasn't as smart as she thought."

"That's the kind of thing you should not be saying," said Justin.

"It's the truth." Amy rubbed her knees. She spread her fingers across her leg. Her fingernails needed touching up, the chlorine in the hot tub had dulled them. The police could ask all the questions they wanted, she was not going to let them blame her for Jane's death.

Chapter Thirty-three

JANE'S FUNERAL WAS HELD in a large church that boasted a towering A-frame ceiling supported by exposed beams. Abstract chunks of stained glass formed a floor to rafters window at the front. Rachel marveled at how a building with a modern design still managed to create a sense of awe that the universe was ancient and filled with unanswered questions. It must be the sheer size that created the quiet air of mystery.

Trent and Sara huddled close to Greg's side while Rachel walked a few feet behind as they made their way down the side aisle. None of the mourners walked down the center aisle where they would be forced to come face-to-face with that enormous, glossy wood box edged with gold handles.

When Greg reached a half-empty pew near the front, he stepped to the side to let Rachel go first. She eased onto the long wooden bench. She scooted as far down as she could, wanting to keep space between her and Greg. It felt as if a wall of thick glass had slid between them. She couldn't sort out where grief for Jane stopped and grief for her marriage began.

Beyond her feelings of sorrow was a trickle of fear that Amy had watched Jane die and done nothing to help. There had to be a logical explanation, but the murmuring thought refused to leave her alone. She closed her eyes. All she had to do was center her mind on Jane's family – Peter, and Dana and her brothers. If she watched the backs of their heads, averted her eyes from that box, she'd be fine. She prayed Amy and Justin would sit behind her. She didn't want to think about Amy at all, didn't want to be required to watch her during the service. She needed to get through the next hour. Later, she would think about the rest.

She crossed her legs, folded her arms around her ribs, then unfolded them because it seemed too defensive. Trying to calm her mind wasn't working. She couldn't take her eyes off the coffin. Her thoughts raced in a circle, replaying the part of the evening she'd witnessed, trying to create a scenario that left Amy blameless. Destroying photographs, complaining that she wanted to be rid of a woman who seemed to be flirting with her husband – those things were minor. Allowing a woman to drown while you sat in a chair and did nothing was beyond horrifying. Amy was a moral woman. She would never ... unless she'd had too much to drink? Unless Jane had said something even worse than those vicious, degrading words, *I think you have a rape fantasy.* Unless those seven words were enough.

People filtered into the church without speaking, as if all the breath was sucked from their lungs the moment they passed through the open doors at the back of the sanctuary. High heels and men's dress shoes clicked on the concrete floor. Soon every pew was filled, people pressing closer together to make room for more.

The service passed in a blur of sound. Piano music, an interlude from a harpist, voices murmuring and praising Jane, sobs that were quickly muffled. There was an underlying air of outrage. A young mother, not even forty years old wasn't supposed to die. Yet, the eulogists kept their words controlled. They said nice things that ended up sounding as if they were saying nothing at all. They mentioned awards and promotions at work, anecdotes from family camping trips, charming stories about Jane's devotion to her children and her love for Peter. One or two spoke about her large group of friends. A woman's life summed up in her dedication to her family and her job. Was that it? Life boiled down to nothing but a few bland stories? Rachel wondered whether her own life was that unremarkable. And right now, she felt as alone as Jane in that box. She uncrossed her legs. It was difficult to think of Jane's body inside the coffin, confined to a space that barely provided enough room to wriggle her hips.

After the service, a man wheeled the coffin up the center aisle. The pallbearers walked helplessly at the sides. By the time the crowd filtered out, the back door of the hearse was closed, the windows shaded by dark curtains. Only Jane's family was going to the grave. Jane's friends and neighbors would nibble tiny sandwiches in the church social hall until the family returned.

Outside in the heat, Rachel immediately felt damp in her navy blue dress and jacket. Her pantyhose dug into her waist and stuck to her thighs. The sun beat down on her head. Her hair acted like a layer of insulation, shielding her neck and shoulders from the slightest breeze. She grabbed her hair, twisted it and lifted it to the crown of her head. After a few minutes her arm grew tired and she let go. She wished she could take off her jacket, but the dress was too tight around her arms. She moved out of the crowd and into the shade under a large oak tree at the edge of a grassy area. At the far end of the complex, Greg and Trent were walking around the rose garden. Sara had gone off with Kit's daughter, Renee. She glanced at the open doors of the social hall and saw Amy headed in her direction. Amy must have sent the twins to school rather than bringing them to the funeral. When Amy reached her side she patted Rachel's arm. Her nails were freshly painted – dusty rose. Her large diamond was turned to the side, resting on her pinky finger.

"That was painful, wasn't it?" said Amy.

Rachel pushed Amy's fingers off her arm. They slid away like vines trailing across the sleeve of her jacket.

"You'd think she was the perfect woman, with all those stories of motherhood and her fabulous career."

"Don't," said Rachel. "She's dead and it's not right to criticize her. Of course everyone focused on the best parts of her life. That's how it should be."

"I'm just saying, she could be a real bitch sometimes. And she drank too much."

"Stop it," said Rachel.

"What are you so grouchy about?"

Most of Amy's face was hidden behind her sunglasses, making it impossible to read her expression.

"Our friend is dead. I'm ..." Rachel didn't even know what to call it. She shouldn't have to explain grief.

"We're all upset. But you seem like you're angry with me. It wasn't my fault," said Amy.

"No one said it was your fault." A shiver passed through Rachel's shoulders. She didn't want to talk about what had happened. All she wanted to do was smile at a few acquaintances and then get home and out of her stifling dress and do something to take her mind off the feeling that her life was being sucked down the drain. She wanted Greg to comfort her, to apologize for the way he'd abandoned her when that detective was asking questions, hinting at something Rachel still couldn't identify.

"Jane drinks too much – *drank* too much. We were always commenting on it," said Amy.

"I wonder how Dana and the boys are doing. Do they understand?" said Rachel.

Amy turned to look across the parking lot. Her expression was hidden by the shade and the angle of her head. "Did that police officer talk to you?" she said.

The remains of her meager breakfast – a slice of toast – lurched in Rachel's stomach. Amy was definitely worried about something. There was no other explanation for her fixation on the events of Jane's death rather than the loss of a friend. "A detective asked a few questions."

"What did you say?"

"I told her what time I arrived and when I left, stuff like that."

"Did you tell her I was still there when you left?" said Amy.

"I think I said I wasn't sure."

"Good."

"What do you mean, *good?*"

"It was obviously an accident and there's no need for the police to be snooping around," said Amy. "Have you talked to Kit?"

Rachel shook her head. "I tried to call but she hasn't called me back."

"I wonder when they found her, what she told the police," said Amy.

"What time did you leave Kit's house?" Rachel's voice trembled. It wasn't right to be talking about this here, Jane's body just a few yards away, her family stunned and bereft, but she had to know.

"Are you going to be suspicious too?"

"I'm just asking. It seems strange."

"What seems strange?"

She studied Amy's face. A heavy coat of liquid foundation stretched across her jaw. Her lips were creamy with the same dusty rose as her fingernails. Was it her imagination that Amy's makeup had been applied with a heavier hand these past few weeks? If she scratched Amy's face, she'd come away with a clump of goo stuffed behind her fingernail. She didn't remember noticing that before. She sighed. Why was she tiptoeing around the subject? Wondering what Amy knew, where she'd been. Questions had tormented her for three days. She might as well say it. No one was paying attention to them, huddled away from the rest of the crowd. "It's strange that Jane would stay in the hot tub after all of us left. Why would she do that?"

"How should I know?" Amy took a few steps back. The narrow heel of her patent leather shoe caught on the edge of the concrete and her ankle turned at an awkward angle. She regained her balance and folded her arms across the front of her black silk jacket.

"It doesn't make sense," said Rachel.

"Ask Kit."

"Did Kit come back outside after I left?" She couldn't back down now. She had to know. "Were you there when Jane passed out?"

"Why would you ask me that?" Amy turned and tiptoed through the border of wood chips that separated the grassy area from the parking lot. When she reached the blacktop she walked quickly to where Justin stood talking to Jane's neighbors.

Rachel slumped against the tree. A branch snagged at the top of her hair. She tried to disentangle herself, but it grabbed more firmly and her hair seemed to intentionally wrap itself around the twigs. Tears burned in her eyes as she struggled without being able to see what she was fighting against.

***

AMY STOOD CLOSE to Justin. She pressed her shoulder against his arm, forcing herself not to look across the parking lot at Rachel. It had startled her that Rachel was so bold – accusing her of sitting near the hot tub, doing nothing while Jane slipped to her death. Rachel skirted around most subjects, downplayed her thoughts with suggestions and hints rather than coming right out and asking direct questions. Rachel and the police acted like Amy's whereabouts made a difference. The truth was, Jane drank at least five enormous glasses of that deliciously buttery Chardonnay while sitting in a tub of steaming water. Everyone knew hot water and alcohol made a deadly combination. It wasn't her fault, and she resented all the questions, hinting she was to blame.

The hearse still hadn't left for the cemetery. It was difficult to think someone her own age was lying inside. Jane would never speak another word. Nothing seemed real. It was almost impossible to believe that a friend, someone she'd spent countless hours with, no longer existed. She kept her gaze fixed on the hearse, ignoring the conversation around her, something about property taxes. The bright sun and the smell of mowed grass flooded her senses. A group of people stood on the steps of the church, staring at the sleek black car with the swollen back end, designed to contain its alarming cargo. Standing apart from the others, near the open church doors, was Charlotte. What was she doing here? For once, she wore clothes that looked somewhat normal, a longish skirt and sandals. Her hair was in the same style as always, spiky and clotted with gel at the dark tips, and Amy was certain the tiny diamond was still stabbed into the side of her nostril. She wore a short black jacket over her tee shirt and her taunting breasts were covered, for the moment.

Amy slipped her arm out of the crook of Justin's arm. She strode across the pavement as fast as her high heels would allow. She teetered at the edge of the step below Charlotte. "Why are you here?" said Amy. "Jane wasn't a friend of yours."

Charlotte looked down at her. She wasn't wearing sunglasses and she squinted into the glare. She turned her head away, looking past Amy.

"I asked you a question," said Amy.

"Why do you have to be the center of attention? One of your friends is dead."

"Exactly. Jane was a close friend of mine. You hardly knew her, so why are you here, pretending to be sad?"

"I'm not pretending anything. Please leave me alone."

"It's rude. Gawking at her death. Haven't you figured out that you don't belong?"

Charlotte looked at her but said nothing.

"This is a nice community," said Amy. "We don't need ex cons or someone dressed like a ..." She flapped her hand near her jaw. "...trying to lure men away from their wives."

"I have no interest in any of the men around here," said Charlotte.

Amy didn't believe that for a minute. It simply proved Charlotte had not only been flirting with Justin, she was a liar. Amy had seen them cuddling over their wine, what further proof was needed? In the few minutes she'd been talking to Charlotte, the sun had shifted and the building cast its shadow over both of them. The air was suddenly cooler. "Too bad it's not you in that coffin," said Amy.

From the corner of her eye, Amy saw Kit separate herself from a group of other moms from Spruce. She walked along the same step on which Amy stood and stopped a few feet away. She offered a gentle smile to Charlotte.

"So awful," said Charlotte.

Kit nodded.

When was Kit going to stop cooing with Charlotte? There were some questions she needed to answer, but Amy wasn't about to ask them with Charlotte eavesdropping. Amy had hoped the remark about the coffin would force her to leave, but Charlotte was a very stubborn woman. She'd made it clear in so many ways that she wasn't easily intimidated. Tell her she didn't fit in, destroy her photography, make sure her daughter wasn't invited over to your home, and all she did was turn those steely gray eyes on you.

Amy looked at Kit. "Are they having a get-together at the Goodman's for close friends, or is this it?" She waved her arm in the direction of the church hall.

Kit put her hand on Charlotte's arm. "Will you excuse us? I need to talk to Amy."

"I imagine you do," said Charlotte.

Amy took a step down. It was difficult moving down and backwards in heels, but she was no longer sure she wanted to ask Kit anything. Kit was likely to turn the conversation into an interrogation, just like Rachel had.

"I should get going." Charlotte took the steps two at a time.

Kit's face was pale beneath her sunglasses; even her lips were washed of color, hardly moving as she spoke. "Were you there when Jane drowned?" said Kit.

Amy sucked in a puff of air.

"Don't act surprised," said Kit.

"I could ask you the same question," said Amy.

"I had a back spasm when I was cleaning up the glass. I thought if I took a muscle relaxant and laid down for a few minutes, I'd be ok."

"And?"

"I fell asleep. I come outside to find you gone and Jane dead in my hot tub. It was the worst night of my life."

"What did you tell the police?"

"That I think you were sitting by the hot tub the whole time. I think you kept pouring wine for Jane when you knew she'd had too much to drink already. And I think it's your fault she's dead."

"It's not. Don't make it sound like you know what happened. You were asleep."

"I'm not going to protect you." Kit turned and hurried down the steps. She walked across the blacktop and swooped past Aaron and her children. They followed her without hesitation, like a flock of birds migrating to a warmer climate.

Chapter Thirty-four

RACHEL STOOD OUTSIDE AMY'S front door, clutching a ceramic figurine in her left hand – a peace offering for her lack of trust. It had been over a week since she'd talked to Amy. Every day since Jane's funeral, Rachel had been seated alone at the picnic table where she and her friends used to wait for their children. Kit was probably busy packing. Amy had started parking outside the school office, remaining in her car until Alice and Amanda were out of school.

She pressed the bell again. The figurine was of a girl sitting on a small patch of sand holding a bucket and shovel. The girl had wavy red hair that reminded Rachel of Amy's. The clerk had tied a purple helium-filled balloon to the handle of the ceramic bucket. The figurine made her think of innocence. It made her feel that it was possible to forget Jane's death, the police, the funeral, and the vandalism. It helped her forget that she'd been so disloyal, imagining Amy sitting in a patio chair, doing nothing while she watched her friend drown. It wasn't murder. It was an act worse than murder, in some ways. Murder happened in a fit of rage. Sitting idly on the sidelines observing someone's death meant there was nothing but a dead heart.

The drapes on the living room window hadn't moved. Amy would peer out to see who was on the porch; she wouldn't rely on the tiny peephole in the door. She would want a full body view. Had there been a flicker of movement? Rachel couldn't be sure. She should have phoned before she came over. She knocked and called out, "Hi, Amy. It's me." She'd taken her eyes off the front window when she knocked and now she wasn't sure whether Amy had peeked out or not. She knocked again, more firmly.

The bolt slid open. Amy opened the door a few inches. "What do you want?"

"To apologize. To tell you I'm sorry for what I said at the funeral. I was so . . ."

Amy shoved her hand through the small opening, her palm facing Rachel. "Stop right there. What you said was inexcusable."

"I know. And I'm so sorry." If Amy would open the door, they could talk, put everything back the way it had been before. "Can I come in for a few minutes?"

Amy sighed. "I was about to pour a glass of wine. Do you want one?"

Wine was the last thing she wanted. It evoked the dizziness she'd felt in the steaming tub after a single glass. She didn't know if she could ever drink wine again without feeling that spacey sensation, without thinking of Jane, but if she refused Amy's offering, the door might close in her face. "Sure. That sounds nice."

Amy pulled open the door.

Rachel squeezed through the narrow space. "This is for you." She held out the ceramic girl. The balloon bobbed against her forehead. She brushed it away.

"Why?" said Amy.

"It made me think of you. She looks like I imagine you looked as a little girl."

Amy stepped behind her, shut the door and turned the lock. "I never went to the beach when I was a child."

"You don't want it?" said Rachel.

"You can put it on the dining room table."

Rachel wanted to hurl the figurine at the tile floor. "Well it reminded me of you. Sorry if you don't like it."

"I didn't say I don't like it. I just said I never went to the beach," said Amy.

"I wanted you to know how terribly sorry I am for asking you all those insulting questions." She followed Amy through the dining room, stopping to place the figurine on the table. The balloon tapped against the chandelier.

In the kitchen Amy took a bottle of Chardonnay out of the refrigerator and pulled out the cork that was inserted halfway into the top of the bottle. She stood on her toes to take a glass out of the cabinet and put it next to the one already on the counter. Wine gurgled into the glasses. She handed one to Rachel and raised her own. "Cheers." Without waiting for Rachel to respond, she took a long swallow.

Rachel took a small sip. The wine tasted sharp, not like Kit's buttery Chardonnay. There was a roaring in her ears, like the rumbling sound of the hot tub. She took another sip, hoping more would push all the uncomfortable thoughts to the back of her mind. She'd felt lost this past week without Amy's constant chatter. The strength of Amy's opinions and the sheer force of her presence had always made Rachel feel like she had more substance. Without Amy, she'd rattled around her life, unsure whether she really existed.

Amy led the way into the family room adjacent to the kitchen. "I want to show you something," she said.

Rachel settled into the chair near the French doors. The drapes were closed. The room was so dark she could hardly see Amy's face. "Can we open the drapes?"

"I like them closed."

Rachel sipped her wine then held the glass on her knee. She felt like Amy's slave, following her around, offering an unwanted gift, obeying her commands. But there was no choice. She had to hang on to her one remaining friend. She'd waited her entire life to find close friends. She wasn't going to throw that away over a misunderstanding fed by an over-zealous police detective. She would stick it out, show more sympathy for Amy's fears. Anyone who had seen her mother raped, who knew the man that did it, and felt forced to keep a secret like that through her entire life would be damaged. Did Amy ever wonder if that secret had contributed to her mother's suicide? Then to be accused of fantasizing about rape, and have her best friend suggest that she sat by and watched a woman drown – the pain would be unbearable.

Amy picked up her purse off the coffee table. It was much larger than the purses she normally carried, made of soft camel-colored leather.

"Is that new?"

Amy nodded. "I had to get something bigger than usual."

Rachel sipped more wine. The sudden infusion of alcohol softened her anxiety.

Amy placed her glass on a coaster and reached into the purse.

Rachel leaned forward.

Amy pulled out her hand and turned it over. Lying in her palm was a small gun. "Isn't it cute? Did you know they made guns this small?"

Rachel flopped back in her chair. Wine sloshed out of her glass and landed in droplets on her beige cotton shirt. The gun reached from the base of Amy's wrist to an inch or two past the end of her fingertips. It was flat, silver with a black handle. "Where did you get a gun? Put it away," said Rachel.

"I know how to use it. My father bought it for me when I moved into my own apartment. A long time ago, before I was married to Justin."

"Why do you need a gun?" Rachel set her glass on the strip of hardwood floor between the large area rug and the French doors.

"You know why."

"No, I don't." Rachel tried not to picture all the things that could go wrong. The twins getting their hands on it, Amy accidentally shooting herself, or freaking out over a cat using her yard as a litter box.

"Because of what happened to Jane."

"What does Jane have to do with this?"

"We all assume she drank too much and passed out. But how do we know someone didn't come into the yard and hold her under the water?"

"I don't think that's what happened," said Rachel.

"But we don't know, do we?" said Amy.

"You're safe here." She could tell by the pinched skin around Amy's lips that was the wrong thing to say. "You could get a security system."

"What about when I have to leave the house? I can't even take out the trash without feeling scared."

"Don't you think you might be over-reacting a little?"

Amy shoved the gun into her purse. "I'm tired of everyone thinking I'm over-reacting. Nothing bad is going to happen to me, or my family. It's my job to keep them safe."

She looked so frail, incapable of keeping anyone safe. Rachel wanted to laugh. She also wanted to cry. "What if you hurt yourself? Or shoot someone accidentally? Do you even know how to aim?"

"I already told you. Plus, I found a shooting range. I've been practicing almost every day."

"What did Justin say?"

"I want to be safe. And this is the only way." She zipped her purse closed.

"You leave it sitting on the coffee table? What if Alice or Amanda gets her hands on it?"

"They never touch my things without permission."

Rachel's tongue swelled against the roof of her mouth. Right. No child ever did anything without asking permission.

The glassy look in Amy's eyes told Rachel there was nothing more to say.

"Relax. Drink your wine," said Amy.

"I shouldn't have any more. I didn't eat lunch, so I'm kind of light-headed," said Rachel.

Amy took a long swallow of her wine. Her glass was almost empty.

Rachel stood up. Her knees trembled, either from the alcohol, or standing up too fast.

"If you don't want it, I'll take the rest of your wine." Amy picked up Rachel's glass off the floor and poured the wine into her own.

"I should go. I need to get dinner started," said Rachel.

Amy followed her to the front door, sipping wine with each step. Rachel turned the deadbolt. She stepped into the sharp afternoon light that hit the porch as the sun moved toward the tops of the houses across the street. She turned to face Amy. "I'm worried about you."

"I'm fine. You should be worried about yourself. Walking around believing this is the safest community in the world."

Rachel nodded. Tears boiled behind her eyelids.

Amy lifted her wine glass as if she was making a toast and shut the door.

Rachel turned and walked down the path to the sidewalk. Her feet felt thick and slightly numb. She got into the car, rested her forearms on the steering wheel, and closed her eyes. Images of Amy flashed across the backs of her eyelids – Amy smashing the display cases, sitting alone in the dark beside Kit's hot tub, tripping around her house with a glass of wine in one hand and a gun in the other.

Chapter Thirty-five

CHARLOTTE FELT STRANGE MEETING Justin and his friend at the office complex. She still couldn't get a sense of whether Justin was motivated by guilt or admiration for her work. It seemed as if he suspected Amy was involved in the vandalism, but had she actually confessed? Charlotte was almost certain Amy knew nothing about Justin's effort to promote her photography. Experiencing Amy's subtle and not-so-subtle assaults, yet enjoying talking to this man who was so excited about the possibilities for expanding her potential audience, made Charlotte feel as if she was living in two worlds – one somewhat frightening, and the other a thrilling step forward in her career.

The building complex where she'd arranged to meet him consisted of three towers; six stories each. It was built on landfill near the southwest side of San Francisco bay. Blue tinted glass shimmered in the late morning sun. She opened the lobby door and was bathed in a draft of climate-controlled air. Justin stood near the receptionist's desk. As Charlotte extended her hand, he reached past it and wrapped his arms around her in a light hug.

"How are you?" he said. "Sorry I wasn't able to talk to you at the funeral."

As she returned his hug, she felt his spine, prominent through the fabric of his dress shirt. It startled her and she pulled away quickly. "It doesn't seem real. It's so hard to believe someone could drown in a hot tub," she said.

He shook his head. "They said her blood alcohol was .16%."

"How did that happen?"

"Her husband said she'd gone out for drinks with a friend from work before she went to Kit's. Then she got in the hot tub and kept drinking. Apparently the combination of hot water and alcohol can really shoot up your body temp."

"Still..." said Charlotte.

"I know. You'd think someone would have noticed."

She didn't say anything. It was difficult, impossible really, to believe the other women had suddenly walked out and Jane had remained in the hot tub by herself. The police were checking into it. She'd heard they'd questioned all three women, but it looked like Justin wasn't going to mention that. Did he wonder at all whether his wife knew exactly what happened? He must believe whatever story she'd told the police. Charlotte didn't understand how he could cope with even a sliver of doubt over whether his wife had been present when Jane died. Perhaps when you lived with someone, you didn't notice disturbing behavior until it was too late.

"Bruce can't join us after all," said Justin. "But I still wanted you to see the layout, so you could figure out how many photographs will fit in the available space."

She was disappointed that Bruce wasn't here to confirm his interest. Would Bruce ever show up? Did he even exist, or was Justin simply stringing her along, trying to make her feel better? Maybe she was stupid for buying in to his enthusiasm.

"He looked at the files you gave me," said Justin. "He's excited about your work. He has his fingers in a lot of community projects, including a homeless shelter." Justin poked her arm. "Maybe he'll buy your whole series. Wouldn't that be great?"

They walked around the lobby, silent except for the scuff of Justin's shoes and the echoing thud of her boots. Every few seconds the phone on the receptionist's desk warbled like water bubbling up in a fountain. Narrow, free-standing panels of wood circled the lobby, offering a prominent place for hanging artwork. Even though she was disappointed that Bruce wasn't available, she was glad she'd come to see the place herself. Since the layout of glass and wood was symmetrical, framing the photographs in a variety of sizes would create a more interesting look.

Justin stood close behind her. His sleeve brushed against her bare arm. She moved away, walking up to the next panel that contained an abstract watercolor. "Will mine be the only pieces on display, or will these others still be here?" She swept her arm around, pointing at the other paintings occupying a few of the wood panels.

Justin shrugged. "I think he'll let you have the whole space."

He'd closed the gap and was once again standing only a few inches away. Her face and neck were so warm she wondered if the air conditioning had cycled down. A thin layer of sweat spread across her forehead and along the sides of her nose. She looked out the window at a reflecting pool with lilies floating on the surface. She wanted a glass of water. Instead, she pulled an index card out of her pocket and wrote down the number of wood panels – thirteen. She continued around the room, then paused and closed her eyes, picturing where each photograph would fit.

While she tried to envision her work, Justin chattered away about how talented she was, about how envious he was of her dedication. As he talked, Charlotte couldn't shake Amy from her thoughts. She was certain he knew nothing about Amy's half-ludicrous but half-frightening remark about the coffin, hinting that she wished Charlotte was dead. The comment was so out of place, it made her laugh. Or was that a mistake? Maybe she should be more scared. He also wouldn't know about the shipment of garbage. The package seemed too silly to mention, but it still bothered her. Meadow had seemed quieter since that day. No matter how many times Charlotte reminded Meadow the package hadn't been addressed to her, Meadow's eyes sparkled with tears whenever she talked about it. And she talked about it often.

Justin seemed so friendly, she wanted to tell him everything, but she didn't really know the guy at all. Obviously he stayed married to Amy for some reason. He must love her.

He wasn't likely to take kindly to a suggestion that his wife was mentally unstable. Charlotte needed him for this display. She didn't want to jeopardize that, but walking around with him, listening to him chat as if they were friends, as if none of those things had happened, made her feel anxious and angry at the same time. Why was he so supportive? Was it guilt, or was something else going on? She wanted to go back to talking about Jane's death. She wanted to find out how he felt about it, whether he had any questions about what had happened that night. After the things Amy had done, Charlotte wasn't sure whether she should be mildly disgusted or truly afraid. Except for the vandalism, they were small things, weren't they? Unless Amy had been involved in Jane's death. Charlotte longed to ask him, but that might force him to defend his wife. She didn't want to dampen his enthusiasm or distract him from thinking about her photo essay.

Finally she couldn't control herself. "How is Amy doing since Jane's funeral?" she said.

"She's fine."

"Does she feel guilty?"

"Of course not."

"They don't feel any responsibility?"

"What do you mean?"

"Nothing. I thought … because of what you said earlier about how unbelievable it is."

"It was a terrible accident. There was nothing anyone could have done."

"I know. I'm sorry." She expected him to reassure her, tell her it was a natural question. But he let the silence grow thicker until it seemed the warbling of the phone had turned into a huge sucking sound, water pulling her under. Had she blown her chance? She needed this so much; it was the best opportunity she was going to get in the foreseeable future. Yet she felt like a fraud, accepting his help while allowing all these unspoken thoughts to accumulate between them, pretending that nothing was out of the ordinary.

He seemed angry that she'd suggested the drowning was suspicious. Didn't everyone already know that? The police were looking into it. Of course, the police were always looking into things, like they were looking into the vandalism. Now that Jane was gone, Justin was her only friend, if you could call him that. She wanted his support. She wanted that feeling she'd had at the carnival, when he looked so stunned, so outraged, as she told him about the destruction of her photographs. Obviously he knew nothing about what was going on right under his nose. He had no idea what his wife was up to, how threatening she was. Charlotte knew she should tell him, but even hinting that something was wrong with the drowning had made him stop talking. A few minutes ago she'd felt they were connecting, now she felt that she was walking around the lobby alone, unsure why she was even here. She wanted to tell him she'd seen enough, but at the same time, she didn't want to leave, didn't want to be left hanging out there without reassurance that this display was actually going to happen.

"When will I be meeting Bruce?"

"He said he'd call you."

"It's kind of expensive. I'm nervous about spending all that money before I meet him. Are you sure he's definitely planning to hang them?"

He stared at her. "He said he was."

"It's … it's a lot of money. I'm on a tight budget."

"You have to spend money to make money, right?" He winked.

She nodded. She slipped her hands into her pockets but it didn't make her feel any more confident. At first she'd been glad of the chance to look around, but now she wanted the mysterious Bruce to be present, to give her some kind of promise that she wasn't about to spend hundreds of dollars for nothing.

Something didn't feel right, but she wasn't sure if it was her own desperation or Justin's proximity. She felt his gaze on the side of her face, smelled the clean scent of his skin. The air conditioning was blowing harder now and the chill air made her nipples harden. She worried that he was staring at them. She didn't want to look at his face, didn't want to know. She was standing in a lobby with a man who said he wanted to help advance her career, but was a riddle of mixed messages. She wasn't sure whether he was attracted to her, or wanted something else from her. For all she knew, Amy had put him up to this. Perhaps they intended to humiliate her by raising her hopes. Maybe it was all a show, aimed at making her give up entirely.

Chapter Thirty-six

WHEN WAS THE WARM weather going to end? Rachel didn't recall it ever lingering so far into October. Seven o'clock in the evening and the temperature in the kitchen was eighty-one, gripping the heat of the day like the house itself was holding its breath. On the back patio, she and Greg sprawled on cushioned chaise lounges. Trent sat in a chair, cross-legged, with his sketchpad balanced between his knees. He was drawing with a soft pencil Greg had picked up at an art supply store.

Rachel sipped her coke. She was still waiting for Greg to apologize for the way he'd acted when the detective came to question her. He'd done nothing to take her side, nothing to defend her against the questions laced with suggestions of negligence. Usually they resolved disagreements and misunderstandings in a day or two. This time, the silences between them were broken only by the conversations required to manage the business of living. If anyone dissolved the impasse, it was going to have to be her. Was it always the female that needed to soften the rough spaces between a man and a woman? It seemed that men accepted superficial calm as proof that everything was good. Greg probably wasn't even aware there was anything wrong. Now that so much time had passed, she'd come to realize all he'd done was try to be cooperative with the detective. A voice at the back of her mind whispered that the detective had done nothing more than speak out loud the questions festering in Rachel's own mind.

Trent slid off the chair and placed the pad on her lap. "Look."

The page was consumed by yet another drawing of a snail. The antennae were pale with strokes that made them look almost transparent. The shell was an intricate blend of lines and smudges indicating the three-dimensional swirl with vivid shadows. The face, without being cartoonish, looked as if the snail had intelligence, a sentient being gazing at the viewer with an affectionate expression. "That's amazing, Trent. It looks so real." She hugged him and held the drawing up so Greg could see.

"Very impressive," said Greg. "Good job."

Trent smiled, but he didn't grin and prance around like Sara would have. He almost looked embarrassed by the attention. "I practice a lot," he said.

"It's really good," said Rachel.

"Maybe I can be an artist. Like Meadow's mom," said Trent.

Rachel nodded.

"I would feel really bad if something happened to my drawings. Like what happened to her pictures."

Rachel closed her eyes. What would her son think if he knew the terrible thing his mother had done to a woman's artwork? Tears pooled in her eyes. Lately, she cried so frequently, she'd stopped wearing mascara because she constantly had to scrub the black smudges off the fragile skin under her eyes.

"Great work, buddy." said Greg. "Now it's reading time. Thirty minutes. Upstairs."

"Ok." Trent picked up his pencil and went into the house.

Was that all it took? A few words of praise for something he cared about and suddenly he was agreeable and good-natured? If only he hadn't mentioned Charlotte's photographs. She sipped her coke.

"Are you crying?" Greg set down his glass and put his hand on her ankle. He stroked his hand along the bone. His fingers were cold and slightly damp from his glass of coke.

She ran her pinkies under her eyes.

"I know you're upset about Jane," he said.

"It's not just Jane."

"What else?"

"It feels like the detective is blaming us for letting her die."

He pushed her legs toward the side and moved onto her chaise lounge. "No she's not."

"Some of her questions made it sound that way. And you acted like I was being difficult. Like you thought it was our fault. Like you thought Jane was murdered."

"I'm sorry," he said. "They have to ask questions when someone dies unexpectedly. But of course it wasn't your fault."

She swallowed. "It's ok."

"It's not. I didn't mean to act like you did something wrong."

"I did."

"You weren't even there. The whole scenario is almost unbelievable and the questions, having a cop in the house, threw me."

"But I did do something wrong. Before that."

He ran his hand further up her leg, slipping it under the hem of her skirt and moving his fingers along the inside of her thigh.

"Amy and I are the ones who destroyed Charlotte's pictures." She put her hands over her face, crying harder.

He pulled his hand out from under her skirt.

"Don't stop. I need to feel you touching me," she said.

"You trashed her photographs? Why?"

"I don't even know. Amy was so upset. I looked fat. And there was a shot of Trent that made him seem … I don't know, ostracized, or something."

"Why would you do that?"

"I told you. Please don't hate me. Please put your hand back where it was."

He slid his hand back up under her skirt. His fingers were warmer now, soothing. He grinned. "My little vandal."

"Don't laugh about it. I feel terrible. I wasn't thinking. Amy told me her mother was raped."

Greg stared at her but said nothing.

"People gossiped about her family. She can't stand having people stare at her, or something like that. Thinking about how awful that must have been for Amy, for her mother, and then seeing that picture of Trent, I stopped thinking."

"It does help explain why she's kind of messed up."

She felt her body softening under the continuing pressure of his fingers on her thigh.

"But even so, you can't get caught up in her issues," said Greg.

She nodded. "I know. Although part of me wanted to do it. I hated Charlotte for making Trent look so forlorn."

"That's all in your own head."

"I guess it is. I want him to have friends."

"He will. He does."

"What should I do?" said Rachel.

"At least offer to pay for the damage. She'd probably feel better if she knew who did it, if you explained how you felt."

"But what about Amy?"

"What about her?"

"She'll be angry."

"So? You have to do the right thing."

"She's my best friend." If she told him about the gun, Greg would yank his hand off her leg. He would tell her she needed new friends. Although maybe he was no longer thinking about Amy, now that he'd slipped his fingers inside her underpants.

"You'd better stop that," she said. "The kids may come down. And you're making me crazy." She wondered if she looked as hideous as she felt with puffy eyes and a red nose, trying to smile through the slick covering of tears on her face.

He moved his hand a few inches lower.

She wanted to relax. It helped, knowing the distance between them was filled. Once Sara and Trent were asleep, they could make love. She would keep her thoughts focused on Greg, not on her friends. It was a relief having him know about her part in destroying the photographs. She'd thought he'd be angry, disgusted with her, but that didn't seem to have even crossed his mind. How had she gotten so lucky to find a guy like him? Sometimes with homework and soccer and yard work and the constant chatter of their children, she forgot how much she liked him. It was possible he had always been her best friend, not Amy. She immediately regretted the thought. Was she the kind of person who abandoned her friend the minute there was a problem? Maybe Amy was right for wanting the gun. She'd made a good point – how did they know the rapist hadn't entered Kit's backyard? Maybe he'd found Jane weak and tipsy and held her under the water. Any number of things could have happened.

Later, as she lay with her head on Greg's shoulder, brushing her lips against the hair of his chest, feeling his muscle firm beneath her cheek, she thought of Amy again. Amy was going through a rough time and needed her best friend now more than ever.

Chapter Thirty-seven

AMY PULLED THE CORK out of a fresh bottle of wine. She was glad to have a few minutes to herself since Rachel had offered to bring the girls home from soccer practice. Although later tonight she wouldn't feel as pleased about being alone – Justin had gone to Houston for two days. He'd been completely unsympathetic about the danger she faced without him there to protect her at night. The wine helped calm her, it was the only way she'd make it through the long hours of darkness. That, and the confidence she was getting more skilled with her gun.

Rachel might not have been so willing to drive the twins home if she'd known Amy had gone to the shooting range during soccer practice. She was surprised by how much fun she had putting the pads over her ears, stabilizing the gun with both hands, feeling the recoil vibrate through her body. It had only taken three trips to the range before she was getting bullets within the outline of the human head and torso. Everything she'd learned when she was twenty had resurfaced, the visceral memory retained all these years.

She grabbed the wine bottle by the neck but before she could tip it over the glass, the doorbell chimed. She placed the bottle on the counter. With the living room drapes pulled tight and the garage door closed, there was no sign anyone was home. She lifted the bottle and filled the glass almost to the rim. The bell sounded again. It couldn't be Rachel. It was only four-thirty; soccer practice wouldn't be over for another half hour. Why didn't they go away?

She picked up her glass and took a quick sip so the wine wouldn't slosh out as she walked. Carrying the glass in her left hand, she went into the living room and slid her finger between the drapes. The idea of the caller actually being the rapist was hard to grasp. Despite her anxiety she never really imagined he would show up as a delivery man. It seemed more likely that he would break into her house at night when Justin was away on business travel. But the person on the front porch was familiar – that detective. The officer had probably noticed the parted drapes. Weren't they paid to observe details like that? Would she call for backup, set up camp outside now that she knew someone was inside the house? Justin had said not to answer any more questions without an attorney, but telling the cop she wanted a lawyer would make her look guilty. Maybe she should call him and ask what to do, but he was probably at a client dinner by now.

She carried her wine back to the kitchen. There was no choice but to answer the door. Hopefully she could keep the detective on the front porch, but it wouldn't look good to be clutching a glass of wine. She returned to the front door. "Who's there?"

"Detective Roberts, Ms. Lewis. I'm following up on our last conversation."

"Now isn't the best time."

"This will only take a minute. It's better if you cooperate with us."

What was that supposed to mean? How was it better? And who was the "us" she was talking about? Amy turned the deadbolt and opened the door.

"May I come in?"

"Can't I answer your questions here?"

"If you prefer. I'm here because we think Ms. Goodman died between 8:30 and 9:30pm. From what I can determine, you were still at the Shepherd home during most of that hour."

"How can you know where I was?"

"Ms. Shepherd indicated that Ms. Matthews left about 8:15. Did you leave at the same time?"

Amy closed her eyes so she didn't have to see the detective's slightly protruding eyes staring her down. She could say yes, but the police were so cagey. What if they knew something else? Kit said she fell asleep on her bed, but did she really? Had she been peeking out the bedroom window, spying on Amy? Was that why the detective refused to give up?

"Did you leave immediately after Ms. Matthews?"

"Pretty soon after. If Jane died at 9:30, I was definitely gone by then."

"I said between 8:30 and 9:30. So your official answer is that you don't know what time you left?"

"That's right."

The officer wrote in her notebook. "What medication are you taking?"

"My husband said I don't have to tell you."

"You don't have to tell us anything. Eventually we can find out, if we have to."

"Fine," said Amy. "*Xanax*. It's for anxiety. But I don't see what that has to do with anything."

"And you're supposed to avoid alcohol with *Xanax*, correct?"

"I don't always take it."

The detective scribbled in her notebook.

"Are you implying I was passed out too?"

"Were you?"

"No."

"Then what happened? What was Ms. Goodman's condition when you left?"

"She was sitting in the hot tub." Technically, this was true.

"Was she conscious?"

"How should I know?"

"Please don't play games with me, Ms. Lewis. It would be fairly obvious if an unconscious woman was floating in a hot tub."

"You think I pushed her under the water? Someone who outweighs me by at least fifty pounds?"

"I don't think anything yet. All I want to know is Ms. Goodman's condition when you left the pool area."

"I'm a small person," said Amy. "And Jane was huge, a hundred times stronger than I am."

The detective scratched the pen on the notebook as if she was trying to get the ink to flow. What was she writing? "You're trying to make it sound like I..."

"Was Ms. Goodman conscious when you left?"

"I don't know. I didn't see her."

"Then where were you?"

"You should be investigating the rapes. How do you know some guy didn't come into their yard and try to attack her and he couldn't get her out of the water, so he pushed her under? Kit doesn't lock the gates to the back yard. Did you know that?"

"That scenario is extremely implausible," said Detective Roberts.

"I don't want to answer anymore questions. I don't understand what any of this has to do with me. I've had a long day and I'm really tired."

Detective Roberts flipped closed the cover of her notebook. "You'll be hearing from us again. I need some sensible answers soon."

Amy was silent. If they knew anything, they would arrest her now. If it was even a crime. Didn't a crime require action? She hadn't done anything.

The detective put her hands in her pockets.

Amy smirked. She'd been right – the detective was fishing. They had a young, dead woman on their hands and rather than spending time where they should be, looking for the rapist, they were trying to turn a drunken woman's drowning into someone else's fault. They probably couldn't figure out how to catch the rapist. They had to look like they were doing something to keep the city safe.

"I'll be in touch," said Detective Roberts.

Amy closed the door firmly and snapped the deadbolt into place.

After she finished a glass of wine, she called to order pizza and drove to pick it up, leaving a note on the door telling Rachel she'd be right back. She wasn't about to have pizza delivered to the house with Justin out of town.

After Alice and Amanda had done their homework and were settled with their pizza and a movie, she took her glass, the bottle of wine, and her purse upstairs. She made her way through the stacks of plastic bins toward the back corner of the spare room. She sat in the chair tucked in the corner and sipped her wine. She took the gun out of her purse, laid it on her lap, and stroked the barrel. The wine numbed her brain and the gun calmed her, heavy as Justin's hand on her leg, but colder. No one could hurt her as long as she had it. At least no stranger, she still had Charlotte to deal with. It would be so perfect if Charlotte tried to sneak up on her. It would be Charlotte's own fault if Amy were startled. Just like it was Jane's fault that she went under the water.

She swallowed the rest of the wine and put the glass on the dresser next to the bottle. The wine was getting warm. She should have put it in the tiny refrigerator under the window, but she was too tired to get out of the chair. She hadn't looked inside the refrigerator for weeks. It used to contain an extra bottle of wine, but she'd removed the wine when she started storing ... A shiver ran down her arms. She really didn't want to think about it, but it had made sense, at the time.

It had been four or five months now, because it was at the start of summer when the neighbor's cat began killing small birds and leaving them in her yard. For a while, she'd thought about dropping them back in the neighbor's yard, but had lost her nerve. She hadn't wanted to bury them, it was too sad, and so she'd placed them in a giant zip-lock bag and stored them in the freezer compartment. She couldn't bear to think of them under the dirt, rotting away, but eventually, she had to do something with them. They couldn't stay in the freezer forever.

She picked up the gun and folded her hand around the grip, her right index finger resting on the trigger. She raised it and aimed at the ceiling light. The globe was the perfect shape, the same size as a human head. She narrowed her eyes and held her arm steady. She took a breath. "Bang," she whispered. She imagined the warm shudder of the recoil. She lowered it and cradled it in her hands. Of course, Charlotte would never walk into this room. She wouldn't even come near the house, but it was interesting to think about. That was what fantasy was, wasn't it? Imagining something that might not happen in real life, but it felt sort of like it *could* happen. Or wanting it to happen. She tried to think of a reason why Charlotte might come inside her house. Maybe a sleepover with that sad little girl – Meadow. She didn't know whether she could bring herself to go quite that far. She raised the gun and aimed at different objects around the room, the hatbox on top of one of the stacks of plastic bins, the packages of toilet paper towering near the closets. She aimed at the shelves packed tightly with canned soup and fruit and tuna – food she didn't really care for, but would keep her family alive in a disaster. That was the important thing, taking care of them.

Her arms ached, so she placed the gun on the dresser and poured the rest of the Chardonnay into the glass. She drank it carefully; it was too warm now and didn't have that creamy taste she loved, the texture that made her feel as if she was drinking liquid moonlight. When Justin traveled, she didn't sleep at all. Mostly she sat in bed and flipped through magazines, or tried to rest on the family room sofa, watching old sitcoms. Sometimes this brought sleep for an hour or two. The wine helped.

She stood and wobbled slightly. She put the gun into her purse and carried it downstairs. She'd have one more glass of wine after she shepherded the girls through their washing up ritual and tucked them into bed.

Chapter Thirty-eight

CHARLOTTE STARED AT THE picnic table bench. An inchworm the color of a green apple marched toward the edge. It stepped too far and spun over the side, dangling by an invisible thread. She reached down and put her finger under its nearly weightless body and lifted it back to the bench. Amy and Rachel were seated a few feet away.

"I feel so much better," said Amy.

Charlotte shifted her position so she wasn't looking directly at Amy. How did they manage to make her feel like she was eavesdropping when she was simply sitting in a public space, waiting for her daughter? Sometimes she felt as if Amy Lewis had an aura that controlled everyone and everything within fifty feet of her.

"I don't want to hear about it," said Rachel.

"Because you're jealous?"

"Absolutely not."

"You worry about the wrong things," said Amy. "Too much about Trent playing soccer and not enough about yourself, or Sara, for that matter. That monster could target your home any day."

"I'm trying to stay focused on the things I can control," said Rachel.

"A woman needs to protect herself," said Amy.

Charlotte's fingers trembled in her lap. The inchworm pitched off the bench again. She leaned down and lifted it back onto steady footing.

"You don't need to explain it to me," said Rachel. "I understand why you're scared, but I don't think you need a gun and I don't want to talk about it any more. I'm afraid to come over to your house. You shouldn't keep it loaded."

Charlotte couldn't help turning to look, even though she was making it obvious she was listening to their conversation.

"Oh my God," said Amy. "What do you think is going to happen?"

"An accident," said Rachel.

"What good would it be if it wasn't loaded? It's not like you get an advance warning when you're going to be attacked."

"Would a gun have helped your mother?"

"Don't talk about that," said Amy.

Charlotte saw Amy glance in her direction. Amy's lips were set in a hard line, as if daring Charlotte to acknowledge she was listening. Amy's voice dropped so low, Charlotte couldn't hear. Then it rose slightly. "...and yes, it would have changed everything." Amy stood and grabbed her purse. She patted it as if she was comforting a child. "Without a gun, you're helpless against a rapist, or any kind of attack. So if you want to sit around and worry about the rare accident that happens when people are careless instead of watching out for yourself, that's fine." She walked away from the table. Her narrow shoulders were pinched close to her neck, bonier than ever under a pink shirt that looked like crepe paper.

Goose bumps shimmied down Charlotte's legs. She rubbed her hands along her thighs, but her palms stuck to the fabric of her shorts. How on earth did someone like Amy get licensed to carry a gun? Was Rachel going to do anything about her friend having a loaded gun on school grounds, or just sit and whine that she didn't want to talk about it?

The bell rang and children gushed out of the doors like a spurt of water from a broken pipe. Charlotte hopped to the ground. Meadow and Amanda emerged from the classroom. Amy hurried over to them and grasped Amanda's wrist. Her sharp tone was evident, but Charlotte couldn't hear what she said. There was a connection between Meadow and Amanda that she couldn't comprehend. She worried the only attraction on Amanda's part was to a girl that her mother didn't like. Meadow was so eager, grinning whenever she was with Amanda, as if she was happy just to absorb the physical presence of her new friend.

She waited for Meadow to make her way to the cluster of picnic tables. "How was your day?"

"Amanda's mom is mean," said Meadow.

Charlotte snorted. "Why do you say that?"

"She says mean things. She said, *I told you not to hang around this little delinquent.*"

Charlotte's throat tightened. She felt as helpless as the inchworm, spinning from its silken thread.

"Why would she call me that?" said Meadow.

"She says all kinds of crazy things. We have to try to stay away from her."

"Does that mean I can't hang out with Amanda?"

"Aren't there any other girls in your class that you like?"

"Amanda likes to read a lot, like me. No one else does."

"How about in one of the other classes?"

Meadow fiddled with the spot where her hair had torn, pulling a few strands over the exposed skin.

Charlotte put her arm around Meadow's shoulders. "Let's figure out a way for you to meet some other kids over the next few weeks. It's better to have more than one friend anyway." She really didn't want Meadow around Amanda at all. The thought of Amy walking around with a gun a few inches from her fingertips was more than a little scary. How could they go anywhere without looking over their shoulders? Was this any different than knowing Mark's suppliers might be watching her, keeping an eye on Meadow? Was it better than when she'd known the cops still drove past her apartment more often than necessary?

They walked slowly across the playground toward the front of the school. With each step, she wondered if she should start driving Meadow to school. This was not what she'd moved here for. She'd given up the art community of the city for a safe neighborhood and a group of friends where Meadow could thrive, but it was beginning to look like her decision was a mistake. "Do you ever miss San Francisco?" said Charlotte.

"No. There's more stuff to do here, and it's not so crowded."

Charlotte nodded. She couldn't seem to stop waffling between thinking Amy was just a self-absorbed bitch and thinking she might actually be dangerous. How did you know when someone was a true threat? What she couldn't escape, no matter how many different ways she looked at it, was that Amy already had acted out. The photographs had made her angry enough to destroy them. What would it take to push her into violence again? Or had that already happened with the unexplained details around Jane's death? A chill ran down her spine. One side of her mind told her she needed to do something. The other side of her mind laughed and said she was over-reacting; it was nothing.

WHEN THEY ARRIVED home, she walked through each of their four rooms and closed and locked the windows. She left the front and back doors shut, blocking the flow of air that usually swept through the house in the afternoon.

"It's too hot," said Meadow. "Why can't I open my window?"

"It's not safe to leave everything open. A woman was murdered. Other women have been attacked. We need to be more careful." Speaking the words made her feel ill. She was lying, and needlessly upsetting her daughter, all in a single breath.

"You weren't worried about it before."

"Well now I am."

Outside, Meadow's soccer ball was half-hidden under the scraggly hedge she used as a practice goal. Charlotte turned the deadbolt on the back door. It settled into place with a satisfying clunk. Her neck was sweating and her bare feet squeaked on the hardwood floor. Sealing themselves inside while the sun was overhead bordered on paranoia. Surely Amy wasn't going to come to her house and shoot them. But then why did her hands keep shaking? It was difficult to take a deep breath. They said the first rule of self-defense was to listen to your instincts. But what was the difference between instinctual, protective fear and unfounded worry? She didn't know, but she had to opt for the safe route.

AT TEN MINUTES past midnight, she was still awake, sitting on the couch. A thin sliver of moon was framed in the gap above the blanket that covered the living room window. Her facial muscles and back ached for sleep, but she couldn't lower her eyelids for more than a few minutes at a time. Despite the hot, stuffy air, she was afraid to let down her guard and open even a single window.

This was no way to live; she had to think of a solution, but her mind refused to offer up any fresh thoughts. All her ideas centered around enlisting the help of some other person. At the same time, her experience so far in this idyllic town told her that was the weakest plan of all. She could call Justin, but after his reaction when she tried to ask him what he thought about the drowning, she was quite sure he wouldn't listen to her fears. Jane had been the only nice one in the bunch, a strong, vibrant woman now shut inside an airless box for the rest of eternity. Drowning in a hot tub was the most improbable fate imaginable for a woman with the energy that had radiated from Jane Goodman. Charlotte could still see her well-rounded muscles and her quick walk. How did a woman like that drown in three feet of water? Maybe all of them were involved. Kit was certainly anxious to pack up and move.

She couldn't sit on the couch all night, staring at the smudge of dirt on the opposite wall, which she'd intended to cover with a photograph at some point. She stood and walked to the box of photographs. They were all framed, waiting for the call from Bruce. Yet another irrational fear that wouldn't go away – that Justin was playing her; that he and Amy were both trying to make her life miserable. The first photo in the box was the shot of Meadow when she was three months old. The image captured the soles of her feet, curled slightly so her toes looked like a cluster of small white grapes. Life started out so pristine. How had she ended up here, locked inside in this run down house, perspiring because she was afraid of something she could hardly name? Mark was shut out of her life, dealing with his own kind of loneliness. She had planned that as soon as Meadow made a few friends, she would arrange an all day play date and make a trip up to visit him. But Meadow's only friend so far appeared to have a sociopath for a mother. Now it had been two months since she'd seen him and it made her chest ache, feeling that he was disappearing into the history of her life. When she closed her eyes, his face was blurry, yet she couldn't bring herself to look at the hundreds of photographs she had of him.

She flipped the picture forward. The next one was smaller, a five by five shot of a three-year old girl's feet in sandals standing in tall grass. As she moved it forward, the metal frames clicked against each other.

"Why are you awake?"

She looked up. Meadow stood in the doorway. Her nightgown clung to her stomach in a damp spot and her hair was wet around the edge of her face.

"I can't sleep." Charlotte draped the sheet over the pictures to protect them.

"It's too hot," said Meadow.

"I'll get some water." Charlotte went into the kitchen and took two bottles of water out of the refrigerator. She used a towel to release the seal on the caps and went back to the couch where Meadow leaned against the arm.

"Why can't we open the windows?"

"I don't feel safe right now."

"I do," said Meadow.

Charlotte smiled. All the worrying that witnessing Mark's arrest and the attack by the officer would traumatize Meadow had been for nothing. The bald spot on her scalp was starting to fill with fuzzy hair. Now, despite all her good intentions to raise a self-confident child, Charlotte was the one instilling fear into her daughter. She put the water bottle to her mouth and took a long swallow. Watching Meadow's expression in the dimly lit room, she saw a reflection of Mark's charming smile. The longer she and Mark were separated, the more she saw his gestures and the movement of his hips mirrored in Meadow. The smile was the eeriest. She felt he was sitting next to her in another form. His confidence, his Zen-like acceptance of whatever rolled his way filled the shadowy corners of the living room.

"Let's sleep on the floor out here. It will be cooler," said Charlotte.

Meadow shimmied off the couch. "I'll get the sleeping bags."

Charlotte laughed. "And I'll get some sheets and crack open the window." There was something about Meadow's excitement that erased Charlotte's fears.

It took some jiggling to get the window to slide back open in its gritty frame. Finally she managed to create a six-inch space. A breeze swam into the room. It felt good to refuse to live like a prisoner. They settled side by side on the opened sleeping bags. Charlotte pulled the sheet up to her waist. Her mind was loose and easy. She had everything to look forward to – Meadow was excited about school and soccer. Charlotte felt that same confidence spilling over – her photo essay was going to be displayed at an upscale office complex. Time would pass quickly and before she knew it, Mark would be with them again. She wouldn't allow Amy to nail her into a virtual coffin. That silly, nervous woman didn't have the courage to do anything dangerous. Wasn't that the definition of a vandal – someone too cowardly to commit a real crime? She closed her eyes.

Chapter Thirty-nine

THE MORNING WAS COOL and gray, covered by the wet blanket of fog Rachel had been waiting for all these weeks. She sat on the back patio drinking coffee from a mug Trent had given her on Mothers' Day – *World's Best Mom*. Instead of soothing her, the fog was a damp, dull reminder that everything in her life seemed to be coming to an end. Jane was gone. Kit's house had a sold sign out front. Not that Kit ever talked to her old friends any more. Since the funeral, she only waved from the opposite side of the playground or the soccer field. Sometimes she didn't even do that. There was no hint that Kit thought she was leaving anything important behind. Nor did she seem to care about what had really happened in her backyard. Amy seemed to be lost in a world no one else could see. She pulled her knees up and rubbed her shins to warm them. In some ways, her friends had been a more pervasive part of her daily life than Greg or her children. Greg went off to work every morning believing she was happy raising Sara and Trent, taking care of their home. And she was happy; but motherhood could be a lonely occupation. Having companions to walk beside her made it so much more enjoyable – friends whose voices wove through her own thoughts, adult conversation, and a sense that they were all in this together.

It might still be possible to fix things. Amy was under so much pressure right now. All she needed was a little time. Once the rapist was caught she would relax, lock away her gun. If Charlotte could give her a little breathing room, Amy might come around. She might find a way to work on whatever was wrong in her marriage that made her view Charlotte as a threat.

She hadn't touched her coffee for twenty minutes. Now it was cold. She poured it on the flagstone where it formed a puddle. She went into the kitchen, rinsed the mug and put it in the dishwasher. She'd planned to make a trip to the store this morning, but a visit to Charlotte was more important right now. It wouldn't take long. Groceries could wait.

***

THE FOG WAS dissipating quickly. Sun flooded Charlotte's front porch even though wisps of vapor lingered above the rooflines across the street. The yard was silent. She lifted her camera out of the backpack and went out onto the porch. She sat on the top step and held the camera, waiting for inspiration to strike. She squinted at the yard. The light was so sharp, but she was fairly certain she couldn't even come close to capturing that effect in a photograph. She closed her eyes and lifted her face, letting the sun wash over her skin. The confidence of last night, that her daughter was thriving, and they only had a few years to wait until Mark could join them – those feelings couldn't be photographed either.

She heard a car slowing down and tires scraping the curb in front of her house. Her eyes flashed open. Her muscles tensed and she put the camera on the porch behind her. She recognized Rachel's *RAV4*. Surely Rachel wasn't dropping by for a friendly visit. The pleasant mood floated away from her as if she'd lost her grasp on the ribbon of a helium-filled balloon.

Rachel got out and stood near the open door of her car. "Hi," she said. She shut the door and walked up the path. Her feet kicked at the fallen magnolia leaves. The stiff leaves scratched at the concrete as if they were scrambling to save themselves from Rachel's careless footsteps.

Charlotte leaned her shoulder against the porch rail. "What's up?"

Rachel stopped a few feet from the bottom step. She was silent for several seconds. "I have a favor to ask. Do you mind if I come inside?"

"We can talk out here."

Rachel's lips remained parted. She looked surprised that she hadn't gotten her way.

"So what's the favor?" said Charlotte.

"I know Amy hasn't been very nice to you. I wanted to help you understand what part of the problem is."

"I'm not interested in what her problem is. What's the favor?"

"Can I tell you a bit about what she's going through?"

"Let's not pretend this is a friendly visit. Tell me what you want so I can get back to enjoying my morning."

"Amy's had a hard life."

"Haven't we all," said Charlotte.

Rachel inched closer. Light filtered through the nest of hair surrounding her face, creating a halo effect. "What I wanted to ask you is – does Meadow really have to play soccer? It might be easier if she found another activity. You must notice how tense Amy is when you're around. She's so stressed, and I don't know what she'll do. It's not like Meadow played soccer all her life. She could …"

Charlotte bolted to her feet. "What is it with the women around here that you think you can dictate what other people do?"

A mourning dove that had been perched in the magnolia tree took off, flapping its wings madly.

Rachel took a step back. "It's not that I'm telling you what to do. I'm just asking. I'm wondering if Meadow wouldn't be happier in another activity, where she could make other friends, since Amy doesn't really want Amanda to hang out with her."

"You wonder? You know nothing about my daughter. How arrogant do you have to be to suggest activities for children you don't even know?"

"I'm trying to help. I'm not trying to chase Meadow away. I know that Amy's really upset and I don't want to see Meadow get her feelings hurt. I don't want anything to … happen."

"What would happen?"

Rachel looked at the ground. She kicked one of the leaves.

"Meadow wants to play soccer," said Charlotte. "If the girls on this team are so cruel that Meadow will get her feelings hurt, then all of you need to wonder what kind of mothers you are."

"My daughter isn't cruel. It's that Amy is … she feels …"

"Amy. Amy. Amy. And Amy has a gun, I understand. What is she planning to do? Yank it out on the soccer field and start taking out people she doesn't like?"

"How can you say something like that?" Rachel had taken enough steps back that the sun was no longer providing her with a halo of any kind. Instead, it shone in her eyes, causing them to glitter.

"If Amy makes a single aggressive move toward Meadow, I'll get a restraining order. Then we'll see whose children need to find another activity."

"Please don't make this worse."

Charlotte walked down the steps. "I'm not making anything worse. I moved into this supposedly pleasant community to start a new life. Since then I've had my artwork destroyed and my daughter's been told she's not welcome. Well that's bullshit." She turned and walked back up the stairs and across the porch. "See you at soccer." She picked up the camera and opened the screen door.

"Wait. Can't we talk about this?" said Rachel.

"There's nothing to talk about. I don't know what kind of hold that woman has on you, but no one is going to prevent my daughter from doing what she wants."

"Please. I'm really trying to help. You don't know her. Amy is so upset. I know it's pretty much unjustified, but you have to understand what's she's been through."

"Pretty much unjustified? It's completely unjustified. And I'm not afraid of her. So she has a gun. Does she know it's illegal to carry a concealed weapon?"

Rachel walked back to the porch and put her foot on the first step. "I don't want anything bad to happen. I don't think you do either. Can't we figure out a solution?"

"No. If something bad happens, it will be Amy's doing, not mine." Charlotte opened the door and stepped into the living room. "So nice of you to drop by and tell me your friend is crazier than I realized."

She let go of the screen door and it clattered shut. She took a deep breath. Her knees and hands shook so she had to sit down on the floor. She pushed the door closed and leaned against it. All the feelings of being trapped in her home rushed back, as if the fog had reversed course and blown back into the yard. So much for a peaceful morning, they weren't going to leave her alone.

Chapter Forty

THE *IL POSTALE* RESTAURANT was on the corner of Washington in the historic section of Sunnyvale, housed in the old post office that had been built in 1917. One wall was the original brick, giving the building extra charm, along with its homemade pasta. The mid-day crowd was comprised mostly of employees of nearby high tech companies. Rachel thought lunch with Amy on neutral turf might help Amy see that the world was the same as always, there was no need for a gun, for living in fear. A nice lunch out would divert Amy from her daily habit of watching Charlotte's every move. They could talk about normal things.

Amy wore navy blue stovepipe pants and a white shirt with the collar turned up and navy blue leather pumps with four-inch heels. Her nails were painted pink. Next to Amy, Rachel felt more frumpy than usual. She'd tried painting her toenails, but the polish was a bit sloppy; a puddle had oozed onto the cuticle of her big toe and she'd had a hard time wiping off the stain. Her skirt was too snug around her waist and she knew her stomach would feel like it was strangling by the time she'd finished eating.

They placed their orders without looking at the menu – angel hair pasta with sautéed vegetables for Rachel and a Caesar salad with chicken for Amy. Rachel resented Amy's ability to restrict herself to a salad that she probably wouldn't finish. Maybe she shouldn't be looking forward to slurping up calorie-coated pasta. She shook off the thought. She wasn't paying for a lunch out and then suffering through an ordinary salad. This was a treat and she planned to enjoy it. Nothing Amy said would get under her skin today. She would not allow more than ten years of friendship to evaporate into nothing. So what if Amy had a gun. Lots of people kept guns in their homes for protection. Lots of women knew how to handle a gun. Yes, there was still the nagging whisper of doubt about where Amy had been when Jane drowned, but there was no good reason to doubt her sincerity.

"Did you see that another woman was raped?" said Amy. "At night. That's four rapes and the one stabbing. In just two months."

"Let's talk about something nice. Can't we go back to the way things used to be?"

"It will never be the same. At least not until they catch this guy. And we're rid of Charlotte."

Rachel picked up her coke and took a small sip. Why did her anticipation of a conversation always fail to take into account the reality of the other person's opinions and desires? Why did she persist in thinking people would be different than who they were? It was the same with her children, with Greg. It was the same in her recent, failed encounter with Charlotte. She imagined a conversation and managed to forget that she had no influence over what the other person would say or do. She tore a piece of bread off the chunk lying on a plate at the center of the table. She dipped it into the dish of olive oil and balsamic vinegar. Chewing the bread would prevent her from talking too soon, from saying the wrong thing.

"I don't know why they can't catch him," said Amy. "I thought there were all kinds of scientific tests to identify criminals. Did you see that they questioned a guy for the stabbing and then let him go?"

"I'm sure they're working on it."

"But why would they let him go?"

"Maybe it wasn't the right guy. Maybe there are two guys. They said it was unusual that one woman was stabbed and not the others."

Amy flapped her hand near the side of her head. "It's taking too long. I don't like staying locked up in my house all the time. I'm afraid to let my girls go anywhere. I'm afraid to leave my own bedroom."

Rachel took another small bite of bread. Their lunches were delivered and they started eating. "Can't we please try to forget all that? Why don't we ask the guys to cheer for us at the game on Saturday and you and I can go shopping? Or get a manicure."

"Maybe." Amy poured sparkling water into her glass and took several rapid sips. "I don't know if Amanda and Alice are going to play soccer any more."

"Why not?" Rachel put her hands in her lap and squeezed them into fists. Not only couldn't she lead Amy to a more pleasant topic of conversation, she was constantly tripped up by new information.

"That girl is always there. And her mother."

Rachel wanted to ask what girl, but she knew better. "Can't you ignore her?"

"No."

"I could drive the girls to practice for awhile. You don't even have to see her."

"It doesn't matter. She's there at the games, wiggling her body at Justin. I can't let him leave the house without sitting there biting my nails until he comes home."

Rachel looked at Amy's hands. It was a ridiculous description for her worry, with those acrylic spears on her fingertips. More likely, Amy was drinking wine while she worried about Justin. Rachel turned her fork, winding the pasta into a neat bundle. She put it into her mouth. The olive oil melted on her tongue. She poked her fork at a shitake mushroom and a piece of yellow pepper. "I wish you wouldn't think about her so much. She didn't do anything. It's not like they had an affair."

"Not yet."

"It seems like he ignores her at the games."

"No man can ignore her."

Amy was twisting it into something more disturbing than it was. Did she really believe Charlotte was going to drag Justin off against his will? Or was she so afraid for her marriage, she thought he wouldn't put up much of a fight? "Are things okay between you and Justin?" said Rachel.

Amy dropped her fork on the tablecloth. It left a pale smear of salad dressing. "Of course everything is okay. We have a perfect marriage."

"Then I don't see why you're so worried. He might look, but he's not interested."

"That doesn't matter. She could still try to steal him away," said Amy.

"How? If Justin is happy with you, no one can steal him."

Amy picked up her fork and laid it across her plate. She pushed the plate to the side. She folded her hands and rested them on the edge of the table. "I'm not interested in arguing about my marriage. It's perfectly happy. Better than yours."

Rachel felt as if the fork had been shoved in her throat. She opened her mouth, but no words formed. She closed her eyes and tried to catch her breath.

"But that doesn't mean I want a woman prowling around with her eye on seducing him. I'm not going to pretend she's harmless." Amy sipped her water, put down the glass and pushed the slice of lime around with the tip of her fingernail. The water beaded up on her nail. She blotted it dry on her napkin.

"I just wish ..." Rachel stabbed at the mushrooms left on her plate.

"Wish what? That I wasn't concerned about someone drinking wine with my husband behind my back, rubbing her breast on his bare skin?"

"When did that happen?" said Rachel.

"I'm tired of talking about this. Everything started to go wrong when she showed up, starting with those obnoxious pictures. You seem to have forgotten all about that. If she touches Justin again, I'm ready to take care of it now." She reached under her chair and patted her purse. She sat up and curled her fingers like she was holding a gun. "Bang."

"Amy!" Rachel looked at the other tables, set close together along the length of the brick wall. She pushed her plate away. "Don't do that."

"If she comes anywhere near my husband, I'll shoot her."

"Lower your voice. Don't say things like that. I know you don't mean it."

Amy leaned forward. "How do you know what I mean?"

"You can't think about killing someone. For no reason."

"People make too big a deal out of death. It's not that bad. One minute you're here, and then you're gone."

"Then why do you need a gun? If you're not afraid to die? You're not making any sense."

"Sometimes it's better to die. My mother would have been better off if that creep had killed her. She acted like she was dead anyway. And in the end, he made her kill herself. So it's almost the same thing. And some people deserve to die. They put themselves in situations where it's their own fault."

Rachel's thoughts floated upward, like the bubbles in her coke rose to the surface and dissolved. She felt light-headed. Was Amy talking about Jane? Was she admitting she'd been there when Jane passed out and slipped beneath the water? It sounded like she was hinting that she'd done nothing because in some convoluted way she thought Jane deserved to die. Who was this person sitting across from her, eyes widened by the effect of thick brown liquid liner, varying shades of brown shadow? Amy's eyes seemed to be sinking into her head. Rachel barely recognized her, as if some other being had taken over her best friend's body, or at least her thoughts.

She looked away from Amy's clenched face, searching for their waitress. What if someone at a nearby table heard the insane words hissing from Amy's lips? Spots of perspiration grew on Rachel's palms and the back of her neck. It was difficult to breathe, whether from the unyielding fabric of her skirt that was now trying to restrain a plateful of pasta inside her belly, or because she was suffocating under Amy's staring eyes and disturbing ideas. She tucked her cash into the black folder the waitress set near her plate.

"What do I owe you?" Amy picked up her purse and peered inside. "You know, I've really wondered what it would be like. To shoot someone."

"Oh my God, Amy. Stop." Rachel pushed back her chair and without waiting to see whether Amy followed, rose and walked to the door.

Outside, Amy stood too close, clutching her purse to her ribs with the top opened. She fiddled with the contents. "Haven't you ever wondered?"

"No."

"Especially after Jane died. You find yourself thinking about what it's like to die. To see another person die."

"I don't think about that at all," said Rachel.

"I do. One pop and Charlotte would be out of my life, no more prancing around our husbands, making them think they can have something better."

"I know you don't mean all this." Rachel started to cry. "Even if you really feel that way, you'd never get away with it."

"People get away with all kinds of stuff."

Rachel feared she might lose her pasta on the sidewalk. "It would destroy your life, and it wouldn't be Charlotte's fault."

"If I don't, she's probably going to destroy my life for me."

"Why are you so convinced she's trying to get Justin? I don't understand."

"Because he's the best looking guy around. She obviously has no money, no man in her life, no father for her child, and is blatantly hunting for sex. It's a simple matter of adding up all the evidence."

Chapter Forty-one

AMY SQUEEZED HER WAY past the shoulder-high stacks of boxes in the spare room. She wound her way along the narrow path to the back corner where the armchair waited for her. She set her purse on the dresser and stepped out of her favorite Cole Haan pumps. A glass of wine would be so nice. Rachel should have suggested wine with their lunch. Her nerves felt like fabric that had been rubbed until the loose threads were exposed, picking up every sensation, magnifying each one so that even the chirp of the finch outside her window sounded like a shriek. Her pulse hammered in her throat. She never should have eaten that Caesar salad. The dressing was rich and now she tasted anchovies, a thick, stomach-churning texture. She'd ordered the salad without the anchovies, but she sensed the aroma was still there, laced in the dressing.

She leaned on the small fridge beside the chair. She opened the door and eased open the tiny freezer compartment. The large plastic bag lay in the center with the air pressed out and the zip-lock sealed tight over the preserved bodies of the murdered birds. Suddenly, she wasn't sure why she'd kept them all this time. Mostly because she wouldn't have been able to close her eyes without seeing their bodies smothered in dirt, decay setting in deeper each night. It was better to have them in the icy compartment where their beaks remained smooth and sharp. But they wouldn't last forever. Despite the protection of the freezer, the feathers were starting to get a fuzzy, disintegrated look to them, and the eyes were covered with a dull film.

It might be better to be rid of them now. She could finally give them a burial and force herself to suffer through wakeful nights, thinking of them underground. Eventually the image might fade. But then again, it might not. It wasn't as if other frightening images of her life had ever grown blurry. Not even at the edges. What was all that talk about time healing so you could move forward? Did that really happen to other people? It certainly hadn't worked out that way for her. Every painful scene of her life was as sharp in her brain as the day it happened – her mother nearly ripped in two by that man's force. The picture of her eleven year-old self, hiding in the closet, clutching her bony knees, feeling she couldn't breathe, was as distinct in her mind as the lunch she'd just eaten. And she could hear, even now, the sound of forks clinking on the edges of plates; the roaring voices from people unconcerned about whether anyone was annoyed with their tedious lunchtime chatter. It might have been just a moment ago when she saw Charlotte leaning too close to Justin, the light hitting her breasts so they quivered like liquid, bobbing closer until they brushed his bare skin. The expression on his face burned into her memory. There was a melted look to his jaw, a looseness around his mouth and eyes, the look of hunger, almost starvation.

She eased open the bag and pulled out one of the birds and cradled it in her cupped fingers. It was so cold. Why did she feel sorry for them? They were frail, so easily broken. She hated how that cat had been able to kill them with a few swipes of its paw. When she was a child her mother had tried to reassure her, *don't worry about the birds. It's easy for them to escape danger.* What a lie! She wouldn't have a freezer bag stuffed with seven dead birds if their wings protected them. Why did people always lie about how safe you were in this world? Telling stories to shut you up, to keep you from worrying yourself sick.

Maybe seeing these birds would prick a hole in Charlotte Whittington's arrogant lack of fear. There was something about Meadow that gave her a bird-like quality. Her long, uncombed hair made her look like a wild creature. No one had ever explained that weird bald spot, and Amy still worried it was some kind of disease. A few helpless birds left on the front porch might finally shatter their feeling of safety. They wouldn't know what it meant, wouldn't know who had done it because there was no way to get fingerprints off bird feathers.

When she'd talked to Rachel, mimicked the act of taking a shot at Charlotte, it sounded exciting, but she couldn't really do that. She liked the idea, holding the solid weight of the gun in her hand, feeling the power that exploded out of it. But she wasn't a murderer. Not unless she was attacked, of course.

She opened the mouth of the bag and placed the bird inside. Then she had to look away. They were so lifeless.

Chapter Forty-two

CHARLOTTE SAT ON A PATCH of scratchy grass under the pear tree in the back yard. She pressed her spine against the trunk. She lifted her mug to her lips and blew on the cinnamon tea. The air was still damp with fog but the chill wasn't doing anything to cool her tea. A crow sat on the edge of the neighbor's roof and cawed. Its black feathers were shiny against the white sky. What was it about fog that made the crows seem more active? Or was it that she noticed them more because their haunting cries made the fog seem more dismal?

Meadow appeared just inside the back screen door. She wore her pale yellow nightgown that had dragged on the floor when Mark bought it for her. Now, it flowed around her calves. "I went to look for you out front," said Meadow.

"Good morning, Angel."

"There are dead birds on the porch."

"That happens sometimes when they fly into the glass. As soon as I finish my tea, I'll bury it."

"Not one. There are a lot of dead birds."

"That's strange, but I guess it could happen. There are plenty of cats around here. You know how they like to leave their hunting gifts at the door."

"Seven. There are seven dead birds. And they look funny."

"Seven? That's kind of a lot." She stood up.

"That's what I told you. And they look funny."

"Funny, how?"

"Arranged."

"What do you mean?"

"Come look. They look fake and lined up."

It took only three strides for Charlotte to reach the back steps. She climbed up two at a time. Tea splashed out of her cup, the drops like hot needles on her fingers. Meadow wasn't usually squeamish. She was disturbed when she saw a dead squirrel or bird, but right now her voice sounded frightened. She left her cup on the windowsill, walked down the hall to the living room, and looked out through the screen door. Three feet from the threshold were seven dead birds. They were placed on their sides, all of them facing toward the right side of the house, feet pointed toward the doormat. Meadow was right that they looked unusual because they were so perfectly laid out. The wings were folded loosely over their bodies. It certainly wasn't the work of a neighborhood cat, and they hadn't simply fallen there. It looked as if they'd been dead for quite some time. There was a matte finish to the eyes and the feathers were crumbled at the edges. "Go inside, Angel. I'll bury them."

"I want to help," said Meadow.

Charlotte didn't want Meadow to help. She needed time to think about answers to the barrage of questions that was sure to

come. A part of her wanted to be alone, to grieve for the poor
creatures who should have been buried weeks or months ago. It
was irrational to think immediately of Amy, but who else? She
didn't want to consider why Amy might have a collection of
dead birds. She took a long, slow breath. Her focus should be
digging a hole and wrapping the creatures in a shroud. "You can
go get the spade," she said.

Meadow ran through the living room and down the short
hall. As she darted out to the yard and then back into the house,
the screen door slammed in quick succession.

"Are we burying them out front?"

Charlotte nodded.

"They scare me," said Meadow.

"Why?"

"Because someone put them there. Who would do that?"

"I don't know." She hated lying again, but what else could
she do?

"They make me feel like someone wants me to cry."

"Why is that?"

"I feel so sad for them. And I'm scared. I don't want
anything bad to happen to us. To Daddy."

"Why do you think something bad will happen?"

"I don't know. They seem so, I mean, there's so many of
them. It makes me think about how everyone dies. All the birds
will die." Tears spilled onto her lower lashes, catching there,
then dribbling over. "Daddy might die. What if he dies before
he gets out of prison? What if you die?"

Charlotte dropped the spade on the dirt. The metal blade
clanged against a rock. She walked over to the porch steps and

hugged Meadow. She smelled Meadow's hair, clean and soft against her cheeks. "Daddy will be ok, and I'm not going to die for a long time. We're young."

"So was Dana's mom."

Charlotte pulled Meadow closer, squeezing her ribs through the nylon fabric of her nightgown. "Jane's death was a freak accident. Bad things can happen, but lots of good things happen too." Was she going to lie to her daughter from here on out? It made her feel ill, but if she didn't try to reassure Meadow, restore her sense of security, what kind of mother was she?

"You could get hit by a car. You could get cancer."

If Amy was within sight this minute, Charlotte would grab the gun and shoot her. Amy was clever about finding ways to torment her that left no room to fight back. The things she did were impossible to link to her. Sneaking onto the porch was trespassing, but how would she prove it was Amy? And even if she did prove it, what were the consequences for trespassing? Probably nothing. She released her grip on Meadow's shoulders. "Let's give those poor creatures a warm spot in the ground. Go get some paper towels to wrap them in."

Meadow returned with a roll of paper towels. Charlotte climbed the steps. She tore off a sheet and laid it on the porch. Using the spade and a stiff leaf from the magnolia tree, she rolled the first bird onto the paper towel, folded the edges around the body and tucked the excess underneath. The corpse was as insubstantial as the down inside a pillow, ready to collapse at the least bit of pressure. Tears trickled down Meadow's face, but she didn't speak.

"Go get one of those boards from the side of the house so I can carry them down to the grave."

Once the birds were placed in the wide space she'd dug, they covered them over with dirt. Meadow found seven small rocks and placed them in an oval on the freshly packed soil.

WHEN THEY WENT to the soccer game at nine, Charlotte left her camera on the foot of her futon. She couldn't devote herself to taking photographs today. There was no telling when Amy's behavior was going to escalate further. She had to confront Justin and make him see what Amy was doing. She couldn't let her ambition get in the way of protecting her daughter. If Justin was so small-minded that he persuaded Bruce not to show her work after all, then she'd have to live with that.

Meadow ran to find her place with the team. Charlotte scanned the women sitting in their lawn chairs at the side of the field. Amy wasn't there. That might make things easier. As usual, Justin stood under the fruitless mulberry tree with Rachel's husband and the other men, watching the game from the perspective of the goal line. He wore a gray sweatshirt and a navy blue baseball cap. He and Greg both gripped *Starbucks* cups.

She walked across the grass and stopped a few feet away from Justin. "I need to talk to you for a minute."

Greg put the cup to his lips and peered at her over the top. He moved to the side, but not far enough so that he wouldn't overhear.

She turned and walked away from the tree. She didn't pause to see whether Justin followed, trusting that he heard the coldness in her voice. When she reached a quiet area and turned, he was right behind her. "You have to do something about your wife," she said.

"What do you mean?"

"In case it isn't obvious, she's the one who destroyed my photographs."

He nodded.

"Did she admit it?" said Charlotte.

"No, but I thought she might have done it."

"Then why didn't you do anything?"

"That's why I'm trying to help you get them shown."

She would have preferred hearing that he was so impressed with her work, he wanted to help, but she wasn't surprised. "She had a package of rotten food delivered to my house. She sent Rachel over to tell me Meadow shouldn't play soccer. And now she's left dead birds on my front porch. Meadow found them and it scared her."

He put his cup to his mouth but didn't drink, and stared past her at the soccer field.

There'd been such a rushing of blood in her ears; she hadn't been aware of the shouts from the field and the sidelines until he looked in that direction. Even now, the noise sounded distant as her pulse thumped in her temple.

"What makes you think Amy put them there?"

"For whatever reason, she wants to frighten me. At Jane's funeral, she said I was the one who belonged in a coffin."

He pulled the bill of his cap lower on his brow, yanking it hard as if he thought it might help him think of a response. "What do you want me to do?"

"She's *your* wife."

"I'm trying to make up for your loss."

"And I appreciate that, although it's kind of twisted that you think it's okay to cover up a crime as long as you help the victim."

"And it's ironic to hear you concerned about someone breaking the law."

"That's not fair. But I'm not here to talk about me. It's one thing to attack me; I can take care of myself. Going after my daughter is unacceptable."

"I really don't know what to do, Charlotte. I'm trying to help. I don't know what's wrong with her."

"She's running around with a gun in her purse. Did you know that?"

"What?"

"I overheard her arguing with Rachel about carrying a gun. I should go to the police, but I know they'll refuse to do anything until someone gets hurt."

He tipped his head back and took a long swallow of coffee. The sun broke through the fog. Charlotte put her hand across her brow to block the rays and get a clear look at his face. For several minutes he said nothing while the coach droned in the background, *play your positions*. She wondered if that phrase would haunt her for the rest of her life.

"I guess I'd forgotten that her father gave her a gun. It was a long time ago. I thought it was in storage." His voice was hoarse. He cleared his throat. "I'll try to figure out something. It's really difficult, you know."

There were more shouts from the field. She turned. The Emerald Tigers had scored a goal. Amanda Lewis was squeezing Meadow's shoulders, lifting her feet off the ground. Meadow grinned as the girls screamed. "Score! Meadow!"

Charlotte's throat tightened. She raised her arms overhead and clapped until Meadow looked her way.

Chapter Forty-three

THE *EXPEDITION* ROCKED AS it hit the apron of the driveway with too much force. Amy gunned it up the slight incline and into the open garage. From the corner of her eye she saw Justin standing on the front porch. She was late. She'd stopped for a glass of wine at *Il Postale*. Getting her manicure and pedicure made her edgy ever since reports had circulated a few years ago, warning of disease, and sometimes even death, resulting from un-sanitized foot spas swarming with bacteria. Supposedly they'd immediately cracked down and imposed fines on the offenders, closed some shops, but she wasn't sure she believed it. While her feet soaked in the tub, she stared into the moving pool of water and worried. She pictured invisible germs eating at her skin. It made her angry that something pleasurable had been spoiled. She spread her fingers across the steering wheel and admired her nails, hard and shimmering magenta. She wiggled her matching toes. Her beautiful nails were worth the anxiety, but the wine had been nice, easing the tension.

Unfortunately, it made her late and now Justin was worried about her.

She climbed out of the SUV and walked along the stepping-stones that led from the driveway, through the side gate to the main path. The mellow feeling she had while she was drinking her wine had already started to fade. She longed for another glass, but Justin would say it was too early. "It's sweet of you to be watching out for me. I'm sorry I worried you," she said.

"I'm not worried because you're late."

"Were you thinking something happened to me?" She stood on her toes and kissed his jaw.

"You've been drinking."

"I had one glass of wine. I haven't been *drinking*."

"Why did you have wine? I thought you skipped the game to get your nails done?"

Amy reached for the handle of the front door.

He put his hand on her wrist. "Wait. I want to talk to you out here."

"Why? The neighbors will wonder what we're doing."

"I don't care what the neighbors think. I have one thing to say and I don't want Alice and Amanda to hear me. I know about the gun and I want you to give it to me."

Amy wrenched her arm out of his grip. "No."

"I'm not going to argue. Give it to me now. I'm getting rid of it."

"You can't. It's mine." She backed away from him. Why was he turning on her like this? Everything had been fine when he left for the game. The cherished feeling she'd had when she saw him waiting for her popped like a balloon. He didn't care for her at all. He wanted to take away the one thing that made her feel safe, the one thing that allowed her to leave the house, or stay in the house when he wasn't home, for that matter. He didn't care about the nightmares she'd battled all her life. He didn't care that the haunting memories of her mother's assault might play out in her own life. He didn't care that she was being harassed by the police or had to live with the agony of watching a woman seduce him.

"Give me the gun, Amy."

How did he even know she had the gun? "I need it. You aren't going to take away the one thing that's keeping me safe."

"A gun won't keep you safe."

Tears spilled out the sides of her eyes. She could feel her mascara smearing across her cheekbones. "Why are you doing this to me?"

"I want you to talk to a therapist so you can learn to recognize healthy fear. All these things are in your head, and you're going to infect Alice and Amanda with your hysterical ideas."

"All of a sudden I'm a bad mother and I'm paranoid?" said Amy. The tears were gone. Her voice rose. "You don't care about my peace of mind."

"I heard some disturbing things about you."

"What disturbing things?"

"I talked to Charlotte at the game."

She backed to the edge of the porch and stepped down onto the path. "I should have known. Why would you listen to one single word she has to say about me?"

"She told me you're carrying around that gun your father gave you." He held up his fingers, pinched together like he was gripping the space between the two of them. "She said you came this close to making a death threat."

"You can't believe anything she says." Amy sat down on the edge of the porch and hugged her knees. She pressed her face against her forearms, letting her hair fall forward so he couldn't see her swollen face.

"This is why I don't want a gun in the house, much less in your purse. You're too unstable."

"I'm not unstable." Her voice was too loud again, shrill, but it was his fault. "All women are emotional," she said.

"Look at you. You're falling apart just because I talked to the mother of Amanda's friend."

She straightened her back and glared at him, hating him. "That girl is not Amanda's friend."

He gripped her upper arm and tugged. "Stand up. Talk to me like an adult if you want me to believe you're not unstable."

"You don't get to decide who's stable and who's not. Whatever that means anyway. Why do you get to make the rules?"

He yanked her arm harder. "I didn't make any rules. That's how it is for normal people. Now stand up."

Amy wrapped her arms more tightly around her legs and pulled her knees close to her chest. He wasn't going to tell her what to do. He acted as if she were a child.

"Charlotte told me you left dead birds on her porch. That's really sick."

"How does she know who left them?"

"I don't know."

"Well it wasn't me."

"Why don't I believe that?"

"Because you can't even think straight. All you can think about is climbing into bed with her. A woman you hardly know says I put birds on her porch and you believe her? What proof does she have it was me? None, I bet."

"I'm tired of arguing," he said.

"You didn't even deny that you want to have sex with her."

"Give me the gun or I'll get it myself."

"Maybe I'll shoot you before you can get it."

He squeezed the bridge of his nose between his thumb and index finger. He suddenly looked old.

"Don't say things like that," he said.

"I need to protect myself. I need to protect our family."

"You said you want to shoot me. Shoot me or protect me, which is it?" He laughed, but it had a vacant sound.

He reached for her purse. She grabbed it and shoved it under the arch formed by her bent knees. She pinched her heels closer to her body, pinning the purse between her heels and her hips. She moved her arms lower so they sheltered the opening on either side of her legs.

He shoved his hand between her thighs, forcing them apart, and trying to get at the soft leather top. She pressed her legs together as hard as she could.

"Let go," he said.

"You're not taking it away from me."

He tightened his grip and tried to pull the purse out between her thighs. It hurt, the force of the bag full of makeup and keys and wallet and the gun against the backs of her legs, the strength of his arm trying to force its way through her clenched thighs. Why did he refuse to deny he was attracted to Charlotte? That's what made him look so old, the guilt and desire for another woman's body gnawing at him. He deserved to be shot. Men were animals. She'd learned that when she was eleven years old, and now she realized – it wasn't only some men, it was all of them. They didn't want anything but sex, and they didn't care how or where they got it. All these years she'd thought her mother should have done something to stop that creep from violating her. Not only had her mother been helpless under his force, her own husband had turned on her, acting as if it were her fault she'd been assaulted. And Amy had believed him. She started to cry harder. She had been so wrong. She had abandoned her mother, leaving her with nothing but the echo of her own voice, whispering to herself; what could I have done? It wasn't her mother's fault at all.

Suddenly Justin let go of the purse. He pulled his arm out from between her legs and stepped back toward the front door. "It's me or the gun, Amy. Hand it to me right now or I'm taking the girls and we're going to stay with my parents. Today."

She stopped crying. "You won't do that. It would devastate them."

"Not as badly as an accidental shooting."

"I don't believe you."

"Give me the gun before I count to three or I'm going inside to pack."

"What am I, two years old?"

"One."

"Stop it. You're being ridiculous."

"Two."

"God, Justin, I'm not a child."

"Three."

She laughed. "See, you won't do it."

He turned and opened the door.

"You can't leave me here all alone," she said.

"You have your gun to keep you safe."

"I'll still be scared. I'll be lonely."

"Then go stay with Rachel." He went into the house. The bolt slid into place.

She stood slowly. Her hips were cramped from sitting on the concrete. He couldn't possibly mean it. She would be terrified alone in this enormous house. At least when he traveled, the girls were here with her. The presence of other human life, even if they were children, kept the worst demons at bay.

She took out her keys and unlocked the door. He didn't mean it. The girls would refuse to go. She went inside, climbed the stairs and entered her spare room, shutting the door behind her. She would take a few minutes to hide her purse, and then she and Justin could sit in the living room and have a glass of wine; heaven knew, they both needed one.

Chapter Forty-four

THE LUNCH PLATES WERE stacked to one side on the patio table. Sara and Trent were in the corner of the backyard, hunched over a depression in the lawn under the lemon tree where water from the automatic sprinklers pooled, leaving the grass moist all day. Trent was showing Sara the fifteen snails he'd coaxed into the area. Sara's bent head revealed the pale skin of her hair parting as she stared, enraptured with the slimy community.

Rachel and Greg watched them from the patio. "I had lunch with Amy yesterday," said Rachel.

Greg drank his coke with a loud slurping noise. "How did that go?"

She hesitated for a moment. Should she tell him? Once the words were out, there would be no going back. "She was wondering what it would be like to shoot someone. She was going on about keeping Charlotte away from Justin."

Greg set his glass on the table. For a moment, he stared at her without speaking. "We should call the police. Maybe she did have something to do with Jane's drowning."

"No, it's nothing like that. She didn't say she was planning to kill her. Or actually thinking about killing her. She was saying she thought about what it might be like to shoot someone."

"They don't have a gun, do they?"

"She does. Her father bought it for her. A long time ago."

"We need to report it. Or at least give Justin a wake-up call."

"I don't mean to make it sound worse than it is."

"It can't possibly sound worse than it is. Speculating about killing someone can't be made to sound one way or the other."

Rachel pulled a piece of wilted lettuce to the side of the plate. She curled it into a thin tube, then spread it flat again. "I feel so helpless."

He pushed back his chair. The iron feet scraped like talons on the flagstone. He walked behind her, lifted her hair and put his hands on her shoulders. He kneaded the muscles at the base of her neck.

"I don't know what went wrong," she said. "There must be something I can do to help her." She put her hands over her face, wanting to stuff the dampness back into her eye sockets, tired of crying. "I'm losing all my friends."

"You can find other moms to hang out with. In the meantime, you have me."

"We've been friends since our girls were babies. Doesn't that count for something?"

"You put too much into it. If you spread your circle wider, wouldn't you be happier?"

Maybe he was right. It was so easy for Kit to walk away, and Amy shrugged off Jane's death, as if she deserved it. Were those really the words Amy had used? Some people *deserved* to die? Maybe Amy had always been off balance. Wrapped up in her own thoughts, imagining things that weren't there. Ignoring everyone else's problems because her own insane stories seemed more real. Had she ever been the friend Rachel craved? Did any of her friends make her feel like she really belonged? She'd always thought it was something in her, causing her to feel like an outsider, but maybe it wasn't her at all. If they were truly her closest friends, why did she feel awkward and unimportant around them? Did the friendships she clung to really exist at all? Maybe she was living in a distorted reality, just like Amy, an imaginary world that was nothing more than the projection of her own thoughts. And here she sat, with an intelligent man who made her laugh, who adored her and listened to every word she spoke. She realized she didn't feel flabby and out of place when she was focused on Greg, it was only when her thoughts skittered sideways to her friends. When her mind was filled with him, she felt comfortable and safe and feminine.

The patio grew cooler as the sun crept across the house and the fall air sharpened into the crisp scent it was supposed to have. After awhile, Greg pulled her up from the chair and put his arms around her waist, turning her to face him. He tightened his grip and kissed her deeply, letting it stretch out until her thighs and knees felt like jelly. If he loosened his hold on her, she might collapse in a puddle. They hadn't kissed like this in a very long time. Six months? More than that?

Finally, they eased away from each other and went into the kitchen. While Greg rinsed the plates, she wiped the counter. Her cell phone rang. She walked into the family room and plucked it out of her purse. Amy. She swallowed and pressed the answer button. Amy's voice drilled into her ear. "He left me! Justin packed up the girls and went to his parents' house. I'm all alone here."

"What happened?"

"What do you think? It was her. I told you. Women know these things; it's a sixth sense. I wonder if he's really with his parents. Maybe he dropped the girls there and he's going off to meet her."

"That's crazy." The water stopped running in the kitchen sink. A moment later Greg appeared in the doorway of the family room.

"Don't call me crazy. I told you she was out to lure him away."

"Why did he say he was leaving?" said Rachel.

"It was some pointless excuse."

"What did he say?"

Greg walked into the room and stopped right beside her.

"It was about the gun. He said if I didn't give it to him, he was leaving. But I know it's because of her. She told him lies about me, and he decided it was too dangerous for me to have a gun, or some stupid reason like that which makes no sense."

"He's right. I'd feel safer if you got rid of it."

"*You'd* feel safe? What about me? I'm all alone here and there's a rapist looking for a woman without a man in the house. Can you come over? Stay with me until I figure out what to do."

Greg moved around so he faced her, mouthing the word *no*. "Hang up. Tell her you can't listen and you can't help. She is ... Not. Your. Friend."

"Hold on a minute." Rachel pressed her thumb on the small speaker. She held the phone down by her hip. Amy's voice was still going, but Rachel didn't lift up the phone to hear what she was saying. "I don't know what to do. I feel so bad."

"If you go over there, you're as crazy as she is. You're throwing away me, and our kids for a mental case. She has the potential to hurt herself. Or you." He backed away from her, with an expression that said his own life was crumbling. He touched his finger to her lips and walked out of the room.

Rachel lifted the phone to her ear.

"Are you listening to me?" said Amy.

Listening? When had Amy ever listened to *her*? For weeks, she'd tried to talk about her fears for Trent's future. If Amy even acknowledged she heard a word Rachel said, all she did was belittle him, brush off Rachel's worries like lint from a sweater.

"Well answer me. When can you come over? I can't stay here alone."

"You still have your gun, don't you?"

"But I'm scared. I need someone here."

"I can't help you. I'm going to hang up now."

"Don't hang up on me. I need you. You're supposed to be my best friend. I need you to help me figure out how to get rid of her before Justin leaves forever."

"I'm sorry. I can't. Good-bye." She pressed the button to end the call. She felt empty, and guilty, but a little relieved. She couldn't listen to Amy's paranoid stories any more. She was exhausted and numb from all the drama. She tossed the phone on the couch, flopped down and stretched her legs over the arm. She wanted to cry, but the tears were dried up. It wasn't right to hang up without explaining why she could no longer be the kind of friend Amy expected. A true friend would explain why she couldn't come over, why she was worn out. She felt her mind drift, craving sleep, escape from her thoughts. She would take a quick nap and then when she woke up, she'd call Amy back. Or go over there. She turned on her side and let sleep come.

When she woke, it was ten past four. Her neck was stiff. She heard Greg talking to someone at the front door. She sat up and wiped the crust from the corners of her eyes. She tried to run her fingers through her hair but they caught in the tangles. It must be Amy, soliciting face-to-face help. Amy wouldn't accept a simple good-bye.

She got up and walked down the hall to the foyer.

"She's sleeping," said Greg.

"I'm awake," said Rachel. She walked to his side. He opened the door wider, lifting his arm so she could duck under it. Charlotte stood on the front porch. Rachel could see past her to the curb. Meadow sat in the front seat of the *Jetta*, her head bent over, reading a book. Her long, reddish-blonde hair fell in cottony strands, catching the late afternoon sun that poured through the open window of the car.

Charlotte wore her *Doc Marten* boots, knee-length shorts, and a pink tank top so pale it revealed the outlines of her nipples. Rachel was forced to look at her feet to avoid staring. She really was spectacular looking, but Rachel didn't feel lumpy or out of place. She felt comfortable, standing with her shoulder under Greg's arm, small and soft next to his height.

"Hi. Sorry if I woke you up," said Charlotte. "I need your help. I don't know where else to go."

Rachel waited. Greg's upper ribs were solid and warm against her.

"I know I blew you off yesterday, but now I'm really a little afraid of Amy. I tried to talk to Justin but I didn't get the impression he's going to do anything."

"What can we do?" said Greg.

"I've tried to stay away from her, but she's getting scarier."

"What happened?" said Rachel.

"She left a bunch of dead birds on our porch. Meadow found them. They looked like they'd been dead for a while. Like she'd been saving them."

"How do you know it was Amy?" said Rachel.

Charlotte stared, silent for a moment. "She's the only person I know who would even think of something like that. When I told Justin, he didn't seem surprised."

"That's disturbing," said Greg.

"It upset Meadow. A lot."

Rachel nodded. She could imagine Trent finding something like that.

"What do you want us to do?" said Greg.

"I feel like I'm trapped. I know she wants us to go away, that she thinks I don't fit in here, but I can't afford to move. It's not right, what she's doing. I'm afraid she'll hurt Meadow."

"You might be able to get a restraining order," said Greg.

"Amy wouldn't care about a restraining order," said Rachel.

Charlotte looked at her gratefully. "Can you talk to Justin?"

"You should call the police," said Greg.

"They won't do anything," said Charlotte.

Rachel stepped in front of Greg. "I'm really sorry for all this, but I don't know how we can help."

Charlotte rocked back on her heels. "I don't even know what I expected you to do. I'm desperate and I'm not used to feeling this way. I hate it."

"Amy's full of a lot of angry words," said Rachel. "But she's more afraid than anything else."

Charlotte stepped off the porch. "At least you made me feel like I'm not over-reacting." She smiled weakly, then turned and walked along the path to the sidewalk.

Greg closed the door. "I wonder if we should call Justin."

"I could try to talk to Amy."

"Haven't you tried that? More than once?"

She pulled her hair to the side and wound it into a coil. "It just doesn't seem fair to turn my back on her without explaining why. I feel like I should ..."

"I don't want you going over there. That thing with the birds is really weird."

"If she did it." She looked at him.

His eyes were tight with frustration.

"Ok. I know she probably did it," she said.

Greg walked around her and into the living room. "It's still not that cold. How about if I barbecue chicken for dinner?" He went to the window.

She moved next to him. "We could go together."

He put his arm around her. "I'll go over there after dinner and check in on her. Does that work?"

Rachel nodded. She pulled him close and they stood in front of the window for a long time. She felt the rise and fall of each synchronized breath.

Chapter Forty-five

CHARLOTTE SAT AT THE kitchen table staring at yet another cup of cinnamon tea as it cooled. How many cups of tea had she made and let cool without drinking over the past few weeks? Why couldn't she seem to make up her mind whether or not she should be afraid of Amy? Rachel and Greg had seemed concerned, but not enough to speak to Justin or offer any help. It was unlikely Justin would figure out a way to influence Amy's behavior. The fact that he suspected his wife had vandalized Charlotte's photographs, yet chose to help with a new display rather than doing anything about the crime itself, proved how weak he was. All of them had stared at her with expressions of quiet, helpless frustration. It seemed as if they wanted to believe Amy's outbursts were harmless idiosyncrasies, rather than the truly disturbed behavior Charlotte recognized. What did people always say after someone went berserk? *We had no idea. He seemed like such a nice guy. She kept to herself.* Not that there were many women who went on killing sprees, but it happened. Like that prostitute who was a serial killer.

She picked up her cup and gulped down the icy tea. The texture was thick, with a sweeter taste now that it was cold. Inaction was making her skin crawl. She crossed her arms on the table and rested her forehead on her wrists. The next three years without Mark stretched ahead like an endless tunnel. This wasn't a life. She hadn't taken a photograph in ages. All her ideas were as blurry as an out-of-focus image. After the game this morning, she'd finally received a voice mail from Bruce, but returning his call would have to wait until tomorrow. She wasn't sure she could have a lucid conversation with him right now. Despite the thrill of scoring during this morning's game, Meadow's conversation was still consumed with morbid questions about the lurking nature of death.

She carried her cup to the sink and rinsed it. The water sprayed out of the cup over the backs of her hands. She dried them and went to the living room window and looked out at the street. At the side of the yard was the fresh dirt and small ring of stones covering the birds' grave. They slept safely now, tightly packed beneath the earth, like Jane, lying in a hillside cemetery, dirt pressing down on her, an airless, silent world. She clenched her hands so hard her fingernails dug into her palms. She pressed her fists against the window. The urge to pound on the glass was overwhelming. Why was she allowing Amy to create a frightening world for Meadow? She unclenched her fists and shoved her hands in her pockets. There was only one thing left. It looked as if she'd finally been dragged down to Amy's level. She went down the hall to Meadow's bedroom and knocked on the doorframe. "I'm going out for awhile."

Meadow looked up from her book. "Why?"

"I need to take care of something. Promise not to go into the living room, even if someone comes to the door. Just stay in here. Okay? I'll be back before dark."

Meadow nodded. Her eyes appeared teary.

Charlotte looked away for a moment. She stepped into the room. "I want to hear you say it, please."

"Okay. I'll stay in my room." Meadow turned her gaze back to the book.

AMY'S HOUSE DOMINATED the cul-de-sac. Between the stone façade and the sharply peaked roof, it looked like it had fallen out of the set for a horror movie into the sculpted yards of Silicon Valley. All the drapes were closed. Charlotte pulled her camera out of the backpack and closed the car door. She unlatched the gate and walked up the path. She popped off the lens cap and raised the camera to frame the bright red *No Solicitors* sign nailed near the door. She pressed the shutter release. She stepped onto the porch and hammered the side of her fist on the door. The force hurt the small bone of her wrist. She hoped the sound echoed through the entire house, made Amy and her family stop whatever they were doing. She raised her fist and pounded on the door again. The house remained silent. She stepped off the porch and looked at the picture window to her left. Not a flicker of movement. It was possible no one was home, but she refused to accept that. She lifted the camera and focused on the gardenia growing near the porch. The scent was syrupy, like the odor in a funeral home. She stepped to one side so she could capture the glossy white petals, formed as perfectly as if they were carved of wax. She bent her knees slightly and framed two blossoms and the metal plate that continued to insist – *No Solicitors.*

Taking photographs was calming. She should divert her anxiety into taking pictures of the entire house. Something to utilize her adrenaline-laced nerves in the event no one ever answered the door. She backed further down the path, keeping the camera close to her face, letting the lens find the next subject, rather than relying on her naked eye. She scanned the front of the house, the garage, and the upstairs windows. Nothing pricked her imagination. The blank, curtained windows made her think of soul-less eyes, but they wouldn't have any impact in a photograph.

She heard two soft clicks. At first, she thought it was her bracelets knocking against the side of the camera. Then, the front door swung open with a crash.

Amy stumbled onto the porch, clutching her stomach. She lifted her hands and pointed a tiny gun at Charlotte. "What are you doing here? Put that camera away. How dare you trespass on my property and take pictures during the worst day of my life."

Charlotte snapped a picture.

Amy lunged down the steps.

Charlotte zoomed in for two close-ups. She wasn't sure if they were focused. But as she moved down Amy's body the viewfinder was filled first with Amy's contorted face, then her hunched shoulders, and finally the glint of the sinking sun on the barrel of the gun. She lowered the camera and backed toward the sidewalk, keeping her gaze on the gun. Her heel slipped off the path and the thorns from one of the rosebushes tore at the backs of her legs. What was she doing? Already sidling away. Why did this skinny, hysterical woman fill her with such dread? If she kept retreating, her world would shrink with each step. She had to go back and do what she'd intended. If Amy didn't shoot her first. Could she really aim? "I have a photograph of you pointing that gun at me," said Charlotte.

Amy moved down the path, seeming to forget the gun as she waved her left arm in the air. "Give me the camera."

"I'm not putting up with your insanity any more. Those birds were pathetic."

"I don't know what you're talking about."

"All you need to know is that I've had enough." Charlotte's damp fingers slipped on the camera body. She pulled it close to her stomach and walked up the path. Now she was only three or four feet from where Amy stood. The gun was half-hidden behind the silky fabric of Amy's slacks. "I took pictures of the birds. I also took pictures of what was left of my photographs and frames inside the school dumpster."

Amy swung her right arm back and brought it forward, slamming the gun against Charlotte's upper arm.

With one hand firmly on the camera, Charlotte raised her other hand and slapped Amy's cheek. Her skin had the consistency of tissue paper. She slapped her again, harder, then stepped to the side and grabbed Amy's right arm below the elbow. Her long fingers folded all the way around the thin bone and almost non-existent muscle of Amy's forearm. She yanked Amy toward her. The camera banged against her ribs and she steadied it with her elbow. Amy stumbled and flapped her left arm but couldn't make contact with any part of Charlotte's body. She grabbed Amy's opposite shoulder and squeezed hard. Amy yelped and tried to kick at her shins, but her backless sandals prevented her from getting traction.

"I could break your bones if I wanted to," said Charlotte. She pushed her face close to Amy's and slid her hand down to Amy's wrist and wrenched it hard. Still Amy managed to keep the gun secured in her hand. Charlotte dug her nails into the tender flesh on the underside of Amy's wrist, scraping down to the joint, tearing at the skin. In one rapid movement, she let go of Amy's wrist, stepped back and swung her foot, slamming the toe of her boot into Amy's shin. She kicked again. A soft, breathless squeal came from Amy's lips, but she didn't scream. At the third kick Amy lost her balance and sat down hard on the stone path. Charlotte kicked repeatedly at Amy's knees and hips, not caring if she was doing significant damage, and not caring if anyone watched from behind curtained windows. A strange euphoria filled her. She could say good-bye to Justin's help displaying her work, but she didn't care. She had to keep this demented woman away from her daughter.

She grabbed a chunk of Amy's hair and tugged her head sideways. The cartilage cracked inside Amy's neck. Amy dropped the gun and grabbed Charlotte's wrist. Their fingers twisted around each other and Amy's diamond sliced across the back of Charlotte's hand, drawing out a thin line of blood. Charlotte grabbed Amy's ring finger and bent the nail until the acrylic tip pulled away from the natural nail. Amy screamed.

"Leave us alone," said Charlotte. She kicked Amy's foot, sending her sandal spinning onto the lawn. She turned and walked down the path. She left the gate swinging open.

Although the muscles in her arms and legs shuddered as if the air was unbearably cold, sweat covered her back. She managed to walk the final steps to her car. She got in and put the camera on her lap. The engine started with a roar from too much pressure on the gas pedal. Her hands trembled so that she could barely maintain her grip on the steering wheel. She looped around the cul-de-sac, drove to the end of the street, and turned right. After a few blocks she pulled over to the curb. She placed her camera on the passenger seat and leaned over the wheel, pressing her head against her hands. The blood on the back of her hand was damp on her forehead. She lifted her head and wiped it away.

After a few deep breaths her heartbeat slowed. Amy Lewis had succeeded in turning her into the opposite of everything she wanted to be. Where was the calm, meditative life she'd hoped to create? Where was the vision for her photography career and her daughter's tranquil childhood in suburbia? She'd been reduced to sneaking out of her house, issuing threats, and assaulting a woman with a gun so small it looked like a toy. She put her camera into the bag and zipped it closed. She pressed the gas pedal hard, taking corners too fast so she was shoved against the car door and the tires whined on the pavement. The person driving her car was someone she didn't recognize.

At home, she made tacos for dinner and urged Meadow to talk about the goal she'd scored, the book she was reading, anything she could think of. Anything that helped steer her mind, even for a moment, away from what she'd done. And, as she was increasingly realizing, what she'd left undone. It was unlikely that a few bruises, a string of angry words delivered in a voice higher than her normal tone, and a broken fingernail, no matter how bloody, would do anything to stop Amy.

She'd never felt so utterly alone. Her mind leapt from packing Meadow and her camera in the car and driving to San Francisco, trying to scrape together the crumbs of her old life, or driving back to Amy's to inflict some real damage. Maybe she could provoke Amy into shooting her in the foot, force her to do something that would finally get the attention of the police. She laughed to herself. Maybe that wasn't such a bad idea, it wouldn't leave her any more helpless than she was right now.

Chapter Forty-six

AFTER CHARLOTTE'S CAR TURNED the corner, Amy remained seated on the stepping-stone. Her tailbone ached from her fall. She pressed the gun against her chest. Why hadn't she fired? It had been the perfect chance to be rid of Charlotte. It wasn't that she'd been afraid to pull the trigger. Charlotte hadn't given her a chance, grabbing her, kicking her with those heavy boots. She'd known from the first moment she saw those strange clothes, those boots, that it wasn't the kind of clothing a normal woman chose to wear. Charlotte must have known Justin was gone or she wouldn't have been so confident about coming onto their property, attacking her like a wild animal.

She rested her arms on her knees. Welts ran from her wrist bones to the inside of the elbow on her left arm. Her finger burned where the nail had torn off. Her shins and hips ached so badly, she didn't know how she would stand up, but she needed to get inside the house. The yard was in full shade now, the leaves and thorns of the rosebushes looked as black as the iron fence. She was completely exposed, surrounded by nothing but shrubs. The front gate hung open over the sidewalk. The rapist could be watching her from any one of the yards in the cul-de-sac. Staring at her, ready to force his way into the house before she had time to slam the door and lock the deadbolt. Her heart thumped so hard she thought it might explode.

After several long minutes, she stood. Pain shot from her hip down her leg. She picked up her shoe and inched backwards up the path. The door had been open the entire time she was outside. What if someone had snuck into the house while she had her back turned? Slithered up the steps and slipped inside without disturbing the position of the door? She gulped in air. She looked at all at the other houses, the erratic shadows that could be trees or light posts or a man. What to do? Go inside and lock the door, possibly sealing the rapist inside with her? Or go straight to the garage and drive somewhere safe? But she didn't have her keys. There was no choice but to go inside the house.

It took forty-five minutes to walk through every room, checking closets, and under beds. And then she had to do it all over again in case the intruder had changed positions while she searched another area. It was an enormous house, too big to keep one person safe. There were too many rooms, too many corners, far too many closets, bathrooms, and frosted glass doors on showers and tubs.

By the time she completed her second search she was exhausted. Was it only this morning that she'd been sitting with her feet in a whirlpool bath while Charlotte fed lies into Justin's ear? Only two hours ago that Justin had packed up her girls and left? And now she faced a night alone in a house she still wasn't convinced was secure. Justin didn't have to worry at all, casually suggesting she could stay at Rachel's. Some friend, hanging up on her like that. She was stuck here alone. Thank God she had her gun.

She should attend to the bleeding fingernail, the scratches on her wrist and shins, but she needed a glass of wine first. She went into the kitchen and put the gun in her purse. She pulled the cork out of a nearly full bottle of Chardonnay. There was one more bottle still in the refrigerator. Would the two bottles get her through the ten or eleven hours of darkness that lay in front of her? She poured a full glass and drank two large swallows. She picked up her purse, carried it into the dining room and placed it on the mahogany table. She sat in Justin's chair at the head of the table and set the wine glass in front of her. It wasn't good to place the glass directly on the polished surface. Once the moisture dripped down, it would leave a ring. But what did it matter? She might never serve dinner at this table again.

No. She couldn't think that way. Of course she would serve dinner here. Justin would be home soon, once he cooled down. Once he had time alone to think, he'd realize the gun was necessary. One good thing about him being at his parents' house, he would be out of Charlotte's range. She smiled. Maybe this was for the best. There was time to clear her thoughts, to figure out what she should do next.

She pushed the chair away from the table and opened the lower right hand door in the breakfront to get a coaster. As she peered inside she saw them, shoved to the back. The two old photo albums, filled with pictures taken before the twins were born. She pulled one out. It was from so long ago, when she and Justin were engaged and he couldn't keep his eyes off her. Those were the days when he found her fears charming. He said he wanted to protect her. He said he was her knight in shining armor.

The album cover was cherry red with ivory silhouettes of women's heads. It had thick cardboard pages with frames cut out of the center to hold the photographs. Each page held a single picture. There was a sheet of rice paper between each page. Justin's loving camera lens and the soft lighting had made her look spectacular. In one photograph, her black nightgown with a lace bodice showed her breasts like small peaches. The book was filled with images of her with longer hair, softer and not as styled as it was now. She wore black eye liner that gave her an exotic look. The angle of the camera elongated her slim legs. In another picture she wore nothing but a dress shirt of Justin's, suggestively showing the last inches of her thighs before the rounding of her hips. Looking at them now, she couldn't believe she'd allowed him to take such erotic poses. She couldn't believe she'd left these in the dining room where the twins might have stumbled across them. She turned another page, remembering Justin looking over the top of his camera, gazing at her as if she were the only female on earth. He'd had the same soft look to his mouth and the widened pupils that he had when she caught him looking at Charlotte, as they stared at each other over a glass of wine.

She slammed the book closed. Since that woman had shown up, Amy's life had unraveled one piece at a time. Charlotte had stolen her self-respect and the adoration of her husband. She finished the glass of wine and returned to the kitchen to pour another. She felt mildly hungry. She peeled the plastic wrapping off two pieces of string cheese and nibbled through both of them, then instantly regretted it as her stomach felt bloated. She poured the wine and sipped it carefully. The alcohol was making her light-headed – she was drinking it too fast. She carried the glass into the living room and set it on the coffee table. She went into the downstairs bath to bandage her fingernail and attend to her scrapes and bruises.

When she was finished, she sat on the sofa and took a few more sips of wine. Her eyes felt gritty and unfocused. Her body longed for sleep. She got the chiller out of the freezer and slid the bottle inside. She grabbed her purse and managed to juggle chiller, purse, and a clean glass upstairs. It was already five o'clock. She'd take a quick twenty-minute nap before checking the house and turning on the lights for the long hours ahead. She tossed her pants and top across the armchair near the foot of the bed. She removed her contacts and washed her face. The cotton sheets were cool and soft on her arms and legs, caressing her skin with gentle pressure. She set the alarm on her cell phone.

IT WAS TOO dark when she woke. She blinked and looked at the illuminated numbers on the clock. Almost ten o'clock? It wasn't possible. She never slept. Now she had to face a dark house. Why had she been so stupid, thinking she would rest for just a few minutes, not turning on the lights first? She grabbed her cell phone. It was still on vibrate from when she was at the salon. The thrumming on the nightstand hadn't woken her. She reached down and patted the floor near the bed. Her heart raced as she groped further out. Her purse wasn't there.

She sat up and reached for the lamp, but before her fingers touched the switch she heard a sound on the first floor. Maybe. Or was it the stairs? A creak on that fourth step from the top that prevented anyone from ascending in complete silence. Had she really checked the house as thoroughly as she should have after Charlotte left? How could she have been so sloppy? Her thumb and forefinger touched the switch. Her lungs were airless, but she heard nothing. If she turned the switch, the sound might drown out whatever noises were whispering in other parts of the house. She wouldn't know whether or not she'd heard the creak on the stairs. The darkness pressed against her face. All she could make out was the shape of the armchair, the half-opened door of the bathroom, and the glow of the bathroom mirror.

Light was imperative. She turned the switch. It didn't feel much better with light spread across the corner around the side of the bed. The rest of the room looked empty and distorted. Justin wasn't here and the girls weren't sleeping down the hall where they should be. Beyond her bedroom were three other bedrooms, a hallway, the bathroom, the stairs, the foyer, the expanse of the living room curving around into the dining room, the pantry, the kitchen, the breakfast area, the family room, the laundry room, and the downstairs bath, all of it dark. She yanked the comforter up to her breastbone, folding the heavy layers of fabric around her arms. She tried to keep her breathing shallow, not wanting even the flow of her blood to prevent her from hearing every sound. Nothing. Perhaps a faint clicking, like the sound the electric stove made when it cooled down. Or was the sound in her head, mucous popping deep inside her ears?

She was supposed to be looking for her purse. It wasn't on the floor anywhere around the bed. She stared at her silky pants and top on the armchair. The lump underneath could be her purse, but it looked too small. What had she done with it? She wouldn't have left it downstairs, come up to bed unarmed, with only the wine. Would she? She lifted the bottle out of the chiller and poured half a glass. She took a sip. She thought back over her movements after Charlotte had left. Was the purse still on the kitchen table?

When she'd come upstairs she desperately had to pee, and she'd rushed directly into the bathroom. She must have left her purse on the bathroom counter. She flung back the covers. The corner of the comforter caught her wine glass and tipped it onto the carpet. Wine splashed out and the stem snapped. Tears spilled onto her cheeks. She didn't need this. Why was everything so horribly wrong? She picked up the pieces of glass and placed them on the nightstand, then went into the bathroom. Her purse. Sitting on the counter where she'd left it. She reached inside and grabbed her gun. It was hard and cold. She held it against her collarbone. What sounds had she missed from the far corners of the house while she stood in the bathroom? She stepped back onto the bedroom carpet and walked slowly until she was a few feet from the door to the hallway. She was not crazy. There was no doubt she'd heard a sound, either a creaking stair or the stove cooling, or something.

She backed toward the bed and put the gun on the comforter where it sank like an egg into a nest. She crept to the walk-in closet and yanked on a pair of yoga pants and a small white T-shirt. Creaks and whispers flooded her ears, but she couldn't determine the source. She sat on the edge of the bed and held the gun in her lap. She couldn't sit here for the rest of the night, but the thought of making her way down the stairs, trying to second-guess what room she should enter first, groping for light switches, made her feel like sobbing. She bit her tongue hard to prevent the sound from coming out of her throat. This was so unfair. Justin should be here taking care of her, not stealing her children and running to his mother's, if that's where he really was. Maybe he and Charlotte had been plotting this over their wine that day. How many times had they met and Amy hadn't seen them?

Maybe he really was at his mother's. Could it be Charlotte making the sounds downstairs? It was possible she'd come back to finish her attack. She was so angry about those birds; Amy had really struck a nerve with that. She laughed soundlessly. If Charlotte snuck into the house, this was Amy's chance to finally be rid of her. In the front yard, she'd been taken by surprise, not prepared to shoot. But now she was ready.

She heard another sound drift up from the first floor – a tapping, like a glass placed on a table. The living room? The dining room? While she was asleep someone had broken into the house. These were not the sounds of a structure settling into the earth, not the normal cooling of wood and tile and stucco that happened at night. The air outside was still, not a single leaf fluttered. She crept across the pile of blankets to the nightstand.

She picked up the wine bottle and put it to her lips. She took several long swallows, feeling the lovely soothing liquid against her throat.

She was cold and tired. She was afraid to go downstairs and afraid to stay in her room. Everyone had abandoned her. She'd tried so hard to make her life good, to raise her children to be sweet and well-behaved, to keep their minds untarnished by the evil world reaching out its fingers to grab their thoughts. She was a good wife and she kept herself looking nice, the slimmest and best-dressed mother at Spruce Elementary School. She couldn't see any obvious mistakes in her life, couldn't understand what had gone wrong to leave her in this position. Every single thing she'd done was designed to avoid ending up with a broken life where the neighbors whispered about you and your husband said you dressed like you were looking for sex and your daughters were left to raise themselves as best they could. She'd prepared for every disaster. She took good care of her family. Why had they left her?

There was another tap from the first floor. It had to be coming from the dining room. She stood. Her bare toes clenched the fibers of the carpet. She walked to the bedroom door. She was forced to step into the hallway and walk toward the top of the stairs. The tapping sound. Something on the table. The foyer was dark. The thick drapes in the living room blocked the streetlight.

Standing at the top of the stairs all night was not an option. She raised the gun. She loved her gun, it was the only thing between her and total collapse right now, the only thing giving her the strength to walk down, one step at a time. She avoided the spot that creaked. The tile floor in the foyer was icy, like walking onto a frozen pond. Her feet cramped. She moved silently until she reached the step down to the living room. The only interruption in all that blackness was the slight glow of the stove light that spread to the doorway of the kitchen.

A figure stood at the dining room table, hunched over. Her breath stopped. Her body stiffened and she felt like her heart was no longer beating. Charlotte? She squinted, wishing she'd taken time to put in her contacts. Or was the figure too tall? Charlotte was an unusually tall woman. The figure wore what looked like a hooded sweatshirt bunched around the neck and a baseball cap, so it was hard to tell, man or woman? It must be the rapist, finally in her house after all this time. She'd known someone had crept inside while Charlotte was attacking her! A tiny puddle of light from the kitchen stove hit the corner of the dining room table. The creep was looking at her photo album. The heavy cardboard pages tapped against each other as they turned. Pictures of her almost naked, parts of her body exposed. He leaned over it, drooling. She'd known he would find her. As if she was destined to suffer the same fate as her mother. But she wouldn't.

She raised the gun and held her right arm straight like she'd practiced. She fired. The first bullet sank into the center of the figure's back. There was a grunting sound. The next two bullets hit the breakfront and shattered the glass doors and several of the crystal goblets lined up on the shelves. The fourth bullet hit the area around the neck and the figure slumped down. His upper body and head smacked the table and collapsed on the floor.

The recoil vibrated through her arms and down her spine. The explosion rang in her ears. At the practice range she'd worn protective pads and hadn't realized how deafening the shots would be. They echoed inside her skull, but the aftermath was strangely noiseless, as if all sound had been sucked out of her head for a moment.

On her tiptoes, hugging the gun to her stomach, she took a step toward the figure on the floor. It felt good to finally use the gun after all this time spent wondering what it would feel like, the various possibilities playing out in her mind. Could this be what sex was like if you had an orgasm? That buildup and sudden explosive release that felt so calming?

She took another step then looked away. The awkward position of the head against the leg of the table made her queasy. The blood seeping through the sweatshirt was too real. Even in the faint glow coming through the door from the stove light, she knew what all that wet stuff was. It was getting all over the carpet. She'd have to replace it. Justin wasn't going to be happy about that expense. The thought dissolved and she felt another surge of pleasure. She was pretty sure it was a man with his body bent around the table and chair. She really wished it could have been Charlotte, but getting rid of the rapist was just as good. Someone had invaded her home, leering at her photographs, and she had been forced to shoot. Finally she would have some peace. The cavernous house still frightened her, but the number of potential threats was reduced by one.

She stepped closer. Blood spread as if it had a life of its own, not pumping rapidly as she would have expected. She was standing next to a corpse. She should call the cops. That would make that detective realize Amy wasn't a killer. But she was curious. What did he look like? No one had given a good description, just bits and pieces – medium build, that was true. The baseball cap covering his hair. They'd also described fat lips, but she couldn't see the lips. It was a non-description. She moved around the chair. Blood that had soaked the carpet oozed on the soles of her feet. She didn't want to touch the body, but the need to look consumed her. Would he have an evil face? Would those fat lips, slack in death, haunt her dreams? Would his eyes be open, staring at her? She didn't want that image burned into her brain, like those poor birds with the open, staring eyes. He might look like he was at peace because she'd released him from his torment. She'd never seen Jane's face that night. Had it been calm? Or did it show fear of what she was facing next?

If she was going to look, she had to do it soon. Then she would have a small glass of wine to celebrate her courage before she called the police. She knelt and leaned over the body. The head was turned so awkwardly. It looked like she was going to have to touch it. Well, she'd poked for a moment at Jane's body, floating in the hot tub, and that hadn't been so bad. She pushed at the head, trying to move it, but the shoulders were turned in the opposite direction, making her effort futile. She stood and went around the other side, pulled the chair out further and knelt again. Now she was in the faint pool of light coming from the kitchen. She leaned closer. Justin. No.

She must be feeling shock. Her mind was playing tricks on her. She'd had too much to drink and her head was fuzzy. She looked again. She used the tip of the gun to push the baseball cap off the side of the face. It definitely looked like Justin, but that couldn't be right. He was at his parents' house with the twins. Or with Charlotte. Either way, he wasn't the rapist. She stared at the face, the half closed eyes. Even in the darkness, she would know that sleepy, sexy look anywhere. How could this happen? What was Justin doing prowling around in the dark? Scaring her to death? He couldn't be dead. A husband didn't sneak into his own home in the middle of the night, not letting her know he was coming. Standing in the shadowy light, staring at pictures of his wife when she was twenty-three years old.

She slugged his shoulder, but he didn't object. "How could you do this to me? You can't be dead!" She stood and raised her face to the ceiling, letting out a long, aching howl. She looked at the cute gun. She raised it and fired two shots at the photo album. The bullets ripped into the thick pages, tearing holes in the pictures of her seductive young face, blasting an ugly burned spot in her partially exposed breasts. Then she turned and hurled the gun across the living room into the foyer. It slammed into blackness, skittering across the tile. She fell on the floor and curled herself around Justin's legs and feet, the only part of him that wasn't oozing blood. She'd used all her bullets. Now she was completely vulnerable to an intruder.

Chapter Forty-seven

CHARLOTTE STOOD IN THE line that wound through Starbucks. While she waited, she leaned across the narrow space and plucked a newspaper off the rack, folded it and tucked it under her arm. She listened to the drone of orders – *double shot, low fat, non-fat, soy, extra hot, Grande, Venti.* The descriptors mushroomed in clusters of words that made her wonder how the baristas kept the intricate requests straight in their minds. The shop was cold, still running too much air conditioning after the weeks of unseasonal heat. She rubbed her arms. Her fingers scraped against the edges of the newspaper. She gave her order for a *Grande Berry Chai Tea* drink and moved aside.

When she had her tea, she settled at a round black table in the front corner near a window. It faced the patio area that ran out to the parking lot – a less than idyllic view, but the chatter of conversation and the aroma of the tea soothed her. She set the newspaper on the table. At the top of the front page was a small update from Friday's report that the Sunnyvale police had taken their original suspect back into custody, charging him with murder as well as the series of rapes. Investigators had uncovered the fact that the murdered woman had been in a five-year love affair that ended badly. She had decided to keep her suburban life in tact, but her lover wanted her to himself. He'd committed the other rapes in an attempt to cover up the stabbing.

She sipped her tea, enjoying the slight ache in her feet from her attack on Amy. Did the arrest mean Amy would finally put away her gun? Either way, hopefully Amy would leave her alone now. She flipped the paper over to read below the fold.

Sunnyvale Woman Shoots, Kills Husband

She stared at the words until they turned into a blurry line. There was a photograph of Justin. Or was it? She blinked and studied it more carefully. It looked like him – that chunk of pale hair – but not like him, his smile seemed narrower. She read the caption: *Justin Lewis, age 41.* She picked up the tea and slurped. It flooded her mouth, burning her tongue and the back of her throat. Was she reading it wrong? A different Justin Lewis? But how many could there be in Sunnyvale? She read the brief article.

Amy Lewis, 38, shot her estranged husband in the dining room of their Maple Court home Saturday night. Mr. Lewis died before paramedics arrived.

"I was putting my trashcans at the curb when Justin pulled up," said Robert Crowder, a neighbor. "He asked me to keep an eye on the house because he and the twins were staying with his parents. He said Amy was at her girlfriend's while they worked out some problems. He was just

running inside to get the girls' laptops. Next thing I know, I hear four or five gunshots."

Ms. Lewis was sedated at the scene and is currently under medical observation. She was recently questioned in the death of Jane Goodman, also of Sunnyvale.

Charlotte looked up from the newspaper. Her lips were inflamed from the burning tea. She stared at the other patrons, gulping coffee, reading newspapers, and pecking at laptops and smart phones. She took a small sip of tea trying to figure out what she was feeling – sadness at the loss of Justin or elation over finally being rid of Amy. Surely this meant Amy would be locked up where she belonged, whether that was a hospital or a prison. A knot of muscle that had taken up residence between her shoulder blades began to unwind itself. She had been the only one to recognize that Amy was truly ill. She felt vindicated, but also utterly depressed that Justin had to lose his life before anyone acknowledged Amy's madness. Tears filled her eyes and dribbled down the side of her face. If only he had listened. How many times had he shrugged his shoulders, stared blankly into the distance as if he wasn't even trying to think of a solution? If he hadn't been so anxious to protect Amy, things could have been different.

Two people were dead. The only ones who had offered even half-hearted friendship – a mother and a father, ripped from their children's lives. She swallowed a large gulp of tea, hoping the burning would take away the deeper pain. It was selfish to think about her photography display right now, but she couldn't help what flitted through her mind as she continued to stare at the newspaper. Suddenly, she was eager to return Bruce's phone call. She leaned back and looked out the window. After weeks of nervous habit, she scanned the people walking past for signs of that skinny figure with red hair, marching along in high-heeled sandals. She stretched her arms behind her, feeling the release between her shoulder blades. Amy wouldn't be walking past. She drank the rest of her tea, letting her thoughts drift.

After a while, she walked out the door and breathed in the cold October air. An idea for a photography series on images of eccentricity in suburban life flooded her mind. It was as if Amy's presence had clogged her creative flow and it was now trickling back to life. This was a good day to start over, for the second time.

***

RACHEL HAD BEEN standing at Kit's front door for at least five minutes, afraid to ring the bell. She was worried that Kit would refuse to answer, or answer and look at her with those hard, dark eyes and tell her to go away because there was nothing to talk about after all. It felt as if there was a windup toy in her stomach, jittering and lurching, like the rabbits she used to buy the kids at Easter. Even though it had been two days, she still couldn't believe what had happened. Nothing seemed real. Every time she thought about Greg's broken promise to go over and check on Amy that night, she collapsed on whatever piece of furniture was nearby, short of breath and light-headed with relief. How close she'd come to losing him. She wasn't sure whether she'd been a loyal friend to the last bitter moment, or the most naïve woman in the entire state of California.

She pressed the bell.

Before she had time to take more than two breaths, she heard Kit's footsteps on the pebbled concrete behind the atrium wall. Kit opened the door then stepped back to allow Rachel to enter. "Like I told you on the phone," said Kit. "I only have time for a quick cup of coffee."

They walked through the atrium. The built-in bookcases immediately inside the sliding glass front door were bare. Neatly taped cardboard boxes were stacked four high down one side of the hallway leading to the bedrooms. The walls were stripped bare of artwork and photographs.

In the living room, there were two mugs on the coffee table. Clearly Kit intended to make this visit as efficient as possible. Kit settled on the sofa and Rachel took a seat in the wicker rocking chair across from her.

"So what did you want to talk about?" said Kit.

"I didn't want you to move away without me apologizing. Or something."

"What do you have to apologize for?" Kit reached for her mug and cupped it in her hands but didn't drink the coffee. "You know I'm only moving ten miles away." She smiled.

Rachel shifted in the chair, the fibers creaking around her. "Not apologize. Everything's just … wrong. I feel like everything we had is gone."

"Not everything," said Kit.

"Our group."

Kit nodded. "I think our group was falling apart for awhile."

"Not like this. Jane dead. The shooting."

Kit nodded again. The blinds on the opposite side of the room were open. Sunlight streamed across the carpet and the top of the table and formed stripes on the sleeve of Kit's white shirt. The light washed out her face, making it difficult to read her expression.

"You seem so cold about all of it," said Rachel. "Don't you feel sad for what we've lost? What we had when our daughters were babies?"

"That seems like another life," said Kit.

"It does." Rachel reached for her coffee. She wasn't sure why she'd come over here. She'd thought Kit would make her feel better, would be friendlier now that Amy was out of the picture. "Do you think Amy knew it was Justin she was shooting? The paper said she thought he was the rapist, but I wonder ..."

Kit was quiet for several minutes. Finally, she said, "Who knows what she was thinking. I don't mean to be cruel. I know you and Amy are so close. But she has mental problems and I suppose none of us noticed in time. Or maybe we noticed and just didn't want to do anything about it."

"I tried," said Rachel. "I tried to make her see things differently."

"It's kind of ironic that they identified the guy before Amy started shooting."

"That's what I meant," said Rachel. "Do you think she knew they'd already arrested him?" It didn't really matter. In some ways, the last few times she'd talked to Amy, it seemed as if Amy had wanted to shoot someone, anyone, that she wanted to cause damage, death without really caring whether it had anything to do with her.

"I knew from the minute I found Jane in the hot tub that Amy was seriously disturbed," said Kit. "We should have known from her obsession over Charlotte. Her fixation on the rapes."

"She had good reason for that." Part of her hoped Kit would ask why. Yet even now, she didn't want to break Amy's confidence, as if she still needed to protect her from something indefinable.

"Look how that turned out. The woman who was murdered was cheating on her husband. It was someone she knew, just like they'd said all along."

"Amy was still right to be afraid," said Rachel.

"Cautious. Not afraid."

Rachel blew on the surface of her coffee. She was pretty sure it was cool, but she blew at it again, mesmerized by the ripples caused by her breath.

"I'm sorry for Alice and Amanda, and sorry Justin's gone – he was a good guy. But, God, he should have gotten help for her. He had to see it, more than any of us," said Kit.

"Don't you feel sorry for her?"

"No. I'm looking forward to a fresh start."

"So I'm left all alone," said Rachel.

"You can change that. There are lots of fantastic women with children at Spruce."

"But you won't be one of them."

Kit stood as if she'd been conducting an interview and now it was over. "You need to move on and so do I. We need to put Amy out of our minds."

OUTSIDE IN HER car, Rachel felt her attempt to say good-bye to Kit had been awkward, and cold – an exchange of meaningless words. Why had she even bothered? Nothing had been resolved. She backed her RAV4 out of Kit's driveway. There wouldn't be any more hot tub and wine parties at Kit's house. The moving van was coming next week. The houses that had been the backdrop for her children's lives were slipping away, one by one. She'd no longer be visiting 462 Maple Court; a house that would be difficult to sell once word of Justin's violent death took root. Occasionally she might still visit the Goodman house on Oak Circle, picking up Sara from a slumber party, or dropping off Jane's motherless daughter after soccer practice.

Dana and her brothers, Amanda, and Alice – so many children who weren't going to have the safe, well-organized lives their mothers tried so desperately to give them.

Instead of turning right, she drove toward Maple, wondering whether Amy's twins would ever attend Spruce again, or if the grandparents would start the girls in a new school. She'd left a voice mail for Justin's parents, but they hadn't returned her call. She'd have to give it another try, tomorrow. It wouldn't be easy for the twins, if they continued at a school where everyone knew your mother had shot your father in the back. As she turned the corner, she took her foot off the gas pedal and let the small SUV roll slowly on its approach to Amy's house. There was a ribbon of yellow plastic tape draped across the front porch. She pressed on the brake and paused in front of the house next door to Amy's.

Charlotte Whittington was across the street. Rachel hadn't seen her at first because she was almost hidden by the low hanging strands of a willow tree. It looked as if she was taking shelter under a large umbrella. She had her camera equipped with the lens that protruded so far she had to steady it with her left hand. She wore a paper-thin brown and shimmery gold skirt, a long-sleeved black T-shirt and her *Doc Marten* boots. She was in a half squat, snapping pictures of Amy's house. It wasn't hard to imagine how many unattractive features she was focusing on. Two newspapers, still in their blue plastic bags, were kicked to one side, sodden from the automatic sprinklers. Dandelions that had somehow appeared when Amy's vigilance failed sprouted unruly leaves and pulpy stalks under the rose bushes. Long, thin weeds like stray hairs in an old man's nostrils were scattered across the lawn. The garbage can that had been left at the curb on trash day last Friday had its lid flipped open. Two crows swooped down to scavenge for food. They pecked at garbage that had fallen out of the container when the automated arm of the truck swung it up in the air to empty trash into the receptacle. Amy would be devastated, if she knew.

Rachel pulled out from the curb and drove around the cul-de-sac. She glanced from the corner of her eye as she passed within four or five feet of where Charlotte stood. Charlotte didn't acknowledge her. Or see her? She looked so happy, relaxed, in her unconventional clothes, free to invade Amy's life now that Amy wasn't there to defend it.

Rachel couldn't help the disloyal thought that Charlotte would make an interesting friend. After all, their daughters were the same age. They played soccer on the same team.

About the Author

Cathryn Grant's short fiction has appeared in *Alfred Hitchcock's Mystery Magazine* and *Ellery Queen's Mystery Magazine*. Her short story, "I Was Young Once" received an honorable mention from Joyce Carol Oates in the 2007 *Zoetrope All-story* Short Fiction contest. Her flash fiction has been published in the ezine Every Day Fiction and at her website under Flash Fiction for your cocktail hour. Visit Cathryn online at http://cathryngrant.com.

CPSIA information can be obtained
at www.ICGtesting.com
Printed in the USA
LVOW12s0247110917
548250LV00002B/441/P